PRAISE FO.

Early in <u>ANGEL HOUSE</u>, one of the characters thinks "As soon as one thing becomes uncanny, everything else follows," and, in this novel where everything is at once familiar and deeply strange, you would do well to heed those words. If you like the idea of Marwencol as scripted by Daniel Paul Schreber with punch-up by Ben Marcus, this is the book for you.

Gabriel Blackwell, author of <u>Madeleine E.</u>

Videotapes that create portals to other worlds, children levitated by a radio announcer's voice, and a decaying town where women are a hazy memory—that's just the set-up for David Leo Rice's engrossing <u>ANGEL HOUSE</u>. This fantastical novel unravels expectations on every page, while the stories it tells about identity, memory, and community begin to feel hauntingly familiar.

Jeff Jackson, author of <u>Destroy All Monsters</u>

David Leo Rice's <u>ANGEL HOUSE</u> could be described as the story of one year in the life of an isolated town, and the dreams and frustrations of its conflicted residents. But that might not be entirely accurate, because it's also a headfuck of utterly monumental proportions – think endlessly transforming bodies, bifurcated consciousnesses, sinister entities transcending time and space, and terrifying bear-people. If Julio Cortazár wrote cosmic horror, it might look something like this.

Tobias Carroll, author of <u>Reel</u>

Unlike anything else you will read this year, David Leo Rice's ANGEL HOUSE is at once an ode to memory, a de- and (re-) construction of what it is to be human, and a writer's-eye look at how and why we make stories and civilizations. Spinning outward from a core of surreal humor, Rice's second novel is the work of a fantastic and growing talent, one who aims to alter our very perceptions of reality. Evoking Sterne's Tristram Shandy in its sense of narrative whimsy and Pynchon in its use of multivalent symbology, ANGEL HOUSE presents the possibilities of meaning and nihilism, often simultaneously. For readers anxious to be intellectually challenged, this book is a treasure drawn from the eternal depths of our own Inland Sea.

Kurt Baumeister, author of <u>Pax Americana</u>

To Brenda
(only)

ANGEL
H O U S E

10.2.19

A novel by
David Leo Rice

xoxo

KERNPUNKT ⬤ PRESS

Cover Art: Ted Closson
Book Design: Jesi Buell

1st Printing: 2019

ISBN-13 978-1-7323251-2-8

KERNPUNKT Press
Hamilton, New York 13346

www.kernpunktpress.com

This book is dedicated to the memory of
Pleasant St. Video in Northampton, MA, which served as
one of the temples of my childhood, just as its fictional
analogue serves the lost souls in the town you are about to enter.

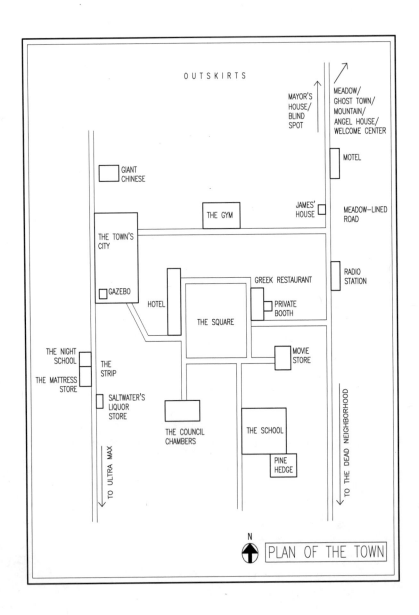

OUTSKIRTS

MAYOR'S
HOUSE/
BLIND
SPOT

MEADOW/
GHOST TOWN/
MOUNTAIN/
ANGEL HOUSE/
WELCOME CENTER

MOTEL

GIANT
CHINESE

THE GYM

JAMES'
HOUSE

MEADOW—LINED
ROAD

THE TOWN'S
CITY

GAZEBO

HOTEL

GREEK RESTAURANT

THE SQUARE

PRIVATE
BOOTH

RADIO
STATION

THE NIGHT
SCHOOL

THE MATTRESS
STORE

THE
STRIP

SALTWATER'S
LIQUOR
STORE

MOVIE
STORE

THE COUNCIL
CHAMBERS

THE SCHOOL

PINE
HEDGE

TO ULTRA MAX

TO THE DEAD NEIGHBORHOOD

N

PLAN OF THE TOWN

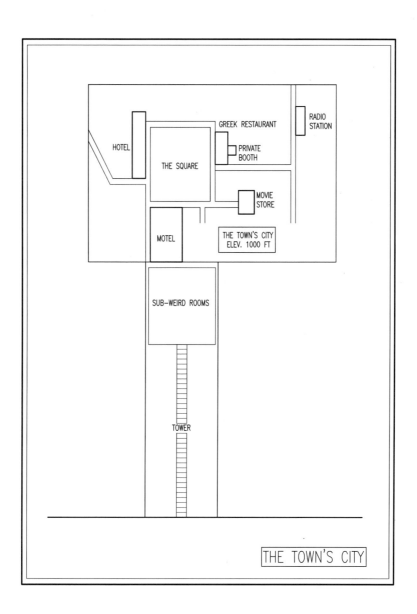

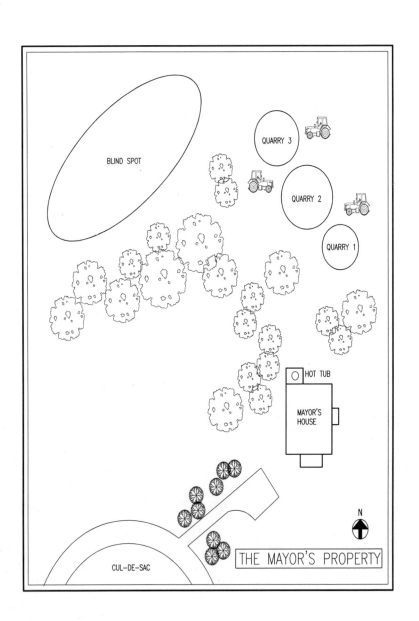

BLIND SPOT

QUARRY 3

QUARRY 2

QUARRY 1

HOT TUB

MAYOR'S
HOUSE

N

CUL−DE−SAC

THE MAYOR'S PROPERTY

the town as it was the town as it was the town as it was
the town as it was the town as it was the town as it was
the town as it was the town as it was the town as it was
the town as it was the town as it was the town as it was
the town as it was the town as it was the town as it was
the town as it was the town as it was the town as it was
the town as it was the town as it was the town as it was
the town as it was the town as it was the town as it was
the town as it was the town as it was the town as it was
the town as it was the town as it was the town as it was
the town as it was the town as it was the town as it was
the town as it was the town as it was the town as it was
the town as it was the town as it was the town as it was
the town as it was the town as it was the town as it was
the town as it was the town as it was the town as it was
the town as it was the town as it was the town as it was
the town as it was the town as it was the town as it was
the town as it was the town as it was the town as it was
the town as it was the town as it was the town as it was
the town as it was the town as it was the town as it was
the town as it was the town as it was the town as it was
the town as it was the town as it was the town as it was
the town as it was the town as it was the town as it was
the town as it was the town as it was the town as it was
the town as it was the town as it was the town as it was
the town as it was the town as it was the town as it was
the town as it was the town as it was the town as it was
the town as it was the town as it was the town as it was
the town as it was the town as it was the town as it was
the town as it was the town as it was the town as it was
the town as it was the town as it was the town as it was
the town as it was.

      – The Mayor

PART 0
Squimbop Comes

Professor Squimbop sets out in ANGEL HOUSE to force this year's town into being.

By the time he reaches the middle of the Inland Sea, the Totally Other Place has vanished behind him and this year's assignment has begun. Now, his point of departure exists only in memory, as the source of the Lectures that will drip into him as soon as he arrives. Until then, he slumbers dreamlessly, staring up at the ceiling without seeing it.

Occasionally he climbs upstairs to the Captain's Chamber and steers the ark with the giant Wooden Wheel, but not often. The course is mostly straight; any fear of arriving at the wrong destination is mostly hypothetical.

There is nothing more in ANGEL HOUSE than the luggage of a traveler heading for a town he plans to spend a year in. This is as long as Squimbop spends anywhere, and as long as any town exists for. A whole history in that much time, the pasts of all the people there struggling to cohere, and then he's gone, and so are they.

The towns are all the same to him, though by the middle of each year he falls deep into wherever he is. His memory of all previous towns diminishes, refreshed only at the end, as he embarks back across the Inland Sea, beneath which every town that has ever existed, submerged, turns slowly to sand.

The people that populate these towns are not created from nothing, nor are they hatched from eggs like flies. They are, rather, dredged from the depths, recombined, stuffed with the memories of previous people, as if the Inland Sea were nothing but a pit in which the remnants of every person that ever existed were melted down and stewed together and ladled into the heads of everyone new, as soon as they are called upon to exist.

Needless to say, they turn out strange. Stranger and stranger, Squimbop is finding, as his decades of doing this stretch into centuries, with no promise of ending, nor of revealing their ultimate purpose. He serves the Totally Other Place and that is all. Anything more is not for him to wonder. Though he does wonder.

Coming to rest at last, the town solid around him, he drops the ANGEL HOUSE anchor through the surrounding mud, in what is fast becoming a Meadow. It sinks all the way down to the soft, semi-aqueous layer deep underground in which the collective memories of these people flow together into a Pornography, to which their hastily-assembled minds, ill-equipped to bear the strain of living, will soon yearn to regress.

Here, the anchor finds purchase, forming a seal against the Inland Sea's incursion, where it will remain until he pulls it up at the end of the year, inviting the floodwaters to come.

The ark has landed, he thinks, catching his breath.

Like so, ANGEL HOUSE came to rest in the Meadow with the Mountain behind it and Squimbop in the Master Bedroom.

Queasy from the landing and the sucking sound of the Inland Sea receding to reveal dry land, he walked to the bathroom, squeezed his bowels but found nothing ready to move, so he sat on the toilet in the dim purple glow, panting like he'd run all the way here.

An hour later, near dawn, he found himself standing before the bay window in the living room, looking at the sunrise over the Meadow, and, because the terrain was flat, the sprawl of the town beyond.

Looming in its center stood a Tower splintering at the top into a skyline, with giant slabs of cement hanging out on every side, almost overshadowing the town below. An elevated city that appeared as tall as any of the town's streets were long.

A ruin.

He sank to his knees, daunted by the sight of it.

The Tower exuded a nativeness that the structures in these towns were not supposed to; it seemed organic, not created by the Totally Other Place, though he knew it only seemed this way. He knew his mind was incapable of seeing a world, or any object, as real outside of the Totally Other Place's will. Still, there were moments, in some of the towns he'd passed through, when he felt that some things, even some people, must be more than figments.

He couldn't shake it: the Tower, as it appeared now, seemed too ancient to have been conjured by his arrival. *Maybe*, he found himself thinking, *I have it wrong… maybe all of this predates me and I'm nothing but a lone figure lost within it.*

A man in exile.

His tether to the Totally Other Place already felt slack.

Maybe this is the only town there's ever been, and everything else, the Inland Sea, the Totally Other Place… nothing but memories of dreams built up over a lifetime of living here, yearning to break free while fearing that possibility in equal measure.

No. He knew what was true, he knew what his purpose was, but still, he had his doubts, and his doubts about his doubts, and…

He shuddered and pulled himself back from the brink, closing his eyes to block the Tower out.

What would he tell the children when they'd taken their places on the ground in the School on Monday morning and the heavy Chamber door had swung shut, sealing them in, and they all looked up at him, in his suit and tie, cheeks and chin angry with aftershave? The smoldering of the everlasting pyre of the damned? The genesis and training of wild beasts, slavering to suck the spirit of youth out through one's intestines? The overture to the universal holy covenant of... the swearing and breaking of oaths and rending of sinew and gristle into the shells of giants thirty stories tall, with teeth made of... piles of gagged mouths weighted down with rocks or chips of boulders, stretching up to the...

No. He caught his breath. He would begin, as he always began, with the Inland Sea. The distant lights along the edges of his course, dim and scattered and filtering into his Death-dream, where he liked to imagine they were distant shores but knew they were distant stars and planets at the very nearest... the blue-green of sunrise and sunset, the blue-black in between.

This was the only inroad, the only reliable way to begin to tell the children what they needed to know, what he had been summoned here to say: *your town exists inside a reality whose full breadth you will never perceive.*

Everything you thought was everything is nothing compared to the Inland Sea, which will swallow you all without its level rising, and cast me back out across its endless calm surface to do it all again.

I am all that will survive.

He looked back at the Tower, picturing it sinking under the waves, down and down until only its massive, manifold roof remained visible, and then even that would sink under, turning back to the sand it was made from. His doubts subsided. *Just the jitters of arrival*, he thought. *Everything is as it should be.*

This town is nothing and I am its God.

Both exhausted and relieved, Squimbop was now ready to eat.

The ANGEL HOUSE basement was full of ground beef, which he tended to gnaw frozen. There was enough for a year, assuming he ate some meals in the town and supplemented it with tallow from the children once they were clustered on the ceiling.

4

Sometimes during winter in the towns, when school was out and he didn't need to shower in order to prepare the next day's Lecture, he'd lie with a chunk of this beef in the bath and let it thaw around him, rubbing its blood along his chest and inner thighs to redden himself before sucking it down, slightly greyed if the water was hot enough. But for now, he'd simply lean over the open freezer and sup from his hands until his nerves were steady and he could think of what to do next.

After swallowing six handfuls of beef in the basement, where the freezers were floating in seawater that'd seeped in and would never seep out, Squimbop decided to go for a walk. Though he usually slept, showered, and shaved before exploring a new town and setting his cameras up, right now he was too agitated to stay indoors.

So he pulled on his red leather boots, took up his briefcase, and set out for his first walk through this town, legs rubbery after so long at sea.

He cut a straight path across the Meadow, past a cluster of wet-looking wooden buildings, their workmanship crude and moldering, and proceeded along the dusty, two-lane road that ran toward the Tower. Looking up this road into the shimmering heat, he could see the canal it would become when he pulled up the ANGEL HOUSE anchor and sailed back across the Inland Sea at the end of the year, leaving only water behind. He kicked up dust and watched it diffuse through the seawater that lingered in the air, wondering if the End he could foresee in some sense existed already.

Time-as-space, an old thought that leads nowhere except to more speculation, he thought, as he stopped under a telephone pole and opened his briefcase. Reaching inside, he fished out the first of five cameras. Warming it in his palm, he felt it shudder as it came online. He exhaled, relieved. Each time he made the journey across the Inland Sea, he feared that something would happen to the cameras in transit. That they'd crack with the jostling of the waves or prove incompatible with his new environment, stranding him alone in one of these towns, with no means of converting his experience into footage, and thus leaving it, he supposed, as some sort of unprocessed, meaningless raw material instead. Pure, indigestible reality. Chaff.

But the cameras hadn't failed yet. They were probably as robust as he was, as robust as ANGEL HOUSE itself, though he was given a fresh set at the start of each journey since the old ones were inevitably lost in the sunken wreckage of the towns he left behind.

He reached as high as he could and affixed this one to a telephone pole on the side of the road. It beeped once, flashed red, then began its silent work. The link was instantaneous and automatic. *Already*, he thought, as he walked away, *footage is streaming onto my hard drive which, at the end of the year, I'll present to someone far form here, someone who will make sense of it in ways I never could, and thankfully don't have to.*

He walked on toward the center of town, his mood lightened now that he'd remembered that interpretation wasn't his responsibility.

In the Square, he took a seat alone at a booth in the only restaurant he could find, directly across from the Hotel. These appeared to be the only two public establishments in the center. In all the towns he'd caused to spring up over the years, none had come with more than a minimum of detail, but he'd never seen one as desolate as this.

The sign outside read "Greek Restaurant." As he settled in, he wondered what place the notion of Greece held in the minds of the people here. *What is Greece to you?* he imagined asking them, as if they were the children he'd be teaching when his class began. Had he asked himself the same question, he knew that he wouldn't have gotten any more of an answer.

In the booth behind him sat eight heavyset old men. They muttered in such a way that they sounded like they were speaking freely but, Squimbop knew, they weren't. They were just glitching along

6

through the ruts their minds had been created with, like wax cylinders producing music when cranked. They reminded him of fish breathing in dirty tanks, mouths popping open and closed against the glass.

"Do you think we'll see…?"

"I wonder how… is doing?"

"How long's it been since…?"

Squimbop closed his eyes and focused on blotting out the names they were using. He made a concerted effort never to learn more than the few he'd have to use during his tenure in each new town. He could tell the men were staring at him, trying to figure out where in the scheme of the coming Reunion he fit. He didn't turn to face them, and wouldn't even if they'd asked him to.

You and all your memories are tinier than a single plankton on the seafloor, he thought, holding his hands open on his thighs under the table. He pictured crushing these men between his palms like papier-mâché effigies.

"Coffee, pancakes," he muttered when he sensed a waiter standing nearby. His voice, so long unused, sounded foreign in his ears, and he feared for a moment that he wasn't speaking the same language as the people around him, but the waiter seemed to understand.

Squimbop cleared his throat and stared at the table, resolved not to look up until his food arrived. By the time it did, he was shivering in the air-conditioning, regretting having come out so soon after arrival. He gulped his pancakes down as quickly as he could and got up, leaving a crumpled $20 bill on top of his unused napkin.

The Totally Other Place afforded him an allowance that was well beyond adequate for a year in these towns, so he took some minor joy in over-tipping.

After this, he set out to explore the backstreets.

He caught his reflection in the window of an out of business hardware store, marked only with a hand-lettered sign that read Nails:

$1/bunch, and stopped to scratch under his mustache, which he had just shaved around this morning. He licked the underside with his tongue, then breathed in sharply with his nose.

He looked good, he thought, tired from the journey but not weak or softened or old, strong still, though soon he would have to resume his workout regimen in the Master Bedroom. He affixed another camera to the upper left corner of the hardware store's front window and walked off without looking at himself again.

Re-crossing the Square, with the Greek restaurant behind him and the Hotel up ahead, he saw those same old men sitting in plastic chairs around a dormant fountain while a few others traced circles around them, their shoelaces untied, all wearing baseball caps high up on their heads, the adjuster straps on the back pulled too tight.

"Hi, hi, how are you?" they muttered to one another each time they passed, "uh-hmm, hi, sure, hi, how are you?" they answered. Squimbop fell momentarily into orbit with them, trying to let a modicum of the familiarity they seemed to feel for one another rub off on him.

What if I truly believed I'd spent my whole life here? He indulged the thought just beyond the point where it was pleasurable, feeling it morph into a vision of a carousel erected on this ground, its roots planted in the center of the fountain, its horses riding the same loop over and over, rusting as they took in the Hotel on one side and the Greek restaurant on the other, never-ending music plinking from a speaker, its cone filling slowly with wasps.

His second orbit around the Square concluded, he turned down a narrow side street with a toy store that looked like it had never been open. Two wide-eyed mannequins leaned against the glass, their breasts in clearings of dust.

The street widened after a few more storefronts, and soon there were large gaps between the buildings, patches of weeds and grass sprouting between cracks in concrete, half-finished strips of mall

8

and auto dealerships fronted by burned-out sedans on cinder blocks.

All of this furnished by the Totally Other Place, to make the town look real.

Pine and oak trees started growing a block further out. Cresting a slight hill, he turned back toward the center and saw the construction site surrounding the ruined Tower he'd seen from the window of ANGEL HOUSE, a mess of wires and fiberglass panes and stalled heavy machinery. Then he passed a fireworks store and a gutted drive-through hamburger joint with only its intercom still standing.

Up ahead he saw another tower, much smaller than the ruin. This one looked like a broadcast tower, protruding from a wide, one-story building with a parking lot on one side. A marquee above the building looked like it was trying to spell RADIO but only the R, I, and O remained.

As he stood under this marquee and looked up at the tower, a man exited into the parking lot through a side door with 'Employee's Entrance' written over it. He wore whitish jeans and sneakers and a blue plaid shirt, tucked into a thick brown leather belt with a gleaming buckle. The shirt's shoulders supported blonde hair that looked heavy with grease.

He looked like a man in his late thirties who'd been up all night, regarding Squimbop with a dazed wariness, like he was taking in the trauma of this stranger's intrusion to ruminate on later, when he had the energy.

Squimbop stood very still and regarded him back, immediately aware that this was one of the few people whose names he would have to learn.

"Night broadcast?" he asked.

The man nodded, pulling keys from his breast pocket and opening his car, sitting down in the driver's seat without closing the door.

"Every night. Now's when I sleep."

"Got a house?" asked Squimbop.

"Hotel. Long term."

Squimbop took this in. "I ate across from there just now."

"Pretty much the only place, unless you drive out to Giant Chinese."

Squimbop pointed to his feet to show he didn't drive.

"Nice boots," the man said. Then he looked into the distance, at a pile of uprooted road signs lying in a ditch.

Squimbop couldn't tell if, in this man's memory, the signs were old or new. He didn't ask.

"Well Broadbeam," said the man, putting his car in gear. "On the air, I'm called the Radio Angel. Maybe I'll see you around."

He pulled out, looking at himself in the rearview mirror.

When he was sure the man was gone, Squimbop reached into his briefcase and affixed his fourth camera to the drainpipe running off the radio station's roof, along the side entrance to the ground.

After this, he continued on, up the Meadow-lined Road in the direction of ANGEL HOUSE, forcing himself to think of this as the way home.

The shadow of the Mountain did nothing to cool the late summer heat.

Standing by the edge of the Meadow, he could tell that, if he kept walking in this direction, he'd reach the sphere of Outskirts that every town had. This was the buffer zone between the inhabited, history-soaked inner town and the unadulterated nothingness of the Inland Sea, the zone that kept the people in town from reaching the edge, or knowing for sure that such an edge existed, whatever suspicions they harbored in private.

In some towns, these Outskirts produced semi-lucid people, dumber and less filled-in than the people in the center, but alive nonetheless. In other towns, the Outskirts were completely sterile. His hunch was that here they were living, but he didn't venture in to explore.

He stared instead at a flat basketball in the center of the road, meditating on the man who called himself the Radio Angel and the relationship they might in time develop. He felt his journey here fade into prehistory as the town became fully real, the limits of his world shrinking vertiginously.

Sweltering where he stood, he looked up at the sky and thought, *Water my lawn.* In the confusion that had been thickening since his arrival, he couldn't remember if he had the power to call down the rain, or if he had to wait like everyone else. As he stood and pondered this, the sky only grew more humid with the air of Reunion, heavy clouds clotting into an overarching atmosphere of shared history.

The rain would not come and the heat kept him from returning to ANGEL HOUSE, which he knew would be hotter still. So, after ten minutes of indecision, he set off, back into the town along another route, seeking elevation, where, at the very least, a faint breeze might blow.

After passing lone houses along the road and then clusters of them on the side streets, he emerged at the bottom of a hill.

Trudging slowly up it, his leg muscles weak after his long slumbering journey, he passed one dead-looking house after another, all of them shuttered, too vacant to be haunted.

As he'd hoped, the air cooled off, thanks to the breeze and the presence of Death, which hung heavily up here, especially at the very top, in a small park with a wooden model boat in the center. Its Wooden Wheel creaked as Squimbop climbed up and took it in his hands, pretending to sail the town through the void, captaining a ship of dead souls, casting himself as the Figure of Death.

He took his hands off the wheel when the vision grew overwhelming and looked at the houses on either side of the park. He saw the face of a child in the upstairs window of both houses. They appeared to be coming out of a deep sleep, fighting for orientation now that they were awake. Turning his head side to side, he made hard, significant eye contact with both of them before affixing his last camera to the center of the wooden boat's wheel, where it had a clear view of the two houses.

When he was sure it was online, he walked back down the hill, through the hellish heat, up the road along the Meadow, past the cluster of wooden houses in the center, and back into ANGEL HOUSE, its anchor now as stable as any foundation.

Back in ANGEL HOUSE, Squimbop sat on the floor of the Master Bedroom, opened his laptop, and logged onto his private Wi-Fi network. First, he opened a program called Cameras 1-5, and verified that all five streams were flowing. Everything looked good, the whole town sweltering, no one but old men wandering the streets.

Then he opened his Internet browser and began to compose the year's first email.

Dear Master,

Have arrived. Passage was tedious but uneventful. Inland Sea seems to grow larger each time I cross it, or perhaps it is only that I forget its true breadth between crossings.

New town is small, dusty, grim, little to recommend it. Cameras are up and running: will return with footage.

The atmosphere is oppressive and feels incestuous. It appears to be one of those towns populated solely by men. A dismal sign, indicative, I believe, of a cruder-than-usual combination of psychic matter from the Inland Seafloor. A volatile and imbalanced mixture, though not, if memory serves, an unusual one. Not for the smaller and more destitute towns, anyway.

All for now,

Prof. Sq.

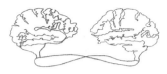

The two nine-year-olds felt the Shadow of Death cross them where they lay dreaming in their Dead Houses. Their whole lives up to this moment faded into a warm, amniotic glow as soon as they rolled over and looked out their windows at the monstrous figure steering the Wooden Wheel in the park, staring first at one of them, then the other.

They yawned, rubbing their hair in unison, trying to massage away the headaches that only got worse the longer they stayed in bed. *Time is already ticking*, they thought, in their shared mind, heartbroken to feel the years of cozy, safe dreaming slip away. *We can't stay here much longer.*

So they rose, dressed for the first time in what they now called *our real lives*, and felt what it was to be embodied, to need to pee, then to eat breakfast, then to put their shoes on and trudge through real space, along a single path rather than through the simultaneity of imagination, in order to accomplish something real.

They met in the park between their Dead Houses after each had locked his front door and hidden the key under the mat. There was no one else around. All the other Dead Houses were clearly vacant; a few were caving in. They had the distant sense that other children existed— that they were, in some sense, two of many—but these others lived elsewhere and were irrelevant to the life the two of them were embarking on now. *There is something meant for us alone,* they thought, *but if we don't find it, we will end up in the same place as all the others.*

There will be no proof that we are different, and that will be our hell.

Setting out, they eased into the feeling of being one person in two bodies. They could feel something pulling them toward the Meadow like a harness hooked under their arms and over their chests. Without quite knowing it, they were following Squimbop's footsteps back to

13

ANGEL HOUSE. They followed them through downtown, past the Hotel and the Greek restaurant and the Movie Store, and onto the Meadow-lined Road, so straight it looked like a dry canal.

It had come to be truly hot. There was water in the air, but that only made it hotter, and bent the light in the distance. Reptiles on the asphalt watched the duo pass. Despite the sluggishness of the atmosphere, they maintained a diligent pace. They could tell it was important to enter the workday with the militant feeling that only such a pace could drum up.

This pace carried them over the lip of the Meadow, away from the road and through the marshy grass. The Mountain loomed behind it, so high it appeared to tip forward, forming a partial roof over the sky. Beneath this roof, the air was a gray haze.

There was something they were looking for, and they could hear a timer ticking down to when they would find it as the marsh water began to seep through their sneakers and socks, encasing their toes in aspic.

ANGEL HOUSE sat in a declivity on one edge of the Meadow, far back from the road, the shadow of the Mountain almost all the way over it, deepening its purple glow, which turned the air suddenly cold.

There was deep déjà vu as they sensed that the cold was localized, such that if they took a few steps back they would meld into late summer, while if they took a few steps forward, ANGEL HOUSE would freeze them solid.

So they stayed where they were, sinking into the marsh up to their shins. They couldn't quite see the interior. Something was shimmering over its façade, blocking it off. Maybe it was only sunlight, or the déjà vu again, or the sensation of life sloshing into the empty spaces within them, frantically filling in nine years of emptiness.

It started to feel like they'd been standing here too long, their skin puckering with the awareness that the inhabitant of this house

14

would soon appear.

As they stared and waited, they felt their eyes straining. They leaned into this strain, trying to find a balance that wouldn't break as the uncoiling in their centers grew fast, nine years of dreaming expanding to fill the town from a single dense point. They could feel the house's interior taking shape as the déjà vu kept growing, the feeling that whatever had cast the Shadow of Death over them in their beds was connected to this place, emanating from it, and that it would not stop until it possessed them or they found a way to possess it.

They took a single step forward and were frozen into scarecrows.

Under their feet, they could feel the entire town opening into a maze of tunnels and vaults, caverns, catacombs, all the sunken chambers they would need to fight their way through to make it out of the past. They could already tell that the town would kill them if they stayed in it. They could feel it hungering for them.

As they stood like this, they barely noticed that their arms were being cranked upward, opening to the sky and the light of ANGEL HOUSE, while, deep in their cores, the Pretend Movie was being born. It was called *The Dream of Escape* and it would be their religion, the one thing they'd serve and worship in exchange for a redemption that they alone, of everyone in this town, stood any chance of achieving, as all the others fought miserably to reenter the past and drowned in the process.

Only Movies, they thought, *can make public what is privately bubbling up inside us now. And only by making it public will we find a world to live in, sanely, outside the town… outside the past…*

Let us never forget this, no matter what else, in time, Movies may seem to be instead.

As they stared at ANGEL HOUSE through eyes too frozen to blink, taking in both the magnitude and the improbability of its arrival, they thought, *This, right now, is our one moment of vision. This is given. Everything else, we'll have to fight for.*

The nine-year-olds found the strength to force their way backwards, out of the scarecrow state and away from ANGEL HOUSE's pull. It wrenched something in their backs and legs, but for the moment they were free.

They turned and ran, limping when they had to, until they reached the grassy median of the Meadow-lined Road.

Here they lay down, curled their legs against their chests, and closed their eyes. As soon as they fell asleep, they were incarnated as the nineteen-year-olds, summoned to town to star in the Pretend Movie that had just been born.

The nineteen-year-olds had been on the road a long time, driving in circles on a featureless ring of highway so wide they'd never known what they were circling. A holding pattern, an unbroken stretch of time in which their only mandate had been to keep driving. But this morning they'd felt something land in the distance that told them their trip would soon come to an end. An ark, a center of gravity sucking them off the road, out of orbit and toward a fixed location, where they'd have to face whatever they'd been avoiding all this time.

We're about to end up somewhere, they thought. *And only by going there and fighting our way through it, down through its dirt and out the other side, will we at last stop circling. Then our real lives will begin. Our adult lives… in which the stakes will be higher, the rewards more tangible.*

In the hours since they'd felt the ark land, the countryside had taunted them with its emptiness and sudden, strange pockets of settlement: drunken men waving from wheat fields, gas stations with their pumps dredged out of the ground and left cracked and rotting on the concrete like sharks dumped onto a dock with their fins cut off. Enough of a sense of things had developed in these hours to make it seem to the nineteen-year-olds that they weren't blipping into existence right now, even if, in reality, they were.

They took the first exit the highway offered them, coming to a halt in an abandoned parking lot at the edge of what appeared to be a town, and went into a glass and cement structure with a giant sign out front that read 'Welcome Center.'

They settled into a booth in the empty Welcome Center restaurant and ordered meatloaf and mashed potatoes and beer from the waiter, who came over eagerly, almost desperately, as soon as they sat down.

Looking out the window, they saw the highway crumbling, turning to dust. The exit they'd taken was gone. Now they were only here, no longer on their way to someplace else.

After laying out their food, the waiter asked if he could do anything else for them. Neither could think straight. Their plan had simply been to keep driving, despite the fatigue, so now the notion of the vanished exit held more terror than promise. They wanted to ask the waiter for help but couldn't think how. They said no. He nodded, a little disappointed, and walked off.

They began to eat, regarding each other, trying to stabilize.

"Somehow," one said to the other, "the time has come. This town is the place where we'll do whatever we're going to do. The thing that'll set our real lives in motion."

The other nodded, agreeing without quite knowing what the thing was, nor how the process of finally doing it might unfold. The notion seemed somehow redundant and menacingly uncharted at the same time. "Ready or not, here we come," he said.

They both laughed feebly.

The waiter sent out slow waves of interest from his station

17

behind the register, which faced an open indoor plaza with coin-operated massage chairs and a giant-claw prize machine. Openly eavesdropping, he smiled whenever they made eye contact with him.

When he came back to the table, they ordered coffee and grasshopper pie. This time, he asked what they were up to here.

"There's no more road for us," they replied, in unison. "Our plan was to keep driving, but then the exit appeared so we took it."

"The exit?"

The three of them looked out the window, where there was only dust and haze in the air.

The nineteen-year-olds shrugged. "Can we have our coffee and pie now?"

The waiter nodded and came back with it a moment later. Putting their plates and mugs in front of them, he announced that he had an idea. "There's a Hotel in the center of town. I haven't stayed there myself, but I would. Not too expensive, not too cheap. It'll fill up for the Reunion this weekend, but you should still be able to get a room there tonight. If you're gonna be here a while, I mean…"

They smiled and said thanks, trying to imitate the friendliness in his eyes, as if that way they might trick themselves into feeling it. After they paid the check, they got back in their car, which they could tell would die as soon as they pulled up in front of the Hotel, never to start again.

They peeled out, past ANGEL HOUSE along the Meadow-lined Road, almost running over the nine-year-olds where they lay dreaming in the grassy median.

The nine-year-olds bolted upright, tearing out fistfuls of grass as the car vanished up the road.

They sat there looking past each other, their eyes glowing ANGEL HOUSE purple. It was a while before they remembered to breathe. As soon as they did, the specifics of the dream faded. Only

18

broad strokes remained.

They looked at each other, confirming that they'd witnessed the opening scene of the Pretend Movie. Not only witnessed it. Directed it.

They're in town, they thought, standing up and beginning to walk down the Meadow-lined Road in the direction the nineteen-year-olds had driven, imagining them pulling into the center, parking, and checking into the Hotel under false names like a pair of seasoned outlaws.

By the time the nine-year-olds had made it back to the Dead Neighborhood, the nineteen-year-olds were settled into their room, booked for a weekly rate.

The Pretend Movie has begun, they thought, settling back into the beds that Squimbop had woken them from this morning. Their sheets and pillows still felt cold with the Shadow of Death, but they knew that they were no longer powerless to resist it.

PART I
The Reunion

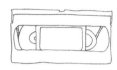

Wednesday

As soon as ANGEL HOUSE came to rest in the Meadow, James found himself standing in the center of the town's abandoned bus station, holding a duffel bag in a pile of broken glass. He wasn't sure it was good to be back, but after ten years of struggle in News City's merciless film world, he allowed himself to feel some relief.

He caught his breath, choking on the dust in the air, and walked the rest of the way across the abandoned concourse, kicking his sneakers side to side to throw off the glass that stuck to the soles. The unreal already hung over his journey here—what had he passed on the way? How long had it taken? He couldn't remember.

The ARRIVALS/DEPARTURES board that hung against one wall was a blur of smudged chalk. Suppressing the urge to turn back and check if the bus was still in its parking space, or if any other passengers had disembarked with him, he hurried through the doors and onto the street out front.

The Outskirts, he thought, letting it all come back to him. The cracked weedy sidewalks, the detached culverts rolling in the wind. *As far out there as Ben and I ever got, until the day we came in here and took the bus to News City...*

He felt like a liar trying to get his story straight. Again he shook it off, hurrying toward the town along what had back then been known as the Meadow-lined Road. He was twenty-nine, a little soft in the gut, his eyes permanently watering from the hours he'd spent staring at screens over the last decade in News City.

He had to stop by the side of the Meadow-lined Road to catch his breath and yet again shake off the feeling that he'd never left the town. A train of geese crossed the sky and they looked exactly like the geese that had crossed it when he and Ben had come up this way to board the bus for News City ten years ago. He had the awful impression that they'd been paused in mid-flight all that time and some malevolent force had just now permitted them to resume their journey.

He spat into the grass and hurried the rest of the way into town, thinking, *As soon as one thing becomes uncanny, everything else follows, and I don't want to be standing out here alone when that happens.*

He emerged relatively intact into the Square, the Greek restaurant on one side, the Hotel on the other. A banner that read REUNION: OUTSKIRTS OPEN hung over the Hotel's doorway, already sagging.

As he was working up the courage to walk under it and ask about a room, a thick, heavy palm landed on his shoulder. He spun around and stood facing the current incarnation of one of his oldest friends, now ten years older and a good two hundred pounds heavier.

"Hey," panted the Mayor. "Welcome back. Glad you made it."

James stared at him, trying not to fixate on the spittle on his lips or the sheen on his forehead. For a moment, he expected the teenager he'd known to step out of this gargantuan man's body, pulling jelly from his healthy frame like a newborn animal.

But that didn't happen.

Fearing that James didn't recognize him, the Mayor added, defeatedly, "It's me, the Mayor."

Instead of fixating on his bulk, James tried to remember what his name had been before. This effort exhausted and disoriented him so much that he fixated again on the sheen and spittle, gladly, gratefully even.

"Hi," he managed, barely. "I think I need to sit down."

The Mayor nodded. "Yeah."

They both sat on the Hotel steps and tried to think back over the past decade, trying to grasp how it'd culminated here, the two of them less than a foot apart after all the miles that one of them had traveled.

James looked up at the REUNION: OUTSKIRTS OPEN banner, then back at the Mayor, gagging as his eyes got lost in the sweaty folds of the man's neck. His eyes swam and he knew that if he didn't rent a bed and get into it in the next few minutes, he'd pass out where he sat.

"I'm a little, uh, this is... can we talk later?" James managed, before turning away from the Mayor and beginning to cry, overwhelmed by the sudden realness of his return.

The Mayor, looking in the opposite direction, began crying as well, mopping his face with his giant palms and inner arms.

Neither said anything when, a few minutes later, James got to his feet with the help of the handrail and dragged himself into the lobby.

The Mayor listened to him go without turning to watch and then, drying his eyes with the hem of his shirt, got to his feet using the same handrail and lumbered across the Square and into his station wagon. Driving along the Meadow-lined Road, disappointed as he was that no more had transpired between them, he had to admit that he was grateful for the chance to go home and think about James' return before taking any further action.

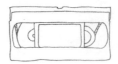

Back home, the Mayor opened his refrigerator and took out all the butter he had. While he waited for it to soften, he replayed his memories of this morning, when the arrival of ANGEL HOUSE had woken him up.

His first thought, upon waking, was the awareness that James was back in town. With this awareness came his first glimpse of the gigantic Movie that James, now the he'd become an actual Director in News City, would make for him. Like a dream that was slipping away as he came back to consciousness, he fought to hold onto this glimpse. *A Movie to end all Movies,* he thought. *To canonize the town so that, finally and forever, this place will be the only one, and all the people here will be only here, never leaving, never aging, and I will be their God.*

This was the mood he'd been in all day, but now, returning home from seeing James in the Square, he was shaken, unsure of himself again. *Omnipotent, not impotent, omnipotent, not impotent,* he chanted as he mixed brownie batter in his kitchen, but the mantra only wound him up, doing nothing to steel his nerves.

He had one Movie left, sitting in its clear plastic Movie Store box in his basement. He'd been saving it, like a dying man refusing to take his final breath, but now, though he knew he'd regret it as soon as it was done, he was about to go down and put it in the VCR. It was the only way forward, out of the decade in which he'd ruled the town alone, and into whatever this new era was, now that both Ben and James were back from News City.

There is no News City, he tried to convince himself, as he stirred butter into the chocolaty sugar. *There is only the town, there is only the town… the town as it was the town as it was the town as it was. In time, Ben and James will remember this.*

He was fuming now, struggling to regulate his breath, his groin pulsing in anticipation.

When the batter was ready, the Mayor took it down to the basement. He put it on the coffee table next to the Movie box and lay down on the couch, again trying to catch his breath before proceeding.

He tried to orient his thoughts toward how things had been before today:

The Movie Store rented Movies by other Directors, predecessors of the Mayor, people he didn't know, collectively fleshing out a vision of the town as it was, before his time. These were the only visions of the town's history that existed; his only means of feeling as though he was part of a lineage and not marooned on an island in time. There was no record except for the Movie record.

This record, taken collectively, had so far been erotic and tangible enough to couple with and sire the town's children, all of whom were now nine years old.

But all that was coming to an end; he could feel life as he'd been living it receding into the past, while some new, daunting present crested the horizon.

He mashed a pillow into his face and tried to picture what James could make for him, a Movie tens or hundreds of hours long, telling the full story of their years—his and James' and Ben's—in the town, the ledges they'd crept onto, the secrets they'd collectively unearthed, their all-night conversations at the Greek restaurant, their thrilling and dangerous proximity to the divine, all before turning nineteen.

He mashed the pillow tighter against his face, trying to keep these images from escaping. Almost suffocating, he saw his teenage years with Ben and James flickering like eels, deep in the Pornography, the only place where life was pure, fresh and uncontaminated by the desire to return to a yet-deeper source. The Oasis in the Desert of Nostalgia.

During this past decade, from nineteen to twenty-nine, the

Mayor had burned through the entire Movie Store's collection, using each tape as a doorway, a means of walking through his TV screen and into the town as it was. Before he was born, before he'd begun losing the things he loved.

But this was a cheap and temporary solution, each tape only good for a single visit. He'd used them all up, tainting the Pornography with his old sperm, fathering a school's worth of children in the effort to ward off suicide, night after night after night, down here in his basement.

Now it was time to go deeper, all the way down, to the fresh, clean Pornography at the bottom, enough to last all his life, if he could only convince James to make a Movie that would crack it open, granting him total private access to their lost years without recourse to the Movie Store.

He sat up, his ass cheeks spread on the couch, his pants and boxers around his ankles, and imagined spending the rest of his life like this, never coming up for air, approaching a state of continuous orgasm, which he'd enter through the doorway of James' Movie, in which he, Ben, and James would forever approach the asymptote of their nineteenth birthday without ever falling off the far side.

Detaching his underwear from his pants, he folded both neatly on the armrest of the couch and turned the screen on, luxuriating in his nakedness as the cathode tube warmed up. When it had, he opened the Movie Store box, removed the tape, kissed all six of its sides, and then, kneeling and closing his eyes, inserted it into the VCR.

When it had been swallowed up, he opened his eyes, exhaled, and crawled back to the couch, retrieving his bowl of brownie batter. He stirred it with a long finger and began to sup as the image expanded from the center of the screen.

He could see objectively only for a moment: the Movie opened on the Town Square, the Greek restaurant on one side, the Hotel on the other. In the center, a group of people the Mayor didn't recognize but felt instantly familiar with stood around, smoking, making small talk, looking

25

up at the sky, then back at the ground, at their feet and one another's, endlessly reconfirming the fact that here they all were, together in the town, and that there was nowhere else they'd rather be, nothing encroaching.

"The town as it was," he sighed, feeling his heartbeat quicken and his eyelids flutter. "The town as it was the town as it was the town as it was."

Slipping into the trance these images always induced in him, the Mayor sighed and let go. The screen opened as the images melted together into a portal. It called to him, inviting him back in. He heeded the invitation, walking toward it, his body already glistening.

He stood before it and saw moist ground with sprouting vines curling around their own roots in the foreground, humps of reddish mountains far off in the distance. The air, reeking of wine and perfume, came straight through the screen to meet him, mixing in his nostrils with the brownie taste in his mouth and throat.

He wiped the chocolate batter all over his penis and testicles, and pushed some up into his rectum, tasting it with the far end of his intestine. Then he heaved a sigh, felt his reproductive system churn, and, still muttering, "the town as it was the town as it was the town as it was," stepped all the way through, pushing the screen open with the tip of his penis, leaving the real town, in its precarious present tense, far behind.

The Orchard enveloped him.

It smelled like molten chocolate and wine and mud and sex. Death was real in the public concourse of the town—at the Welcome Center and the bus station and on the Hotel steps where he'd met James—but in the privacy of the Orchard there was no such thing. In here, life could only begin and begin and begin.

Now he was in the innermost part, where the vaginas grew. His penis swelled at the thought, then the sight. He took it in his hands, squeezing it like a blister that he didn't want to pop just yet.

He walked the rest of the way up to them, stretching as far as he could see in one direction. They grew on fleshy stalks out of the moist ground, opening at waist level, ringed in hair and already wet. They made a low dovelike cooing that grew louder the closer he got.

They all turned toward him, like sunflowers. He walked up and down the row, trying to find the one that tonight's Movie corresponded to. All the others—those of Movies he'd seen long ago—were decaying inside, filled with ash and rotting tissue, enticing only on the surface.

The Movie continued to play in the far distance, the edge of his vision crackling with scenes of old men sitting at tables in the Greek restaurant or working on cars on their lawns, but he was so deep inside the Orchard now, so nostalgia-drunk, that the images he saw might as well have been his own thoughts.

He stroked himself as he went, trying not to imagine the vaginas in their decay, though, of course, imagining only that, growing ever more erect as he saw his penis vanishing into Death and emerging on the far side, longer and thicker than any snuffing force the universe could devise.

Finally, he came to tonight's vagina, less ashy than the others, smelling more strongly of life. "You are my last Movie," he bent to whisper into it. "I love you the same as all the others, but, tonight, a little more desperately."

Returning to his full height, he eased his penis inside.

He sighed, feeling old and worn out, as he guided his penis deeper in and then pulled it out slightly, then guided it in again, breathing through his nose, his ankles digging into the soft mud. The point of contact was way beneath his belly, so he couldn't see it, but the feeling was real.

The disjunct between sight and sensation so occupied his mind that he didn't notice himself coming. By the time he did, it was too late. He pulled out, spurting cold gouts onto his feet.

Spooked, he turned and trudged back through the screen.

It hurt to leave the Orchard like this. Fear and shame clotted over him as he crawled back into his basement.

He put his robe on, yawning, and switched off the TV, tossing the remote onto the couch, where it sank into the well-worn cushion. When he pressed Eject on the VCR, the tape emerged ashy and spent. He pulled out the hot plastic and squished it back into its box, to be returned to the Movie Store after the Reunion.

Then he climbed the stairs out of the basement, passing a gamut of bear eyes arrayed in his backyard, where they'd congregated to keep him moving toward his car.

In the garage, he got in his station wagon and sat there for a moment before shifting into neutral. He thought, as he often did at this point in the ritual, how close he was to full dominion over the night, how close to self-sufficient his world in the basement could be. And yet it wasn't.

The Blind Spot gaped open. Although he could resist for hours, forcing his way into secret compartments in the night, the bears would push closer and closer, right up to his flesh, eventually forcing their way down his throat and into his brain, furring his whole system, until he finally relented.

Awful totems, the bears wouldn't rest until they'd forced him out, back into nightly confrontation with his tininess. This was their duty.

And now my last Movie is gone, he remembered, as if things hadn't been bad enough already.

He looked in his rearview mirror and saw that the bears had come into his garage, as they often did when he sat too long behind the wheel. So he honked angrily and switched into neutral, beginning to roll down his driveway, around the cul-de-sac, and into the dark of the town.

The Mayor drifted all the way to the Blind Spot in neutral, hands in his

28

lap, watching the wheel steer itself in grim parody of a kiddie ride at a funfair, the kind that used to arrive in the Meadow every August.

He passed the rock quarries behind his house, from which, as far as anyone knew, all the raw materials of the town had been sourced by previous generations. From here, he continued along the lonely, untraveled back roads, the ones without streetlights.

Like a tree that only blossomed one day a year, he could smell the Reunion through his cracked windows. It made his eyes water in a reaction part sentimental, part allergic. Everything he rolled past was reverting, taking on the guises of what it had been, pretending that the lost world everyone was forever striving to return to was not lost. *How could it be?* The air whispered. *It's all right here.*

A Home Built of Past, he thought, looking at the dark houses, quoting a standard Reunion line that was back in the air tonight, finding its way into people's throats to be uttered at the School this Saturday, when everything was set up and everyone was there to remember when they'd all been in that same building as much younger people.

Passing through more open territory now, his station wagon crushing the weeds that had overgrown the train tracks, he opened his body further to the roving spirit of Reunion, and began to revisit the trips he took out here with Ben and James in high school, when they were seventeen and eighteen, before nineteen came and News City fractured their trio.

It all came to him now, through the station wagon's windows, as easily as the car's progress in neutral, as he traced the edges of the Outskirts, which he could hear creaking open like a giant vault, coming unsealed as they prepared to release their hordes for the Reunion.

He could picture the nights when he and Ben and James would drink and smoke in the cul-de-sac at the end of his driveway and then walk all the way out here, to stand on ridges and gaze up at the peak of the giant Mountain at whose foot the town sprawled, in terror or worship or both, and, if they walked in a certain direction, at the deep ravines of the quarry that stretched all the way to the woods behind the Mayor's house, where the rusted-over tractors and backhoes that had been used to build the town were parked.

Often they'd stand on one of the ledges and look back at the sporadic lights of the town, and imagine the skyline swelling up into spires, minarets, obelisks, citadels.

They saw themselves as explorers, mutineers from a larger expedition, breaking away from the open road and the march of progress to discover a mammoth, abandoned city, free for the taking.

Let's settle here, they'd think. *And live for Movies like we've always wanted to. No longer refusing to grow up because growing up will no longer mean giving in.*

Many nights, the fantasy spun on and on, into dreams of prosperity and power, of turning the town physically into all that it had become in their minds, filling with matter all the blank spaces they'd so far filled only with fantasy. *This,* they'd thought then, *is the only righteous segue into real life. Not the putting-behind of childish things, but the imposition of those things, forcibly if need be, brutally even, onto the postlapsarian things of adults.*

Eyes misting over, the Mayor enjoyed this spell of unabashed Reunion thinking, incarnating the three of them at seventeen, looking out at the skyline that had no towers except those they dreamed of building.

But, with a smell of burning plastic, the image twisted into now, twenty-nine, alone in his car, surrounded by bears, wrapped in a robe sticky with brownie batter.

"It's impossible to be in two places at once, but one is always in many times," he whispered, quoting another Reunion classic as the bears pressed close to the car to read his lips.

He was at the Blind Spot now, preparing to face the pit, the pure, unrendered space, the hole in the heart of the town. Perhaps the gateway to hell. He was losing his wherewithal, lapsing into Death-think. Soon he'd be barely human, a husk with glazed eyes riveted on nothingness.

But first, one more flurry of memory.

He could see three figures in the distance, framed by his windshield and glowing orange, like the inner part of a forest burning while the outer part waited its turn. This could be the opening scene in the massive Movie he would commission from James. He pictured himself naked in his basement, watching it on his TV, where the scene would be less fleeting and thus more real.

He knew the figures were himself, Ben, and James, and knew they could feel themselves being watched because he remembered it from when he was on the other side, all times being equally present within the Psychogeography.

The three of them weren't so powerful they could reach across the intervening decade and touch him, and neither could he touch them, but he could tell they knew he was here, and that their spines were quivering with the possibility of contact.

The thrill and discomfort were mutual, the watching himself as a younger man and the being watched by himself now.

He became aroused but suppressed it as best he could, adjusting his robe, knowing that to let sex out of his basement would contaminate the entire town.

From his current remove all he could recall from that moment was that the three of them had come very close to seeing the Blind Spot for what it was.

The truth had been there back then, as they wobbled before it in their shorts and sandals with their long puffy hair and barely grown-in beards and teeth scummy with pot smoke.

But they'd written it off, and then Ben and James had applied to college and gone to News City to become professionals, as if that escape route were real.

They'd attributed the vision back then to drugs and drink and being teenagers, full of impulse and empty of context and training. The Mayor knew there'd always been a part of Ben and James that yearned to give up the Pretend Movie and become artists-in-the-world, paid real money and written up in magazines for the delectation of strangers.

The reality of the Blind Spot could only mock them for this.

If the three of us, then, had accepted that the Blind Spot is real in a way that nothing else ever would be, the Mayor was thinking now, *I wouldn't be here alone tonight. We'd all three be ruling this empire together, and the town would be a paradise.*

They would have known never to leave.

He could see the bears grimacing, growing bored. A speck of strength within his blubber tried to hold out, but the rest of him said, *Obey.*

He sighed, closed his eyes, and opened his mouth, letting the Blind Spot speak through him as the last of the vision dissipated. His headlights illuminated nothing but the pit now. "I am nothing, I am nothing, I am less than nothing," he heard himself confess, like a radio tuned to a private channel, to the audience of bears that had thronged his station wagon.

"I am nothing, and the town is nothing. We are all just blips, abandoned and marooned in the vastness of the world, a world we will never know because we aren't strong enough to take it in. The town as it was is the town as it is and the town as it is is nothing."

 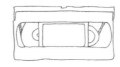

Thursday Morning

After the Blind Spot released him, the Mayor wasn't ready to go home. So he cruised downtown in his station wagon, which he was now able to take out of neutral.

Where the Meadow-lined Road entered town, he turned right instead of going straight, and found himself coming to a halt by the fence that surrounded a construction site, where Ben was standing with a cup of Greek restaurant coffee. It must have been 6:30 a.m.; the Greek restaurant opened at six.

The Mayor got out, wheezing, tasting copper.

Ben came over but didn't say anything until the Mayor caught his breath, holding his robe closed with both hands.

The construction site was choked with white mist, like something in its materials was generating it.

"Checking up on things?" asked Ben, sipping his coffee, which he had indeed gotten at the Greek restaurant as soon as it opened, having found it impossible to sleep past sunrise in the Hotel where he'd been staying since last year, when the Mayor had summoned him back from News City and given him the order to design the thing in whose shadow they were now standing. He stood with his back to the wooden gazebo the contractors had fitted with a vault-quality lock to store the blueprints he'd drawn last year. He supposed the gazebo itself must have been in his blueprints somewhere as well, but he couldn't remember drawing it.

The Mayor nodded. "Yeah. Let's do a walkthrough. See how things are coming along."

Ben shrugged, swallowed a mouthful of coffee, and ducked under the fence, turning to help the Mayor through once he'd found his footing on the other side.

Now they were in the construction site, straddling nail-stuck planks and looking up at the Tower.

But before either of them could ask or say anything specific about things as they stood now, the Reunion spirit in the air looped them back to last year. The Psychogeography was open, rendering this year momentarily indistinguishable from the last.

"How is it being an architect in News City?" the Mayor had asked. "Lots of people calling you up with jobs? Designing skyscrapers and art museums and high-speed train stations?"

The interval between the call and Ben's return to the town had been nonexistent, like one moment he was stewing in his News City apartment, trying to expel the terror that came with being broke, and the next moment he was checking into the Hotel, preparing to meet the Mayor at the bar.

They'd sat at the Hotel bar, not tasting their drinks, plunging straight past the complexities of having not seen each other for nine years, like the foundation for the Town's City had already been laid and now they were standing in it, envisioning the structure it would soon give rise to, with or without their participation.

Like now, thought Ben, holding his coffee with the Mayor in the fog of the present, looking at the construction site, which struck him less as a work in progress and more as a ruin, something whose apex had come during an earlier era and was now meant not for contractors but for archaeologists. *Maybe these archeologists,* he thought, *will manage to find some meaning in the ruin that the contractors failed to find, or failed to understand, in my blueprints … maybe, centuries from now, it'll become clear what went wrong.*

Ben had no concrete memories from last year in the Hotel, drawing the blueprints while falling more and more into what he now, with a few months of hindsight, recognized as a form of insanity, the first flowering of the thing he'd felt latent in his brainstem since his late teens.

He'd fallen into something, or let it swirl up in him, as soon as the Mayor commissioned the plans, like all the anxiety and terror he'd built up during his years in News City had popped and bled out of him onto his drafting paper. By Hibernation of last year, he was saying goodbye to himself every night and cautiously meeting himself again every morning.

But he emerged in spring with the plans under his arm and handed them to the Mayor, who'd hired a team of contractors and told them, "Buy your materials at Ultra Max and bill me for whatever they come to. Get to work right away and don't stop until it's done."

They'd done just that, and now here was the result. The Mayor stood with Ben and gazed up at it, trying to see it as it actually was, as opposed to how he'd always seen it in his mind and, more often than not, saw it still.

In today's early dawn, the suggestion of a wider skyline hung in the haze above the central shaft of the Tower, and the Mayor permitted himself the thrill of pretending he lived in an actual city, the Town's City, one that wouldn't dwarf him because he was its father. *There is no other place, nowhere else I ought to be. No dichotomy between the tininess of the town and the vastness of the City… because both are here, unified, indivisible… belonging entirely to me.*

"Remember our first talk at the Hotel bar last year?" The Mayor understood by now that the walkthrough was nothing but a Reunion ritual, and so saw no alternative to embracing it as such.

Ben took another gulp of coffee and nodded. Sitting in the Hotel bar, the Mayor had begun to free associate about urban scenes, pastiches of cities he'd never been to, places he'd dreamed of as a baby or imagined were in the Bible, trying to spark in Ben what would, given time and money and whatever expertise Ben had managed to accrue throughout his twenties, turn into blueprints.

Ben had sat quietly, looking somewhere between the Mayor and the rest of the bar, the shell of downtown visible through half-curtained windows.

"The rain falling past neon onto awnings and stalls and whipping up a harbor full of ships from every country, sailors cursing in a thousand languages, animals that no longer exist in the wild preserved in cages, prostitutes spreading exotic disease... a near future that looks the same as the recent past, on street level, but on the rooftop level it looks like the distant future," the Mayor had said, as the sun set outside the windows of the Hotel bar last year.

"An underbelly. Something seedy, rife with dark potential. Seed just sitting there, waiting to sprout. Do you know what I mean? Rain falling on thick cuts of meat steaming on portable grills, guys with guns in sweaty undershirts standing nearby, spirits roaming blind alleys, looking for bodies to inhabit. An autopsy happening behind a curtain. Do you know what I mean by this? The autopsy doctor fumbling to work under the blanket, the corpse so secret even he can't see its face." The Mayor could barely fit his stomach behind the bar. Parts of it crept over the edges of the chair and under the armrests.

"I think I can relate to that scene," said Ben. He experimented inside himself to see if he could, aware that he'd said it with no gut sense of whether it was true.

He imagined the Hotel bar spilling onto a street where hooded men were grifting on the corners, maybe in some far eastern country during a war, a foreign occupation, always in the rain, gangsters playing

36

cards and turncoats marked for death coming out of revolving doors, stepping into limos with tinted windows that pulled up while a white-gloved man inside reached across the back seat to haul them in. Exquisite etchings on the doors of hotel bathrooms, fine linework and frosted glass disguising unspeakable things inside.

He and James had grown up casting the town into guises, developing the ability to see everyone around them as a troupe of actors, ready for whatever roles the Pretend Movie assigned them, every rundown street and storefront waiting to be turned into a set, and thus liberated from whatever dull role it had played in reality.

This was, throughout Ben's and James' childhoods, the only reason all these people and places existed.

"Inside this structure," the Mayor concluded, at the Hotel bar last year, "there will be mostly empty space, hallowed space, where the aspects of our beings that are now loose on the streets, at odds, will be able to go, and establish residence. It'll be the town's brain, its temple, its emanating point and eventual sarcophagus. An antidote to the rot of foreclosure, which, as you can see, has been the fate of almost every real structure here. Take what you remember of News City and improve upon it, to the point where the notion of leaving the town will be reduced to the kind of absurdity we'll be able to enjoy most when we're old. In short, make it as if News City had existed here all along and there was never an outside place you and James felt you had to go to in order to become adults."

Wiping his mouth with the back of his hand, the Mayor added, "Basically, make it so that there's no threat of another place in anyone's mind. Make it whatever you want, so long as it includes everything there could possibly be."

Returning to the present, they finished the walkthrough. Neither of them could tell if they'd just circled the whole site or paced back and forth over a couple of square feet. They coughed as the Psychogeography

37

released them.

Ben swallowed the last of his Greek restaurant coffee and threw the cup into the mud of the construction site, on top of the hundreds of similar cups the contractors had left behind. It felt good to be part of this material record.

"Okay," said Ben. "I hope you're happy with things as they stand. See you at the School on Saturday?"

"Why don't I come by the Hotel and we'll get breakfast before heading over together?"

Ben nodded, then climbed under the fence, helped the Mayor back through, and set out toward the Hotel, where he hadn't slept more than two hours any night this year.

Thursday

Shaken with the sense that he and the Mayor had just reenacted their entire discussion from last year, and thus that the Reunion was in full control of his thinking now, Ben got in bed in his Hotel room and tried not to think at all.

He was on his back, aiming his toes at the window pretending each was connected to the trigger of a machine gun on the Hotel roof, mowing people down in the Square outside. He knew the Hotel would soon cease to be as empty as it had been all year, when Well Broadbeam had been its only other resident. Though he could accept that there was no preventing the influx of Reuniongoers, he felt called to defend it against intrusion, despite remembering how the loneliness of the empty hallways, the empty restaurant, and the empty lobby had pushed him close to suicide more days than not. *Loneliness is the worst thing*, he thought, *until the threat of intrusion becomes real.* He felt like the Hotel had turned him into its protective ghost against his will.

Now all he wanted was for it to be last year again. But the Reunion would turn it into an entirely different structure, like a massive renovation was about to begin here as well, the contractors from the Town's City trudging over en masse with their jackhammers ready to break ground under the lobby.

His machine-gun toe cramped and he thought, *Out of ammo.*

I did what I could for you, he explained to himself, then closed his eyes and watched as the Reunion hordes tore him into fistfuls that they sprinkled with salt and swallowed raw.

He almost fell asleep, but came to on his bed and got up, returning to the window. Back in the dead of summer, he'd set himself the strict deadline of Reunion Weekend Friday Night—the last weekend in August, before the new school year began—for being "totally recovered," and determined that thereafter he'd begin the next phase of his life.

So tonight was the borderline, the last of the old before the dawning of the new, just as he remembered his last night in News City before getting on the bus to come back here at the Mayor's behest last year.

Staring out the window at the skyline he'd caused to rise from the one- and two-story sprawl surrounding it, he felt the cramp in his toe and remembered his actual gun.

A week ago, he'd awoken very early, put his sneakers on under his pajamas, and walked out into the sweltering street, down an alley that led across a parking lot and onto the Strip, past the Night School to Ultra Max, where he bought a handgun but no ammo.

He'd taken it back to his room and put it in his mouth and pulled the trigger. He did this every night thereafter, like it was an asthma

39

inhaler, thinking, *I hereby kill the old day inside me and tear the birth-hole of the new, through which a better me will appear.*

Now, he fished it from the back pocket of his jeans slung over his desk chair and brought it to the window, aiming it as far up the street as he could, in the direction of the Outskirts. *Round two*, he thought, pulling the trigger several times, hearing it click, perhaps as loudly as it would have if it'd been loaded.

But the longer he shot toward the Outskirts, the more his imagination strayed from shooting bullets. He began to feel the gun barrel emitting a kind of welcoming signal, partly auditory—a hum—and partly visual—a glow.

I'm calling them in, he couldn't help thinking, and he felt the roof of the Town's City out the window glow in assent. Some beacon was up there as well, sucking life from the Outskirts into the town's center.

Without me they wouldn't have come, he couldn't help thinking. *Try as I might to repel them, I can only call them in.*

Enervated, he dropped the gun and curled on top of it, finally stealing half an hour of sleep as the town filled with Reunion traffic.

When he came to again, it was fully dark.

Determined to leave the room rather than turning the lights on, he went out into the hall to get a soda from the machine and ran into James, drinking tonic water. Ben got a tonic too.

The two of them sat down on the bench in the hallway, mutually watching the machine like it was a fish tank. One of the fluorescent lights overhead had burned out; the other strained to fill a space that was now too big for it.

"Just getting in?" Ben finally asked.

James nodded, swallowing.

They didn't mention News City, where they'd barely interacted over the latter years of the past decade, despite the shared mission they'd arrived with. Neither could decide whether meeting the other back in town was better than being here alone. Time, each supposed, would tell.

James nodded again and said, "Want to get dinner downstairs?"

Ben took his turn to nod. "Sure. Give me an hour."

After spending the hour sitting right where he was, drinking tonic after tonic, Ben went down to the Hotel bar, where James was waiting.

They each ordered rum and cola.

James chewed ice. Ben watched his melt.

"Want to get a table?" Ben asked after a while.

"Sure."

The spirit of the Reunion hovered in the dining room around them. Although most of those who'd checked in today had eaten earlier and the place was now close to empty, the waiters were still on edge, unused to the fraught atmosphere and to crowds in general.

Ben and James were seated at a white tableclothed table set for four, where they ate pork with mustard sauce and rice pilaf and shared a bottle of red wine.

They asked their waiter to close the curtains and stand behind them, out of sight, so there was nothing to see but rows of glasses and bottles behind the bar, and swaths of curtain and carpet, all of which could have been anywhere, aboard a luxury liner on the Inland Sea or inside a lodge on the summit of the Mountain.

Both of them considered these possibilities but held off on mentioning them. The era of casting the town in pretend guises felt like it'd ended long ago, though it didn't feel like any new era had taken its place.

So they sat in silence as they ate and drank, not quite at the stage of making deliberately pointless small talk, though they could see that stage coming. At the very least, they hoped that the next time they met up wouldn't feel like the first time. If nothing else, tonight could take care of that.

They both noticed that all the women were gone, off in News City, surely, where everyone sane must be. Everyone hoping to live a life. Each struggled to remember the women there used to be, what they'd looked like, what their names had been. Neither could summon a clear enough image to mention it, so neither did.

A welcome shift in mood came with their coffee as the nineteen-year-olds passed by the edge of the dining room, on their way to their own room upstairs.

They regarded Ben and James, who turned to regard them back after they felt a shadow cross their graves.

The decade that separated them from nineteen began to vibrate in their stomachs, sending sweat down their necks and into their shirts, as they felt the hand of the Reunion materialize to choke them.

We could be nineteen again, we could do it all over, do it right this time... we could be legends by twenty-nine, they both fell to thinking, their minds conjoining and losing integrity.

One of us writes the script, the other builds the sets... and like so the Pretend Movie becomes real.

The actual nineteen-year-olds had moved on, but Ben and James wouldn't recover until the waiter cleared his throat, announcing that it was time to pay the bill.

Easy to fall in, easy to fall in, they thought, in the hallway upstairs, leaning against the soda machine where they'd met earlier. They each got another tonic before parting ways, tearing their minds back into separation for the long, slow attempt at sleep.

Each in his own room was visited by the feeling of having been in the town all along, of having wanted to go to News City without ever having gone. The News City years were boiling off in panic sweat, leaving their bodies slack in the belly and humped in the shoulders. As they tossed and turned in their rented beds, they both felt their cloaks of professionalism—the filmmaker, the architect—boiling off as well, and they knew that they would never fit again, not even as costumes.

Thursday Night

Well Broadbeam woke in his room in the Hotel, a few floors above where Ben and James were trying to sleep, in the early evening of what would soon be Reunion Weekend.

He woke up every evening at exactly this time, and lay just like this thinking of the sentence he'd bring to the station, printed on a card he'd press face down on his desk beside his takeout dinner, just under the mic. It would be the first sentence he'd utter, as the children were brushing their teeth and putting their dirty socks in their hampers.

By the time they were crawling into bed, with their radios set at just the right volume under their pillows, Well would utter this first sentence, easing into his Radio Angel voice, finding the frequency that only those under ten could hear. Then he'd put the card away, under the rock that held down the pile that had accumulated over nine years of broadcasts.

At this point in the evening, his work was done. The children were already floating, bound to his voice, their minds shut off. Now, all he had to do was guide them out of their beds, up the Meadow-lined Road, and into the Ghost Town, the vast set he'd constructed in the Meadow to model the town as it'd been when he was their age, thirty years ago.

This was his reward, his particular means of constructing a

bearable life: if he could force the dreaming children to dream of the town as it'd been for him, not as it was for them, he could feel the clutches of Death easing slightly from around his neck, if only for as long as he went on talking, alone behind the mic.

Back in the Hotel, he stretched out his toes and fingertips, reaching off the mattress and into empty space. One wall was stained with water damage that looked like a turtle slowly climbing to the next floor.

Well treated it as his companion, the only other being he could claim to know in any profound sense, and dreaded the day it finished its climb and disappeared.

Aside from this, all he had were a few clothes he never wore, his shaving kit and toiletries in a cardboard box in the bathroom, and three notebooks that periodically got soaked in the bath and then dried, blimping out on the windowsill.

He rolled over and yawned. Whatever he said first would be the sentence he'd print on his card. Tonight's was: *In that place where they all lived, there was one who did not.*

As he lay like this, listening to the empty rooms surrounding him fill with Reunion arrivals, his mind drifted to the streets of his Ghost Town, touring them in their emptiness until he could no longer bear to. Only the children's arrival, borne on the waves of his voice, could save it from shriveling out of existence, leaving him truly at large in the world, a state he did not believe he could survive in.

The further he stretched his limbs, the more it felt like he was floating, witch-like, out of the Hotel and across the town, up the Meadow-lined Road to the marshy site of the Ghost Town, into the house he'd grown up in.

He could feel his thought-pattern turning dangerous, the possibility of mania beginning to loom. Too long inside that house and he'd spend the night moaning in bed rather than getting behind the mic where he belonged.

44

So, shouting, "C'mon man!" he swung his feet onto the thin carpet, stood and got dressed, entering a window of time that had little room for error. He had to get in his car, pick up dinner, and make it to the station in time to be behind the mic and have uttered his first sentence just as the children were closing their eyes, easing their way over the cusp of consciousness and into the kind of earnest dreaming where they would follow his voice anywhere it wanted to take them. If he missed his window, they'd end up deep in their own dreams, beyond the sway of the radio, useless.

So he quickly did his stretches, showered, combed his hair, buttoned and tucked in his shirt, put on his shoes, and left the Hotel.

The gloved hand in the Giant Chinese takeout window handed him his chicken stir-fry and soy sauce packets in a paper bag, and Well held out the credit card the Mayor had equipped him with when he hired him nine years ago, to shepherd the town's dreaming children through the nights so they didn't drift into the Orchard when he was alone with his Movies, seeing him at his most vulnerable, as he feared they might otherwise do.

"It's just a matter of keeping the channels clean," the Mayor had said. "Keeping the nights open just for me."

Well pulled out onto the Strip, passing the Night School and the Mattress Store, which together comprised the town's only site of non-solitary sex.

Each was lit brightly, the Mattress Store blue, the Night School red, cars piled up in the lot, Reuniongoers looking to get sleazy right away.

He parked at the station and went in through the employees' entrance.

After rinsing the laminated astronomical chart he used as a placemat, he placed his big glass of water atop the mess of stars at the center, which he called *View from the Upstairs Bathroom When I Woke*

45

Up to Pee in the Middle of the Night, Age Seven. After securing the door behind him, he carried a chair over to the table, opened the paper bag, and unwrapped his Giant Chinese.

He ate as the children in their houses around town shuffled unsupervised to bed. When it was time for the broadcast, they collapsed under an exhaustion that hadn't been creeping up on them. They were fully awake, going about their business, and then snuffed.

They waited in bed, eyes closed and ears open, wearing sleeping caps just as Well did. He removed his from a drawer beneath his placemat, pretending that he, like them, was about to settle into his childhood bed, all of life ahead of him, all of the universe open to receive his dreaming body wherever it happened to float.

The time had come. He put his leftovers in the bag, then took out his keys and unlocked his inner office, which was pitch black and cold. He took his fur coat from the hook where it waited all day in the dark, and bundled it around his neck and shoulders, so that the fur came up around his mouth and nose and ears, overlapping with his sleeping cap, and then he picked up the headset from another hook, put it over his head, and turned it on.

There was an ideal volume for his broadcast, not so quiet that it passed into the warm mud beneath hearing, but also not so loud that it disturbed real sleep and brought the children too harshly back to an awareness of their actual beds. And certainly not loud enough to breach the realm of adult hearing. All manner of perverts, he knew, were listening in, and it was up to him to ensure that they never gleaned more than a distant sigh.

When he'd gotten the knobs to this exact point, he began with the sentence he'd prepared: "In that place where they all lived, there was one who did not."

The children's radios under their pillows spit this up into their ears through several layers of cloth and feathers, and soon they were

46

on their way. They'd been traveling on Well's voice all their lives, so the Ghost Town was, to them, as ancestral a place as any.

The broadcast was unspooling and gaining speed. They had taken off from the earth, broken free from their beds and passed through the roofs above them.

Well held the mic very close to his lips. His legs felt far away beneath him, stowed under the table in a tub of soothing gel. One arm hung by his side, over the armrest of the chair, while the other held the mic against his lips, his teeth against the grate and his tongue pressing into the hole.

This hole in the mic was analogous to the hole in space, which had opened over the roofs of all the houses in town in which the children slept, sucking them gently from their beds and into the regions above.

"There are things you can't know but you can know are there… things you can't see but you can feel see you… things calling you to them that don't want to hurt you but won't let you go…"

Tonight's broadcast was taking on the momentum of a litany, as many of them did. It was a gentler journey for the dreamers than when Well got to ranting, as he did on other nights, snarling curses and describing torments the body would undergo in the hidden torture chambers of the sky, where the clouds muffled the sound of breaking bones and tearing muscle.

"There are roads that look straight but aren't, turns you make that you can't unmake, roads that are seams on the earth above other earths below that whisper up through them, whisper *asphalt, asphalt, asphalt*, because all earths want to be roads and all roads want to go on and on."

He was singing now.

To pass from this town, here on earth, to the Ghost Town as it stood in the bulging country of the mind at night, there had to be some borderland, a period of hard travel before the wonders began. So the children, in their pajamas and sleeping caps, floated up the Meadow-lined Road, struggling to stay aloft and to avoid the snagging telephone wires, shivering in the high air.

When they reached the Meadow, bathed in the purple glow of ANGEL HOUSE, they turned in toward it, over the marshy cold that surrounded the Ghost Town, which quivered, as Well quivered, to welcome them.

Well's voice coursed through their brains as he threw all his strength into pulling them out of the air and planting them inside the Ghost Town, setting them on a course toward his house, where, he prayed, they'd crowd into the upstairs bedroom and keep his childhood bed from ever going cold. "Down... down... down... softly down," he whispered, guiding them into a landing without breaking their bones.

Once inside the Ghost Town, the children were free to wander and play.

Massed on the Ghost Town streets, they commingled to reincarnate Well at that age, a group-body that resisted the weight of years which, as an individual, had made Well the man he was, killing the boy he'd been.

He would've loved to go further, to direct their behavior even within the Ghost Town, reiterating exact days he'd spent there as a nine-year-old, sitting in the summer sun and contemplating eternity, fitting the exact words he'd said and thoughts he'd thought back then into their mouths and minds, but this was beyond the power the radio granted him. At this point of the night, his was the role of a parent at a park, sitting on a bench while his children played, developing their own personalities a little at a time.

This was the farthest-in part of the night for Well, the waiting in blankness while the children did their living in the Ghost Town, before settling into his house to sleep. He could picture them in there, but only as clearly as he could remember his own nine-year-old body, in that same bed, thirty years ago.

48

The Ghost Town was thus a fertile but blank set for the children to populate in a different way every night, even though, in its essential character, it was always the same.

Well sighed and whispered into the mic, though now his voice was only background noise: "I found a lizard one day in July, on the street you're walking down now, its teeth so sticky that when they bit me they almost became part of my hand…"

He dug his feet and legs deeper into their gel bath under the desk, trying to keep them from jerking with excitement.

"In the heart of the woods is a heart," he went on, "and in that heart is a bed, its sheets made of thick heart-paper, its will obscure to all but its maker, who slumbers eternally upon it."

The children roamed the streets in twos and threes, overturning rocks and rotten logs, standing on benches, making bets with one another or talking to dream-dogs tethered to street signs, playing in unstaffed pool halls and mashing the buttons of arcade games, their screens forever blinking INSERT COINS.

Well stopped pronouncing full words and let out a low, constant hum, interspersed with sighs and exhalations that were only air.

Finally, of their own accord, the children entered his house, sticking close together, bound magnetically into the shape of a single body, climbing the stairs, approaching the bedroom and the bed.

When they lay down upon it, Well pushed his head hard against the leather of his chair in the Broadcast Chamber, as close as he'd ever come to feeling his childhood pillow again, and exhaled slowly, admitting that if true peace existed, then here it was.

When it was time to lead them back to town, near dawn, he sent out a signal, like a flare, over the slack airwaves.

"The road back is the short road, the boring road," he began. "The grim surrender to time, and gravity, and school." His return

49

broadcast was necessarily more concrete, and never a part of the job he relished.

They lined up without fuss, exiting his house and beginning to separate. Sometimes he wished they'd resist, beg to stay longer, as he wished he'd begged to stay longer when he'd been nine, but they were docile, even eager to return to the town, not yet knowing what Squimbop's arrival portended.

They marched out of the Ghost Town, past the specter of ANGEL HOUSE and Squimbop at his window in the Master Bedroom, back along the Meadow-lined Road toward the edge of town, past the radio station where Well sat, his feet waterlogged and his sleeping cap sweaty and wilting.

When they'd returned to their daytime houses, he turned off his mic, removed his fur coat, pulled his feet from their gel bath, dried them on a towel, turned everything off, and left the Broadcast Chamber to drive blearily back to the Hotel, where he'd wait in silence until night fell again.

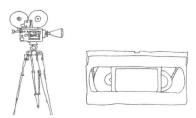

Friday Night

The Mayor cruised the few streets of downtown, killing the hours before it was time to meet James. This time, he was determined to get the ball rolling.

As a Director, he assumed that James kept late hours, or wanted to be seen as though he did, so he'd scheduled their meeting for midnight.

James said he'd be waiting at the Night School, where he hadn't been since his eighteenth birthday. Neither had the Mayor. He pictured it now: two stripping waiters who served wings and beer until dawn, bending over for dollars dropped on the floor. One dressed as a woman, approximating those features as well as anyone could remember or imagine them—and thus never stripping all the way—while the other remained a man, appealing to a smaller but far less conflicted clientele.

The Mayor rolled his window down, leaning his wrist out as he drove. It was ten p.m.

Several times he closed his eyes and almost crashed, either not braking at a red light or nearly missing a turn. He indulged images of driving slow and in style down a hot, palm-lined boulevard in the Town's City, figures of superhuman beauty gliding up to his window whenever he came to a stop, checking out his money roll, hiking their skirts up as they asked what his heart desired. He imagined they knew the answer better than he ever could.

After two more hours of cruising, the Mayor pulled into the lot in front of the Night School.

The doorman, his gut hanging out of his canvas jacket as he hunched on a stool out front, nodded, took the Mayor's five singles, and grunted in the direction of the area beyond the windowless front door.

Peanut shells on the floor, chicken grease and Ultra Max aftershave in the air, the voices of Reuniongoers echoing with arousal through the din of the sound system… the interior was bigger and louder than he'd remembered, the presence of sex outside of Movies more than he was ready to confront.

He rushed to the bathroom, stepped in vomit on the threshold, and found himself balanced on one foot with the other in the sink, trying to wash the sole without soaking his sock, braced with an elbow on the soap dispenser, looking at himself stretched across two mirrors.

A man in the bathroom stall masturbated frantically, throwing himself against the plastic dividers, unless it was two men…

Then James came in and stood at the urinal.

The Mayor heaved his shoe down from the sink and put his hands under the hand dryer, even though they weren't wet.

Help me, he wanted to whisper, terrified of failing to connect with James for a second and possibly final time.

He stepped back from the dryer and stood blocking the door, his width significantly exceeding its frame. This way, he'd both block anyone new from entering and keep James from getting out.

James, in a black blazer over a white T-shirt and black jeans, flushed the urinal and turned to face the Mayor. The bathroom now felt like an office where the man or men in the stall were workers in another cubicle. After all the work he'd put into preparing his house, it now seemed like the meeting might simply occur here. "Hey," began the Mayor. "If you've... done what you came to do in here, do you mind if we head back to my place now? I'm not feeling so great."

"Okay," said James.

In this light, combined with the expression he was now wearing, James looked a lot like Ben, except his hair was lighter and he was bigger through the chest and shoulders.

The Mayor fixated on his face, trying to understand how it'd changed in the past decade, but he was thwarted by the part of himself that refused to believe it had.

"Okay," said James again, slightly brusque, pulling the Mayor out of himself.

They exited the bathroom into the main fray where the waiters were circulating, trying to herd those who were ready across to the Mattress Store.

One brushed against the Mayor, carrying two pitchers of beer, and he shivered. He wished he had a third hand tucked under his clothes to wipe off the place where he'd been touched. He could feel stranger-sweat festering on him and turning to boils. Years and years in the Orchard had turned his skin into an organ not equipped to suffer the

52

touch of stranger-skin in a place like this.

James said he'd settle his bar tab and be right out.

The Mayor made his way back to the parking lot. Standing by his car, he looked out at the Strip, deserted but for a few figures walking up and down. Looking at the lights of the liquor store just up the way, he longed for the warmth of his basement, his TV opening into his Orchard, and thought for a moment of trying to go behind his car and quickly masturbate, but then the door opened and James came out.

"Okay," said the Mayor, pulling his hand from his pocket and opening the passenger door of his station wagon before going around to the driver's side.

With James in the passenger's seat and the children of the town floating overhead, the Mayor drove up the Strip past Ultra Max before cutting across onto the Meadow-lined Road, just before ANGEL HOUSE, which both of them saw but neither remarked on, lacking the words to broach the topic.

If I get James to start the Movie before I have to think about what that glowing building is, there's a chance it won't overtake me, the Mayor thought, careful not to speed up as he drove by.

They parked in the garage and went in through the side door, into a house thick with white smoke.

The Mayor realized he'd left the oven on, forgetting to remove the brownies he'd put in to bake, having feared that pure batter wouldn't send the right message. But they were black hives now and the house smelled like a plastic factory, so he opened all the downstairs windows and stuffed ten of them down his throat before throwing the rest away. Then he got a six-pack from the fridge and said, "Let's talk in the basement."

James descended slowly, trying not to arrive in the basement before his mind had processed the fact that he was back in a site he'd consecrated to memory, certain he would never return.

In the basement, they settled onto the couch, just the two of them, beside the Mayor's last Movie, melted in its Movie Store box.

The Mayor hung back, letting James get acclimated, hoping the Director inside him would come to life in the midst of this shrine.

"I remember you slumped against that wall," the Mayor finally said. "With a yellow legal pad and a blue pen, in your jeans and white socks, writing out equations to govern all the human behavior fomenting among the stoned and horny people we'd just seen at the Greek restaurant's midnight breakfast."

James smiled a little too, picking up on the change in the Mayor's tone. He'd decided not to bring up their last meeting, on the Hotel steps. That already felt like a long time ago, like there was no solid ground to keep any event from sinking all the way down into myth as soon as it occurred. "I used to archive those notepads, in my first apartment in News City. I'd refer to them now and then, try to unscramble the code I used when the epiphanies came faster than I could write. I think I lost them when I moved to my second apartment, where I still… am."

The Mayor could see the bears pressed against the windows, at ground level near the basement's ceiling. The night was pushing him, as ever, toward the Blind Spot, regardless of what else he had planned.

This forced him to concentrate. He didn't have any lingo to share with James; he could only talk worshipfully about Movies and hope James was capable of translating it into whatever terminology it took to actually put something on tape.

I want to have children again, new, strong children… and through my new children grow bigger than the Blind Spot, live forever as emperor of the town and the Town's City, with you and Ben as my lieutenants.

How much translation this thought needed depended on how much James had changed.

"I can't re-watch what I've already seen," he began. "I've gotten what I can from the Movie Store, from the fetish-memories of others.

54

From graven images of the town as it was. Now I need to dig deeper, all the way down to the aquifer, where the real, fresh Pornography bubbles forth. My story. Our story, up there on the screen, boiling through it to open onto a field of vaginas that..." he paused, choked up. "Can you understand that?"

"Sure."

The Mayor saw a cloudy mixture of sympathy and money-lust in James' face. That was alright. He couldn't imagine what it was like to be broke in News City, in an apartment with roommates—to have someone else's problems in place of his own—but he could understand that the prospect of being paid to make a Movie would compel James to say yes, even if it meant relocating back here, putting on hold whatever he'd been working on out there.

Even with his TV off, the Mayor could smell the Orchard rotting, worms growing teeth, turning snakelike in the soil, eating the roots of the vaginas that were already rotten inside, dripping wet ash.

Sensing a lull in the exchange, the Mayor went upstairs and came back with two frozen glasses and a bottle of whiskey on a tray. He'd changed into buffed leather and fur slippers and a red robe, and started pouring as he sat down next to James, breathing through his mouth.

Each of them sipped. A look came across James that betrayed both his discomfort and his pride in this discomfort, like he believed that being uncomfortable in the houses of others was crucial to his profession. Despite the depth of his past with the Mayor, he let himself see the moment now as that of a professional artist accepting a commission from an eager, slightly deranged patron.

"Do you want me to tell you about the work I do?" asked James. "My style?"

"No."

James sipped and nodded, hurt but not enough to say anything.

The Mayor wanted to say, *From now on you will be a Director in*

55

the same sense that Ben is an architect. Someone with a raw skill that I can exploit to my exact needs. Those are the terms of your return here.

"Are you able to stay a while?" The Mayor seemed to take up the entire room.

James nodded.

"What I have in mind will be very, very long. Maybe it'll take a year just to watch. I don't know. The longest Movie ever made."

James made it clear that he was still listening.

The Mayor refilled their whiskeys, then went on to describe the great Movie of the spiritual life of their era, divided into installments like a television series, but not to be broadcast. To be archived and watched only in this room, by him alone.

"The Movie will be a testament for all time. A record of our lives, when we were all rooted here and everything was possible, vault after vault after vault opening before us, all the locks yielding to the power of our tripartite intellect, the crucial days that amounted to the crucial years, when we touched the divine and felt it touch us. Before the dream that there was more out there made it seem like there was less in here."

I want access to it all the time, autonomous and unconditional access to those years, here in my home. To live inside them—as us at eighteen, just before we turned nineteen—forever.

He didn't say this. He said, "The Movie will be of such magnitude that it will encircle the Blind Spot, at once enshrining and choking it off. Filling it in, making of it a ground I can gallivant across, triumphant and almighty. It will make the Blind Spot a symbol, and, as such, render it powerless over me. No longer will I cower before it like a... a..." He didn't want to say what he felt like when he faced the Blind Spot. It was something too low for words.

With the Movie powering his whole house from the basement on up, the Mayor's nights would stretch on and on without any reminder of his mortality, and he'd live in his Orchard as a warrior-king, siring multitudes every night, all of whom would live only to glorify his name,

56

and that of the town, which would by then be synonymous.

"You can build sets, you can scout locations, anything you see fit. You can record people verbatim or doctor it as far into the surreal as you are psychically able to go. It just has to be true to the spirit of our teenage years. Name a price."

"$800,000."

The Mayor had always lived in this house and surrounded himself with expensive-looking things, but James had never known how much actual cash he had access to. He had always, simply, been their rich friend. Now, the way things were going in News City, James would have accepted a tenth of this figure.

"Fine," the Mayor replied, his lip curled like a prehensile tail. "Half now and half when it's done. And you'll need a house, where you can live and set up your office. I have one for you. On Monday, we'll move you in."

"Okay," said James, halfway thinking that he'd go to sleep tonight and, when he woke up, there'd be no record of what had just happened. He pictured waking up in his apartment in News City, but couldn't fill in the image beyond placing a generic bed in a generic room.

The Mayor could hear the bears tapping at the windows.

"You'll have to... excuse me," he moaned at James, who'd been trying to find the right moment to say the same thing.

Sitting in his car in the garage with the engine idling, the Mayor closed his eyes and indulged in a fantasy of watching the final cut of James' Movie right now. *It's really happening!* he thought, aware that his life had just changed in what might be a fundamental way.

He imagined ejaculating into his Orchard in a stream as thick and long as a piss after several nights' sleep, a God making more Gods, spraying them out like sweat from his pores, so great was the excess of his power.

The bears were in the garage now, pressed up to his car

windows. *You know what you have to do*, he imagined them thinking. He could feel the weight of their bodies as he sat there, starting to swoon, imagining the Movie enabling him to fly over the Blind Spot, hovering in the night as his offspring filled it in, turning it into a flat field with all of Death and weakness buried in its depths.

The feeling surged up and up into an echelon of exhilaration he'd never felt before, and he thought he was close to the top, about to discover what it would mean to be superhuman. But when he got there, to the true top, the feeling was terror. His head knocked against the headrest and his eyes rolled and his arm spasmed, hitting the garage-door switch beneath the rearview mirror before jerking the stick shift into neutral.

Outside the window of Ben's Hotel room, dejected, featureless figures were thickening into a crowd. They walked with their hands in their pockets and plaid shirts unbuttoned or windbreakers unzipped, cargo pants over scuffed white sneakers.

Ben nursed a bottle of wine he'd pilfered from the bar downstairs and watched them, wondering how much of their confusion he shared and how much, because of the work he'd put into becoming an architect in News City, he'd transcended.

He lay down on his bed and tried to forget that they were out there, swarming the center of town, desperate for reenactment. His plan was to stay in the rest of the night, sleeping.

He took off his shirt and pressed it over his eyes, trying to work his way asleep by picturing a congested alleyway he'd drawn into the plans for the Town's City, an urban corridor choked not with Reuniongoers but with strangers whose lives intersected only in the basest, most physical sense. Those who shared no common origin.

But tonight he saw himself draped in rags at the alley's mouth, a penitent or fallen holy man, covered in scabs and sores, mumbling prophecies no one would believe, or even try to parse, hands extended for alms that did not appear.

Far from sleep, he sank deeper into this vision, letting it overwhelm him, until he found himself in the Square outside, draped not in rags but in his old jeans and a T-shirt, a sweatshirt hanging open over that, with no money or keys in his pocket.

Nothing but his gun, unloaded and tucked into his waistband.

When he reached the Strip, he stopped at the liquor store across from the Night School and went straight to the back cooler, picked up a six-pack, and brought it to the counter.

The owner was an ancient, nearly mute man named J. Andre Salwator, whom everyone called Saltwater. He had a number of roles within the town, running from counter to counter and then sitting quietly behind them for hours on end. He spent his days at the Movie Store, nights at the liquor store, and did inventory and stocking at the Night School in between, blowing up new sex dolls with a hand pump, and stuffing the old ones into antiseptic surgical trash bags.

Ben hadn't seen him since coming back to town. Tonight, he wore a tall fur hat and eyed Ben suspiciously.

"I have no cash right now, but..."

Saltwater sighed, nodded, and pulled a legal pad and a pen from under the counter. Ben wrote "BEN" at the top, underlined it, and wrote "1 SIX-PACK" under that. He pushed it back across and Saltwater put it away without looking at it.

The air over the Strip outside was oppressive.

Even before entering the Outskirts, Ben could feel the imbalance that the Reunion had created by opening the sealed border and inviting everyone from out there to come in.

The town felt dense now, its pressure rising. The awful, self-conscious pain he'd felt while designing the Town's City was crowding back in, urging him toward the Outskirts with the vague promise of relief, as if that far out the air would be thinner.

He was on his third beer by the time he made it under the underpass where he'd first seen two people seriously kissing when he was thirteen. He paused, leaning against the wall that one of them had pushed the other against. It still felt hot from that charged contact, sixteen years ago. He tried to remember if it'd been a man and a woman, but could only picture their outlines. Both could just as well have been dolls.

As soon as he set out again, discarding a third empty can in favor of a fourth full one, the shittiness of the Strip gave way to the spookiness of the early Outskirts, where stragglers were milling around wearing more sinister expressions.

Ben stepped over debris that he didn't look down to examine, ignoring the forms rustling in the underbrush. He wanted to be brave enough to speak to them if they'd listen, but could tell this wasn't the time. He wasn't ready, and perhaps they weren't either.

So he pushed further in, feeling the air lose heat as the town receded into the distance behind him. Soon, he'd be deeper in than ever before, inside the genuine Outskirts which, but for the Reunion, were cauterized from the town. *The veil,* he thought, is lifted. *The worlds of town and Outskirts, living and dead, past and present, are closer tonight than on any other night.*

Closer than they should be.

He heard people out here now, in fields of splintered cornstalks and in the gravel lots of auto repair shops and the hulking frames of

60

gutted strip malls and garden supply depots. They were crawling through and standing around in the big field where the town's school bus and snow plow used to be stored at night, and elsewhere they were sitting on plastic chairs and leaning against diagonally-jutting posts among acres of loose piping and stretches of fence and barbed wire.

After another half hour of walking, he met the train tracks, which followed and occasionally crossed a dry riverbed where, on a school walking tour of nature, he and James and the Mayor had seen a man lying dead and their teacher had refused to admit he could see anything at all.

Later on, the three of them had hiked out here on weekday afternoons to smoke and lie down under the sky, speculating on reincarnation while trying to guess what it'd be like to be pinned to the tracks with a steam train thundering down to behead them.

This was the farthest out they'd gone, even in those far-out days. Now Ben permitted himself a thrill to think how much farther he could've made it since then, imagining his twenties as a straight line, proceeding unwaveringly toward a distant but attainable horizon. *It's all coming together*, he thought, trying to convince himself. *All the years I've put in have prepared me for whatever's going to happen now.*

The few people out here watched as he passed by, shuffling around with their headphones on. He nodded when he had to, never stopping to talk, well aware that they were all wondering why he was headed in the wrong direction.

Some cars parked with their headlights on cast enough light that Ben could make out a few details, but he didn't linger until someone tapped his shoulder and he turned around.

A man held a flashlight to his face, studying it. Ben studied him as well, as best he could through the glare. But there was nothing to glean from his face; it only rang a distant bell of semi-familiarity. This face had no name to him, only the possibility that they'd gone to school together, passing unremarkably in a hallway that seemed now to belong

61

more to legend than to any personal past.

"I know you, don't I?" asked the face.

Ben couldn't answer.

"I do," it went on. "So you haven't left for the Reunion yet?"

Ben pictured the Reunion as a great going-away party rather than a coming-together, an emptying of the Outskirts into the town which, from this vantage, seemed the greatest Outskirt of all.

I'm not from here, he wanted to say, scared that the man had mistaken him for a fellow Outskirts dweller, but he let his head fall into a nod.

"Well, it's great to see you again," said the face, pulling out a pair of headphones from its sweatshirt pocket and switching off the flashlight as it walked away.

Tracing the length of a disconnected culvert in the dry riverbed across from the train tracks, Ben settled into a wandering rhythm, abandoning thought and trusting this rhythm to take him where he needed to go.

His ears were ringing as he walked up and down the train tracks, staring at the culvert, trying to understand how he'd gotten so turned around. He'd crossed the riverbed several times, going in both directions until the inevitable moment of panic, when he decided to reverse course and found that such a notion no longer meant anything. The Town's City appeared in the far distance on occasion, but it never grew closer. He felt like a satellite in a fixed orbit.

People streamed past him in one direction, heading toward town and the Reunion, but he couldn't seem to follow. Every time he did, the pain in his ears and sinuses grew so acute he had to hunch over, exhaling hard with his hands around his knees. He had to accept that the Outskirts didn't want to let him go, not until he'd seen or done something further, or perhaps not ever, though his mind filled with shrieking noise at this thought.

In the midst of this, he felt a disturbance in the air overhead and looked up, but saw only the whitish traces of the parade of children, floating like dead fish in what he believed was the direction of the Meadow.

Just before they disappeared, they illuminated the distant structure of the bus station, where the Meadow-lined Road met a country road that had no name. He ran toward it, afraid it would disappear if he didn't catch it before the light was gone.

The bus station was a squat cement structure with a paved lot in front, cracked now into concrete islands in an ocean of dirt and weeds.

Most of the windows were broken and there was no door in the doorway he made his way through. He stood in the empty hall in the pitch dark, smelling cement and urine and old paint.

His spine tensed at the thought of rabid animals huddled in here, but he walked further in, looking up into the dark where the giant ARRIVALS/DEPARTURES board hung, smudged beyond language.

The pressure was even denser in here, so much so that he had to lie down, massaging his temples on the cold concrete and looking up at the cracks in the ceiling, as if stargazing.

He closed his eyes, dreaming of the onramp that used to connect the bus station to the highway.

An hour later, he awoke from the memory of his departure here with James, the two of them on the day they'd turned nineteen, huge backpacks on their backs and rolling suitcases on the ground beside them, college acceptance letters in their pockets, the Mayor standing in the parking lot, refusing to come in because he'd started to cry.

The bus hadn't said *NEWS CITY*, but it'd been the only one, making all the stops through the Outskirts and a few along the highway after that, before pulling into…

Ben found he couldn't remember what the News City station looked like, nor, now that he thought about it, how he'd managed to return to town last year.

Presumably by bus, since he couldn't think of any other way, but he had no memory. He fought hard to regain it, but nothing came.

His head started to hurt again, and soon the entire bus journey with James ten years ago felt imaginary. He had to let it go.

He sat up fast, hoping to tip the News City years back into genuine memory, but it was too late. He was on his feet before he had his balance, his arms thrown out in front of him, afraid now not of lurking animals but of people... Outskirts people... *Sub-Weird.*

The term slammed back into his head like it'd been thrown hard from a corner of the station, and he bent forward and vomited on his shoes, heaving several times after everything that was going to come up—mostly tonic water—had come.

He heard horrible laughter but assumed it was internal as he spat, wiped his forehead on his upper arm, and walked out with feigned dignity, feeling a hard ball of Sub-Weird thoughts bouncing against the walls of his skull.

He knew it would unravel in the Hotel hot tub and that, this time, he would find his way back to town. *I wasn't ready to exit the Outskirts before, but I am now. I survived longer out here than I thought I could, and have something inside me to show for it.*

You don't know what you're prepared for, he added, recycling one of the Mayor's old lines in the spirit of the Reunion.

Now the lights of the Town's City consented to guide him back to the Square.

The Square at dawn was littered with drunks and the very elderly, who'd already begun their circuit of the cobblestones. "Hi, hi, how are you?" they whispered, hats high on their heads, everyone asking, no one answering.

The Greek restaurant had its lights on and a few people were setting up inside, but it wasn't open yet. He could see the day's first pot of coffee filling in the machine behind the cash register, but unlike yesterday he decided not to wait until it was ready.

Ben passed through the doors of the Hotel, taking the elevator straight to the top floor, where the hot tub waited.

He stripped quickly and sank in. Under the hot water with the lights off, his head expanded and the hard, fatty tissue that had congealed in the bus station began to unfurl. It was a feeling of improbable and painfully accomplished relief, like passing a kidney stone.

His head soon felt detached from his body, the body brute and inert against the jets, its shoulders humping and bubbling in time to the water, while his head bobbed farther out, into a part of the hot tub that grew suddenly deep, as if there were a pit in the center that opened onto a stream that linked all nighttime thinking in the town, a group-mind that he, James, and the Mayor had incarnated for whole years' worth of nights.

The Psychogeography, he thought, the town within the town, where all salient points are adjacent and the extraneous doesn't exist.

This led him to remember *The Heads in the Brew… the three of us as dreaming Godheads, conjuring the universe from scratch, forcing it to exist solely for our amusement.*

He wasn't sure if he was drowning, but it felt good. It was all coming back to him, his mouth chewing at the edge of the water, tasting the chlorine and the Outskirt-tang boiling off his body.

So, the Sub-Weird, he thought. He saw them streaming into town, grey sweatshirts over black T-shirts, baggy cargo pants over unlaced white sneakers and white socks, guts hanging low over their pants, faces purged of all specificity, pockmarked and reeking of time gone by.

The Holy Book of the Sub-Weird, which he and James had drafted on legal pads at 17 and 18 in all-night work sessions, delineated the Sub-Weird as a buffer between the normal and the genuinely weird,

65

both of which were recognizable for different reasons, and, each in its own way, less complex. The Sub-Weird were liminal, unstable, people from the town who'd drifted into the Outskirts or let the Outskirts drift into them, rather than actual Outskirts-people, the truly weird, the wildmen of the surrounding countryside who were essentially a different species and would not show up at the Reunion.

The Sub-Weird are everyone we used to know, they'd written, as far as Ben could remember, picturing the people he'd seen tonight, and would see again at the School tomorrow.

The vast, vast majority of the people we were once among will become Sub-Weird in the coming decade, he'd written a decade ago. *They're changing even now, during the last years of school, as they drift off in twos and threes, crossing that line into mediocrity we'll fight so hard not to cross.*

As he tried to remember *The Holy Book,* Ben found himself rewriting it, bobbing up and down in the hot tub just enough to keep his buttocks from going numb.

There's no failing to recognize them—no overlooking the Sub-Weird—and yet also no getting to know them, no real recognition, certainly no putting names to their faces, though they can never be dismissed as strangers.

He felt around the tub edges for his gun and found it in his pants on the floor, bringing it down into the water with him.

It's best to treat them as a separate, collective category, no longer individuals, he went on. *The Outskirts whittled all that away.*

These last words Ben could see clearly on a legal pad, scrawled in James' handwriting back when the Greek restaurant had a midnight breakfast on weekends. These had always been their core writing sessions.

They're what we would've become if not for News City, he thought. *If James and I hadn't been driven there in pursuit of recognition on a global scale, that would be us now, morosely scanning bar codes* in the Ultra Max check-out aisle, or frying burgers on the line at the Greek restaurant.

The Sub-Weird are those who, while not insane, find life in the town to be the natural condition of life itself.

Ben exhaled, exhausted. He felt like he'd just written *The Holy Book* again.

He flipped in his memory to the pages that dealt with the possibility of the town without the Sub-Weird: *There'd then be an empty layer that would soon collapse, the far Outskirts with their full-weird—creatures from the Inland Sea, for all we know, living out human evolution on a different scale of time than the rest of us—billowing into the center and infecting everything, burying us in a scum we'd never scrape off.*

Then, instead of a town, we'd be one more corner of the demon-realm that underlies everything. Undifferentiated. With nothing specific to make us who we are.

Ben could tell that hot tub saturation was close. His brain had burned so much fat it was about to start burning muscle. Just before heaving up onto his arms and out of the tub, he glanced at the window, catching the lights of the Town's City through the steam. Had he gone over and wiped that steam away, he would've seen a train of Sub-Weird casing the fenceline, looking for a way in.

Back in his room, he lay down in his wet clothes and unpacked one final line before closing his eyes and trying again to sleep: *If the Void is a cave with the town nestled in a chink in its floor, the Sub-Weird are the bats, each clinging to its own crevice in the high, high ceiling.*

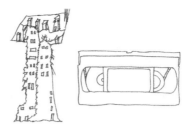

Saturday Morning

Ben got dressed without having slept, scratching along the line where his stubble met his neck. He checked the clock and saw there was no time to shave before meeting the Mayor in the breakfast room, so he went straight down, still scratching.

He was seated across from the Mayor, both of them cracking their knuckles, when the coffee and fresh orange juice arrived.

Ben said nothing of his trip to the bus station, and the Mayor said nothing of his night with James. Instead, they closed their eyes and breathed slowly and evenly, letting the spirit of the Reunion fill them.

We know everyone here, and everyone here knows us. They repeated this thought until they were both nearly hypnotized, docile and thus able to eat together in peace.

The shape of the Tower and the cloud of dust surrounding the construction site was visible out the window, its base thriving with Sub-Weird, but, for today, the two of them receded deeply into the feeling of being in a town, forgoing all talk of building a city.

These few streets… these few shops… they're all there is and ever was.

"I… um," began the Mayor, trying to break the spell, but he couldn't get the words out.

Eggs, bacon, and waffles arrived and both tried to stuff it all into their mouths so as to tamp down the words that were bubbling up their throats.

As he ate, the Mayor looked around, drifting into a fantasy of this scene recreated in James' Movie, himself and Ben played by younger, more sure-footed versions of themselves.

Ben thought only of the Outskirts, of getting back out there today.

When the food was gone, the need to speak returned.

"All these people in here… you remember them all?" Ben asked.

The Mayor began to survey the faces but nodded before he was done. "Of course. They've been at the peripheries all along. The padding of our lives when the three of us were here, and the padding of my life when the two of you were gone."

Ben tried to entertain the image of the Mayor running into them at Ultra Max, chatting politely, arms full of lubes and lotions.

He laughed.

"What's so funny?"

Ben shook his head, swallowing his smile. "Nothing."

They sat there silently again, waiting for more coffee that didn't come. The Mayor was about to bellow for a waiter when Ben blurted, "Remember the Sub-Weird?"

The Mayor looked back at him, forgetting the coffee though feeling its lack more than ever.

"You know," Ben went on, "all the people we used to know who lost part of themselves in the Outskirts after School … who got sanded down into genericness?"

"Genericness?"

Ben shrugged. "I don't know any other word for it." Outside the hot tub, he found he couldn't visualize *The Holy Book of the Sub-Weird* well enough to quote it accurately. "Never mind. Just a Reunion feeling."

More coffee finally came and the Mayor slurped it down, his body glistening under his clothes like it did when the bears leveled too much attention on him when he was naked in his basement.

There was a commotion at the door. A person was caught trying to come in while another was trying to get out. The waiter ran over to help and several Reuniongoers slipped away without paying.

Ben closed his eyes as a wave of exhaustion made him

69

feel boneless. When he opened them again, a wiry, fiftyish man was approaching their table.

When he got close, Ben's mind surged with long-dormant recognition. "Janitor Pete?"

Janitor Pete nodded while the Mayor motioned for the waiter to bring a third chair and another breakfast.

"Janitor Pete, you remember Ben, don't you?" asked the Mayor.

Janitor Pete nodded, tipping back a flask he'd produced from under his shirt. "Of course."

The Mayor turned to Ben. "Janitor Pete's been busier than ever since you've been away. Working at the School, the Gym, the radio station... driving the school bus."

Janitor Pete smiled. "Just trying to keep things moving around here. Trying to keep them from getting strange."

There was something so sinister in his face, so utterly complacent, that it turned Ben's stomach. He gagged and wiped sweat from his forehead. "I'll be back down in half an hour," he said, hurrying out of the restaurant. "I need a shave."

He ran upstairs for his gun and clicked it in his mouth three times with his eyes closed.

As he did, he saw Janitor Pete's face behind the grimy window of the art room at school, where he'd stayed late into the night at sixteen, seventeen, and eighteen, frantically drawing blueprints for the sets of the Pretend Movie whose script James was supposedly writing during those same hours. Every time he looked up, Janitor Pete had been there in the window, leering at him with his vacuum on his back.

He slapped aftershave onto his stubble, tucked the gun into his pants, laced up his sneakers, and walked as slowly as he could back down to meet the Mayor and Janitor Pete by the door, where they were ready to head out into the Reunion Parade that was making its way over to the School they'd all attended in a past they were working hard to feel as though they'd really shared.

 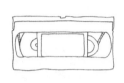 

The Square was full of Sub-Weird, all the same medium amount overweight, with acne pits and rashes along their cheeks and necks.

As soon as Ben, the Mayor, and Janitor Pete exited the Hotel, they started moving toward the School.

James entered the flow behind them, carrying a camera. "Hey, sorry I missed breakfast." He wore sunglasses and a black baseball cap, and looked as tired as Ben felt.

Ben and the Mayor nodded casually, neither acknowledging that this was the first time the three of them had been in the same place since the current era began.

They were leaving the main square now, merging onto the road that met the road that led out of the Dead Neighborhood, where Ben and James had lived as children.

We're children making our way to school, thought the spirit of the Reunion, possessing everyone present, townspeople and Sub-Weird alike.

We're off to meet our friends and listen to our teacher and wait for the Recess Aides to tell us it's time to play.

The Parade hummed with memory like an appliance filling with more charge than it could hold, about to begin sparking.

"Hey, good to see you," said a voice behind them, as they stopped at a free donut stand at the bottom of the hill that stood between the edge of downtown and the School. "Been a long time."

James turned with his camera, watching the face through the viewfinder. Even with his attention thus mediated, he could feel the eeriness of semi-recognition, the Sub-Weird as potent in his mind as they were in Ben's.

"Yeah," he said, as the nameless face drifted off.

"Isn't this great?" said the Mayor, his voice spooky and distant, barely his own.

Chewing donuts and breathing through their noses, they crested the hill, which had once seemed mountainous but was now barely an incline.

Ben licked crumbs from his palm and wiped them on his pants as he looked down over the School grounds, all the way from the portico to the main building to the recess yard, at the back of which stood the pine hedge where he and James had staked out their Pine Hedge Office, production headquarters for the Pretend Movie.

"Are you crying?" asked James, from behind his camera.

"No," said Ben, turning toward the Mayor, whose fat was quivering in the fraught atmosphere. He imagined it melting like butter and felt his own skin crawl as Sub-Weird pressed in around him and he and James were separated from the Mayor, dragged down the hill and across the portico and then across the threshold, into the School itself without a moment of grace.

Somewhere past the Front Office, where they'd been counted present every morning for the first half of their lives, James too vanished into the fray.

Now Ben hustled along with his donut-sticky hands over his face, trying to retain the shred of self-awareness that would let him escape without being sucked all the way in.

The crowd was moving as a herd, everyone breathing in the molecules hovering around the neck of the person in front of him, passing the gym, then the art room with the milk dispenser outside, toward the room where all their classes had been held.

Along the way were folding tables laid out with pitchers of grape juice and Ultra Max strawberry wafers.

Everyone was regressing to their nine-year-old selves. It was a shameful process, and a private one, but it was too crowded for those assembled to give each other any space.

Before long, they were crawling on their hands and knees, speaking in fey high voices, saying things like, "Did you know dinosaur pee is still in our water?"

Grape juice spilled over Ben's face and collar and he shivered, feeling the sugar cluster in the stubble his razor had missed.

"Do you know when our homework on fractions is due?" asked a voice in his ear, close enough that his spine seized up.

He reeled away, among more faces and soft husky bodies crowding into the doorway of the classroom, where Acting Mayor John Lester Wind waited with a hot mic.

The Mayor was the progenitor and Godhead of the town, but it fell to the Acting Mayor to safeguard its smooth-functioning in the real world, dealing with everything from taxes to road cleaning to zoning what was left of the Central Business District.

They all stood back up as he put the mic to his lips, sweating and filtering Sub-Weird musk through his nose. Ben couldn't see the Acting Mayor over the crowd, but he could feel his blood cool and thicken as the benevolent voice began to speak.

"I know how much you all yearn to regress," he began, shouting over the rising cheer, on tiptoe so his mouth wasn't mashed into the heads of the Sub-Weird around him. He was conspicuously twirling his hair around his finger and scratching it off, as he must have at age nine.

"So do I. That's why we're all here, to let the Reunion override the otherwise slow, mediocre functioning of our bodily systems as they age. To replace chaos with ritual, as we wish we could every day."

73

The Sub-Weird sighed in assent, partially listening and partially lost in private regression, their dead childhood cells springing back to life.

"My speech today will be short. It is barely autumn. We have many months until Hibernation, at which point the borders of our town will be resealed, and all Outskirts traffic will cease. The past will no longer be present then. For now, enjoy. We live while we can. We remain awake in order to remember, and we sleep in order to dream of childhood. The great vault of the Outskirts is open, so that all those we've lost touch with may drift back in and bind themselves back together with us, even if only for a short while."

The cheer rose. Ben closed his eyes, which had begun to sting.

"Let us all, be we from the center of downtown or the edge of the Outskirts, bathe together in Our Common Past, which is all too easy to lose hold of in the course of daily life. Today, and all weekend, we let Our Common Past wash over us, binding, even gluing us together, reminding us that, yes, we are all from here. We all grew up together and we live our lives together, as people born of and devoted to this town and no other place."

The cheer was so deafening the Acting Mayor had to shriek in order to make his command known: "Tip the bag! Tip the bag!"

Ben looked up as the Sub-Weird leapt with outstretched hands, tearing at a giant hanging trash bag painted with the words OUR COMMON PAST.

They split it open and a yellowish, gluey substance that looked like a mix of raw egg and whole milk rained over everyone beneath it, covering their faces, necks, and hair.

"We're all from here! We've all lived here for years and years!" they shouted, sticking together into a clump.

"There's no disparity among us! No distinctions! We are one flesh! One town! One flesh and one town!"

The next ritual was bread effigies. Effigies of everyone as a child—there was James, there was Ben, there was the Mayor—had been set out, barely baked through, to symbolize how fresh, almost raw, they'd all been then.

It was everyone's job to get on his knees and eat all the bread of himself at nine, subsuming it into himself at twenty-nine so that the past might never be forgotten, physically as well as psychologically.

Ben, James, and the Mayor, covered in the sticky milk of Our Common Past, were on their hands and knees in the hallway outside the art room, regarding themselves in bread.

Sub-Weird were chomping all around them, gasping, desperate to swallow themselves before they were swallowed by others.

Without using their hands, James and the Mayor tore into their nine-year-old bodies, sucking down all they could, breathing through their noses, trembling as the carbohydrate rush hit their brains.

But Ben couldn't get more than a few mouthfuls down. The scene, for him, had gone beyond aberration and into disgust. He was about to be sick. So, at the risk of sacrilege, he came up from his hands and knees and ran, jumping and stepping over Sub-Weird, into the nearest bathroom, which had an emergency shower beside the toilet.

He peeled off his clothes and hauled the shower dial as hot as it would go, ripping the slime from his hair and throwing it toward the drain.

Then he filled his hands with soap from the wall dispenser and rubbed them between his legs, trying to purge every strand of what had fallen from the ceiling, as if any remnant left clinging to him when he finished showering would be enough to turn him Sub-Weird.

He stooped under the child-sized showerhead and opened his mouth, spitting up all the bread he'd eaten, which had remained packed like insulation in his throat. It came out wet and mealy, expanding on top of his feet, turning them into those of an effigy-Ben he feared would overtake him.

75

As he turned off the shower and pulled his soiled clothes back on, he could hear the Reunion continuing in the recess yard. Sub-Weird—with James and the Mayor somewhere among them—were romping on the kickball field, chanting the names of former teachers and rehashing old feuds, challenging each other to wrestling matches and shouting that the devil was real.

Ben slipped through the door at the edge of the gym, which led back across the portico, skirting the recess yard without going through it. Much as he wanted to overcome the Reunion, he couldn't deny the thrill of sneaking out of school before the day was over.

It didn't take long to get through downtown, as the streets were completely dead. It was only him and the heat waves. He hustled up the Strip and onto a side street that passed the back of the radio station before meeting the Meadow-lined Road. This he took quickly as well, head down to ignore the purple glow of ANGEL HOUSE until it was far behind him.

Now there was a heaviness in the sky that hadn't been there before. It portended lateness, an abrupt shortening of the days; the year, with its progression into Hibernation, was commencing in earnest.

Monday morning is on its way, he thought, glad to hear his own voice rather than that of the Reunion in his head. He quickened his pace even more, crossing the unsealed border between town and Outskirts without stopping to acknowledge it.

He was now back among the loose culverts, strewn along the road in an array that he and James had understood, at nine, to be a map of the underground tunnels, pointing the way out to those brave enough to see the signs for what they were.

Letting his mind wander through memories of these tunnels, Ben found himself in the parking lot of the Motel. The arrow-shaped Motel sign had VACANCY printed beneath it, without a NO option, and, beneath that, a smaller sign that read NO CLEANING OF DEER OR OTHER GAME IN GUEST BATHTUBS.

The abandoned two-story structure—the glass broken in the windows of the Front Office, a crow eating a bag under the ice machine—struck him as a way station between the town and the Outskirts. A place to stay the night while traveling in either direction, just like climbers were advised to do when scaling the Mountain, so as not to pop from the altitude.

The air pressure changed more; the storm was drawing closer.

Half-thinking he might spend the night out here, he approached the Front Office, counting the dried moths on the sill, picturing them coming back to life when the rain soaked them through.

From here, he climbed the external staircase and started along the row of second-story rooms like the owner on patrol, making sure all his guests were safe in bed before the lightning hit. He could tell he was using up the energy he'd reserved for a longer trek into the Outskirts, but it felt right. This was the day's destination, again less ambitious than he'd intended.

He walked up one row of doors and turned and kept going, one hand on the railing, crushing wasps' nests and spiderwebs and more moths. After he'd made one complete revolution of the upstairs, he returned to the Front Office, past the RING BELL FOR SERVICE sign, and set out to make a revolution of the downstairs, this time knocking on each door as he passed, waiting until the sound filled the room, chasing out the silence that had compounded in there.

Alright everyone, he imagined shouting to the ghosts inside, *checkout time!*

Time to get some new blood in here.

He couldn't yet say why, but he could tell that the Motel was a crucial location on his personal map of the town, a place he needed to keep in mind no matter how much confusion intervened between now and the next time he found himself out here.

He burned off the rest of the afternoon in this fashion, waiting for the storm to break, making the Motel less abandoned with each circuit.

He couldn't help seeing it as a disused Movie set, somehow contiguous with the Town's City, seedy in a compatible way, introducing an aspect of the urban into the vacuum of the town. He knew not to push the connection too far, but he could feel it taking root. This feeling—its promise of a new chapter—brought further relief from the Reunion.

When the sky cracked straight down the middle in a blade of lightning that cut across the entire valley, he was standing in the Motel parking lot. A cloud bulged downward like a sac full of crushed grapes, then shivered and spilled open on him.

He started to run.

The Meadow-lined Road flooded so fast that Ben soon found himself swimming down a canal past ANGEL HOUSE.

The water was warm and fetid with Outskirts trash—hair, skin, foam, rinds, wrappers—all washing into town with him, borne as steadily by the rain as he was, all of them drawn to the beacon of the Town's City, shining ever more brightly as the storm blackened the sky.

Ben's eyes were open but, aside from the beacon, he saw only water and wet wood and the pulp of Ultra Max coupons. Then a wave pushed him under, and he flailed without direction or any sense of self until he surfaced inside the construction site, rattled with the premonition that, when the End came, it would look and feel just like this.

Ben found himself lying on the cement floor, flakes of skin protruding from his shoulders and belly, his shirt gone, his pants matted to his legs. His gun, soaked and covered in weeds, lay beside his left ear.

He stuck it in his mouth and pulled the trigger. This grounded him enough to grab one of the flakes on his shoulder and pull, removing all the hair from his upper arm to his wrist. He did the same on the other side, completing the renewal that the sticky Common Past concoction had perhaps intended. He was a slightly new man now, bleeding in dots as the tender inner skin toughened, becoming the outer.

When the dizziness subsided, he stood, sucking in his gut and sweating out more blood, smelling the fresh cement of the lobby.

The cement is wet but it's not wet cement, he thought, on the verge of giggling aloud, aware that he was finally about to enter the thing that had defined itself through him on his drafting pad last year. It felt like approaching the verge of being unborn.

Acknowledging this possibility, he picked up his wet gun and tucked it back into his pants and began his first trip across the lobby, toward the dark rooms behind it.

Noticing a pressure against his shins familiar from wading through the flooded streets outside, he looked down and found them buried in the piled remains of Giant Chinese containers, like the boneyard of some man-sized falcon. *The contractors must have eaten it every day for lunch,* he thought.

He pushed through a tarp, out of the lobby and into a room on the same floor whose place in the blueprints he couldn't remember. The light from the lobby diffused and there was no deeper light behind it.

Everything smelled both new and old, like the materials it'd been made with had been rotten right out of the box. The paint, cement, and metal, somehow wet though Ben couldn't see where the rain was coming in from, melded into an odor that seemed out of time, not likely to get worse with age but far from the new-building smell that had once been so seductive to him.

He pressed through the room behind the lobby and into the one behind that, fighting the urge to turn back. His bare feet glided across the smooth concrete of the floor, drier this deep inside, and his mind began to let go of the town, acclimating to the interior of the Town's City instead.

At the end of the longest corridor he'd so far traversed, he shouldered his way through another tarp and saw a gray light shimmering on the far side.

He took in all of the empty space before his eyes settled on the back of a figure slouched on a high stool at what looked like a marble-topped bar. As if feeding off his ambivalence about approaching any further, the figure sat up, and, without turning around, said, "Join me," in a low, authoritative voice.

Unable to refuse, Ben sat down on a stool and laid one arm on the marble countertop, letting the other dangle by his side as he faced the stranger, who had an immaculately trimmed and combed black mustache and black eyes to match it, thin tight cheeks, and a smiling mouth that wouldn't resolve into warmth or menace.

He wasn't Sub-Weird.

"We'll have two, on the rocks," the man said softly.

Nothing happened.

"There's no liquor," the man explained, after they'd waited longer than anyone in a bar would wait. "But it's still important to order.

80

We wouldn't be able to sit together at this bar otherwise. Don't you agree?"

This made a certain sense to Ben.

"The whole structure appears to be a ruin. A remnant of some long-buried society. Who knows. The missing bartender is the least of its problems. Though it is a problem for us."

Ben could sense that the man was baiting him, waiting to see what he'd say. He knows I'm the architect, he thought, unsure whether this meant he should trust or fear him. "It looks pretty bad," he agreed, scanning the area behind the bar in case there turned out to be a bottle after all.

Then he turned back toward the man, who'd been staring at him all along. He couldn't remember the last time he'd had the experience of meeting someone genuinely new.

"Been here long?" he asked, trying to inject his voice with the casualness of one stranger meeting another at a dive bar in News City.

"Since yesterday," the man replied. "There was a festival going on that I wanted no part of."

Ben tried to resist thinking The Reunion, but it came into his head. Try as he might to feel like a drifter in the Town's City, he remained an ambassador from the town.

"The Reunion, yes," the man said.

Ben flinched, but the man continued with no change in tone or speed. "The structure drew me to it. Courting my approach, it declared itself a place not of this town, a haven for strangers like myself. Far from the fray of reversion, incorporation, ritual..." He smiled like he'd made an effort to simplify a complex thought for the sake of a child.

Ben licked his lips and pretended the moisture came from a drink he'd just finished. The man watched him do this, then added, "This weekend belongs to all of you. Come Monday morning, the year belongs to me."

"Belongs to you?"

The man nodded. "At the School. The children are waiting for me. Can you hear them now, in their beds, waiting? I am their new Professor."

Ben shivered and remembered he was shirtless. He could feel his veins seizing up.

"I will Lecture to them. Tell them things they've never heard. They will call me Professor Squimbop and know me as their God. What do people know you as?"

Ben could barely pronounce the single syllable of his own name.

"Hello Ben," said Squimbop, happy to assist.

"So you've just been sitting here all through the Reunion?"

It'd taken an hour for Ben to summon the energy to speak again.

Squimbop smiled into his mustache as his body stuffed its coarse brown coat fuller than it had a moment ago.

"Yes I have. I considered climbing to the upper floors, but I decided against it. There will be time. I'm still tired from my journey."

"J–?"

Squimbop halted the question with his hand. There would be no discussion of the Inland Sea, the Totally Other Place, the raising of the town from total submersion.

Ben swallowed and blushed.

"As I had no Lectures to deliver these mornings," Squimbop continued, "I had no need to sleep and dream in my own bed. So I took the opportunity to explore. On my way in here, I saw as much as I needed to of the people on the streets. They struck me as very ill. People who walk through this world without living in it. I was afraid for them. Afraid of the toll my presence would take if I went among them while they were so..."

"Vulnerable?"

82

The Professor nodded.

Ben felt a burst of energy in his gut, a call to defend the Sub-Weird. *I am their Prophet!* he thought, and blushed again, aware that he'd be unable to assist them in any real way if it came to that.

"Those people would've done better to stay where they came from," the Professor added. "They'll see."

Then he held up his hand again to show that this part of the conversation was also over.

Another silence, until he said, "I need something to eat."

Ben's arm flew out, desperately grateful for the opportunity to act. "I... I can call," he stammered, feeling around in his wet pants for a phone without finding one.

When he was sure it wasn't there, he put his hands on the bar and looked at Squimbop in terror, feeling like he'd just failed a test.

"Check behind the bar."

Ben stood up and his gun clattered to the floor. He crept around behind the bar without picking it up, and there found a rudimentary cell phone covered in dust, probably left by one of the contractors.

He picked it up, coughing as a cloud rose from its keypad. He turned it on and, coughing again and closing his eyes to focus, dialed the Giant Chinese number from memory while Squimbop examined the gun.

He ordered a feast. "Forty minutes," said Sam Ren, the delivery boy. He didn't evince surprise when Ben told him the address.
"Come to the fence," he said, and hung up.

Ben hung up too and turned to face the Professor, who'd taken the empty clip from the gun. He put it back in and handed it over.

"Charming," he said.

Ben tucked it back into his pants. The barrel felt hot, almost molten, where it'd been touched.

Unable to sit still for forty minutes, Ben got up and mumbled, "I'm going to walk around until the food comes."

Had Squimbop said no, he would've sat right back down, but there was no response.

So he left his stool to pace in agitation, looking for a bathroom like this really was a bar. After a few trips around, wobbling on ankles that felt close to collapse, he made his way out through the tarp he'd come in through and into another network of darkened corridors.

I'm glad it's too dark to see. I'm not ready to take the whole structure in. Not yet. He let his mind wander back to his earliest days of architectural stirring, sketching sets and maps for the Pretend Movie while James paced around the Pine Hedge Office at recess, blocking out scenes, impersonating characters, speculating about which of the people they knew were acting already.

Speeding up, groping through one tarp after another, he made it back through the lobby and into the rain over the construction site.

Despite the likelihood of nails and broken glass, he ran into the mud barefoot and pulled down his pants, squatting over one of the pits, shaking with how much he suddenly had to go.

The stars through the rain glowed gray.

As he squatted, a pair of headlights appeared in the distance, growing closer and stopping at the fence, illuminating him and the locked gazebo that held his blueprints.

He put his hand in front of his face, as if this might preserve his privacy.

When he'd finished, he pulled up his pants and walked over to Sam Ren, who stood in front of the idling Giant Chinese van with the bags out.

Ben winced, making a show of checking his pockets. "You're here already? Look, I have no cash, can I start a tab? I'm at the Hotel. You'll know where to find me."

Sam Ren sighed, as Saltwater had, nodded, and wrote down a

84

number on a small pad inside his jacket.

Ben took the food and turned, then turned back just as Sam Ren was getting back in the van.

"Hey, got any beer?" he asked. "You can mark it down double on my tab."

Sam Ren pulled a can out of the glove compartment and tossed it to Ben, who failed to catch it. He watched it roll through the mud as the van sped away.

Kneeling down, Ben drank it on his knees, then wiped his ass with one of the napkins from the bag of food.

Fixing his pants as he stood up, he took a moment to catch his breath before heading back in to Squimbop.

Ben tried to keep his balance while heaving the immense quantity of food across the construction site, picturing himself with two broken legs at the bottom of a pit, in shock, a scarecrow packed in by a layer of noodles and diced meat.

Back at the bar, he arrayed the food up and down the countertop while Squimbop watched. He laid out two paper plates and two red paper packs of chopsticks, waiting, afraid to start on his own. Mouth-breathing around all the dust in the air, he tried and failed to hold back a sneeze.

This jolted the Professor awake and set him to devouring madly from the open containers, not stopping to put anything on his plate or to use his chopsticks.

Ben watched until the Professor sat back, licking grease from his teeth and mustache. Then, tentatively, he began to scoop out what little was left. He could tell this was the exact portion the Professor had set aside for him.

Except for the slithering of noodles, the only sound was a low churning coming from the Professor. Ben continued to eat, listening to this sound without turning to look.

He's converting that food into something other than human

85

energy.

The Professor looked at him, nodding. Then he got to his feet, adjusting his coat so it hung cleanly from his shoulders. Ben swallowed and reached for one last bite but stopped, reading on the Professor's face that the time to leave was now, not one bite from now.

"All that I've put in my belly is pulling me down, down, down, and I must get into my bed to go where it is pulling me. I came here to avoid dreaming, but now it's time. Monday morning is almost upon us."

So Ben stood up, pushing the rest of the food off the bar and onto the floor, watching the various similar meats and sauces run together. He kicked them into the corners, to join the other Giant Chinese detritus piled there.

As soon as they exited the building, Squimbop made a sharp left across the muddy ground and stepped over a low section of the fence, disappearing.

Ben found himself back on the street, alone in the watery dreg-end of Reunion Weekend Saturday Night. Instead of heading back to the Hotel, he ambled toward the Strip, too unsettled to face the ordeal of trying to sleep. After discovering the Professor in there, the estrangement of his Tower felt complete. *Never again will I feel as though I am the architect. Something drew the plans through me last year, and now that thing's moved on.*

A bell rang as he entered Saltwater's store. Saltwater looked up from behind the counter, then sank back into enervation.

In the back aisles stood a few Sub-Weird, running their fingers over the embossed labels on bottles of rum and whiskey. Ben passed behind them, avoiding eye contact.

He picked up a bottle of vodka with a cartoon image of the Mountain as its logo, and held it up to Saltwater on his way out, indicating that this too should be added to his tab.

Back at the Hotel, the elevator doors dinged open and he stepped in and leaned against the wall, sinking into a pacific vision of himself already submerged in the hot tub.

His eyes had closed but the elevator doors hadn't. A hand came through the seam and a teenager got on, clearing his throat.

"There's two of us," said the teenager, when he caught Ben's sleepy attention.

Ben looked at himself, and then at the teenager. "There would seem to be," he agreed.

The teenager grinned. "No, I mean, two of us with me. Me and my friend. We're sharing the room, but we didn't want to pay for two, so we're trying not to be seen together. He's up there now. I'm telling you so you don't rat us out. We're nineteen. We just got to town, so we're trying to meet people."

"Thanks for letting me know," yawned Ben, as the doors opened on the third floor. The nineteen-year-old nodded and got out.

By the time the doors opened on the sixth floor, Ben had taken his pants off and kicked them on top of the vodka bag in the back corner of the elevator.

His last prayer of the night was that the hot tub would be empty. This prayer, for once, was answered.

Entering the hot tub room, he sucked in as much steam as his lungs could hold and breathed it out in pure relief. Then he went to the temperature control and turned it as high as it would go, slipped his boxers off, cracked the seal on the vodka bottle, and toasted the rain through the window.

After several dancing trips through the steam, he slipped under the water without testing it with his toe, waiting for Squimbop, the nineteen-year-olds, and everything else that was hard and knotty in his brain to turn to jelly and then to liquid as he drank and soaked his head.

Sunday

No one who'd had any integral role in the Thursday-Saturday run of the Reunion went outside on Sunday.

The rain continued to pound, steady and deliberate, purging the streets of the Reunion scum that'd built up, pushing it down the storm drains and into the ground, where it'd seep into the Pornography and finally back to the Inland Sea.

For Ben, it was as though he slipped under the hot tub late Saturday night and came up for air on Monday morning, his skin wrinkled into a prayer shawl.

James spent the day on the upper floor of the house the Mayor had rented for him, shuffling about on the naked floorboards and pulling used-smelling blankets from the linen closet, wrapping them one after another over his shoulders until he was too thick to feel himself at the center.

The Mayor, except for two trips to the Blind Spot, spent the end of Saturday night through Monday morning licking brownie batter in his basement, watched by the bears and by his reflection on the screen he could no longer penetrate.

Well Broadbeam kept to his nightly schedule at the radio station, pushing the children harder than ever into the Ghost Town, and holding them in there longer than was safe, up in his childhood bedroom in the house that would go extinct without them, sheltering them from the pull of the new thing that had arrived in town and was already—he could feel it on the airwaves—disrupting its gravity.

The nine-year-olds spent the weekend in thrall to the Shadow of Death and the vision of the Pretend Movie it'd engendered inside them. Deep under their covers, they kept their eyes closed and fought to inhabit the nineteen-year-olds, plotting their Escape from the town.

After leaving the Town's City and walking back up the Meadow-lined

Road to ANGEL HOUSE, Squimbop sprawled on his mattress in the Master Bedroom. Blinking in the purple glow, he opened his laptop, checked the camera feeds, and composed an email.

Dear Master,

The Reunion is complete. Everyone in this town now believes they know one another, and have for many years. A shared history has solidified inside and among them.

After spending the weekend in an odd, hulking tower I discovered in the center of the town—an irregularity, I believe, despite my admitted inability to remember the specifics of towns previous to this one—I have returned to ANGEL HOUSE and am ready for any and all material you deign to transmit into me. As ever, I will deliver it as close to verbatim as I am able when I begin my appointment at the School tomorrow morning.

Whom have I met? I have met a rather distressed young man named Ben who is, in some capacity, the author of the tower I refer to above, and another, slightly older man named Well whose profession, as far as I understand it, is to co-opt the dreams of sleeping children via the radio, and compel them into a cluster of wooden buildings—I can see them from my window now—which he believes to be the town of his boyhood, no doubt a version of the town I find myself in now.

All for now,

Prof. Sq.

PART II
Procession into Autumn

Monday Morning

Squimbop woke up to his alarm going off. The sound melted in his head, dripping into the pool that contained his Lecture, threatening to overflow and soak his pillow. He flailed, throwing off the sheets, still mentally in the Totally Other Place, slapping his mattress in search of the sound. The more he flailed, the louder it got, like he was making the sound himself. His skin started to pucker and seek shelter against his bones.

Finally, yawning, enough air reached his bloodstream to let him sit up and flop his arm around until it hit the alarm.

He got out of bed naked and lifted the shade to look out at the Meadow, the grass beginning to dry after the weekend's rain. He saluted the sunrise, feeling it on him, letting his mind wander back to the Town's City where he'd spent the weekend. He shuddered and looked back up at the sky and pictured the Totally Other Place beyond, apologizing for this momentary lapse of attention.

When he'd regained composure, he turned his back on the window, lumbered into the bathroom and ran the shower, sitting on the toilet with his head in his hands as he waited for the water to warm.

When it had, he stepped under the steam, closing his eyes and imagining it shearing off his skin as painlessly as wool from a shaggy sheep, revealing the leaner, better man beneath.

He began to lather himself, body and hair.

A frothy substance like rendered fat rose to the surface of his skin as the central tenets of the dream firmed up and took shape in his mind. As soon as he stepped out of the shower, the amorphous Lecture that had dripped into his head overnight would begin to drip into his mouth as fully-fledged language.

He scraped off the excess in thick handfuls which he shook down toward the drain, where it pooled around his toes until the water runoff washed it away. There wasn't pain, but there was pressure. It grew in his head, armpits, and groin.

Scraping off the last of it, he almost lost his balance and fell on the slick tiles. He righted himself by grasping the water knob, the momentum of which turned it sharply to the right.

Now that the spray was freezing, he lathered his armpits and groin again in ice water, feeling righteous and smooth and too big for the space he was in, the pain a blessing on his first day of school.

Then he stood before the mirror and shaved around his mustache without using shaving cream, so soft was his skin after the shower.

He dressed, tucking his shirt into his jeans, and put on a jacket but no tie, his collar open to his chest. Then he stepped into his dark red leather boots. He wore no deodorant, aftershave, or cologne, nor did he look at himself in the mirror as he took up his keys and briefcase and went out.

He walked up the Meadow-lined Road to the Greek restaurant, where he ate alone at the counter, chewing strawberry pancakes mainly to practice working his mouth, unsticking it from the silence of ANGEL HOUSE, where there wasn't and would never be occasion to speak.

When the check came, he paid again from the allowance the Totally Other Place afforded him, and strutted out past the cowed eyes of the elderly, who would spend the day sitting where they were sitting now.

91

He cut across the Square and onto the street that led to the street that led to the School, carrying his briefcase and licking bubbles of prematurely delivered Lecture from his mustache.

In these same moments, the children were streaming forth, newly returned from their night's journey to the Ghost Town.

They'd had less than an hour after their return to switch their radios off, yawn in the new sunlight, press their sheets close to wick off the cold and the wet of Well's voice, and then stagger to their feet and into their showers.

In sync, they toweled dry and got dressed, consumed their cereal and orange juice, sat on their stairs to lace up their sneakers, shouldered their backpacks, and headed out their doors, down their driveways, and onto the street where they began to converge.

As they did, they looked up and nodded to one another, exactly as their adult counterparts had at the Reunion. Then they put their heads down and trudged on in silence, either all the way to the School on foot or, if they lived far enough out, to wait at the first intersection for Janitor Pete to pick them up in the school bus.

The duo, meanwhile, was exiting their Dead Houses, reentering their nine-year-old bodies after having been nineteen all night, wandering the corridors of the Hotel, ruminating on their vision of a Comedy Troupe in the Oasis in the Desert.

They felt small in their bodies now, seething with a sexual excess they could do nothing with except channel it back into the Pretend Movie as its Directors, no longer its stars. To be nine years old and trapped in the town, in bedrooms that they knew were not their own—the ephemera that Ben and James had left behind surrounded them everywhere they looked—after having been nineteen and newly arrived in it after months on the highway, was a rare and awful sickness.

The Dream of Escape was all that stood between them and

wishing for everything to end right now.

Still, they stretched their legs gratefully as they walked down the hill and out of the Dead Neighborhood, past the camera Squimbop had planted, lagging behind the faceless mass of other children, with whom they felt no bond aside from a shared mandate to go to school.

Squimbop's class had a support staff of two Recess Aides, neither of whom ever left the School. They'd been there all weekend, helping clean up from the Reunion, and were now ready to devote themselves to the year ahead.

Lurking by the front door, they corralled the children into a tight and orderly line as they arrived on foot or descended from the school bus, idling in the traffic circle. With one at the front and one at the back, they led them through the hallways and down the staircases, past the gym and the art room, around the corners until they reached the door of the Chamber. This was open just enough for the children to push through in single file, which they did, powerless to resist.

When they were all in, the Recess Aides sealed the Chamber door and took their seats on folding chairs outside, unwrapping sticks of sugarless gum, preparing to pass the hours until recess by chewing them down to liquid.

The Professor came in through a different entrance, on the other side of the Chamber, connected to his personal bathroom and a prep room that had a closet and a refrigerator.

All the Recess Aides could hear from the hallway was a low buzz, like the sound of a machine sucking electricity. An eye watching the grounds all morning would have seen only grass drifting through air, and a bird or two leaving its perch before returning to it.

Inside, Squimbop took out a black velvet handkerchief and spat into it, then rolled it up and put it back in his pocket.

The duo stared, recognizing him as the figure who'd cast the

Shadow of Death in the park between their two Dead Houses. *So he is the villain*, they thought, forcing themselves to retain composure. *The only way to keep him from destroying the Pretend Movie is to cast him in it. It must become strong enough to incorporate him. The role of the villain is every bit as crucial as that of the hero, if not more so.*

"Echtchttchththt," Squimbop barked, quietly. Then, louder, "Tschkritchtnicht." He showed them his teeth, then his tongue, white with Lecture.

They tried to shuffle back on their carpet squares, but the look on his face froze them where they sat. They could see one another starting to become scarecrows, but couldn't feel it in themselves.

Lecture run-off, hot and lard-smelling, dribbled down his chin as he took his handkerchief back out of his pocket, wiped himself, and left it on the desk he was leaning on.

It was time to force the Lecture into words.

"It's fucking grimmer out there than you can know," he began, feeling the word-clot in his throat break down and begin to move. "This is what you're going to have to hear from me this year. All of your lives, all of what you've so far known as Life, is not that. Your existences are insectoid at most. This is what I'm here to tell you. You don't think you will die. You don't even know what it is. But you will."

The children, including the duo, were no longer able to move. The minds of the other children were clouding over, growing scummy and turbid, while the duo fought to keep hold of the Pretend Movie, even if it was only a single frame, a still image of Escape fixed in their shared mind like the Pretend Movie's poster. They were already aware that if they lost this, it was all over.

"You'd love to think this town is all there is. I know you would," Squimbop continued, leaning rigidly against his desk without moving his arms. "You were created from that desire and nothing else. The Mayor's arousal at imagining the town's infinitude, its fertility spreading out and out and out before his tiny quivering penis late at night, his belly slick with sugar sweat. Spurting to imagine his dominion over all decay and caving-in. Every town has a Mayor like this. I've seen thousands. But there's nothing substantive about him, or you. The spunk that created you is nothing, just as the Movies that show the same fucking square with the same fucking people standing around in it are nothing, just as this town, like any town, is nothing. Not even a stain or a dot on the real map."

He coughed, wiped his mouth with his handkerchief, and continued.

"There is a vast Inland Sea and I have crossed it, past freakish disembodied things cooing and whispering to me from private islands. Leering at me, saying, "*Oooh, stop here, right here, in the soft, sweet middle. Just stop and rest and don't go where you're going. Let whatever will happen to that town happen. Don't bother with towns anymore.*" You can call the Inland Sea the highway and the ships trucks if it makes you feel any better, or if you find the latter possible to imagine but not the former. It's all the same thing. I came here, rather than stopping in the middle, to tell you this. I completed my journey, as I do every year, for your sake, though I have no good news. I have deigned to let you live so that you might know you will die.

"On the far side of the Inland Sea is the Totally Other Place, and its otherness is indeed absolute. It has nothing whatsoever to do with you. You can call it Death if you like, but all that matters is that it's where you're going, and when you get there you won't be you. You won't be anyone, or even anything. You will be melted down and poured into the Inland Sea, and eventually recombined and dredged back up, dried and let loose into another town just like this one, to listen to the Lectures of another Professor just like me."

Or maybe it'll be me still, he thought, *saying this all again, trying to make it new.* For a moment, he envied them their impending Deaths. Then he got ahold of himself and continued.

"Nothing of what you are or wanted to be will survive. No history,

95

no friendship, no love, no tenderness, no deeds, no calling or yearning or wishing or wondering what might've been. You will all be nothing, true nothing, less than bones, less than rot.

"And I will tower over you as the Infinite, the All-One. I am the only God you will ever know. You can fight it until it rips your veins in half and sucks the fluid and spits it in your face and forces you to drown in it, or you can relent now, succumb, follow me into ANGEL HOUSE. Preempt the slow creep that will otherwise poison every moment between you and it. Accept sleep, laxity, surrender. Let it be painless. Stop praying that an End will come to relieve your fear of the End. Do not pretend it is possible to follow through on anything. Your town is barely afloat; it is, at most, a penny sinking in a fountain, vested with a wish that will never come true. Leap from its cold ruin into my warm embrace. That is all the solace I can offer. And all the solace I want to offer. I would not make the news sweeter if I could. Any thought you may have, anything inside you at all, is only a webbing between you and nullity, gumming up your progress toward the place you are going, making your approach slower and more painful and roundabout, amplifying the confusion and the terror."

He stopped, wiped his mouth again on the handkerchief, and let images of shrieking mouths from under the Inland Sea play behind his eyes as he watched himself sailing by in ANGEL HOUSE, the Totally Other Place receding behind him with the sunset.

"There is a spot on my ceiling for each of you," he continued, after an hour's pause. "You will be bunched together on the ceiling of ANGEL HOUSE, incredibly tightly, with no room to breathe, but the good news is you won't need to. You won't need to gasp in agony as your town goes under, as every adult here will, every last sad husk that begged the Reunion for solace. You won't need to gasp through lifetimes of Reunions like this one, offering your puny viscera to the universe if it'd only let you remember a time that never happened, and pretend to live happily ever after deep inside it, blanketed from a future

96

that will never come. The future that will come is me. It is coming. Here I am."

Squimbop paused for another hour, walking among the rapt children, touching their hair and ears, all equally brittle and waxy, like models of children. Except for two, who remained present, somehow sharper than the others, their gaze upon him. He took note of the duo.

At the sound of the bell, a sluice opened and the children washed through the hallways and out the double doors and onto the playground, carrying lunches they were too dizzy to eat.

Squimbop had a separate corridor by which he exited the School at the bell and, though he came out onto the same playground and existed side-by-side with the children and the Recess Aides, it wasn't hard for anyone to understand that he was to be left alone.

He went to a bench on the edge of the property and sat looking toward the quiet street beyond the fence, one leg tipped over the other and his head cocked pensively like an old man's.

The children paced and drifted about.

They tried to brush off what Squimbop had infused them with, but found their hands sticky and burning when they touched their faces. For the first time, their minds were forced to conceive of a moment in which they would no longer exist, or would belong to other people.

Many of them had dropped their lunches and wandered on without them, stumbling over flat basketballs in the dirt. Those that fell remained face down. Some of the others wandered in small groups, their shoulders brushing together in tidal, bobbing swells, but none spoke or made eye contact. They traipsed over chalk lines on the blacktop, no longer recognizing the games they corresponded to.

The Recess Aides were steely as they looked on, glad not to have heard the Lecture themselves but careful not to show their gladness, one standing on the side of the recess yard nearest the

School, the other on the far side, near the windbreak.

The duo crawled up the hill, away from the kickball diamond, past the swingset and under the lip of the pine hedge, in search of a private space to work. They hurried, wriggling on their bellies among the roots, drawn inward by deep, archaic memories, until they emerged in a central hollow, the walls of pine far enough apart to let them sit up, even stand if they hunched a little. This, they could tell already, was the only place where the Pretend Movie would be safe.

The Pine Hedge Office, they thought, aware that they were not the first to have used it for this purpose, and, depending on how soon the world ended, might not be the last, either.

They lay down on the pine needles and closed their eyes, falling asleep with heads full of froth, saturated to overflowing with Squimbop's Lecture. They could feel the Pretend Movie wavering, the Inland Sea trying to flood the sets and melt them back down to raw notions. The tunnels under the town were filling, threatening to drown anyone who dared to attempt Escape.

The nineteen-year-olds woke up in their Hotel room surrounded by bottles and cigarette butts, too disoriented to wonder where they were.

They sighed and luxuriated in the sheets, pulling them over their faces though they were covered in ash. Some distant urgency burned in their stomachs, but they were too torpid to think, and afraid to sit up in case the hangover hit them all at once when they did.

So they rolled around, restless but awake, unwilling to take on the town just yet.

This was all the time they had.

The Recess Aides blew their whistles, waking the nine-year-olds up, and they had to abort, leaving the nineteen-year-olds where they were.

Dejected, they crawled out of the Pine Hedge Office to line

up with the other children, filing back into the Chamber for the next Squimbop barrage.

At dismissal time, Janitor Pete stood waiting on the portico.

The children came stunned and staggering down the hallway and up to the doors and pressed flatly against them, unable to remember how to make an opening from two panes of shatterproof glass.

Janitor Pete took in the scene, his eyes emanating serenity. Then he stepped forward and pulled the doors open from outside and held them, waiting for the children to scatter.

They didn't.

They stood in place with the Recess Aides behind them, doing nothing.

All eyes lifted in unison when the Professor emerged from a separate door and walked off. No one moved until he was out of sight.

Then the children snapped back to life, running across the portico, into the traffic circle, and back toward wherever they lived.

They had no homework except, as Squimbop had put it, to "Picture yourselves in the light of what I said, and accept that it's only the beginning."

The duo walked among them for the next three blocks, tracing the edge of the main residential streets until they reached the turnoff for the Dead Neighborhood.

After this, they were alone.

Their heads hung even lower than the others' because they were full of the dual weights of the Pretend Movie and today's Lecture, each trying to subsume the other.

When they got to the edge of the Wooden Wheel park, they parted ways, each into his own Dead House to drink a glass of water and dive into bed, groins swollen with a burden only the nineteen-year-olds could relieve.

99

Monday Afternoon, Evening, and Night

The Mayor had spent the day stewing at home, trying to forget that it was the first day of school and that the person or thing from ANGEL HOUSE would therefore be alone in a sealed Chamber with his children. He'd seen it in dreams, twice now over the past two nights: whoever or whatever it was that lived in the ark that had landed in the Meadow would march out of it, up the Meadow-lined Road, through downtown, and into the School. Whatever previous teachers there had been—he could summon no memories of them—wouldn't dare come near. The dream had the force of a process already set in motion, as inevitable as the tragic end of a famous Movie.

Stunned into bleary wakefulness by this vision, he hadn't managed to sleep off as much of the day as he'd wanted to, nor had he mustered the strength to drive down to the Movie Store and return his last, ruined tape.

The rot of the Orchard curling up from his basement was enough to prevent him from going down there. It was enough, even, to prevent him from mixing a batch of brownie batter and eating it in bed.

So he roamed the house in his bathrobe, pretending it was Hibernation already and the robe was a fur coat, and he dozed for a while in every room he came to, dragging the day incrementally closer to night with an effort that exhausted him.

Awakening at dusk in a spare bedroom he never used except for rare naps like this one, he shivered from an unremembered nightmare and hurried downstairs to microwave three pizzas, a box of waffles, and a frozen chicken, which he washed down with a pitcher of chocolate milk. His robe had fallen open and he looked at his gut and thought about the town's history until he got too sad and horny to go on.

This feeling sent him to the edge of his hot tub, but, as the water warmed up, he decided to pay Well a visit at the radio station instead of taking a soak. He could feel, however vaguely, that something would be wrong with the children after their first day of school, and he wanted to see if Well could help him glean what it was.

The central room at the station was empty when he arrived. He took off his windbreaker and sat on one of the chairs until Well appeared.

They acknowledged one another for the first time in what both considered recent history.

Though Well didn't say anything, he didn't try to mask his annoyance at the intrusion this close to airtime. He could picture the children lying in bed above their radios, and he could feel the coldness of his own childhood bed, lost in the Ghost Town without them. It was enough to make him breathe steam.

I know they're your children, but… he thought in the Mayor's direction.

The Mayor smiled, doing his best to feign innocence. "Just thought I'd drop by, since it's the start of the school year. That's not a problem, is it?"

Well, who was on the Mayor's payroll just like Ben and James, burped against his closed fist and shook his head. "No. Make yourself a home."

"What?"

"Make yourself at home," he corrected, turning to enter the Broadcast Chamber alone.

The Mayor nodded, leaning back in his chair and closing his eyes. When he grew too itchy to sit still, he stood up, scratching his love handles and wishing he had a beer. Rummaging in the break room a moment later, he found two.

Panting, he settled back into the chair and sipped from both as Well's broadcast began.

Soon a low, sad moan filled the station.

The children had been lifted over the Meadow-lined Road, high above the telephone wires. The Ghost Town was coming into view up ahead, growing clearer as they approached it like an image slowly developing in the satiny bath of the night.

Well pressed his lips to the mic and stretched his feet in their cool gel beneath him, drawing his cloak closer around his shoulders, trying to cover the cold patch on his back where he felt the Mayor's presence just outside the door. There were few things he hated more than feeling his privacy violated, and thus being forced to remember that the station, the children... none of it was his.

Forcing himself to focus, he swallowed, fingering the notecard on which he'd printed tonight's opening line: *And the dead shot up into the sky like bubbles from under a rock on the floor of a rushing river, seeking the surface.*

He said it again and again, until the words became mere sounds. Then it was time to move on.

"And in between each bubble is another bubble, and between those yet more, and all of them shoot up toward the surface, once the rock is removed that'd been holding them down on the bottom where the crayfish and the bad people live."

Well continued, feeling the children float as smoothly as airplanes, the Ghost Town lighting up with their energy as they drew near. He kept his volume low and resisted the urge to bend the notes toward a chant. If he became too desperate, it would break the illusion that the voice the children heard in their heads was their own.

"The bubbles pop when they reach the surface, and begin to float with the current, but we know they're not really part of it. We know

102

how many things are smoothed together to make that smooth black water seem real."

As he guided the children into the Meadow, something disturbed their landing. They wobbled, skidded, stirred up dust.

Some of them fell and cried out in dog-whimpers.

Well was juddering in the broadcast booth, feeling the controls buck and snarl in his mouth, his voice losing purchase on its passengers. The hypnosis was breaking.

He panted, trying to compose his voice, unsure whether to leave the children that'd fallen and worry about the rest, or stop everything until they got up.

A purple glow rose like the light of a planet on the horizon, seeping across the Meadow and into the buildings of the Ghost Town, filtering through the windows of Well's childhood bedroom and saturating his pillow, making it sick and unfit for dreaming. The Mayor's invasion of his privacy at the station was nothing compared to this.

With his eyes closed behind the mic, whispering, "and the streets spread out from the main intersection under the stopped clock where all of you congregate to scan the sky for clues," Well could feel a merciless wind tearing over the Ghost Town, blanking out its buildings until they were just frames, the outlines of buildings too liminal to support life.

He was barely conscious now, but had enough reflex to turn the children back, out of harm's way, no matter the damage their absence would do to the buildings he was trying to preserve.

Well could feel ANGEL HOUSE opening to suck the children in, and he could just barely conjure a glimpse of it glowing purple from outside and deep orange, almost red within, Squimbop sighing like an ember in the Master Bedroom.

If you go in there, you will be lost for good, Well managed to grunt. The force it took to pull the children away almost ripped his teeth out. He was standing up, yelling into the mic, nearly deafening himself

103

through the headphones.

He heaved them back onto the Meadow-lined Road, but he couldn't keep them afloat. They fell, landing on their faces. Some of them woke up right away, while others remained asleep, lost in pools of dust.

Soon, those who'd awoken would pass the radio station where Well sat in despondency, aware that the Ghost Town would never hold life again.

The Mayor coughed and felt his eyelids rip upward. He found himself in a strange chair with beer pooled around his feet and fluorescent light beaming down.

Well came out, taller than the doorway he stood in, and regarded the Mayor with eyes that looked miserably dry, beyond tears.

"Leave," he whispered. "Please. Just leave me alone with what's happened."

The Mayor nodded, holding out his hand for help standing up.

When Well had gotten him onto his feet, the Mayor trudged out to his car, aware that he'd just witnessed, or at least been present for, a cataclysm in the town's history.

Back in ANGEL HOUSE, once the cloud of children had drifted out of the sky overhead, Squimbop sat on the floor in the Master Bedroom and opened his laptop to check the cameras and then compose an email.

Dear Master,

I have just delivered my first Lecture, on the topic of Death, its inevitability, its ubiquitous reach. I believe the children received it well, insofar as their surrender to ANGEL HOUSE is already imminent.

Furthermore, on the airwaves tonight, as the radio host was attempting to compel them through the sky and into his model

*town, the mass of dreaming children was jolted out of orbit by, I
believe, the weight of Death-fear I'd implanted in them earlier.*

All of which I take to mean they'll be here soon.

All for now,

Prof. Sq.

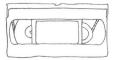

The Mayor was cruising the Strip again, burning off an hour
before visiting the Blind Spot.

He cruised past the Night School and the Mattress Store and
pulled into the lot at Ultra Max, parking in back near the culverts where
dogs curled up to sleep in the hot nights of summer, the last of which
had ended on Reunion Weekend. He shuddered, hurried in to buy an
ice cream cake, and hurried out.

His station wagon brought itself to a halt at the edge of the Blind Spot
and the Mayor undid his seatbelt, got out, and walked up to its edge.

This is no more than a hole, he thought, finding it hard to stop
repeating mantras against his fear that the town was unraveling.

The bears regarded him in silent warning, tonguing their teeth.
A surge of defiance came from his gut, but he gulped it down.

Okay, okay, this is the Blind Spot, he conceded, *where every
spent day of my life ends up.*

He felt as if the upshot of what'd happened with Well was a
deepening of what he was now staring into, a sense that the children
were falling into these same depths, pushed by the Professor he'd still

never met.

The bears groaned, almost purring with pleasure at the sight of him weakened, unsure of himself once again.

When the Blind Spot finally released him, he got back in his station wagon. There, like a passenger who'd climbed in when he wasn't looking, sat the Ultra Max ice cream cake.

He took it out and sat on the hood and popped off the plastic dome that covered it, and began to scoop into it with his fingers. The ice cream was melted just enough to have taken on the softness of regular cake.

When he was done, he wiped his fingers on his pants and wiped his mouth with the edges of both forearms, then carried the carton to the edge of the pit and hurled it in. It fell so far down there was no sound of impact.

He drove home with his sticky fingers glued to the steering wheel.

Down in his basement, he looked at his switched-off screen and empty VCR. Taking his clothes off, he stood naked before it, trying to harden himself at the thought of his Orchard, but there was no life in him now. He walked up to the screen and pressed the tip of his penis against it, at first gently and then hard, squishing it flat against the cold glass, begging it to open and let him through until he couldn't take it anymore and he went whimpering back upstairs, praying to the possibility of James' Movie for salvation.

As he slid into his hot tub and closed his eyes, shaking so hard water sloshed over the edges and onto the floor, he resolved to meet the new Professor soon, no matter what toll it took.

106

The only children outside of the night's disturbance were the duo in their Dead Houses.

They'd gotten in bed immediately upon arriving home, covering themselves with blankets to sweat out as much as they could of what Squimbop had pumped into them, too queasy for dinner. They'd spent the dimming hours of the afternoon descending, level by level, into the bottom broth of their shared mind, which served as the launching point across the scary chasm of nonbeing and into the safety and strength the nineteen-year-olds, who, as both teenagers and Movie stars, were immune to terror. Maybe they were even invincible.

All of this kept the duo from being swept up by Well's voice and compelled to populate his Ghost Town like all the other children.

They woke up as the nineteen-year-olds in the Hotel, lying on the bed feeling clammy and cold, bath towels draped over them as the whole town hummed outside and the Town's City cast a shadow even at night.

They struggled to keep hold of the lives they'd led before ending up in this town. Their car, the road, the endless aimless trip, the Desert and the Comedy Troupe and the Oasis where a new town was forming, the one in which their real lives would finally begin… they held these things like a box of sacred objects given to them by a dying mentor.

We have to find the Oasis, they thought, glimpsing a shore on the far side of the Desert for a split second before the nine-year-olds jolted awake in their Dead Houses at the exact instant that all the other children crashed onto the Meadow-lined Road, some breaking their noses, some chipping teeth, all dusting themselves off and beginning the long, dazed hike back to town.

The duo sat up in bed, panting and feeling sick, as the sun rose outside their windows and they accepted the grim fact that their second day of school was about to begin.

Tuesday Morning

The second day of school was indistinguishable from the first except that all the children, aside from the duo, showed up with black eyes and puffy lips. They processed into the Chamber with their heads down and their arms hanging at their sides, sitting on their carpet squares at Squimbop's feet, ready to absorb whatever he chose to pump into them.

"How much more do you want to suffer?" he began, his Lecture hearty on his lips. "Why postpone relief? Why shrivel in the town when you could bask in ANGEL HOUSE?" He meant these words for all the children, but looked straight at the duo as he spoke them, well aware that the others were already done for.

He was almost sorry to think how easy it'd been. After all these years, a little challenge might've been nice.

The duo stared back at him, trying to stuff the walls of the Chamber, the carpet squares, and the dead-eyed children around them into the Pretend Movie, cannibalizing everything to make it into a scene with Squimbop-the-villain at its center, saying, "How much pain will you heap on yourselves before accepting the only relief there is?"

James slept fitfully through Sunday night's rain and all of Monday in the house the Mayor had rented for him, just off the Meadow-lined Road a few blocks before the Meadow, next to the shell of what had, in his youth, been the tire shop.

He'd lain with his eyes closed on the couch, ruminating on his history as a filmmaker. *What have I actually done?* he wondered. *All those years in News City—did I make anything at all? Did I even start anything?*

He rolled over and over on the couch, trying to get ahold of himself. He could remember his Pretend Movie with Ben, twenty years ago, the two of them scheming in the Pine Hedge Office at recess and at home in their Dead Houses in the evenings... and he could remember departing for News City at nineteen to go to film school... but since then?

If he forced himself, he could picture a hard drive full of script notes and outlines and an office wall covered with charts, even an inbox full of emails, but these images had the vagueness of fantasy, like he was trying to imagine the private life of a neighbor based only on a few casual interactions.

Would it be so terrible to think of this film as my first? He let the question hang in his gut like something he'd swallowed but not yet begun to digest.

It occurred to him that he hadn't spoken since Reunion Saturday Afternoon, when the Mayor had driven up here from the School and sat with him in the kitchen, drinking tap water while they waited for their Giant Chinese to arrive.

Lying on the couch now, cradling the jar into which he'd

whispered his last words—"*highway onramp*"—before falling asleep, so that if he died before waking someone might find them, he went back over his conversation with the Mayor.

"You have total freedom of casting. Anyone you see, take them. They can play themselves, or versions of us. Aspects of us, pieces of our personalities magnified into whole people, as you see fit. As long as the three of us in our prime are well-represented."

"Should I be writing this down?"

"Just listen. You can incorporate notes once you get a system set up. Just think about places you might want to use, and we'll go back to them in the next few days, scout them out. I want you to not worry about time. You'll have as much as you need. And the money is already in an account for you. Here's the card to access it. Time and money should be so far from your mind that you shouldn't even be aware of not worrying about them."

At this—James remembered now, getting up from the couch to try sleeping in an armchair—he'd done a mental reckoning of the most filmically resonant spots around town, and found that every one of them deserved inclusion. There was nowhere that didn't. The only way to overcome the impossibility of deciding where to start would be to start at random: pick any place at all and do the first scene there, with the understanding that every other place would get its turn and that some order would be imposed in the editing process.

When he closed his eyes, now as then, he could see a spool of footage running from the Movie Store to the Meadow to the Night School to Ultra Max and finally back to the Movie Store, where the film would be deposited when it was finished, with his name on it for all to see. Even if the only copy of the tape itself remained forever in the Mayor's house, he'd find a way to get an empty box with the cover image and his name on it onto the shelves at the Movie Store. And perhaps a poster in the window.

"Can I empty houses to set scenes in them?"

"You can empty and fill houses in any way you choose. You can ask Ben to build you a house from scratch, or, if there's a house you want with people living in it, they can be expelled. That's no problem."

When he woke up on Tuesday morning, James couldn't think. He emptied the jar of his last words, then went to the front window and looked out, trying to remember about reality by describing everything he saw as if to a blind person.

"There's a dog looking for a place to shit or trying to hide," he began. "There's a man carrying a sign, but I can't tell you what it says. There's a squirrel clinging to a tree. There's a car slowing down but not enough to stop before it passes the Stop sign."

The more he did this, the closer he came to bridging where he'd been with where he was. He realized this was the first time he'd lived in a house since leaving the Dead Neighborhood. He wondered, briefly, what the status of his Dead House was now, but something in him—decency, perhaps, or some variety of fear—kept him from the thought of walking over to investigate.

When he had the strength, he shuffled to the kitchen and pulled the remainder of a Giant Chinese order from the fridge, eating it with a spoon while he looked out the window at the weedy backyard, wondering whose job it was to mow, and if someone would materialize to give him $5 and a glass of lemonade if he did it himself.

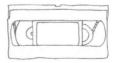

The Mayor woke just past noon, his mouth still sticky with the peanut butter of the ice cream cake he'd consumed at the Blind Spot last night.

He gargled over the sink and looked away as he spat, half expecting a tooth to come out with the brackish water.

Hoping to restrain his mind from spending all day revisiting the disturbance at the radio station last night, as well as to put off contacting Squimbop a little longer, he put on an apron and some rubber gloves and set about cleaning up, determined to instill a modicum of order into the chaos of his house, if only for the day.

He scraped the past few weeks' worth of food trash into a pile in the center of the living room, and another in the dining room, each as tall as the other.

As the afternoon wore on, he came to see this project as that of purging his house of everything from before the Reunion, as if these bags of cake and ice cream boxes and beer bottles and brownie batter were robust enough to represent all the years of abandonment before Ben and James returned, when the town had consisted of nothing but him, his Orchard, the Movie Store, and the Blind Spot.

Rubbing his hands along all his surfaces, flicking all his switches, he fell to thinking about the coherence of his house, the fact that it was everything. All of history, all the seasons, the stars, the possibility of demons and eternal life, boiled down to this place where he was, right now, and no other. He had not allowed himself to be spread thin, to pretend there was a better life in News City. The entirety of his idea of what a house was came from this house. The question of what a bed was was answered by the bed he'd just slept in. There was no taking the average or splitting anything down the middle. Nothing was an example of anything else.

He wore his shimmering red robe as he worked, its sash so long it hung loose around his belly. Touching the walls, scrubbing the floors, growing the piles, he resolved to keep his thoughts anchored amidst the material desolation, at least until he dragged it out back to the gravel quarry.

By late afternoon, all the bags were in a pile by the back door.

He put his boots on over his sweatpants under his red robe and started dragging the bags, their stems bunched in both fists, extending into an ectoplasmic bubble behind him.

When he passed the stand of trees that led into the denser woods, he found a shovel where he'd left it among the ashes of a long-ago bonfire.

There were bear footprints everywhere, marking the trail they took from here to the Blind Spot, outpacing his station wagon as it drifted in neutral. The trail vanished into such deep woods behind the quarry that he'd never been able to follow it all the way. The first cover of fallen leaves, off-green and near-yellow, had blanketed the ground, but the dirt underneath was still soft enough that the Mayor's boots sunk into the bear tracks.

He could smell their fur and dander mixed with the clean, smoky smell of early autumn and the vegetal smell of their droppings, which he couldn't deny he found comforting.

How old am I? he wondered suddenly, tearing up as he tried to count the autumns, and then he heard a voice say, small and timid like a child raising its hand in a classroom, twenty-nine. The rest of the classroom howled with spite.

There were a number of wrecked tractors strewn about the no-man's land of small pits and ditches that led up to the gravel quarry, the first in the long series that terminated in the Blind Spot.

Earlier in his twenties, he had the habit of coming out here at sundown to picture a scene of raucous strangers inhabiting these vehicles, driving them dangerously close to the quarry edges, hooting out the windows. Reenacting the construction of the town, or else constructing it—whether as a Movie set or a real place, or both—for the first and only time.

Earlier still, as a child, before he put on the weight that now severely limited the range of spaces he could enter, he'd pried their squeaky cab doors open and climbed onto the hard, black leather, grinding their stuck gears and pretend-smoking cigarettes with one hand slung over the steering wheel like he was going somewhere fast. He pretended he was the original Director, determining what the whole town would look like, and everything that would happen in it, and what it would all mean.

Goodbye to all that, he thought now, palms starting to lose their hold on the strings of the trashbags.

He gripped them more tightly and crept to the edge of the quarry, which was a sheer thirty feet down. All his life, this had been his dump, the vault of all the trash he'd so far produced.

He breathed the autumn in, letting it mix with the fumes from what he'd buried here over the summer. Then, offering the trash in place of himself, he threw it as far as he could, holding his breath until he heard it land with a wet slap.

This accomplished, he sat down on the pit's edge, dangling his legs over.

The pit would be his grave when the day came, which he sincerely hoped and often believed never would. But if it did, and he was lucid, he would walk out here in his pajamas, barefoot no matter the season, and settle on the edge where he was now, staring down at the trash until it mesmerized him, pulling the rest of his body in the direction his eyes had already gone. He would settle on top and lie there as long as Death took, nestled among the effluence of his life, ready to become part of it, degrading into a compact protein for the bears to eat.

All that kept him from falling in today was the thought of James' Movie. *The byproducts of the Reunion are now disposed of,* he thought. *So the processes it set in motion can proceed.*

This thought was hopeful enough to propel him back inside, not envying the trash as the sky got dark over the pit and the bears came out from behind the tractors to see if it contained anything edible.

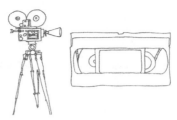

Back in his house with evening filling up the outdoors, the Mayor stood over his hot tub, waiting to see steam.

He made one revolution around the tub's blue outer rim, watching his reflection take shape as the windows darkened, and then he got in, peeing a little as he sat down.

He sank until the water was up to his neck and stayed like that, feeling trash scum detach from his skin, breathing evenly, resisting the urge to go all the way under and enter the different headspace down there. Even at this depth, the thought was clear: *Tonight you confront ANGEL HOUSE; no more will it remain a blot in your headspace, crowding out all productive thought.*

Often, we know things before we know that we know them… but tonight is the night when I admit that I know it's here, and it isn't going away.

Whatever ANGEL HOUSE was, he would see it tonight with as much clarity as he could bear. After that, it would be time to meet the Professor.

Towel around his waist, feet dripping into twin pools on the hardwood floor of his kitchen a few moments later, the Mayor stood with the phone to his ear.

After a few rings, James picked up. The Mayor said, "It's time to check out that thing in the Meadow. Bring your camera."

James said he'd be ready in half an hour.

The Mayor cruised down his driveway, around the cul-de-sac and onto the Meadow-lined Road. He could have traced the route to James' rented house with his eyes closed, but the streets were full of people. He avoided looking at them until their presence grew so overwhelming he had to close his eyes, thinking, *The Reunion's over, isn't it?*

He jolted to attention as James let himself in, hoisting his camera over the trashcan the car had crushed.

"How'd you sleep?" the Mayor asked, as if they'd both spent the night in the Hotel and were now meeting in the lobby for breakfast.

James shrugged, yawning.

They could easily have walked to the Meadow, less than a mile up the road, but they drove. Whatever happened after they crossed into the purple glow, the Mayor wanted his car parked nearby.

When they got to the Meadow, they could see their headlights reflected in the grass, deeply flooded with rain that had thickened into a jelly.

He parked on the other side of the Meadow-lined Road, where it was dry and the terrain tipped sharply into a ditch, so that his car was balanced at the angle of repose. They both climbed through James' side onto the asphalt and jogged across, only slowing when they felt water splash over their shoes.

"Watch out for ticks," was all the Mayor could think to say.

"Thanks, you too," replied James, perching the camera on his shoulder. The spectacle before them was wet empty grass, the fence around the Ghost Town, and the purple glow. The Mountain was too black to be perceived as such; it only bounded the scene on one side, keeping the purple glow from extending infinitely.

When they were all the way into the Meadow, James turned his camera on and began to film, catching the light of ANGEL HOUSE filtering through the wooden structures of the Ghost Town.

The Meadow reminded them of nothing; no series of nights out here ten years ago, no dreams of its deeper significance when they were children. Aside from the Mountain and its timeless grandeur, there was nothing here except what was here now.

They sank up to their thighs and James reached way up to keep the camera dry as the Mayor fell further in, snorting water through his

116

nose and spitting it out. It lapped under their armpits and fought to enter their mouths. They flailed like this, somewhere between stumbling and swimming, until the ground sloped upward and the water level sank back to their waists and then their ankles.

Arrival, thought the Mayor. *Soon whatever landed here will become specific. We'll know for sure what we're up against.*

"What?" asked James.

The Mayor looked over at him and shook his head.

"You were mumbling."

"I'll stop."

They walked deeper in, the Ghost Town behind them now, the purple light of ANGEL HOUSE so bright it became the whole horizon, obscuring the point where the structure ended and the space around it began.

The Mayor's wet body took on a rotten smell and he had to kneel down to catch his breath. His shin bones felt worn away, like pulped cardboard.

"Help me up," he gasped, afraid for his heart as James extended a hand, filming the interaction with the other.

When he could breathe again, he said, "Let's pick up the pace."

Head down, James hurried after him.

The ANGEL HOUSE door hung open, but if there had ever been a question of going inside, there wasn't now. It looked like a dim hole in a wall of light, leading directly out of existence.

James felt his camera arm wilt, so that he had to grab it with the other to keep it from falling. He held it at his center, against his belt buckle. When he tried to look over at the Mayor, he found that he couldn't. His neck was locked straight ahead.

He saw the two of them as scarecrows planted here, at the harsh peak of a bad trip, staring at the lights of a distant lodge shrouded in mist, night birds swooping down from high branches, not afraid to

117

roost on their extremities.

They stood fixed like this for long enough to forget about time. Their consciousness got tiny and dense in their cores while the rest of them turned to roughage in the purple glow.

Trying to keep from pitching forward, they dug their ankles into the soft ground and felt the presence of hollows deep below... corridors, passageways, tunnels, a vast networked geography surrounding the anchor, which anchored not only ANGEL HOUSE but the entire world that had come into being around it.

They remained frozen, feeling their bones tremble, about to break, until Squimbop opened the front door and came onto the porch naked. Just before making the hand gesture that released them, he walked off his porch and down through the marsh, leaning into the Mayor's ear to whisper, "I'll see you at the Greek restaurant tomorrow evening at six."

He had no message for James.

Then he was gone, the door closed behind him, and the two of them were face down in the grass, aching like they'd been dropped from twenty feet and hadn't bounced.

Once they got to their feet, James and the Mayor kept their heads as far down as their necks would allow, walking like apes back to the Meadow-lined Road, James holding his camera against one leg.

They stood in the median, massaging their elbows and shoulders, waiting to think of what to do. Staring at the lights of the Town's City, they refocused on the near distance in time to catch sight of two teenagers straggling along, crushing beer cans and smoking a joint.

Pretending he was back in his basement staring at his screen, where everything happened for his sake only, the Mayor watched them approach, thinking, *That's Ben and James at nineteen... walking out of the past to save me.*

In an imitation of his own nineteen-year-old voice, the Mayor said, "Hey guys."

Diffidently, one of them said, "Hey."

James was fighting to keep hold of the camera, their image slipping around inside the frame. He wanted to tell them, "Okay, you be me, you be Ben. We're leaving town next month and never coming back. That's the story, okay?"

Even more than that, he wanted to turn to the Mayor and say, "Go home. I need to speak to myself and Ben alone."

The nineteen-year-olds smoked and smirked and watched the two older men, in no hurry. They leaned into the camera and made peace signs and stuck their tongues out, laughing.

"I'm James, the Director," James finally said, hoping the declaration would bring some clarity. Their resemblance to himself and Ben at nineteen was starting to weaken his knees and shorten his breath. "And this is the Mayor."

The nineteen-year-olds looked from one to the other, affixing the names to the bodies. "Cool."

"New in town?" the Mayor asked, trying to act comfortable with the concept.

One of them nodded and said, "Yeah. We were on the road. Got tired. Started seeing things. Saw an exit, so we took it. Now we're here. Figure we'll stay until we find a way out. Maybe pick up some work in the meantime."

"Work," said James, fingering his camera again, already several scenes into imagining their performance. "Ever acted before?"

The nineteen-year-olds smiled in unison, like a single spirit was puppeting them both, one of its hands in each of their heads, making their mouths move. "Sure," they grinned. "We're acting right now."

Then they were gone.

Back in their Dead Houses, the nine-year-olds sat up in bed. They looked out their windows and across the Wooden Wheel park at one another, waving to signal that they were alright.

Then they waited out the phantom seconds that always came after being the nineteen-year-olds, the queasy interim during which their bodies felt too small and their limbs strained to control distant fingers and toes that no longer obeyed them.

James, likewise, was back in his house now, sitting at the kitchen table with only the overhead light on. After the Mayor dropped him off—neither had been up for a drink—he'd run straight to the table, grabbing a stack of loose papers and a pen from the living room on his way, in pantomime of a man possessed by a fully-formed idea dying to come out.

Now he hovered over the paper, uncomfortable in his wet shoes, trying to picture what the nineteen-year-olds would do in his film.

They come to town in a car that stops working as soon as they get here, he wrote on the sheet he'd labeled FILM TREATMENT DRAFT 1.

They drive in full of memories that they can't be sure are theirs, like possibly stolen cargo… they're drifters, memory drifters, carting cast-off material that no one wants to own up to anymore… unless maybe there's someone looking for it… faceless people, blank people, swarming in, hungry for this stuff, whatever it is.

He was starting to get into it now, eating the last piece of a cake he'd found in the fridge and squishing the crumbs with his pen where they fell on the paper.

They're from nowhere, willing to be from anywhere, maybe searching for where they're really from but coming to suspect it isn't on Earth…

He could picture the trunk of their car with a box marked ROOTS, like tree roots but ancestral in this case, human roots waiting to be put down, maybe put to rest, in whatever town they finally settled in, calling off their journey either due to exhaustion or because there was something about the place they'd come to that they liked.

They're unencumbered but looking to settle, James wrote. *Maybe someone's after them... dark beings with dripping mouths, trying to steal the psychic matter from their trunk and purge it of whatever spark it has left... but the nineteen-year-olds won't let them.*

They're me and Ben but on opposite trajectories, coming from out there to seek their destinies in here, with an actual wealth of worldly experience—real danger, real entanglements, real sex—rather than Ben and me, who, when we left for News City, had nothing but nineteen years' worth of work on the Pretend Movie to our credit.

He crossed this last part out, content to let it reside in his mind without needing anyone else to see it. He liked where this was going and decided he'd done enough for one night. He thought about brushing his teeth and going upstairs to bed, but decided to sleep with his face on his notes instead, to see how it'd feel to look like a man who's worked himself over the edge and into exhaustion, so that when he woke up in the morning, he'd know the transition into seriousness had occurred.

Tuesday Night into Wednesday

At this point on any other night, Well's broadcast would have been underway.

But tonight he'd taken a Night Off, as his contract with the Mayor permitted, "in such cases as moral collapse is otherwise deemed likely."

He'd never taken one. He'd come close, but the idea of leaving the Ghost Town unvisited had kept him behind the mic through all sickness and upset until now.

Sure, he thought, in his room at the Hotel, *there's an element of cowardice about me, as now is surely when the children need me most. And the Ghost Town...*

The thought of it empty and freezing made him snarl.

He was lying in bed, sweating on top of his sheets, furious that what he wanted most was sleep and he'd gone out of his way to put himself in a position to get some, and still couldn't get any.

He lay like that until anger brought him back to life. Anger at the thing that was pulling the children away, and at himself for his inability to inhabit the Ghost Town without them. He toyed with the notion of storming across the Meadow and entering the Ghost Town himself, insisting it admit him, but he knew—he hadn't yet lost all reason—that the presence of an adult man in his child's bed would only corrupt whatever pure memories he had left.

Life is nothing but middlemen, he thought, and then he kept thinking it, like this was the sentence on the notecard for tonight's broadcast and now it was starting, intended for him alone.

He could feel the rooms above and below him standing empty after the Reunion, like he was perched between empty spaces yawning inward to crush him.

Do it, he thought.

The walls groaned like they were trying, but he remained inviolate.

Frozen on his stomach, he pushed into the mattress like a man lowering his face into a pond, parting the waters in search of something lost on the bottom. Eyes buried in fabric, he saw the streets and houses of the Ghost Town, his perspective sweeping through them, taking it all in, straining to diagnose what was happening.

The streets were empty, of course, but they didn't have the warmth of recent occupancy. Usually, when he tried hard, he could feel traces of the children even when they weren't there, keeping the Ghost

122

Town from freezing over or falling entirely into the past. But not tonight.

Fuck me, he thought, feeling older than he'd imagined it possible to feel, no matter how long he lived. "An icy wind rolls down the streets," he whispered, like his pillow was the mic and a yet-newer broadcast was beginning.

It felt like an Ice Age was almost here.

He tried again to fall asleep, but a vision of the far end of the street kept him awake. Zooming past the familiar houses and storefronts, he could see, dimly, at the very end, a structure he'd never noticed before.

A house.

As the vision brought him closer, he could see a child inside, on the second floor, cautiously descending the stairs into the smell of coffee and toast, seeking warmth, even love.

The house was situated at the end of the dusty street, surrounded by heat rather than ice. Tan-yellow light, motes in the air, telephone wires slack between splintered, maybe lightning-split poles.

Another Ghost Town, he thought. Never before had he imagined there could be more than one. *A Ghost Town built of future, not of past.*

Still out there, uncorrupted, waiting for me...

Another iteration of my Childhood Home, one I'll never have to leave if I can survive the journey between here and there.

A house at the end of a dead-end street, beyond which is nothing. No future, no loss, no Death.

Straining so hard he could feel his neck quake, like he was holding something immensely heavy in his mouth, he focused on the other presences in this house who'd come, or been brought, to live there with him.

As me, he thought. *As me at nine.*

His arm was so frozen he was afraid it would break if he tried to move, but he felt the moment of release coming and knew that if he didn't push the vision to the point of realization before then, he'd lose all

123

he'd just been shown. *If I have to sacrifice the Ghost Town down here,* he thought, *and all the children in it… so be it.*

If that's what it takes to get through the Desert to Dust House…

As soon as the term coined itself and its referent materialized in the Desert, his arm snapped back to life, throbbing like it'd been run over, while the child, or children, on the stairs descended, into the warm bright kitchen of Dust House and the vision dissolved into golden motes.

He leapt out of bed, pulled his pants on, stuffed his wallet in his pocket, and resolved to leave the town and never come back.

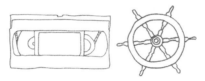

Wednesday Evening

The Mayor microwaved a tub of Ultra Max banana pudding, then got ready to meet Squimbop at the Greek restaurant. His memory of having been invited last night from the ANGEL HOUSE porch was so vivid— he could feel himself standing there, frozen and terrified, receiving the message—that he couldn't dismiss it as having been a dream, though he knew that, like any memory, it might have been.

At the very least, he would eat at the Greek restaurant tonight. If the Professor arrived, they would eat together. If not, he would devote yet another evening to ruminating on what it was to be alone.

He finished his pudding, left the bowl on the counter beside many others, and went upstairs. Pretending his bedroom mirror was a TV screen, he watched himself play dress up, pulling on the good slacks and blazer he wore to Town Council Meetings and struggling to tie his tie.

Breathe, he thought, loosening the knot around his neck. He kept loosening until it fell off. Then, some clarity flowing back into his head, he pulled off this costume and pulled on jeans and a plain button-up shirt. *No need to go into this like it's a date,* he consoled himself, though he'd never been on a date before and could not have said what one entailed aside from, as he imagined it, the hard fucking at the end.

After a short nap in his new clothes, he got up, stepped into his sneakers by the door, and got in his station wagon.

He parked on the street and took the half-staircase down to the Greek restaurant. A few Reunion stragglers were scattered around, mumbling as they ate, but it was empty aside from them.

The waiter forced a smile and told the Mayor to sit anywhere. He loved the tables far in the back, near the kitchen, where there were no windows but very wide booths, tabletops large enough to spread out a map and a set of blueprints if the food hadn't come yet, or if it was long gone.

He had spent late nights here during his teens, when it stayed open for midnight breakfast, drinking whole pots of coffee and shuffling papers around with Ben and James, some to read and others to write on, every hour bringing them closer to the psychic transcendence they'd felt was inevitable. The Face of God, the One True Word…

The waiter came with the menu and a glass of water. As the Mayor was running his fingers over the words PANCAKES and WAFFLES, the Professor slid into the booth across from him. The Mayor looked up, saw the man's thick mustache caked with whitish clumps and smelled his rich breath. Then he looked back at his menu, blushing, unable to hold the stranger's gaze. He fixated on the A and the E in waffles, stretching his entire will to live between those two letters.

The Professor reached out to the two sides of the table and shoved it forward, despite the fact that it was nailed to the ground. Now it pushed into the Mayor's gut, leaving the Professor more breathing room than he needed and reddening the Mayor's face a shade further than it already was.

He smiled. The waiter tiptoed back over as silently as he could, sensing that he was intruding, and put another menu in front of the Professor, who put a hand on his and held it there, reaching a finger up as far as the man's watch before letting him go.

"Thank you," gasped the Mayor. "We'll each have coffee, to start."

The waiter ran off and returned with it a moment later, desperate not to spill any despite his shaking hands.

Squimbop sniffed the cream in the metal canister and made a sour expression, then dribbled some in and stirred it with his fork, which he left in the mug.

The Mayor opened his mouth in a sudden surge of confidence that something cogent would come out, but, meeting the Professor's eyes, he clamped his jaws shut on his tongue, wincing and tearing up. A drop of blood beaded up on his lip and he licked it off with a quick, lizard-like flick of his tongue. Then he put his hands around his coffee mug and kept them there.

After he'd held off as long as he could, he blurted, "I trust you're finding the facilities at the School adequate?"

The Professor looked into the open space of the restaurant like he was trying to remember what the School was. When he looked back, he seemed bigger than he had a moment ago. Capable of greater violence than the Mayor had let himself imagine.

"Adequate," he replied. "Adequate."

"So what have you been teaching the children?" The Mayor had stopped himself from saying "my children," but could feel the Professor gleaning exactly what he meant. He was both impressed and unsettled by this feeling.

"I don't teach. I Lecture. I use up each Lecture as I deliver it, retaining nothing. I could not tell you a single word I have uttered to

126

them so far this week. Nor any that I will utter a week from now, should my services still be required then."

Hearing this last phrase, the Mayor's throat closed up and stayed closed until the waiter came back, standing beside the table until someone spoke.

"We'll each have the buttermilk pancakes, with extra syrup and butter." The Mayor forced the words out, pretending he was in charge.

The waiter had an instinct to look to Squimbop for confirmation, but the Mayor held his gaze, forcefully.

Eventually, he nodded and left.

"They're great. You'll love them," said the Mayor.

"I'll eat later. When I'm too tired to think." The Professor finally pulled his hands back to his side of the table.

The Mayor felt dismay rising from his stomach. He expelled it with a burp when it reached his mouth, trying not to lose his smile as he did. "Sure. More for me." He smiled, resisting the urge to wipe his forehead though he could feel sweat pooling.

"Eat," said the Professor, in a calm voice, when the food came. The Mayor nodded and filled his fork with dough, his diaphragm flapping like a flounder hauled out of a tank with a gaff.

Squimbop sipped coffee and looked at the huge man across from him, choking down syrupy dough and sweating with an unfocused pleading look in his eyes. It was the phase of early evening when he had to start preparing to receive tomorrow's Lecture. So he set to work opening his mind, greasing the cavity for the Totally Other Place to shove itself in when it was ready, all the while retaining a mask of attention on the Mayor.

The Mayor asked him about his trip to town, and Squimbop shook his head. He would not discuss this.

After a brief internal struggle in search of a new subject, during which he considered and rejected the Blind Spot and James' Movie

127

as too intimate, the Mayor said to expect a brutal winter, colder than anyplace Squimbop might be from or have been before here. He talked about snow blocking the doors of shops and houses, people jumping from second-story windows and barely falling, and the ominous red that filled the night sky before the snows came at dawn and lasted into the following night, so red that neither light nor darkness could break through.

"Hibernation: it's like we're all dead for months," said the Mayor, his plate down to one pancake. "Curled up, heads, bodies, nubs of arms and elbows, under felt, down, feathers…"

He can't stop talking, he thought about himself.

He went on: "Once, I was out driving with my friend James just after a storm and a police officer pulled us over when we sped over an icy stretch of the Meadow-lined Road. I was driving, so I got out when the officer asked me to. As I was talking to him, James got out too and walked over to the brick wall of what was at that time the lumber yard and started making snowballs from the piles all around and hurling them at the wall. He did this the whole time the cop was checking the trunk and writing down my license plate number, and even when the cop drove away, leaving a ticket on the dashboard, James just kept hurling snowballs, watching them smash against the wall that was already so snow-covered they hardly made a dent. Then they didn't make a dent at all. Eventually, the wall of snow was so close to him he couldn't throw the snowballs, he just shoved them into the snow that was up against his face. He kept it up all the rest of the day, and throughout the night, burying himself, until I had to go home. I came back the next day to find him frozen solid, like a," the Mayor shuddered at the association with the ugly, grueling memory of last night in the Meadow, "scarecrow. I put him in my trunk and took him to my house and thawed him out in the hot tub. He came back to life, but he was never quite the same.

"The point," he said, panting, relieved that he'd managed to say this much without blurting something shameful or clamming up, "is that

Hibernation can make anyone crazy. If you find yourself wavering in a few months, just call me. There are things that can be done. My hot tub's always..."

He choked himself to a halt at this point, swallowing the rest of his coffee and looking at the dregs on the bottom, certain he'd said too much without knowing where the time to stop might have been.

Squimbop said he was going to the bathroom. When he got out of the booth, the Mayor was surprised at how tall and thin he was, more so than he'd seemed when he first sat down, or in his hazy memory of seeing him on the ANGEL HOUSE porch last night. *There's something beautiful about him*, he thought, involuntarily.

The Mayor also had to go to the bathroom, but he was wedged too tightly between his seat and the table. He clenched his teeth, imagining himself deep inside a Movie written and directed by Squimbop, happily doing whatever the script commanded.

In the time the Professor was gone, the Mayor thought of six things to say but, when he got back, he jettisoned them all and said what came to him right then: "They're my children, you know."

He looked away, shocked that he'd said this, uncertain what the repercussion would be.

"It's not my concern where they come from. My concern is where they go."

Squimbop took in the Mayor, the booth behind his head, the coat rack, and the windows, giving equal importance to each. By the time he refocused on the Mayor, the conversation was over.

The Mayor got a refill on coffee, and told the waiter to give Squimbop one as well, but he put his hand over his cup. The waiter hovered for a minute, the pot extended in his left hand. A hot drop fell on the Professor's knuckle.

All went quiet. The old men at other tables stopped groaning and stared into space.

Squimbop licked up the drop like the first blood from a deep wound. Then he looked at the waiter, dismissing him with a wink.

Everyone exhaled.

"Is the atmosphere here working out for you, in terms of dreaming up your Lectures?" the Mayor asked, when the Professor's knuckle was dry.

"The atmosphere is adequate." Then a different look came over the Professor, like he was finally making an effort to think of something meaningful to say. "Actually, there is one thing."

The Mayor leaned in.

"My mattress. It's… not ideal for this town. It has too many old dreams in it. A silty, stale residue from years and years of travel. These things often need to be replaced, but rarely are."

The Mayor tilted his head back, opened his mouth, and let visions of the Mattress Store flood in. He felt that something important and inevitable would occur there, between himself and the Professor, and that he could delay that thing but not prevent its eventual occurrence. "We can visit the Mattress Store together. It would be my pleasure to purchase a new mattress on your behalf. A little welcome present from me to you."

He looked at the Professor looking at him and wondered how much of his thoughts he'd been able to read. *If you're reading my mind right now*, he thought, trying to keep eye contact with the Professor until the end… but he couldn't complete the message before he had to speak. He cleared his throat. "I'll pick you up this Saturday at 4:30. In the Square outside," he pointed at the half-windows.

"And I'll get this too," he added, when the waiter brought the check, falsely magnanimous since the Professor had only had coffee and hadn't offered to pay.

After he paid, leaving a larger tip than usual, the Mayor said, "Shall we walk out?"

The Professor shook his head. "I'll see you Saturday."

Then, slowly, he pulled the booth back enough to let the Mayor stand up.

The Mayor stood, turned, and found himself face-to-face with Well. He maneuvered around him with a noncommittal "Hi," same as he would've offered a barely familiar face at the Reunion, and hurried to his car without looking back.

Later Wednesday Evening

Well had more energy than he expected to. After his bout of sleep paralysis, he came into the restaurant feeling sharp for the first time since the Reunion. His frozen arm felt like it had grown more muscular, and the image of the house on the hot, dusty street filled him with hope. Determined to leave it forever, the town looked almost sweet to him now. Minor, harmless, holding neither menace nor opportunity. A blip on the radar; a stop along the way.

He sat down across from Squimbop, letting go of whatever enmity he felt about what had happened on the airwaves. *If not him, something else would've come for the children,* he thought. *Ghost Towns aren't built to last.*

The Professor nodded, grinning to show that he agreed.

After a long conversation on Monday night, when both had come in alone but ended up eating together, a sort of ritual had established itself between them. Dinner was the crossover point, the changing of the guards where Squimbop relinquished control over the children in order to prepare for the night's Lecture-influx, and Well, with his sentence printed on his notecard, got ready to climb behind the mic and take over their dreaming minds at the radio station.

But not tonight, Well remembered. *Nor ever again.* All of that was over. Now it was time for something new. He shivered, unable to block an onrush of fear. *Fear of what? That there won't be anything new? That I'll arrive in the Desert and find it just a desert, where I'll wander until I collapse and that'll be that?*

He teared up, putting a napkin to his mouth and surreptitiously wiping his eyes.

Squimbop grinned wide enough to show his teeth, enjoying Well's pain.

The waiter came over and stood beside them for a long time before clearing his throat.

Well ordered the same pancake plate as the Mayor, and coffee. Squimbop shook his head when the waiter looked in his direction.

"What did the Mayor want?" Well asked, when they were alone again.

"To buy me a mattress."

"At the Mattress Store?" Now it was Well's turn to grin.

When Squimbop didn't reply, they drifted away from each other, into their own minds.

"He came by the radio station, which is unusual," Well heard himself say, a while later.

"Who?"

"The Mayor. To audit my broadcast. It's his prerogative, though of course I prefer to work in private. He doesn't do it very often."

"Something's wrong then?" Squimbop refreshed his grin, relishing the act of pretending not to know what it was.

"Yeah. I might be leaving town soon. If I don't see you, uh…"

"Leaving town? Leaving it for what?"

Well shook his head. "I don't know. If I fall off the edge, fine. That's better than living here while my Ghost Town dies. I had a vision, a vision of a… another house. In a hot place, far from the coming frost."

132

Should I be telling him this? He couldn't tell what the risks were, or if any good could come of it. Probably Squimbop already knew. He could feel himself starting to squirm, his thinking looping around, boiling toward panic, until the prospect of lying to Squimbop felt as futile as that of lying to himself.

He tried to stand and knocked over his coffee. Squimbop watched the puddle seep across the table and into his lap.

Well sat back down. "The Desert," he added. He focused on controlling his voice, making it sound voluntary. "First up the Mountain, then across the summit, to the Desert, then… back home at last."

Squimbop looked at him, pity in his eyes. "In that case, good luck. I hope we meet again someday."

Well nodded, got up again, and hurried to the door. Squimbop sat in silence until the waiter appeared, a dishrag in his hands. He mopped the table and then, looking from Squimbop's lap to his face and back again, tremblingly reached down and mopped between the Professor's legs, praying these moments would not be his last.

Later that night, Squimbop sat on the toilet in ANGEL HOUSE, peeing slowly while typing on his laptop, its underside burning his upper thighs.

Dear Master,

An eventful day. I finally presented myself for my first extended interaction with the man who calls himself "the Mayor," though I don't believe he holds any elected office. He is a colossally obese man, independently wealthy as far as I can tell, and ravaged by loneliness. I would not go so far as to say that the man elicits sympathy from me, but there is something endearing about his despair. Despite my admitted inability to remember the specifics of previous towns, I would be willing to suggest that he is perhaps the saddest individual I have ever met.

I cannot say exactly which emotions I elicit in him, but a bond of some sort—one-sided, naturally—is forming between us.

This man seems to consider himself the father of the town's children. Incapable of comprehending the means by which everyone in the town—him included—was culled from the Inland Seafloor upon my arrival, he has grown to believe that he sired them through a sort of mystical masturbation, as best I can understand it, by which he enters his TV screen and fertilizes a sort of human-soil born of cinema (this town is morosely obsessed with movies) on the far side. I am sorry to be unable to provide greater insight into this process, but I trust your understanding, here as in all things, surpasses mine.

All for now,
Prof. Sq.

The Rest of the Week, Culminating in Friday

It took Ben until late in the week to dry off from the rain of Reunion Weekend. It had gotten deep into him and came out very slowly, in waves of cold steam.

He hung around the Hotel, opening his blinds to look out at the Town's City from time to time, keeping them closed aside from that. He kept almost going stir crazy. Each time it came over him, he drew the blinds, stepped into his still-wet jeans and shoes, and went downstairs to the restaurant, where he was always the only person eating.

After the Reunion, the dust in the restaurant settled fast. For all the frenzy of Sub-Weird in the Square outside and around the edges of the Town's City, he could find no definite indication that they'd ever stayed here at the Hotel.

The waiters were surprised, disturbed even, each time Ben

showed up, but they did what they could for him, microwaving leftovers from the kitchen, opening cans, or mixing dry goods with water and heating the mixture in a saucepan. All this went on his tab, which someday the Mayor would settle.

His overlapping sleeping and eating spells during this week came to share a nautical theme, partially due to the dampness that'd seeped into him, partially to the watery, drifting tempo he'd synced up to, and partially to the distant sound of the Inland Sea, lapping against a shore on the far side of the Outskirts, beyond which, in theory, lay News City.

Down in the restaurant, he tried to let go of all specific memories and think only, *I am a drifter here, a sailor on shore leave, rootless among the ultra-rooted, just passing through…*

The Motel was the terminal of this train of thought. *The Motel is the home of all drifters, he thought. The only place where one can live and not end up like the Mayor, desperate for reenactment, or like the Sub-Weird, reeking of how things were back when all of us lived in the town but not in the world.*

In bed, wet sheets pulled up around his neck, he could hear the Mayor knocking on his door, shouting, "Ben! Ben! You in there?"

As soon as he heard the disappointed footsteps retreat, he sat up and clicked his gun, satisfyingly, in the depths of his mouth. Something had changed. In a mental leap he'd just now become capable of making, he realized he could take off his wet clothes for good. Like a monk removing his hairshirt in the privacy of his dim cell, Ben decided he didn't have to get sick and die in his Reunion outfit. He could even shower and shave, more carefully this time. The water was hot and afterwards, to his amazement, the towels were dry.

Standing in his other pair of jeans and a grey T-shirt, he rubbed his smooth jawline, smelled his fingers, then tucked his gun into his waistband and pulled on a crumpled but clean blazer. He felt jaunty and strong. Crossing the lobby, he flexed his lungs, preparing for the first

135

manly stab of autumn.

The first order of business was to visit the Town's City and observe it as it was, accepting that it existed entirely apart from whatever his intentions for it had been.

Then he would penetrate the Outskirts as a purged man, indifferent, with nothing in the town to anchor him. *Anyone can drift*, he thought, lighter on his feet than he'd been all year. *All you have to do is pull up your anchor.*

He leaned on the fence surrounding the Town's City, watching two contractors unload sheets of glass from a pile and bring them through the tarp hanging in the main doorway.

The ground of the site was shredded with deep tire tracks hardened into the mud. He knew that some of the tractors and backhoes parked behind the Mayor's house had been used to dig it, but they'd long since been returned to their original location, overlooking the quarry.

Nails and staples littered every flat surface and clung to the inclines, and there were coffee cups and soda cans in shoulder-high piles. In the center of it all was the gazebo that contained his blueprints, which the contractors would only unlock in moments of doubt.

He tried to remember how the site had looked on Sunday, when he'd sat in the lobby with Squimbop eating Giant Chinese, but he felt the maw of the Reunion opening in his head at this thought, so he closed his eyes, pictured a muscular, tattooed arm growing from his brainstem, and ordered that arm to swat the memory to death against the walls of his skull.

When he opened his eyes, he saw two contractors entering the code to open the gazebo, looking him over before they vanished inside. Looking sharply away, he jerked his head upward until his eyes stopped on the faces of two Sub-Weird in a window frame on the eighth floor, hanging curtains. They leered down at him before vanishing behind black felt.

He closed his eyes and ran, not opening them until he was halfway up the Meadow-lined Road.

The air out here hurt his lungs and the space behind his eyes and set his temples to throbbing. He felt like he was diving down through the Inland Sea, seeking the road on the bottom, along which the course of his future extended.

The only road home.

When the pressure grew blinding, he sat down at the marsh edge of the Meadow, letting the frosty wind off the Ghost Town numb him into submission. He closed his eyes and pictured the Tower.

Sub-Weird were filling all the windows, forcing the spirit of the Outskirts into the Town's City, unwilling to leave though the Reunion was over.

If you won't leave town, I will be your Prophet, Ben promised them, uncertain if he'd had this thought before, or merely a premonition that he soon would. *I will retrieve some message from the far Outskirts, from the shore of the Inland Sea, and bring it back to you, so that, together, we might overcome our past-hunger and free ourselves to exist, even here, as drifters, true individuals inhabiting an actual city at last, free of the town's inward pull… and free of the pain of exile as well. At home in the whole world.*

When he opened his eyes, he was face to face with Squimbop at the edge of the Meadow. He couldn't move. His mouth hung open, saliva crystalizing on his lips.

"Shhh," said Squimbop, touching Ben's forehead, releasing him from the scarecrow state. "Go back to town. Do not try to reach the Inland Sea. It's too far for you, and you wouldn't be happy if you found yourself marooned on its shore."

Ben took an unsteady step away from ANGEL HOUSE, his knees and elbows trembling.

When he came back to himself, Ben was standing alone and dusk was falling. He looked up at a tree, most of its leaves turned by now. They looked like overripe fruit, desperate to fall.

When he looked back at the Meadow-lined Road, he saw a man shuffling along with a leather sack over his shoulder and a giant key dangling from his belt. He looked sad, maybe old, though his face was so expressionless it was hard to be sure.

He stopped where Ben was standing but didn't move his eyes, so Ben crept around behind him to look where he was looking. The Town's City was blinking, drawing him inward.

"Missed the Reunion?" Ben whispered in his ear, following as the man resumed his approach.

"Couldn't wake up for it," he whispered. "I was deep in a dream, sealed in my sleeping bag, but now I'm going home. The sighing of the void woke me at last."

"Are there more stragglers?" Ben whispered. "Are the whole Outskirts emptying out?"

The man sighed. "See that up there?" He pointed at the Town's City. "It's calling us in."

Then he was gone. Ben sat down in the road as night fell. The journey through the Outskirts to the Inland Sea felt insurmountable. Though he was certain it had been clear a few minutes ago, he found he could no longer remember what he'd hoped to find there. The brief, extraordinary rush of prophecy flowing through him had petered out. Despondent with the feeling of having given up on himself, he rose to his feet and began the walk back to town, trailing in the sad man's wake.

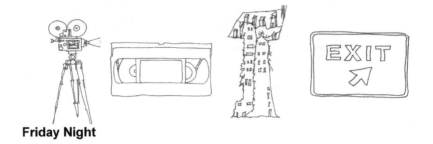

Friday Night

Ben didn't get far before a station wagon pulled over next to him, covering his dry jeans in puddle spray. The passenger's side window rolled down and James stuck his head out and shouted, "Hey!"

"Hey," Ben parroted, too far inside himself to be surprised.

He looked past James and saw the Mayor driving the same old station wagon he'd had when they were seventeen.

"Ben!" shouted the Mayor, in the same way that James had. "Get in. Giant Chinese is on me tonight."

They were at the host stand, looking out at the cavernous, velvet-draped red interior, with the stage for comedians on one side and the neon blue Tiki bar on the other.

The green and orange of the fish tank glowed off their cheeks and the sides of their necks as they waited to be seated at one of the fifty tables. The place was empty, as it always was except back when it used to stay open until two a.m. on Fridays and Saturdays, to soak up hungry crowds spilling out of the Night School and the Mattress Store, and those eager to chase the Greek restaurant's midnight pancakes with something savory.

Eels, crabs, catfish, lobster, and carp—dredged up from the Inland Sea generations ago and bred in captivity since then—looked out at them, faces pressed to the cloudy glass, perhaps the same ones that had looked at them a decade ago, and twenty gutted ducks hung against the steamed-up window of the prep area at the very back.

The host gathered three dinner menus and three for cocktails and led them to one of the round banquet tables, big enough for fifteen, with a Lazy Susan in the center.

The three of them sat bunched together on one side.

It took a long time to get focused on the menus. The Mayor forced his mind to zero in on the fact that the three of them were here together for the first time in what he was determined to call the present. There had to be some good in this. Thoughts of Squimbop seeped in, clouding his mind like the fish tank he'd just been staring at, but he worked to shove them back where they came from, promising them his undivided attention later on, when he was alone.

His eyes clung to the menu, as did Ben's and James', a huge laminated thing with over two hundred items, running into complex combinations of letters and numbers like C33d-4, all of which the waiters had memorized.

Lost among the dozens of pages, hunger overtook the Mayor. It felt like the decade since the three of them had sat here together was how long it'd been since he'd eaten.

When the waiter came, he groaned his order like he was afraid he'd die before it was filled. Ben and James, in a chorus behind the Mayor, ordered one dish each.

Drinks came first. The Mayor raised his cocktail and toasted, "May the sanest man go crazy, may the craziest man survive!"

Ben and James raised their glasses and nodded, pushing through the embarrassment in hopes of connecting with some remnant, no matter how withered, of how it used to feel to make this toast, back when having a drink in hand was something special.

Borne by a fleet of otherwise idle wait staff, their order began to arrive.

They looked down at the platters piling up until each of them was alone behind a mountain of food.

The Mayor closed his eyes and said a small inward Grace: *Let*

140

my world cohere a little while longer. Let me live this night for old times'
sake, as though Squimbop had never come.

There was so much food that for the first fifteen minutes, no
one could talk. Ben and the Mayor were ravenous, while James ate at
their pace just to keep up.

When they reached the point where they couldn't go on eating
at the rate they'd started at, James tried to make conversation by
saying, "There's no hot tub in the house I'm renting, but the water in the
shower is excellent."

No one responded, and, as soon as he'd said it, James couldn't
remember what response he'd hoped for.

Ben was as silent as the Mayor had ever seen him. He
wondered what he'd been doing in his Hotel room all week. He knew
he'd flirted with suicide before, but had never known how close he'd
come. Maybe this week he almost got there.

The Mayor snapped out of mawkishness with a flamboyant
cattle-round up gesture, signaling for another round of cocktails, which
soon arrived. By the end of the round after that, with their plates cleared
away and pulpy orange rinds and fortune cookie wrappers adorning
the check, the front door swung open and two teenagers swaggered in,
surveying the room in light windbreakers, jeans, and scuffed sneakers.

The host, clearly impressed with their attitude, came over and
seated them with food menus and, since Giant Chinese didn't card,
cocktail menus as well.

Ben was looking at his hands on the stained white tablecloth,
but the Mayor and James were looking straight at the nineteen-year-
olds, whom they remembered from the Meadow-lined Road.

The nineteen-year-olds looked over at the three of them and
nodded sleepily, making peace signs with limp fingers. Then they went
back to their menus, the host hanging over their shoulders, watching
them read.

Ben looked up and said, to the Mayor's and James' surprise,

141

"I've seen them hanging around the Hotel."

James registered this without looking away from them.

The nineteen-year-olds had ordered and were leaning back in their chairs, taking in their new surroundings, clearly aware they were being looked at. The Mayor tried to conceive of the reality of being nineteen, at Giant Chinese for the first time right now, giddy with the thrill of having just ordered a cocktail. *In this same room as me, in this same moment,* he thought, *some aspect of the world of ten years ago still exists.* He swooned at the implications as he imagined the two of them as Ben and James in a Movie on his screen in his basement. *Versions of Ben and James prepared to spend their twenties right here, in town, with me... twenties that will never end because they'll never truly begin.*

He burped into his fist and stood up, muttering, "Wait for me in the car."

He tripped on his way to the bathroom, knocking over one of the banquet tables and groaning as Sam Ren and another waiter heaved him back to his feet.

When he was gone, Ben turned to James and said, "Remember how much we used to like to pretend we were nineteen back when we were nine?"

In order to fit behind the wheel of his station wagon, the Mayor had to push the driver's seat so far back he was almost next to Ben in the backseat. He then reached over his belly to hold the wheel with his outstretched fingertips. Sometimes driving was so uncomfortable in this position he looked forward to drifting to the Blind Spot in neutral later on, his hands folded in his lap and his eyes closed.

Heaving up his driveway, he was glad not to see any bears, though he knew they were lurking in the trees. While Ben and James let themselves into the house, he watched one lumber across the yard, pausing to stare at his headlights as they faded out. He nodded in its direction before stepping inside and closing the door behind him.

Looking at their two sets of nearly identical shoes by the door, the Mayor realized that, though James had been here a few days ago to discuss the Movie, Ben still hadn't, not in all the time he'd been back in town.

"No more dogs, huh?" Ben asked from the kitchen.

The Mayor shook his head. "Long, long dead. Buried in the quarry out back." He nodded at the window, catching sight of his reflection in the darkened glass, which looked to him like some ghost-version of his worst self trying to get in.

The Mayor went off to start a fire in the living room while Ben and James opened beers in the kitchen, leaning against the counter where a bowl of brownie batter sat uncovered, filling with dust.

"Hey Mayor!" shouted James, surprised at how good it felt to be back here. "Want a beer?" No answer from the Mayor aside from the rumpling of newspapers in the living room. Again he tried to think of what the Mayor's name had been before, and again he drew a blank. The more he thought about it, the more lobotomized he felt. So he drank more, trying to keep up with Ben, both of them starting new beers before they'd finished the old.

"Those kids at Giant Chinese looked like us, didn't they?" said Ben.

James shrugged, glad that Ben saw it too, but wary of discussing it before his film was underway. If he'd learned anything at film school, it was to keep ideas private until they'd taken definite shape.

He pulled yet another bottle from the fridge, and one for the Mayor, and went into the living room, where the fire was sending shadows up the walls.

The Mayor cracked his open on the couch and exhaled, closing his eyes. As they sat watching the fire, he slipped back into thinking about Well and the children on the road, whatever had happened at

143

the station this week. When these thoughts turned too dark to pursue, he took a long swig and fell to counting the minutes until his trip to the Mattress Store with Squimbop tomorrow. He leaned against the headrest on the couch and hoped his head looked innocuous from the outside.

"Got anything harder?"

The Mayor opened his eyes. "What?"

James shook his head. "Never mind." He left to get yet another beer from the kitchen, thinking, *In my film, the nineteen-year-olds will do real drugs. The kind that can change you.*

Ben couldn't sit still. He was roaming the living room, looking at his reflection in the bay windows that opened onto the front porch and the sloping front lawn, bounded on one side by woods and on the other by the driveway. He ran his fingers along the lacquer of the grand piano and watched himself ripple.

James, close to real drunkenness now, returned from the kitchen with a fresh round of beers and sat on the couch rehearsing his film pitch in his head.

"It used to get so fucking late in this house," said Ben, sitting back down next to the Mayor. "Unbelievable, how fucking late we used to let it get. I wonder what we talked about. Each time felt like the final one, didn't it? The time when we'd finally break through, after the long approach. Into the world we were fighting to be part of, where there'd be no need for words anymore. Where all thinking would reveal itself as a bygone phase of our evolution. Then we'd gorge on pancakes and coffee and talk some more."

He opened another bottle. "If only we knew now what we knew then." Ben spluttered. "Or thought we knew…"

"No," he resumed, after a pause. "What we did know. We really knew it. We just don't anymore."

A bear peered in the window, yawning.

The Mayor was starting to wish that Ben was asleep and James

144

was hard at work on the Movie in another location.

"We let it get so fucking late back then," James added, several minutes later, like it'd taken him that long to think of a retort, "but it was never as fucking late then as it fucking is now."

Now came a silence in which they could hear the firewood popping.

All three of them felt old, but there was too much time still to come, despite how impossibly much there'd already been. None could see how they'd get through it, to whatever, if anything, was on the far side. All three labored to accept the fact that they were still alive. Like they hadn't been sure on their own, but together there was no denying it. Whatever was ahead of them, there was no going around or turning back. Even if they did nothing—perhaps especially in that case—whatever was coming would come.

"I hate to always be the one," said James, "but I'm gonna need to crash."

He stretched out on the couch, moving pillows from behind his back to under his head, hoping that if he fell asleep fast enough, the need to piss would abate.

The Mayor and Ben sat for a brief vigil over James' body. Each made a motion toward reclaiming the more businesslike attitude they had affected during the planning stages of the Town's City, but now that atmosphere wouldn't cohere.

So they both remained alone, locked in themselves, looking out at each other without being quite sure whom they were seeing.

The Mayor felt the basement calling him. He longed to grab the brownie batter and run down the stairs and lock the door behind him, taking his clothes off to stand there in the dark and pretend his Orchard wasn't dead, that there was one more Movie, one more unfertilized vagina in the far dark back, silent and open, waiting for him to find it.

Ben was falling asleep.

The Mayor waited until he was unconscious, then grabbed

145

the brownie batter and almost fell down the stairs to the basement. He caught his balance on a knee and remained in impromptu prayer, giving thanks from the depths of his gut before plunging his face into the bowl.

He felt the Pornography churning deep underfoot, all the way at the aqueous foundation of the town. This was enough to squeeze some life into his penis as he coated it in the batter that remained on his hands. He didn't ejaculate, but there was relief in the nervous pulsing of his balls, same as there had been when he was twelve.

Saturday Morning

Ben left the house just before dawn, as the Mayor was drifting toward the Blind Spot in neutral.

The Mayor's footsteps coming up from the basement had woken him. After he heard the station wagon pass the cul-de-sac, he let himself out through the back door, toward the parked tractors and the gravel quarry.

A decade ago, walking this route at this hour back to the Dead Neighborhood, Ben would always stop where the tree line opened and look out toward the Mountain, wondering if it was true that a fringe group of Sub-Weird called Dwellers lived up there, in a kind of high-altitude peace unknown to the town below. This was the story that everyone told without anyone being able to verify it, except maybe the Ultra Max night shift employees, who claimed that the Dwellers appeared en masse just before dawn on the first of each month, to load up on bulk supplies before ascending again.

Now, it was the Town's City that drew Ben's eye. This habit, too,

146

felt ancient, though he knew it couldn't be. He couldn't see anyone in it, but he could sense Sub-Weird huddled in its unfinished rooms, hanging their curtains and spreading Outskirts materials, beginning to live lives whose nature was entirely unfamiliar to him.

Sessions, he thought, reviving the term he and James had used to describe the activity they'd often perceived on the peripheral sets of their Pretend Movie, among the extras who operated beyond their ability to direct.

An Ultra Max truck passed by and he yawned, as tired as he would've been if he'd been walking all night.

As he continued along a back road that departed from the quarry and eventually intersected with downtown, he saw a few Sub-Weird walking back and forth, listening to headphones and scratching at their collars.

After three vacant lots came the post office, open for one hour on Saturday mornings, and the bank whose front window displayed a sign reading NO CASH ON PREMISES. After this, he passed the bakery that serviced this part of town, which was peripheral without quite being in the Outskirts. This was the bakery, he realized, that had laid out the free donuts during the Reunion parade. He could smell more of them frying now, mixed with the smell of hazelnut coffee.

He went in, ordering two donuts and a large coffee, then he crossed the street and went into the tobacco and stationery store, where he bought six ruled legal pads and six blue pens. Then he went to the real estate office next to the bakery and asked for an office.

"How far do you want to go?" asked the realtor. His face, like everyone's, hovered between the too-familiar and the alien. As long as he didn't make eye contact, Ben no longer found it overwhelming. He wondered if the realtor felt the same way about him.

"Not far."

The realtor showed him the office directly overhead, up a flight of external stairs.

Ben said he'd take it. He explained his line of credit with the Mayor and asked if the realtor wouldn't mind contacting the Hotel and getting the rent from them by asking that it be added to his tab there. The realtor shrugged and said, "Okay." He pried a key off his key ring and handed it over.

After he'd shown himself out, Ben remained in the office. He tried out the lights and the taps in the bathroom, and took his shoes off to feel the glazed wooden floor on his bare soles. He sat down in the office chair, old but still springy, and looked out the window at the street, reminding himself that he was an architect.

He arranged his pens and drafting pads on the desk. On the first one, he drew a small circle and labeled it "town." Then he drew a huge circle around it, which he labeled "Outskirts." At the point where they met, he drew a dot and labeled it "me."

He spent half an hour regarding his day's work, then locked up and left.

Walking back into the Hotel, he passed the nineteen-year-olds smoking on the steps. They acknowledged him, and he them.

Inside, he brushed past the desk and went straight to his room, where he lay in bed with his hands on his chest, coffin-like, and thought, *I now have an office in which I can spend the whole rest of my life as a professional, and no one will ever have to know it still feels pretend.*

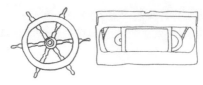

Saturday Afternoon

Squimbop was sitting on a bench in the Square, looking into the autumn sky. He'd found a crate of sweet wine in the ANGEL HOUSE cellar this morning and gorged on it, so his mouth was stained and trembling as the Mayor pulled up in his station wagon and honked. He watched him for a full minute, as two other cars maneuvered around his. Then he got up and got in.

The Mayor was flushed and reeked of cologne, and he'd cut his neck shaving, the wound half scabbed over by now. "No Lectures to write on the weekend?" he asked.

"I don't write them," said the Professor.

The smell of his not having showered was unmistakable. It made the Mayor shiver. He couldn't decide whether to roll down the window or turn up the heat.

As they cruised out of the Square, the Mayor told the short version of the Mattress Store story: the Town Council debated the buyout for years, letting the storefront next to the Night School stand empty.

THE NIGHT SCHOOL IS ENOUGH had been a popular slogan a generation ago, according to one Movie the Mayor had seen. But now the complex of the Night School and the Mattress Store was a central node in the town's nighttime web, a gathering point for most of those who found themselves out after a certain hour.

The Night School alone, where you could eat, drink, and look at the stripping waiters, but not touch or lie down, eventually proved to be not enough. It was the fact that you could go next door, into the Mattress Store, even if you didn't end up going, that made the whole experience

149

fulfilling.

I'm the only one who gets what I get from Movies. For everyone else, they're not enough, the Mayor was thinking, suspecting that Squimbop could tell. *Other people need to touch... something.*

The Mayor listened to his own voice as he talked through the history.

"There was violent crime before... sex crime. People doing what they wanted to each other on the concrete. At least in the Mattress Store, they can do it indoors, for a price, and only the people involved have to see and hear it."

Now they were on the Strip, passing Saltwater's liquor store.

He went on, describing the layout of display beds in the Mattress Store, and where the curtains were and how the pillows and sheets were stacked, falling into a frenzy driven by the fear of silence.

He was in a loop where he connected his voice to the car's engine, fearing it would stall if he stopped talking. "There are three main rooms... once we get inside, you'll see... there are mattresses of lace, satin, velvet, velour, rayon...

"There's what we call the Birth Canal, though it might look like just a hallway, the walls lined with silk, leading from one space into the other, and sometimes you'll seen someone escorting someone else from the Night School into the Mattress Store... and the mattresses are supposed to dampen the sound, but really they..."

The Mayor's eyes felt runny, like undercooked eggs, and now everything had a yolky yellow tinge. They pulled into the parking lot and he cut the engine without putting it in park, panting.

As they walked in past the clanging bells on the blue-lit door, the carpeting grew thick around their boots, the air close and full of the smells of human function grafted onto rubber, plastic, and foam.

The atmosphere was clotted up, bits of cottony debris stuck in the vents. The door to the next room, past the sales desk and the

150

clearance items, was trimmed in blue glow sticks, echoing the motif of the main door they'd come through a moment ago, but more complex, more intimate.

It served as a barrier against casual shoppers. No one passed through this second door without meaning to.

A salesman in a black dress and black leggings leaned against one of the mattresses propped against the wall inside this second chamber. He waved with the fingers of a hand that was also pressed into the mattress, high above his head, spidering them through the pliant foam. The other hand was by his side.

"You two need anything?"

The Mayor heard it, but was already looking at the posters covering all the wall space that wasn't given to shaded windows or propped mattresses. The images were mostly composed of textured darkness, made vaginal by the border of skin, mucous, and membranes surrounding their dark centers. Artistic renderings of what everyone knew existed but no one knew how, or where.

Squimbop ran his fingers along the bottoms of the mattresses laid out in rows, pressing into them, checking their firmness and spring.

"Go all the way into it," said the Mayor, struggling to sound dispassionate.

"Into what?"

"Whatever you do when you sleep. When your Lectures come. Get like you're about to start dreaming, then feel around for which one you'd want to do that dreaming on."

Squimbop's eyes were darkening as the mattresses took effect on him. "I don't have to do anything. It's just me."

"Well then just be you."

They entered the next room, where the only light came from the previous one. The salesman did not follow.

The Mayor settled into an armchair beside a tall pile of sex

151

dolls. Neither explicitly male nor female, they were monsters made of foam, rubber, glue, hair, and meat, with an array of both protrusions and orifices, to be rented out in lieu of actual prostitutes to those customers who came in here alone and wished to be otherwise.

Head against the headrest, the Mayor breathed in the still air and the sweat coming off the dolls, and watched the outline of the Professor moving through the dimness, from mattress to mattress, sinking into each successive one.

Time no longer passed as it did outside. In the Mattress Store everything was slow, sultry, like the Mayor had always imagined the South. As a gesture of relinquishment of control, he held his empty hands palm-up on his lap, letting the movement of hours play across them. *I have nowhere to be*, he thought, hoping that whatever force regulated his anxiety would hear, and believe him.

The Mayor could hear the dolls settling and falling over each other, and submitted to the fantasy that they were breeding, creating more like themselves through a kind of congress they engaged in when no one was around.

When Squimbop was ready, they moved on to the next room, where the mattresses were bigger and less plentiful. Here he luxuriated on each one, stretching all the way out, octopus-like, and then shriveling into a wet speck near the center, like something newly born and abandoned.

The Mayor found a new seat and closed his eyes, focusing on breathing, picturing his Orchard in its prime. He kept his palms up while something dripped on them. He dismissed it as a product of how he felt. He tried not to sob as loud noises began to issue from the mattress that Squimbop had settled onto. The word *Sex* echoed in his mind, but he couldn't bear to explain to himself what it was. He felt equal parts fury at and terror towards Squimbop as he went deep into whomever he'd found under the covers, man or doll he couldn't say.

He hadn't expected to be this shaken. He wanted to go outside but feared he'd never make it back in if he left. So he sat riveted in the chair, feeling some of the scarecrow effect that had come over him and James on the ANGEL HOUSE lawn. Before it completely dominated him, he got up and started groping his way around the room, using his hands for balance and direction.

He touched the dolls on all the mattresses and found that none of them were Squimbop. *Effigies,* he thought, remembering the bread-self he'd eaten at the Reunion. *All we have recourse to are effigies.*

Never had he missed the vaginas in his Orchard more.

Afraid to stop moving, he pushed through the curtain that separated this room from the next, where there was only one mattress for sale.

In what little light there was, he could make out a sleeping form on this last mattress, and, once his eyes and mind had adjusted, he could tell it was Squimbop, dead to the world. How he'd gotten back here the Mayor would never know.

All he knew was that the bill for the services Squimbop had just enjoyed would be tallied at the front door, on top of any purchase they made. Somehow, the management would know.

"Hello?" the Mayor shouted, rattled and ready to leave.

Squimbop yawned and tossed off his sheet, his penis glistening in the dim blue light. It flopped to the side, hitting the mattress with the sound of steak hitting a still-cold frying pan. The Mayor tried to look away and almost fell over.

Falling back asleep, Squimbop didn't snore. He looked sunken in the mattress like a worm in the hardening bed of what would one day be a fossil.

The Mayor stood there, impotent, for what felt like hours.

When he couldn't stand like that any longer, he got on his knees beside the mattress and reached up to shake the Professor, at first gently, then savagely, until he woke up.

153

Now they were nearly face to face, the Mayor kneeling on the carpeting and the Professor lying with his head dangling off the mattress.

"This one will do," he said.

Then he sat up and pointed to a door in the back of the room, barely visible. "I remember seeing that door just as I ejaculated," he said. "Like I had torn it into the wall. What is it?"

The Mayor's first instinct was to avoid the question, but he'd agreed to take on whatever next thing came, and here it was.

"The Final Room," he said. "An entrance to the Psychogeography, which connects all the key places in the town without any of the middle ones."

Squimbop put his penis away. If he caught the Mayor watching, he betrayed no reaction. "Show me."

Back on his feet, the Mayor opened the door.

The Final Room was taken up with a mattress that measured twenty feet by twenty feet, and eight feet thick. Large enough to serve a life sentence on.

Not for sale.

The digital thermostat, glowing in the humid dark, was set at 110. Both of them sank into the rug, watching the mattress loom even higher.

A ladder led from the bottom of the rug up to the mattress' surface, which was barely a human-width from the ceiling. The smell of dirt and blood wafted down from the top, and the Mayor knew that the ceiling would open through the Psychogeography and into his Orchard, just as the TV in his basement did.

They shuffled on their knees to the foot of the ladder and looked up. The fluff of the rug clung to their pants and the Mayor understood that Squimbop had the power to keep him here as long as he chose. Part of him wished he would; he would gladly forget Ben, James, the

154

Movie, the Town's City, if…

"Okay," said Squimbop, standing.

The Mayor likewise pulled himself back to his feet. "Okay what?" he panted.

"I found what I wanted. Buy me the one in the last room. Maybe we'll come back in here sometime. Climb this huge mattress together."

The mattress and the sex services cost $2800 all told. While the Mayor laboriously strapped it to the roof of his car, Squimbop disposed of the doll he'd destroyed, peeling its rubber and hair from his skin and throwing the peelings in the weeds.

"Drive me back to ANGEL HOUSE," he said, getting in the car before the Mayor and leaning his head against the window.

By the time the Mayor was behind the wheel, Squimbop was fast asleep, his pants unbuttoned, his lips churning up Lecture.

Ben and James kept to themselves most of the day.

By evening they were restless, so James called Ben, who said he'd been about to call him. Neither suggested they invite the Mayor. Though nothing concrete had gone wrong at his house last night, they both felt they'd seen enough of him for the time being. The line between reenactment and reversion was fine, and it seemed dangerous to let old patterns reassert themselves too fully.

James had spent the day in his house, watching the air turn to autumn outside his windows while doing pushups and sit-ups in all the rooms on the first floor. After a shower, he made lunch and ate it standing in the kitchen. He spent what time was left after this in his office on the third floor.

Over the past few days he'd come and gone from Ultra Max collecting supplies, all the non-digital ephemera that would go into the planning stages of his film. Mostly pens and paper and ways of storing and organizing those papers: notecards with a blue snap-box to keep them in, binders, and a whiteboard he carried up to his office and left propped against the wall.

With everything from the latest trip out of its bags and piled on the desk, he sat back and tried to feel like the Director of all this material.

"You work for me now," he told it.

When he couldn't sit anymore, he went to the window. He looked down very steeply onto the street, his line of sight almost vertical to the people passing by, so he could see only their bald spots and the whorls and splits in their hair.

He would watch his footage up here, and edit it too—all he needed was a bank of computers and monitors, which the Mayor had said he could pick up at the radio station as soon as he was ready.

His camera was wedged under the desk, charging.

He sat back down and imagined the room full of buzzing monitors, hard drives, tapes and speakers. Not quite napping, he fell into a daze as the sounds of all that equipment melded together. He started to hear something in their commingled buzz. The monitors were picking something up, like a radio signal, something at large in the air. A new weather front, filling his sinuses with pressure. He swallowed and winced, pinching his nostrils and breathing out.

Eyes closed, he tried to discern what it was, as if he were now listening to a rough cut of his film, the footage all there, trying to tell the truth about itself. Here was his one chance to not miss it.

He could perceive his entire film compressed to a density so potent it could only reach him through this buzz, an art form deeper than narrative, a unit of dark matter too heavy to exist in the town without consuming it.

A change is coming tonight, he thought, proud of his insight but despondent at the realization that he could fill all the tapes in Ultra Max and never get at what it actually was. *Is the nature of film the problem, or am I?* he wondered, grinding his teeth. *If I were a better filmmaker, would I be able to get at it? Or is it film itself that can't go far enough?*

This was the point at which he'd called Ben.

Ben could hear it too.

Getting dressed after a long shave, the ringing pressure seemed to emanate from the Town's City, in waves he could almost see through the dark windows of his room, like a broadcast beaming from an empty lot on the Tower's roof.

A radio station up there, to match the one down here... he couldn't quite see it, but could sense it was there, or would be soon, once the contractors executed that phase of the blueprints.

As the streets down here empty out, the streets up there are filling...

He was glad James had called.

Neither of them had a car, so tonight would unfold on foot.

It would be like when, at nine, they'd leave their Dead Houses and walk downtown together to see what there was to do, until they had no choice but to retreat into fantasy, wandering the lower reaches of the Movie Store and imagining what was contained on all those tapes, which they were not yet allowed to rent, developing the Pretend Movie by simple virtue of being conscious.

Tonight they met in the Square, full of the usual old-timers, sedated by the buzz, which was louder outdoors, amplifying the headaches they both already had. It gave off heat, scenting the air with the trace of long-gone summers, implying a coming age when there'd be

157

no more cold.

They looked each other over. James held his camera; Ben had his gun tucked into the back of his jeans, under his shirt. Without saying anything, they could tell they were in the same mood and so set out to get ice cream, as they always used to when it was unseasonably warm in autumn, knowing, as they always had, that this time could well be the last before Hibernation.

On the walk over, they caught up a little more, trying to keep their memories of News City alive. "You know what's the same about filmmaking and architecture?" James asked.

"What?"

"We both have to realize our vision through, and often against, the will of the money people. Producers, clients, whatever… it's someone else's money we're spending to make the thing we want to make."

The image of the Mayor, as their mutual patron, appeared before them, but they shrugged him off, pretending there had been others. Like each of their current projects was one of many.

"Yeah," Ben replied. "That's been my experience over the years as well."

The ice cream parlor looked nothing like it did in real summer, but was far more crowded than it should've been by this point in autumn. Traffic filtering in and out was so constant it held the doors open, letting in the evening's air, which kept getting warmer.

The crowd was all children, chattering, keyed up, half-crazy from the buzz in their ears. They looked bad: exhausted, bruised, like something was eating away at them.

Still, they ordered brownie sundaes with abandon, bigger than they'd be able to finish, but the night called for it. Some of them got a sundae in each hand, sucking them down without spoons, heaving, trying to breathe through their noses so as not to suffocate.

The cashier didn't ring anyone up. He grimaced when Ben and

158

James took free sundaes as well, but said nothing.

As the heat kept rising, the freezers in back started to whir and groan. Soon they shut down and the smell of melting ice cream curled along the counter and out into the eating area. Ben and James could tell it was time to leave.

The exit was so jammed all they could do was get in line, still devouring wet brownie chunks, their chins running with vanilla.

James filmed it all, balancing his camera as best he could while he ate.

The children wore T-shirts that hung to their knees with pajama bottoms underneath and no shoes. They carried their sundaes by their sides like briefcases. These dripped onto their bare feet and helped them glide along, through the heat and buzz, past downtown in the direction of the Meadow-lined Road, the purple glow of ANGEL HOUSE already supplanting the moonlight.

Ben and James were at the back of the procession, following without being part of it.

Late Saturday Night

Ben and James followed behind the mass of children, accepting their position as unofficial chaperones, vested with no power except that of bearing witness. James filmed it without looking through his viewfinder, uncertain if he'd use this footage or even watch it.

All the ice cream was melted. The children were sweating and trying not to bite their tongues, their skin so covered in goosebumps it looked scaly.

They generated a staticky energy that turned them into a multi-limbed blob, moving toward the Meadow on centipede legs. As they passed James' house, they emitted a high-pitched wail in harmony with the lower buzz. It sounded like, *Goodbye, town, don't wait up for us.*

At the Meadow's edge they stood in silence a moment, the puddles lapping at their feet. Then, as one, they turned back in the direction of the radio station, blank-faced and patient, giving Well one last chance to rescue them.

When nothing happened, they turned again and crossed over, through the puddles, past the empty Ghost Town, letting the purple glow of ANGEL HOUSE filter into their bodies and change their blood.

Ben and James refused to think; they gave their minds over to their organs of perception, and just saw what they saw, James letting his camera run without checking focus.

Now they were deep in the Meadow, the scarecrow state overtaking them as the children marched ahead, toward the relief that Squimbop had promised in the School's sealed Chamber.

Like slipping past a second curtain on a stage, between the shallow play and the deep one, the children passed out of the realm that Ben and James could inhabit.

They felt the Meadow cool as the shadows of the children merged with the purple glow. They could tell that the night's warmth would be gone by morning and true autumn would take its place.

In the center of their field of vision, too complex to comprehend, stood ANGEL HOUSE. Its porch and gables were barely visible through the glow, and it seemed to bob slightly.

Ben and James felt the scarecrow state intensify, hardening first their jawbones, then their cheekbones, then their eyes, forcing them to stare straight ahead at nothing. Their last conscious thought before it hardened their brains was, *We are the scarecrows that scare the Mayor away, for his own good, to save him from the sight of what's happening to his children.*

James' camera slipped from his fingers and landed against his knee, still running, capturing the climax of the disappearance at a lurid angle.

The Totally Other Place seethed through Squimbop as he reclined on his new mattress in the Master Bedroom. It stuffed him with more Lecture than his head could hold, and compelled him onto his feet, into a red silk robe embroidered with blue dragons, and across the massive interior to the front door.

He heaved it open in a trance as the children began to stream in, up the steps and through the door, their pajamas trailing behind as the town's feeble gravity lost hold of them.

Once inside, Squimbop returned to his mattress, granting the Totally Other Place private access to its newest acquisitions. It cleansed the children of the dirt of the town, then began the deflation process, undoing the structural integrity first of their skulls, then of their shoulders and hips, then of their spines and rib cages. When they'd gone rubbery and soft, strands from the ceiling descended, growing into their spines and heaving them upward until they were flat against it, covering all of it like a leather quilt.

White chrysalises wrapped them from head to toe and then from toe to head. When they were twice-wrapped, as taut against the ceiling as they could be pulled, their muscles reduced to liquid inside the sacs they were becoming, the doors closed, resealing ANGEL HOUSE against the town it was docked in and ensuring that the true story of what had happened to its children would never be told.

As the children clustered on the ceiling, their moment of pain already behind them, the reality of Death once again absent from their skulls, Squimbop opened his laptop, checked the cameras, and composed an email.

Dear Master,

It is done. The children have arrived, en masse. It took less doing this year than in previous years, I believe. The certainty of Death, which

I impressed upon them day after day in the Chamber at school, was more than their fragile, ignorant systems could process. To face up to the sustained stress of remaining individuals for the length of their lifetimes, despite the knowledge of that effort's ultimate futility... 'No thanks,' they all, in effect, have said.

All for now,

Prof. Sq.

Before sending this message off, he considered adding that there were two children who had not yet crossed over, but he held off for the time being, assuming they would join the others soon enough.

PART III
The End of Open Borders

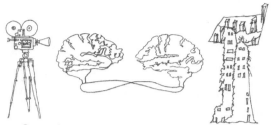

Late That Same Saturday Night

As soon as ANGEL HOUSE released them from the scarecrow state, Ben and James hurried across the Meadow, reminding themselves that they were running toward the town, where people still lived, not only away from a place where people had just disappeared. The prospect of return had never been so welcome.

When they came to a fence, they leaned on it. An evil, frosty wind ripped across the Ghost Town on the other side, stirring up a cinder smell that hit them hard in the face. The wind whipped through buildings that had been reduced to cold jags of wood, sharp and irregular, barely suggesting habitable terrain.

These buildings—low houses and stores along a foggy street, dead-ending in front of what was clearly Well's Childhood Home, the centerpiece of the area, its front path tamped down from years of nightly visitation—came more into focus as they stood there, but their attention faltered when two other forms appeared.

The interruption was welcome. They were more than ready for a return to terrestrial interaction, though their readiness made them feel like cowards.

It was two children. Their postures and expressions exactly mirrored one another's, though they weren't twins.

"Did you lose the others?" asked Ben.

"We saw them," added James. "They went on ahead."

The children shook their heads. "They're gone now. We've been walking around and around, waiting to be sure. We have better things to do than curl up in there." They nodded in the direction of ANGEL HOUSE. "We're making a Pretend Movie, and everything around here is part of it. We tried to stay in bed all night dreaming it up, but the buzz was too loud, so here we are. On the outside looking in."

James recoiled. "A Pretend Movie?"

"Yeah. When we're awake, we're the Directors, thinking everything through, figuring out how it works. When we fall asleep, we become the nineteen-year-olds. They're the stars, a little dumb maybe, but good-looking and practiced at dealing with the world. And possibly invincible, we don't know yet. As them, we're gonna get way down under the town and wriggle through the tunnels, swimming, holding our breath, bracing for the bite of the bone-snakes, until we make it out, into the wider world on the other side. That's why it's called *The Dream of Escape*. The town has been touched by Death. We're not staying here."

Ben took a step back. The interaction was taking on an intimacy that clearly had no space for him. If he'd felt any need to pee, he would've tried to now, despite the cold.

"I make films professionally," said James. "That's what I came here to do."

"Came where?" the duo asked, confused.

"Back to town."

"Where were you before?"

James smiled, but said nothing.

Everyone paused.

"Maybe we'll cross paths again sometime," he said, a full minute later, when the duo turned to leave. "I'd like to hear more about your work."

The duo shrugged and trudged off, kicking at the grass and holding their sides in the frosty wind.

On the far side of the Ghost Town, the duo watched the twenty-nine-year-olds depart.

Then, taking deep breaths like they were about to jump off a dock and through a patch of ice, they toppled over where they stood.

Gathering their knees into their chests and holding them tight with both arms, they closed their eyes and slowed their breathing.

Soon they were inside the nineteen-year-olds, walking up the Meadow-lined Road away from the Hotel, then into the Meadow and onto the ANGEL HOUSE lawn, to see what the disturbance was. They could feel that the ground they were walking on was hollow, with the tunnels coursing directly underfoot. Standing as close as they could without freezing solid, they lit cigarettes and listened to the phantom structure rock with the laughter of whatever was inside.

Sunday Afternoon, Late September

James slept late on Sunday and woke to needles and hammers on his temples and the back of his head where his neck began.

It wasn't until he'd brushed his teeth and showered, and was standing in the hall with a towel wrapped around his middle, that last night began to resurface.

We touched the line last night, he thought. *Life goes on and on and on, but that doesn't mean there isn't a line. And if you touch that line, you pay for it.*

He decided to pay for it by going to the Gym.

Immediately determined to postpone acting on this decision for as long as possible, he let his towel fall and started pacing the house, naked and uneasy, until he gravitated to the windows behind the kitchen, where the sunlight was brightest.

He opened the door and went onto the back porch. The early afternoon sun pushed down on his eyelids and his temples throbbed harder than ever, his chest and back hair standing up in the bright cold. After the porch steps, he came onto hard dirt and patches of trampled grass. There were some long-dead plants in pots by the fence and some in the areas between the house and the driveway, and there was a gutted guitar amp and a mostly gutted TV piled on the metal hatch that led to the basement.

James wandered among these like a visitor at a roadside museum, squeezing his feet into the softer parts of the ground and counting his breaths to keep the throbbing in his temples from knocking him over.

Finally, when he was so dizzy he couldn't see except through panes of water dripping across his eyes, he sat down in a plastic armchair against the fence. One of its legs cracked and he fell halfway to the ground before the plastic jammed together and returned to something like equilibrium. Picturing himself in a makeshift Director's chair, he mused on the nineteen-year-olds drifting into the town of his film, stowing their roots under a blanket in the trunk of their car while they holed up in the Hotel, wandering the streets until they'd learned the town's Psychogeography well enough to understand where their roots ought to be planted.

Underneath this, like a counter-film within the film, he pictured those same nineteen-year-olds fighting their way out of town through the flooded tunnels of the nine-year-olds' Pretend Movie. *This is the central conflict,* he thought. *A conflict between rival versions of the film, rather than within the narrative of one film or the other.*

Or not between films: between the film and the Pretend Movie. And there's a world of difference between those two terms…

His eyes watered more as he pictured himself and Ben departing for News City at nineteen, high on the conviction that they were following the path by which their Pretend Movie would become real, somehow evolving the strength to withstand the financial and industrial processes inherent in the reality of filmmaking.

He shuddered at this last thought and began to feel so queasy that he relished the prospect of leaving the house for the Gym, a state that, he saw now, he'd been trying to put himself into all this time.

Back inside, he pulled on a T-shirt and a pair of shorts, and packed a bathing suit and a pair of pants in a duffel bag, then pulled his sneakers over the same socks he'd worn yesterday. Slinging the bag over his shoulder, he jogged down his front steps and out into the neighborhood.

When he got to the Gym, the chains on the hoops of the outdoor basketball court behind the parking lot hung limp in a breeze that was too light to lift them. There used to be an ownerless ball sat on the court for whomever happened to pass by, but now there were only dry leaves.

He jogged up the rest of the path and into the main building, through two sets of doors. After a stop to stretch and pant, he walked past the abandoned front desk, reaching over to flick the switch that turned on the hall lights.

The chlorine smell led the way to the pool, past the water fountain. He bent over but the water tasted like spit and blood so he didn't swallow.

The glass doors to the adult pool were to his right. He turned and looked through them, all the way across to the next set of glass doors, the ones that led to the heated children's pool. Beyond that, though he could only imagine it for now, bubbled the hot tub, in a narrow cell with no overhead lighting and no ventilation.

The locker room was equally dark. He felt around on the wall until he found the switch. The lights took a minute to warm up, groaning like they were coming out of a long slumber. The plastic stool in the shower area that people who couldn't stand sat on had slid out into the locker room on a wave of soap. He kicked it back and started to undress, shoving the clothes he'd been wearing into the nearest locker, its metal door warped outward.

He burped and tasted stomach acid and lactose from last night's ice cream. When he'd choked this back down, he looked up and saw Janitor Pete, who seemed the same as he had when Ben and James haunted the weight room at fifteen, warning them that they were too young to put on the muscle they were convinced they needed, but agreeing to spot them when they insisted on lifting anyway.

His grey stubble and longish hair were the same; only his torso looked older, still wiry but losing itself in an outer layer of beer and microwave dinners.

"Hey, James. Here's your towel." Janitor Pete smiled as he handed it to him. "Saw you from the towel room on your way in, so..."

"I..."

"You thought no one was here. Nearly no one is. Just me. I man the ship these days."

James stuffed the towel into his locker and stepped forward to shake Janitor Pete's hand.

"I saw you at the Reunion, but it was such a mess I didn't try to say hello."

"I appreciate that," mumbled James, already antsy.

"So you're back in town?"

"Yeah, to make a film."

"A what?"

"A Movie."

"Ah. Gonna be on a shelf in the Movie Store someday? Poster in the window?" Janitor Pete smiled.

"Hopefully."

"Well, if you ever need to do any scenes or anything in here, just let me know." Janitor Pete picked up a towel from under a bench and flicked it in the air to shake the dust off. "I bet we could arrange something. Be nice to see this place get used again."

Then he just stood there, looking at James, not moving. The moment extended into the kind of unease that, if it went on much longer, would develop an edge.

"I'm gonna go see if there's any metal downstairs that needs moving," said James, making for the door.

Janitor Pete stepped aside just enough to let him by. "Watch out for your back, man. Start slow. You young guys don't want to hear that, I get it. But trust me."

James put on the HEAVY ROCK FOR LIFTING mix he found on the shelf by the CD player, the disc sitting out, its box long gone, and flexed for the mirror. His upper body wasn't exactly withered, but he'd have to log considerable hours down here if he wanted to become what he'd been at nineteen.

He got down to it.

When he'd finished his bench press repetitions, he stalked across the rubber mats and over to the CD player, turning up the volume until the speakers shook. Then he filled a paper cup with water from the dispenser that tasted like it hadn't been changed since the last time he was here. He crushed the cup and threw it away.

I own this place, he thought, striding away from the speakers, narrowing his eyes at the mirror-walls. His shoulders and pecs and triceps, though diminished, pulsed from the strain he'd just put them under.

I'm the Director, goddamit.

When he'd lifted as much as his body would allow, he indulged in a series of victory laps around the rubber floor, posing, catching himself in the perpendicular and parallel reflections-upon-reflections. News City had leached a lot from him, and hadn't given much back. He could tell that his film would only grow in proportion to his body—the Director he

169

yearned to see himself as was a bigger man than he currently was, by several orders of magnitude. *Time makes you grow up,* he thought, *but only lifting makes you grow out.* The formulation was clumsy, his mind sluggish with exhaustion, but it rang true. To direct the nineteen-year-olds, if he could get them to star in his film, he'd have to look the part as much as they would.

He flexed and spun again, opening and closing his eyes until he made himself into a zoetrope, conjuring a fearsome, hulking Director out of the skinny creep he currently resembled. *Not for much longer,* he mouthed at himself in the mirrors, grabbing his crotch and sticking out his bottom lip.

When a head appeared in the corner of the frame, he released his balls slowly, like they might crash to the floor if he let go all at once, and turned to see Janitor Pete standing in the doorway.

"What?" He no longer tried to disguise the sharpness in his voice.

Janitor Pete held out a plastic water bottle without coming closer, reluctant to enter what was now clearly James' territory.

James crossed the rubber mats to take it, popping it open and taking a swig, nodding thanks.

"Occurred to me you might not have one," shouted Janitor Pete over the music. "And that's bad business if you're gonna be lifting seriously, which it looks like you are. No need to keep sipping from those dusty paper cups. Take care now."

He turned and was gone, still holding the dirty towel from the locker room.

Glad for Janitor Pete's recognition of the seriousness of his workout, James took another swig as the CD came to an end, grinding as it slowed down.

Back in the locker room, he stripped and walked into the shower.

He pressed the timer that turned on the spray and soaped

up, taking a careful look around before turning into the tiled corner and masturbating, cleanly and methodically, sinking into a familiar scenario of his body as a 30-foot totem on the seashore, surrounded by legions of the faithful, kneeling to kiss his feet, ankles, shins, and thighs. He finished with a minimum of exertion, his arm barely functional after the workout, and washed his hand against his chest, smiling to feel the muscles there pulsing as well.

He had a memory of a man with only one leg sitting on the ground under the shower, in the drain trough, while another man reset the shower timer whenever it stopped. This image returned to him as he dried off and put on his bathing suit.

Bracing for the cold beyond the steam of the shower room, he pushed open the door into the hallway that led to the adult pool. Plunging in without stopping by the edge to prepare, his skin puckered up and the cold pared down the thoughts that the heat of the shower had loosed from their reef.

He plied the pool's bottom, swimming under and among the lane dividers, relishing its emptiness, circling like a blind fish whose gills had healed up and couldn't be reopened, feeding on thoughts that grew on the tiles of the pool bottom. He sucked them up like algae and felt them settle in his gums as he swam along before surfacing for air and diving down for another mouthful.

Nothing conclusive yet, but every shard was worth filing away. The makings of scenes, a word or two that the nineteen-year-olds might say, a gesture, a telling object seemingly abandoned on a shelf.

He already knew he would shoot the film here; Janitor Pete's offer was merely a confirmation. He would make a model of the Hotel that the nineteen-year-olds were holed up in, a model of their car, maybe a graveyard where they'd try to bury their materials… and the pool would be the Inland Sea.

He sank to the bottom, where images came faster: fermenting swamps, lightning-split trees, crawling androgynous hulks with huge bellies, melting wax, stakes driven into the ground, men in chains dragging crosses the size of houses, the grease and leavings of the ten thousand films he'd seen in News City… it was all down here, waiting to be sucked up.

He stayed in for over an hour, surfacing less and less often, until the possibility of never surfacing again became so compelling he terrified himself and flew shivering out of the pool.

Through the next set of sealed doors, he was admitted into the far warmer sanctum of the children's pool, also empty. His armpit hair, clustered painfully around his lymph nodes, expanded in the light steam.

Cartoon hippos and giraffes adorned the walls, cheerfully commanding James not to run, not to push, and not to dive. They looked at him as he passed through, craning their long or squat necks to register his intrusion, reminding him that their faces were his earliest memories. The warm water lapped at the pool's edge.

In the relative dark, he slid in and started to soak, trying to quiet his yearning to go immediately to the hot tub room, which would be the final stop along this circuit.

He slid down the edges until the water of the children's pool covered his mouth. He let some in, swishing it around, trying to taste his and Ben's ancient urine.

Whole thoughts were down here, in the part of his mind that was now softening and opening up, as opposed to the cold cinematic image-meal of the adult pool, but these were massive and lazy, drifting into sight at their own speed, too heavy to grab and haul into the world of art.

So James tried, simply, to remember that he was real, and alive, and in a single location within time and the universe, not on a giant vessel chugging aimlessly across an ocean too wide to cross in his lifetime. For now, this would be enough.

I'm already on the far shore, he thought. *I don't need to spend*

172

my life wondering if I'll ever make it. I need to spend it doing something now that I'm here.

He remained sunk in the children's pool until the sealed door cracked open. It took him a long time to look over and see who it was. Water rushed up his nose when he did.

Janitor Pete stood in the doorway, holding out a towel. "Hey James," he said, a faint note of fear in his voice. "Closing time."

James wrapped it around his shoulders and retreated to the locker room, saving the hot tub for another day.

Monday

Squimbop was at the front of the class, bubbling Lecture into the Chamber that now contained only the duo. He didn't remark on the change, and neither did they.

He'd slept last night on the mattress the Mayor had bought for him at the Mattress Store, lying on his back with his mouth open while the Totally Other Place filled his mind and the children began to drip their numbing tallow from the ceiling. His raw throat was soothed, but today's Lecture was no less vicious.

"And they—those almost-people, whose heads looked hooded until I passed close enough to realize their hoods were faces—leered at the me from the islands I passed, summoning forth bone-snakes from the tidal pools to eat into the foundation of ANGEL HOUSE, and swim inside, where they still are, soaking up whatever warmth seeps down from the upper floors. They probably think they're still drifting through the Inland Sea, if there's anything resembling brains in their skulls. And soon enough, when I leave this town, they will be."

For now, rather than insisting on the grandeur and necessity of Death, Squimbop's Lecture was more abstract, designed to impress upon the duo the immensity and variety of his experience, as compared to theirs. The simple presentation of nullity clearly wasn't enough to get them onto his ceiling.

"The actual world, as it exists both on the banks of the Inland Sea and on its bottom, contains more than your language has the capacity to describe. Lands where the sun never rises, others so blindingly bright their inhabitants have countless layers of skin over their faces and no eyes, nor even noses or mouths. They gain nutrients by wallowing in a sort of muck that smells like…"

Both Squimbop and the duo phased in and out of attention so that, for long periods of the day, he was delivering his Lecture to no one at all.

As the duo pictured it, their classmates were now slowly roasting, releasing their knowledge of Death back into the air. *Back into us*, they thought. *We are the ones who must bear it. If we are to face up to it and not succumb, we must never forget that it is real, and that our time here is limited.*

Closing their eyes but remaining awake, they imagined the nineteen-year-olds casing the tunnels under ANGEL HOUSE, avoiding the bone-snakes as they searched, as ever, for Escape.

"Your place is here with me," said Squimbop, not raising his voice. "Or in the places where I've been, and to which I will return. In dank chambers crammed full of leathery batlike women chained to the ceiling, rotating slowly while hogs with thorny tongues lick their undersides, wearing them away like pheasants on a spit."

At recess they crawled under the lip of the pine hedge, wriggled among the roots, and kept going until they reached the place where they could sit up, the woodwork encasing them in a snug bubble with only a few specks of light shining through.

Over the past few weeks, they'd furnished their Office from Ultra Max, sneaking in on nights they couldn't sleep and dragging whatever they needed out through the side exit without paying. No one tried to stop them.

They'd amassed two plastic chairs, a low desk, and a cooler they kept half-buried in the dirt, filled with beer and candy bars. They allowed themselves one beer each per recess, for help falling asleep.

After they choked these down, they unzipped their sleeping bags and wriggled inside, staring up at the network of branches and needles.

They lay like this in the cold for five minutes of their twenty-five-minute recess, having already spent five drinking and getting into position.

With only fifteen minutes left, they would at most have time to become the nineteen-year-olds and enter the Hotel basement, thinking for a few concrete moments about Escape before they were summoned back into the impotence of childhood.

They had to fall truly asleep before they could enter the nineteen-year-olds; there was no partial becoming. If they only dozed, they were nothing but dozing nine-year-olds, as weak as the other children had been. Becoming the nineteen-year-olds required falling so deeply asleep that they let go of everything, including the mandate to direct the Pretend Movie.

So deeply asleep they were willing to never wake up again.

Let go, let go… the nine-year-olds thought in the Pine Hedge Office, begging their minds to disengage. *We will return to being Directors when we wake up, but for now…*

If they didn't both go under, neither could surface. It was both or neither, here as in all things. Today, mercifully, they got there.

They opened their eyes as the nineteen-year-olds in the Hotel, and lost

175

no time taking the stairs down past the lobby to the basement.

They opened the basement door, shoved past a clutter of cots and spare or trashed mattresses and bulk cleaning supplies, and were in the tunnels, flooded with a thick, salty brine. It lapped at their ankles and burned, clinging to their skin.

There was nothing to do but explore, trying every direction until they found a way out. *The Dream of Escape* would only enter its next phase when they'd left the town forever, and that would only happen when they found their way through, taking on whatever stood in their way.

The nineteen-year-olds knew that standing and looking around while the water seeped into their shoes wasn't good, so they threw off the urge to get their bearings and pushed forward, deeper into the tunnel.

They took three steps, the water deepening with each one, before something much crueler than water bit into them. They screamed and heard it echo.

Just before they tipped backward, they reached down and grabbed the bone-snake, ripping its mouth off their shins and holding it up, wriggling and struggling in their hands, to stare it down. It stared back, Squimbop's face growing seamlessly from its mess of scales, hissing and snapping.

They jerked awake so fast the pine branches scraped their teeth. Looking over, they saw Squimbop standing in the grass just outside the hedge, leering in at them. "Recess is over," he said, and turned back toward the School.

Thank God he can't get in here, they thought, crawling toward the grass on their toes and knees so as to keep their bruised shins from touching the ground. They wished they could be sure this was true.

176

Late October, 3 Weeks Later

Another school day was over.

Squimbop stopped his Lecture a little earlier every day. He would continue until some point after recess, and then just sit on his desk, staring at the clock, daring the duo to fall asleep. Had he stared at them this intently from the porch of ANGEL HOUSE, he would have made them scarecrows right away, but from within the sealed confines of the Chamber, the power that the Totally Other Place imbued him with was tempered by the inertia of the town.

So he was as bored as they were for the minutes after he'd finished today's Lecture. Though they weren't asleep or frozen by his gaze, they still jumped when the bell rang.

They hurried to the door of the Chamber, waiting for Squimbop to press the button that signaled to the Recess Aides that it was time to heave it open, which could only be done from the outside.

At the end of the day, Squimbop would normally depart in the direction of the Meadow while the duo marched in the opposite direction, back to the Dead Neighborhood. But today they'd resolved to return to the Meadow for the sake of the Pretend Movie: they would approach ANGEL HOUSE in daylight and prove to themselves that they could behold it without being sucked inside. They had to know their shared will was strong enough. Then they'd go to sleep in the marsh grass so the nineteen-year-olds could spend the afternoon exploring the tunnels underneath. They waited until the Professor was out of sight, then set off in the same direction.

The Meadow-lined Road took them past James' house.

Just before reaching the Meadow, they saw a train of Sub-Weird processing into town with their heads down and duffel bags slung over their shoulders, listening to headphones whose cords

177

dangled in the air behind them, connected to nothing.

Had they not ended up in ANGEL HOUSE, the duo thought, *our classmates would have ended up like that.*

And if we fail to complete the Pretend Movie, so will we.

They crossed the edge of the Meadow, through the sopping marsh and into the dead grass. Their middle-backs seized up with a preliminary scarecrow shiver, and they could tell that soon they'd be frozen solid if they didn't turn back, which they hadn't come all the way out here to do. So they picked up the pace, praying they could outrun the paralysis as long as they never stopped to watch it set in.

They were past the Ghost Town now, onto the broad expanse that fronted ANGEL HOUSE which, due to the singularity of their purpose, felt narrow. No more than a hallway, a bridge between one Pretend Movie set and the next.

They were walking through the footprints of the other children in the grass, still fresh from the procession. Then they felt their spines go hard, like two erections that no soft other could relieve. Then they felt nothing. They were two scarecrows riveted on an image they could no longer comprehend, their eyes staring without seeing.

Reclining on his Mattress Store mattress inside, Squimbop swallowed a mouthful of tallow and looked out at them, relishing their pain while, at the same time, envying it, wondering what it felt like. He could not imagine the experience of encountering ANGEL HOUSE without knowing what it was.

The duo would've remained scarecrows, the Pretend Movie withering inside them, all day and into the night, had they not felt a hand on their shoulders, painful as a hammer striking frostbitten limbs.

They felt their feet leaving the ground without any sensation of walking.

The moment at which their eyes left ANGEL HOUSE was one of organ-level pain, like their life support had just been turned off and these were their final seconds. *Goodbye*, each thought, and waited for the purple to turn black.

Instead of dying, they found themselves leaning against the fence of the Ghost Town with ANGEL HOUSE behind them, still pinching the nerves in their spines but no longer vivid enough to freeze them solid.

It took them a while to remember that someone had saved them, and even longer to check if this person was still around.

He was, standing right beside them and looking very sadly at the Ghost Town.

They looked up, tugging on the hem of his shirt to indicate that they were ready to see his face.

Tall and thin, with long blonde hair and freckles and a few days' growth of reddish beard, he looked down at them. His eyes were eaten away by sadness, too dry for tears.

"Hello?"

"Hello," said Well. "This used to be my town. Back when I was your age."

"You're the Radio Angel?"

Well nodded, exhaling heavily. "I was. Not anymore though. Look at this place. A kind of hell now."

"So now you're from nowhere?"

This made Well smile. "For the time being."

Then he turned to look at the Mountain, by far the biggest single shape there was. "What do you think's up there?"

The duo answered immediately: "The Desert. The Oasis. Where new towns grow like flowers."

Well closed his eyes. To keep from grabbing the duo right then and dragging them up the Mountain on his back, he sat down in the frozen grass and whispered, half-consciously, "We will meet again in Dust House, we will meet again in Dust House, we will meet again in the deep, deep Desert in Dust House …"

He didn't look up until he was sure they were gone.

After the duo left, Squimbop settled onto his mattress, opened his laptop, checked the cameras, and composed an email. This time, he knew, he had to say it.

Dear Master,

When I said that all the children presented themselves in surrender, I was not quite thorough.

As it turns out, two remained behind. They share a sort of, as best I can explain it, telepathic link. A twinned mental state. This, I believe, is a factor, perhaps the factor, in their decision to go on living as themselves. There is something between them, within them, that differentiates them from the other children, who were—to be appropriately cruel in my assessment—mindless from the start. Not once did I see the spark of presence in the other children that I see in these two.

It is disturbing to behold. I will, of course, persist in lecturing to them, provided you continue to fill me with Lecture, which I trust you will, but I cannot guarantee their surrender. Some more desperate measure may become necessary.

All for now,

Prof. Sq.

Ben was finishing a bag of donuts on the stairwell outside his office. Though he'd made a rule not to eat or sleep in the office, coffee and naps were permitted. Donuts on the stairwell were neither encouraged nor explicitly prohibited. Thus he spent part of every day huffing them down and regretting it.

His walk out here, which he began at dawn, was the only exercise he got before the walk back after the day's work, and the climb up the ladders and then the stairs of his Tower and out to the Town's City, which he'd been patrolling nightly since the children's disappearance.

His work at the office these days consisted of looking out the window. His pens, papers, straightedges, velum, rulers, compass, and protractor were all in place, but he was far from ready to use them in any serious way. His mind, for now, was half vacant and half riveted on the Sub-Weird's continued procession into the Town's City.

He pictured the Outskirts deflating, its denizens scurrying out before its edges crushed them. They streamed past his window all day, carrying pillows and teddy bears and small wax statues, yawning like they'd just woken up.

Ben tried to picture what it was about his Tower that drew the Sub-Weird to it, but could come up with no more than a feeling.

They think it's for them, he wrote on a piece of drafting paper, then drew a very straight line under it with one of his rulers. Under this, like the denominator of a fraction, he wrote, *The thing that the Reunion invited them to regain connection with feels never-lost to them inside the rooms and hallways that I drew. All they want is for the Reunion to never end—to never be banished back to the*

Outskirts—and somehow the Town's City provides this feeling.

If they kept heading inward at this rate, soon they'd pool up, outnumbering everyone else in town. *The Town's City will be genuinely populous, with the town as a minor outskirt on its edge. It will be a bustling, complex, dangerous place, just as the Mayor wanted it to be.*

He wrote this down, circled it, and called it a day.

On his way to the Town's City, he stopped at the Greek restaurant and ate at the counter. Sometimes he glimpsed Squimbop sitting alone at one of the tables, but he never tried to approach him. It went without saying that their interaction in the Tower lobby at the end of the Reunion had forged no special connection between them.

Had anyone asked him what he was doing here, he was prepared to answer, "I'm a salesman," but no one did.

When he left, he fell in among the Sub-Weird in the Square. Their eyes were all over him, trying to ascertain whether he belonged.

"I'm a salesman," he whispered.

One of them turned around, gazing at him hard. "What?"

"Nothing."

Crossing the construction site, where some contractors were fixing a dented saw-blade, he pushed through the hanging tarp and hurried up the stairs and then up the ladder, trying to get above the Sub-Weird before they pushed him into one of the rooms they were colonizing.

He was far from ready to get involved in their urban life, whatever they were doing in those rooms, whether they were the same things they'd been doing in the Outskirts or brand new ones. So he climbed to the roof without stopping, took a lap around, then

182

lay down in the Square with his head on the cold concrete, praying some message would seep in.

An hour later, a sound from below woke him. He got up and hurried to the edge, looking over as James passed along the fence in the distance, talking to himself loudly.

Ben shouted down. James flinched but kept walking. He shouted again, and James stopped, looking around in a wide circle before staring up at the underside of the Town's City.

"Come through the fence!" he shouted. "I'll meet you down below."

As he climbed the ladders and then the stairs to the lobby, unsure if James would be waiting when he got there, he could hear moaning Sub-Weird from the surrounding rooms, some blocked off with pink insulation foam and sheets of fiberglass. He didn't stop before reaching the lobby and pushing through the tarp.

When he got outside, James was leaning on the fence in the dark, hugging his sides, his hair wet.

"Come in."

"This is your house now?" laughed James.

Ben nodded, also laughing, as James entered, pushing the tarp aside and coughing as a dust cloud enveloped him.

Ben found himself leading James through the lobby to the bar where he'd sat with Squimbop.

James followed, settling onto a metal stool.

"You smell like chlorine," said Ben, when they were settled.

"I've been swimming. It's where I work on my film for the time being."

"In the pool?"

James nodded. "Pools. The frigid adult pool, the warm children's pool..."

"What about the hot tub?" Ben could picture the three

183

bodies of water, and the sacred progression through them.

"Not yet. Not until production's in full swing. Need to save something for then."

"When's that gonna be?"

James sat up straighter, stretching his right arm across his chest, hoping Ben could see the slight thickening of muscle that had begun there. "Soon. I'm planning to ask the nineteen-year-olds to play us. But opposite."

"Opposite?"

Ben coughed as more moaning came from one of the first-floor rooms. He was embarrassed for James to hear it.

"Opposite in the sense that they're coming to town at nineteen rather than leaving then. Growing into themselves here, rather than trying to shed the place in order to reach fruition in News City. For them, there's an actual future here."

Ben flinched at the mention of News City. "This here, where we are now, is the only city." He was only partially joking.

"This city?" asked James, wishing the bar they were sitting at was real.

"Yeah," said Ben. "The Town's City. It's all here."

James looked him over, taking this in, considering whether Ben was joking or beginning to fall back into the psychosis they both knew was in him. He decided to change the subject.
"Want to go to the Night School and get an actual drink?"

Ben took out his phone and dialed Giant Chinese before answering. "No. I'll ask Sam Ren to bring some beers when he comes. What do you want to eat?"

As Ben was ordering, a Sub-Weird overhead grunted like a boar, and James wondered if the Town's City had just seen its first murder.

November 5th

The Mayor sat in his car in the garage. It was five p.m., late enough in the season to be almost dark, though last week it'd still been high autumn.

Hibernation was no longer infinitely far in the future. He'd felt paralyzed since buying Squimbop the mattress, waiting for the next thing to happen, but now it was time to start moving, even if there was no clear path forward.

Something rolls in November 5th, he thought, rolling down the driveway in neutral as if he were already being pulled to the Blind Spot. Another Reunion line.

By the time he reached the cul-de-sac, where gravity stopped pulling him and he had to shift into drive, he'd decided to face one of the many aspects of reality he'd been hiding from all year, and set off in the direction of the Dead Neighborhood to see what had become of Ben's and James' Dead Houses.

Over the years of Ben's and James' absence, he'd conscientiously avoided going back there. In the religion he was building with himself at the center, a return to the Dead Houses, so crucial to his first nineteen years, was an unpardonable sin, a looping-back that could not be permitted. *Ben and James are gone from them, so your presence there would be nothing but a haunting,* he'd told himself whenever, in the depths of insomnia, the urge to investigate had grown overwhelming.

But the rules were different now. Things had changed. He couldn't shake the feeling that the Dead Houses weren't as empty as he'd imagined, and he could no longer live with this feeling without yielding to it. He had to see if any of his children were left,

185

or if they'd all been sucked into ANGEL HOUSE. Or perhaps he simply wanted to sin.

Whatever the case was, he floored the gas pedal and almost drove off the Meadow-lined Road as he sped toward town.

The hush of the Dead Neighborhood—which he understood as a place where Death was fundamental, a kind of hell within the town, rather than a formerly living place that had at some point died—came over him as soon as he'd passed the Square, as if the intermediate streets knew where he was going and had recast themselves accordingly, turning into the Dead Neighborhood rather than leading to it.

His first ever encounter with the houses of other people had been with these two, so that they came to form his composite picture of the other house, counterbalancing his picture of my house. There had always been something lewd about the idea of a house housing people who weren't him. He couldn't dwell for long on the idea of them shitting, pissing, and dreaming in there, with him the stranger outside, subject to the weather. *I am not a stranger,* he knew, *so any place that treats me as one is in some way corrupt.*

He was still driving, getting closer.

He took a fistful of marshmallows from a bag wedged under the passenger's seat and bit down, receiving a vision of the night's trajectory as the sugar hit his brain: he would enter the Dead House—he saw that it would be James' tonight, not Ben's—spend no more than an hour exploring, then go straight to the Blind Spot from there, so he could come home to his bed in peace after that, and not have to go out again.

The gas pedal sank under his foot and the backstreets swam. He didn't know what any of them were called. They were ritually renamed by the Town Council every few years. Still, he could see he was getting close, beginning to climb the hill toward

186

the Wooden Wheel park.

He received a memory of what these streets had looked like when he, Ben, and James had cased them on foot, patrolling at two and three a.m., making the rounds up and down the hill, past the other Dead Houses, daring each other to go in.

He tried to slow the car to a walking pace to linger in this mode before arriving, but his foot felt paralyzed on the gas pedal.

The Mayor came to a stop on the lawn and sat panting behind the wheel, mopping his forehead and exhaling as slowly and fully as he could. Then he refilled his mouth with a fresh wad of marshmallows. Chewing more contentedly now, he got out, walked up the front steps, and approached the front door. As he stood there, he found that the marshmallow wad was so impacted it wouldn't budge. It felt like caulking that'd been sprayed into his gums and throat, soon to harden into a cast, guaranteeing his silence.

He pried his nostrils as wide as he could, to suck some air into his brain. Then he rang the doorbell and waited, half-expecting a demon to open up and drag him in. *And perhaps the place it drags me to will be my final resting place*, he thought, almost praying for this to be so.

When no one came, he turned the knob and let himself in, wiping his shoes on the Welcome mat as he crossed the threshold. There was no pile of mail to trip over. The air inside was so cold he thanked God for his fat. Then he thought, *You're welcome.*

In the kitchen he opened the fridge, but closed it without rooting around. He took a glass from the cupboard and filled it from the tap, as he had always done upon making it inside with Ben and James just before morning, gulping huge quantities of water to soothe their throats, which were always hoarse from talking, smoking, and yelling at the sky.

Sitting at the kitchen table with his shoes off, he didn't

know what he expected to find here, but he knew he'd come to the right place. The time, also, felt right; here was the way into the next phase of the year, beyond the long tail of the Reunion.

He enjoyed a minute's reprieve before the solid ground of the present softened into the swampy murk of the past, and the two states merged. He felt his anchor tear.

Swimming gracelessly in open time, he found himself grasping toward a surface that looked as muddy as the bottom he was on now, sucking air around the marshmallow paste in his throat, which the tap water had only caused to expand.

When he had worked himself to the point where he could no longer sit still, he got up and began to drift through the downstairs rooms. Flapping his arms while imagining himself as a swimmer in a deep, warm bath, he propelled himself past all the ephemera of his long-lost nights with Ben and James, when they'd been different people but the rooms had been exactly the same.

He drifted past toy pianos and grandfather clocks, desks with drawers full of pen caps and string, hand-drawn maps of the Psychogeography rolled up with slackening rubber bands, piled in corners and curling off the walls. The house would become a torture chamber if he brooded on these objects, listening too intently to what he knew they were saying: *It's all gone... it's all over...*

He picked up the pace, jogging in a circuit around the downstairs, from kitchen to playroom to living room to study, trying to warm the Death out of the Dead House, as if the rooms might crack open to reveal an inner shrine, the home within the house, an inner refuge where life still dwelt.

A room will open to me... a room will open... he thought, desperate to drown out the last rational part of his mind that knew it wouldn't, that this was all there was and would ever be.

He opened his eyes after tripping over the footstool in front

188

of the piano, but avoided looking at the darkened windows so as not to catch his reflection in them, which he knew would have the effect of making him feel watched by a second, identical Mayor on the lawn outside, as nighttime windows always did.

When he'd made himself too queasy to keep moving, he sat back down at the kitchen table. Refilling his water glass, he pretended it was coffee and the night was young and he was too, the table laid with wide, blank sheets of paper that would be filled before sunrise.

After a moment of silence, he heard footsteps overhead. They sounded so natural it took him a long time to accept that they were real, in the sense of existing outside of him. *I am perceiving something that I am not imagining...*

This was an unpleasant feeling. He closed his eyes and tried to make them stop, or to incorporate them back into himself, but they refused to submit. They continued, autonomous and threatening.

He gulped his water and listened as the footsteps reached the top of the stairs, hesitating before the descent.

In a moment, the past is going to be present, he warned himself, trying to remember that this was what he'd come here for. *The yearning is always more pleasant than the getting.*

Then it was over: the Mayor opened his eyes and regarded the nine-year-old whose Dead House this currently was.

They looked at each other long enough to become acquainted. The nine-year-old could tell that the man had some ancient history in this house—he was no simple intruder—and the Mayor could tell, immediately, that the boy was a version of James. He was not like the other children, Orchard-grown and easily disposed of. Though this was what he'd come here looking for, the fact of its being true was still overwhelming.

As soon as they began to speak, the time for preliminaries

was over.

"Did you have a nightmare?" the Mayor asked, as clearly as he could around the marshmallow wad.

The boy nodded. "A bad one. We encountered disturbances in the tunnels. Bone-snakes... And then the danger felt much closer-by, right downstairs, thumping around... so I came down to investigate."

The Mayor gestured at one of the empty seats at the table but the boy climbed onto the counter and got a glass from the cupboard, taking it to the fridge instead. Watching him fill it with milk, the Mayor was besought by a vision of himself and Squimbop as this boy's parents. He wished he could shake it, but the harder he tried, the more vividly it developed. Soon, he felt like Squimbop was in the bedroom upstairs, waiting for him to soothe their son so they could all get back to sleep.

He could feel his penis recoil, as it had in the Mattress Store. He groaned, loud enough that the nine-year-old stopped drinking and stared at him.

He wanted to groan again, but suppressed it.

After a moment of silence, the nine-year-old took his empty glass and sat down at the table beside the Mayor, playing with his car keys, which sat in the fruit bowl.

The Mayor tried to think of something reassuring to say. "I'm sorry you had a nightmare," was the best he could do.

"They hurt, but they're crucial to the Pretend Movie. They're what make it matter."

"So you're making a Pretend Movie?" the Mayor asked, terrified of breaking down and sobbing about himself and Ben and James, the years they'd lost and would never get back.

The nine-year-old nodded. "Me and my counterpart, who lives across the park. The Pretend Movie is our God. It's all that gives us a chance of making it out of here before it's too late. In the

190

Pretend Movie, there is a world that is not this one. Escape is real in the Pretend Movie because it contains something to escape into."

The Mayor found himself covered in sweat as the child's voice grew more and more like James' at that age, until it was indistinguishable. It'd taken a few minutes to calibrate, but now there was no denying it. The Psychogeography was open, bridging the eras, with the Mayor teetering in between.

"Excuse me," he gasped, grabbing his car keys and crawling to the bathroom while the boy-James watched silently.

In the bathroom he writhed in spasms, his whole head under the running faucet, gagging to clear his throat and the back of his mouth, as if by purging the marshmallow wad, he could purge James' voice from his ears, thick as cotton and growing thicker.

With a feeling of complete surrender, he pushed his teeth against the drain at the bottom and emptied his throat. Had all his teeth fallen out too, the Mayor would have gladly parted with them just to get James' voice out of his ears.

When it was all gone, he wiped his mouth with toilet paper, put on his shoes, and ran through the back door and into his station wagon, digging a deeper hole in the lawn as he peeled out.

Driving away, he had two thoughts.

The first was, *Ben and James, at twenty-nine, will never reenter these Dead Houses. They can't. It falls to me.*

The second was, *There is no nine-year-old version of me to encounter because I still am who I am. I'm the same inside. I never went anywhere. It's only the two of them, who left and came back, that are split or doubled in this way.*

Cruising out to Giant Chinese for a late-night Lo Mein before the Blind Spot took over, he wondered if he ought to feel pride or shame at this insight. *Pride*, he decided, slurping a noodle, *for the clarity of my thinking; shame for its being true.*

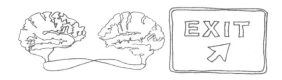

Friday

For the past week, the nine-year-olds had been struggling to control the nineteen-year-olds whenever they went to work on the Pretend Movie. They knew that James had been talking to them at the Hotel bar because whenever they entered the nineteen-year-olds' heads, snatches of their recent memories were still accessible, like echoes. This week, these included the taste of cocktails and the thrill of knowing they were on James' tab.

Thursday at recess, they'd gone to sleep in the Pine Hedge Office and emerged inside the nineteen-year-olds at the bar with James, agreeing to meet him at the Welcome Center restaurant tomorrow night, to discuss his film. "I've always found that a good place for doing business," James was saying. "Its abstraction, its position on the cusp of the Outskirts... I can think there in a way I can't here in town."

All of recess was wasted in witnessing this exchange, which the nine-year-olds were powerless to direct the nineteen-year-olds away from. Apparently, they wanted money from James just as much as they wanted to fulfill the yearnings of the nine-year-olds who, they had to admit, had no means by which to pay. They couldn't be sure how much directorial power they really had, since, in the end, it was up to the nineteen-year-olds to make *The Dream of Escape* real. After all, they were actors, not slaves.

So, in the Pine Hedge Office at recess on Friday, the duo agreed to give in for now and let the nineteen-year-olds do as they pleased. *We have to be open to whatever course the Pretend Movie decides to take. It is using us, not vice versa,* they decided, though it hurt to relinquish control, especially after the Mayor's appearance in James' Dead House this week, which seemed like yet another harbinger of the coming End.

Real art comes from adapting to reality, not from forcing it to be what it doesn't want to be, they reminded themselves, trying to act braver than they felt.

After dismissal, ears weeping with what Squimbop had fed into them, they stomped up the Meadow-lined Road to the tall grass near the Welcome Center, where the meeting with James was to be held. They walked behind Squimbop as far as the Meadow, and kept going when he turned in to ANGEL HOUSE. Crossing into the Outskirts, past the Motel, they felt the temperature drop and the wind slice at their ears.

From their vantage in the tall grass that had grown over the highway onramp, they looked at the tables in the Welcome Center restaurant, in the almost-evening when the inside lights were coming on, and saw two thin bald men sharing a sandwich, their hands unsteady as they picked out the lettuce and tomatoes and laid them on a shared napkin.

As they watched, their mind stirred with thoughts of the nineteen-year-olds, eager to get started. They could feel the ten years hanging over them like storm clouds in the November dusk, about to bury their bodies in time. Though they knew they wouldn't be conscious for the nineteen-year-olds' meeting, they figured that by coming all the way out here before falling asleep, they could maintain a closeness to the event that would've been lost if they were asleep in their beds, dreaming at a distance.

They closed their eyes and saw themselves crouching in this same grass ten years from now. Seventy years from then, if the

193

Pretend Movie hadn't come to fruition and the world hadn't ended, they would only have moved indoors, to take their pick of empty booths in the Welcome Center at five p.m., picking the lettuce and tomatoes from their sandwich, aware that as soon as they finished eating, it would be bedtime, even though it was Friday night.

It was a future at once terrifying in its banality and immensely comforting in its promise of undisturbed routine.

The tall grass got colder and they pulled their coats tight.

Inside, the two old men split the check, leaving warped dollar bills on the table beside their lettuce and tomatoes. The waiter, still young, cleared all this away with an automatic motion he had learned when he was even younger and would still be repeating when he was much older.

Exhausted from the effort of imagining the far future, the nine-year-olds became nothing for a moment.

Then they woke up as the nineteen-year-olds, putting their shoes on in the Hotel. They took the elevator down, walked out through the lobby and into the Square, passed the Greek restaurant, and headed for the Meadow-lined Road, eager to talk to the filmmaker who said he had a job for them.

Friday Evening

James wasn't far behind. He had his pages of film treatment in his pocket, but he doubted he'd use them tonight. The time to discuss specifics would, he hoped, come later.

Basically, your roles are to play nineteen-year-olds having just arrived in town from nowhere, ready to seek adulthood by burrowing into the micro rather than fanning out into the macro, he practiced telling them.

For you, the town is the future, not the past. He could see this as the film's tagline, in twenty-inch lettering on the poster in the Movie Store window.

If he could just succeed in casting the nineteen-year-olds tonight, James believed, the rest would take care of itself. His film would then already be underway, a living organism whose growth he was merely fostering, no longer a looming abstraction impossible to give birth to.

The ding of the Welcome Center door hung in the air.

James crossed the indoor plaza to the restaurant and sat down at an empty booth. A waiter stepped into the circle of his ruminations, puncturing it with the hard laminated corner of a menu. It had a green leather backing and a dab of ketchup between its first and second pages. James wiped this off with a napkin, then ordered the family-style meatloaf dinner with stuffing and mashed potatoes.

By the time it arrived, the nineteen-year-olds were sitting across from him, looking at menus of their own.

When the waiter came back, they ordered pancakes and said, "Thanks for suggesting the Hotel when we first got to town. That worked out well."

The waiter smiled and said, "Good to hear."

"You know him?" asked James.

They said they did, but it didn't turn into a conversation.

He sat there looking at them, one hand in his pocket stroking his film treatment, the other resting his fork on the surface of his meatloaf. The sight of it turned his stomach, but he was determined

195

to make a dent, eventually.

The nineteen-year-olds were mesmeric, holding him in a gaze he could neither break from nor return. He could see them wavering, like a projected image that comes in and out of focus, as the dreaming nine-year-olds, wherever they were, struggled to stay in it.

He couldn't remember exactly what the nine-year-olds looked like, so he couldn't be sure if the nineteen-year-olds were perfect renditions of them at nineteen. Same as himself and Ben: *What did we actually look like then?*

"As long as you show up onscreen..." he heard himself mumble a few minutes later.

"What?" they asked.

He almost laughed with relief at having managed to say something before the silence grew unbreakable. "Usually my casting sessions, in News City I mean, are more... formal, but, in this case..."

He couldn't take the thought any further. There was too little to work with. His meatloaf seemed to be expanding on his plate, defying him to finish it.

"Let me tell you about the Movie Store," he began again, trying to steer his mind toward an area that would let him talk for a while without having to think clearly. "The Movies upstairs are arranged by Director. But only the Great Directors, those few with a truly singular, uncategorizable vision. Most Movies are downstairs, which is laid out as a 1-to-1 scale model of the town. All the downstairs Movies are arranged by genre, depending on what part of the town they're about or take place in."

The nineteen-year-olds ate without relish and watched him ramble.

He explained how, for as long as he could remember until he left for News City, he had lived inside a Pretend Movie with Ben.

But only he, of the two of them, had truly yearned to make it into an actual film that the Movie Store would stock on its shelves along with the others, adding to the filmed mythos of the town, which stretched back farther than anyone could remember, like a well whose water was so deep no one knew if it would ever run out. They were thus compelled to be profligate about drinking from it, though not without a constant undertone of apocalyptic terror.

"You know what I mean?" he asked, as he rambled about his walks with the Mayor through the aisles of the Movie Store at seventeen and eighteen, him picking up boxes and looking at the pictures on the back while the Mayor stroked himself through his pockets, whimpering, discovering the vast reproductive potential he could only activate alone with these Movies in his basement, entering the Orchard through his screen... a potential for creating life that he'd lost and was now desperate to get back, "Through the film I want to make with you two."

James finally spat it out, blushing. "You don't mind if I call you 'Ben' and 'James,' do you?" he asked.

They shook their heads. James decided he would use the names interchangeably, since he couldn't tell them apart and didn't want to try. He would write every line for both of them, letting them decide who would deliver which.

He was aware of the asymmetry—they were two and he was only one, he was real and they were semi-real—but he felt a professional accord firming up between them nonetheless. *You don't need to know much about someone to do good work with them,* he thought. *Provided they're right for the job.*

Keeping his mind anchored in the Movie Store basement, he found the focus to keep talking. "It's the translation from the Pretend to the real, from Movie to film, that makes our lives bigger than they seem to be, and in that sense worthwhile beyond the time they take to live out... This is what lets us live beyond our means,

197

so to speak. It's what lets us contribute to humanity, rather than only taking.

"To the Mayor, there is no such thing as film, only Movies. He prays to them, worships them, fucks them, wants to die in them. His waking life passes him by in terror of the Blind Spot, which is a giant nothingness behind his house. If it weren't for Movies, he would have jumped in by now."

James paused, gathering his thoughts.

"My film will—for the Mayor — be a Movie. That's okay. For me—for us—we're talking about something else. Not Pornography in the sense that the Mayor understands it, but representation, reification, a way of taking the lostness of the past and translating that into…"

James knew he was losing it, barely making sense to himself, unable to put into words quite what a film was.

But it felt good to say a lot upfront, in a tone that sounded something like that of a Director, so as to convince the nineteen-year-olds that he was the real thing.

The waiter brought the check and he paid it with a casualness he hoped seemed habitual, like he had years of practice wining and dining actors.

The nineteen-year-olds started to waver as the nine-year-olds stirred in the grass outside, the expression on their faces drooping.

"All you need to know right now," James said, grimacing with the pain of forcing his mind to produce a concrete thought before it was too late, "is that you two drive into this town from the larger country, which you know exists but no one else here does. You have no pasts, but are looking for one. In that sense, you're drifters. Your trunk is full of psychic material, which in the film will have a shape, like a bunch of trash. But it's not trash, it's roots, and you need to plant them here, so as to engineer a past for yourselves and

198

put an end to the drifting which will otherwise kill you, because the open road has become unsafe. Out there, someone or something is looking for you, trying to wipe you out. Meanwhile, the road out of here is reverting to the Inland Sea, which is aching to overflow its banks and submerge everything. Your only chance of hanging on is to put down roots in the soil of this town, deep in its Pornography, deep enough to find purchase in something solid, no matter how deep the floodwaters go."

He paused, shuddering with the exertion.

"Okay? I'll pay you $50,000 each."

They nodded. "Give us a week to consider. Have a contract for us by then."

Then they slumped over, braindead where they sat.

James looked out the window and felt a rush of horror at the sight of the nine-year-olds watching him from the frosty grass, standing up and wiping sleep from their mouths. Their gaze made him feel eighty-nine.

Talked out and frightened, James slipped away from the Welcome Center booth, leaving the nineteen-year-olds slumped there like a couple of drunks.

After washing his face again in the bathroom, he forced himself into the parking lot, to meet the nine-year-olds where they stood waiting in the grass.

Standing before them, feeling posed, James looked them over, staring openly for the first time. There was no question that they were him and Ben at nine. With the nineteen-year-olds it was hazier, a matter of wishful thinking perhaps, mutual projection, but, with the nine-year-olds, it was absolute and objective. If anything, James found himself wishing there was more room for doubt.

"How's my Dead House?" he asked the one who looked more like him. "Have you changed the sheets on the bed?" It occurred to him that the nine-year-olds were almost identical to one another. He and Ben must have diverged in appearance over the course of the years in News City, as they underwent their separate ravages.

"Pretty good and no," replied the boy-James, not mentioning the Mayor's recent incursion.

Then silence.

I can tell you right now what becomes of Pretend Movies, James thought, and almost said it, but he didn't, partially because it would've been cruel and partially because, right now, he wasn't altogether sure.

You only know what became of your Pretend Movie, he imagined them thinking. *Ours is different.*

Part of him hoped they were right. It was enough to push him to the edge of tears. He found himself silently begging the cold night sky for relief. *Just make it stop… Let me find peace, rest, no matter how much I leave undone…*

Then go to ANGEL HOUSE, he imagined them replying. *Stop pretending to be a filmmaker and give us our actors back.* The Dream of Escape *died in you so it could live in us.*

Now he really was crying, head down against his forearm, running past the nine-year-olds, who turned to watch him go but didn't follow.

James slowed to a jog as he reached the edge of the Meadow, eyes stinging with the tears he hadn't yet wiped away. It was cold out, but he wasn't ready to go back to his house. He knew he'd sit up all night over a sheet of paper, squeezing a pen until it popped.

The fear of being unable to turn the Pretend Movie into an actual film was nothing new, but rarely had it bit him this hard. He could feel its teeth binding with his bones, becoming permanent.

So he stumbled off the road and into the frosty grass, the

once-deep puddles hardened into sharp rifts. This made the going easier than it had been earlier in autumn. Without stopping to pick a direction, he found himself at the edge of the Ghost Town, which looked as desolate as he felt in the November cold.

He leaned on the fence and mused on the mist-shrouded streets, the buildings sinking into the hard ground. The wind was light, and there was no grass to rustle. A few pebbles rattled, but that was all.

The scene was lit by the swimmy purple glow of ANGEL HOUSE, which, even at this distance, froze him with the suggestion of eternal dreamless sleep, warmth, floating... the rest of time with no film to make, no compulsion, no guilt...

He sank to his knees, hands balling into fists, eyes closing, the pressure of doing anything at all receding as his body lost mobility.

He imagined pounding on the door and swearing to Squimbop that he was a child. "I only look twenty-nine," he whispered. "Really, I'm nine, just like all the others. Please let me in. Surely you have room for one more."

"Hey!" someone was kicking him.

He could hear it but not feel it.

"Hey, open your eyes. You okay?"

James opened his eyes with a ripping sensation. His tears had turned to ice.

It was dawn, the Ghost Town lost in fog.

A man stood over him, holding his hand out. James took his time before letting the man help him up.

When he was on his feet, he recognized Well.

"I thought you were a statue," he said.

James tried to smile. "Just cold."

"Freezing." Well shifted his attention to the Ghost Town.

"It's not even a town anymore. Population zero. Guess they'd rather be in there," he nodded in the direction of ANGEL HOUSE. "And never have to wake up for school again."

"Can't say I blame them," said James. "Sorry."

"Anyway," said Well, a catch in his voice, "I'm getting out of here. I've hung around these ruins long enough."

He turned to face the Mountain.

"Ever been up?"

James shook his head. The thought of the summit made him cold, but not as cold as the thought of going back to his house and working on his script for a week while he waited for the nineteen-year-olds to get back to him.

"You're gonna climb it?"

Well nodded. "As high as I can get. If I die up there, fine. If not, I'll do something else. Want to come?"

Though he wasn't sure if he did, James couldn't picture himself saying no. So, after both pissing on the fence a few yards apart, they set out together.

Saturday Morning

After they had walked for half an hour, their meeting by the Ghost Town felt like last night, already part of the past. Now it was today, Day Zero.

They were out of the Meadow, on ground that was sloping upward into foothills. After they ran out of breath, the fact that they had nothing to talk about felt less onerous. The ground lost its grass and the trees got thin and sheer. The pine needles were soon so far overhead that a side-to-side glance revealed nothing but stripped trunks. For now, they followed a rough trail beaten by the footsteps of whomever else had passed this way.

After the first hour, Well's eyes had dried in the sun. He'd lost the look of having stumbled out of the dark in anger and confusion, and regained the look of a man carrying out a decision he'd made regarding the rest of his life. There was a defiance to his step now—abandoning the radio and the town whose children had abandoned him was a reality, no longer an idle notion.

Though he was older, Well was faster than James, whose head was full of guilt and fear about abandoning his film, even if just for now. He knew he'd have to work doubly hard upon his return to sea level and so was in no hurry to climb the Mountain, thereby reaching the point at which he'd have to start back down.

Sometimes Well made it out of sight up the path, around a bend as it snaked back and forth, the grade growing incrementally steeper. When this happened, he kept going, under no obligation to wait for James, whom he barely knew and whose purpose in following him he wasn't invested in considering. James always caught up, but if he hadn't, Well wouldn't have looked for him. He was fixated on the summit, certain the road to Dust House began up there. He held onto the image of himself descending those morning stairs into the smell of coffee and toast like a talisman.

Soon they left the last of the path and wound around the slope to a point where the Meadow was invisible. The panorama would only reopen when they reached the summit.

Well pointed out a pensive-looking vulture to James, and James, catching his breath, told the story he'd heard about the

Mountain's far side, totally impassible, a straight drop down into lands where no one had been but from which, it was said, people had come up, along a path known only to them. "Dwellers," he called them. The word tasted rotten from disuse.

This story didn't expand into a conversation, but it left them both discomfited enough to pick up the pace, exposed, as they were, in a no-man's-land between the pastoral lower reaches and the supposed Promised Land of the summit.

They kept up this pace until Well tripped, landing on his tailbone by the side of the path. Waving James away, he rolled up to a knee, breathed in that position for a moment, then regained his footing and continued on. After this, he kept ahead, striding hard on his long legs despite the throbbing in his back, immersed in images of the Desert, sipping at air he wished he could gulp.

They saw their first Dwellers around noon, having left the path more than two hours ago and scrambled over several hairy patches since.

The two of them looked away, like children cutting across a reclusive neighbor's lawn, ashamed to be seen. Scared as well. It felt obscene to watch beings from folklore materialize. They didn't see any faces, only bodies carrying bulky packages, luggage, and equipment. James noticed that all their bags bore the Ultra Max logo. They trudged by, easily overtaking Well and James without stopping to look at them.

Well was so fixated on imagining his new life on the summit that he began casting these people as subservients without wondering who they were or how he'd conquer them. Some would be guards, some scouts, some workmen lugging lumber and tools to build his new Dust House if it turned out that vision alone wasn't enough to conjure it.

James, meanwhile, tried to reconcile the reality of these

204

people passing by with the stories he and Ben had heard about them over the years. They seemed, upon first impression, no different than Sub-Weird, likewise clotted in the semi-familiarity of the Outskirts, existing at a vertical rather than a horizontal remove from the town, but equally peripheral to it. Hardly the shriveled, super-agile creatures he and Ben had imagined. He had to admire that they'd made a new life for themselves up here, something beyond the purgatory of the Outskirts.

James couldn't tell if their lapse from the fantastical into the human had resonance for his film, now that nothing was off-limits. He gave in to giddiness as possibilities proliferated in his mind, but then he crashed, the altitude and exertion getting the better of him.

Pathos overcame him as his sense of the surreal flagged, leaving in its wake only sadness for the bedraggled lives these Dwellers surely lived, swarming into Ultra Max once a month, then slowly eating through their haul on the cold summit. He panted and wiped his forehead and felt bad.

There was a picnic area around the next bend that looked down one of the Mountain's blank sides, neither at the Meadow nor at the fabled sheer back. This side was just a series of steep drops that led down into a series of interlocking basins and flats, with a thin stream twining among them.

They could smell the smoke from a portable grill set up inside a gazebo. The Dwellers didn't wear masks or veils while cooking, but their faces were obscured by James' and Well's unwillingness to look straight at them. One of them stooped over, squinting at the meat as if trying to see the bacteria on it.

It took James a few minutes to realize how hungry he was. When he did, he went up to the man and, staring at the meat, asked if he and his companion could buy some.

The Dweller grabbed two hocks off the grill and held them out, without buns or napkins or checking to see if they were done.

James grunted thanks and carried them pinched between thumb and forefinger back to where Well was standing, looking away from this interaction.

Well nodded appreciatively as he ate, passing the hock from hand to hand to keep it from burning him.

A pickup truck rumbled by, filled with Dwellers huddled around more Ultra Max bags.

When Well and James were finished, they wiped the meat leavings on their pants, just under their pockets, and got going again, afraid that if they rested any longer, they wouldn't reach the summit by dark.

Repurposing the dreamtime it would have doled out had they fallen asleep, the day grew an unexpected middle. The sky took on a rich purple hue, emboldened by the light reflecting off the Inland Sea, which was nearly visible at this altitude.

All noise grew distant. Pickup trucks still rumbled by, but they sounded like they'd been wrapped in gauze. Dwellers sat in the back like statues being moved from one museum to the next.

For a while, the climb got easy, like Well and James had crossed into a new regime of gravity in which going back down would have been harder than going the rest of the way up.

Then James felt a pressure in his sinuses and a pain in his armpit. He scratched it, and it felt worse.

He kept scratching, slowly, for what felt like hours, trying not to panic. Both armpits now, and the love handles under his shirt in back, and the parts of his groin just to the right and left of his fly. He knew he should resist scratching and wait for the hot tub at the Gym once he got back down, but the raw self-control he'd had at nineteen was long gone.

His body was becoming a farm. He patted himself in the places he'd been scratching and felt tight, knotted clusters.

Well ignored this increasingly frantic behavior, focusing on the path as it wound along, doubling back and forth, preserving a traversable grade. Birds hung immobile in the sky in hours that refused to pass.

James untucked his shirt and ran one hand under it. Touching the sore areas, he felt tight, inward-pulling clusters, moist, soft, extremely painful.

Hives.

Now that he had the word, he put his hand back in his armpit, gagging. The whole cavity was dense with them, dripping musk, the heads crowding each other for space, grasping toward a center as if trying to merge.

He pulled on one deep in his armpit until his vision blurred. Then he waited a second, breathed in, and pulled again, sharp and fast. It came loose in his hand.

It was soft but its roots were sharp, covered with skin and blood and the armpit hairs that it had grown out of. He fell back against a tree and leaned like that for a long time, peeing a trickle down his pants as blood dripped from under his shirt and into his pocket.

When he'd gotten ahold of himself, he put the hive into this same pocket, like an orchid in a bowl of water, and patted his torso again, feeling the clusters nesting in his flesh. It fuzzed his memory of how he'd gotten up here, to the point where he started to feel like a Dweller, half inside of folklore and half out, his future devoid of possibility but perhaps also immune to whatever was coming for the town below.

He groped on, barely cognizant of the topography. If there

207

were drop-offs along this part of the path, he was in grave unacknowledged danger, and Well would have done little to prevent him from falling.

They continued like this until Well stopped to pick up a white sheet, barely visible in the dusk, which must have fallen from one of the pickup trucks. He held it up, dusted it, and smelled it. Then he said, "Cover yourself with this," looking away as James did.

When James was covered, hugging its edges as tightly as he could without agitating the hives, they walked up the rest of the way.

More pickup trucks passed by, headlights on, leaking gas. The Dwellers in back peered out at Well and James, one in the sheet, the other leading the way with slow but confident steps.

Saturday Evening

Soon they reached the highest point where the trucks could park. The Dwellers got out, dragging their Ultra Max bags up the last steep stretch as Well and James followed. No one opposed them.

When the ground flattened out, the Dwellers dispersed into their settlement, which consisted of a series of wooden shacks and tents beyond those, spreading across a plateau.

The layout—as far as James could see through the sheet—was similar to how he pictured the Outskirts, except that the ground here was soft unmarked dirt instead of scarred roads and culverts.

Some of the Dwellers were roasting meat over a fire; others were making what smelled like powdered hot chocolate on a foldout table. Near where they stood, two men with very long hair and patchy sideburns and goatees stood over metal trash cans seething with boiling water. In the water bobbed cans of soda, which the men stirred with wooden paddles.

James pulled the sheet tighter over his face, agitating the hives around his collar in order to see broad outlines through the taut fabric. He breathed in the sheet's smell, naming its musk Essence of Dweller, though he couldn't be sure the smell wasn't his own.

When it was time, the men reached in a hook and removed two cans. They popped the lids with an awl and held them out to Well and James.

Well reached out quickly and burned his fingers on the aluminum, while James took his more carefully, reaching under his sheet with outstretched fingers. The men neither laughed nor recoiled, simply watched as Well dropped it, then knelt down to pick it up again. He sipped while James stood beside him, holding his can under the sheet, trying to bring it to his lips without knocking himself out with hive-pain.

A few Dwellers crowded around to watch them drink. James could tell that faces were focused on him without being able to see their expressions. To help him in this regard, one of the Dwellers took out a knife and cut two eyeholes. James felt his hives quiver as the blade tore through the sheet, tickling his eyeballs without puncturing them. The holes were a little low, closer to the middle of his nose, but if he hunched, he could see out.

"Thank you," he murmured, aware that no one else was speaking, nor had anyone spoken since they'd been up here.

The meat was ready. The ribs of some large animal. Well understood that the Dwellers saw him as the keeper of a leper, and accepted this role as a means of integrating himself, even if James likely wouldn't be here for long.

209

Perhaps, Well thought, as the meat-smoke made him both hungry and queasy, *that's the only reason they're not eating us right now. Afflicted holy men in from the wilderness, seeking succor... maybe they think I'm a priest.*

There had been no convocation around the fire, only a drifting-towards. Ribs were being broken up by hand and passed around. They ate standing up or squatting near the fire, without ceremony.

Bags of Ultra Max potato chips followed, as did cans of beer, plastic bottles of ketchup and barbecue sauce, tubs of coleslaw and potato salad. For these, there were plastic plates.

It was cold out; the Dwellers put on gloves to eat, unconcerned by the grease and mayonnaise sticking to the fabric.

James couldn't sit without squishing the hives around his lower back, so he stood. He held his plate under his sheet, creating a bulge that moved from his stomach to his mouth each time he raised it to take a bite.

Listening to the Dwellers chew, Well looked up at the starless sky, as black here as it surely was over the Inland Sea, and began to fill it with an instinctual broadcast. *I ease my codebreaking kit from the upstairs dresser*, he thought, taking that sentence as his starting point, as if he were back at the station in town and the children were all settling into bed with their radios. *I tiptoe downstairs in Dust House and open it on the couch, and prepare myself for what the frequencies in the night are about to reveal.*

Well barely looked up as he mumbled his broadcast into the back of his hand, given over to imagining his house from the Ghost Town sailing up the Mountain like a giant ship, coming to rest in the depths of the Desert, at the dead end of a dusty street, this time for good.

The fire had simmered down to coals and the Dwellers were finishing their cans and sitting quietly, in no need of entertainment.

Leaving their company, Well followed a hazy red light deeper into the plateau, over to what turned out to be a broadcast tower. Beside it was a small wooden shack, which he knew would contain a table, a chair, and a mic.

There is nothing I need that I don't eventually find, he thought. The revelation felt at once reassuring and ominous, proof from the universe that there would never be any release from the few, repetitive things that had defined his life so far.

"All material is raw material," he mumbled, touching the tower, which felt hot, like it was already transmitting.

He was rehearsing his broadcast and, at the same time, beginning it. It seemed good to him that there should be no difference. Permitting himself this flourish, Well imagined a Dweller asking him what the broadcast was called. "The Return of the Radio Angel," he replied. "A prayer to summon those last two children from the town up here to me."

Saturday Night

James sat on a rock inside the sheet, letting its eyeholes billow as he breathed in and out. The fire was dying. He tossed his plate out the bottom of the sheet without straining to see where it landed. Judging from the plasticky rustling he could hear in all directions, the whole encampment had tossed its trash on the ground.

The cumulative exhaustion of being up all night and climbing all day was hitting him. It made him homesick for the rented house on the Meadow-lined Road, even though that was no home at all. Every time he yawned, his eyes watered with exhaustion, and every time the sheet billowed back toward his face, it dried them.

He wasn't sure what toll staying out all night in the cold would take at this point in his life, but he could tell that no one was going to invite him into their tent. The hives on his ass and thighs were mushed down against the rock, in a state of dormant pain. They hurt when he moved, but this was the only way to warm up, so he worked his way into a trance by mentally juggling the prospects of hive-pain and freezing.

Though he would've preferred to repress this knowledge, he knew what the hives meant: *Retreat. Your work lies below, not up here. If you try to run from it, it will find you. It will burst forth from you. It will kill you.*

Mixed with James' shivering were the sounds of the Dwellers, who continued to sit around the dead fire, making noises that might have been words or merely sighs. Their voices seemed to be in some alternation with one another, but whether this constituted communication or simple turn-taking was unclear.

When it got too cold to stay seated, James stood and walked around the fire, wincing as he went. No one turned to watch him. Circling more and more widely, he found himself at the edge of the encampment, looking off into total blackness, unsure whether it concealed the back reaches of the summit or the Edge, where the habitable world ended and the point of recursion supposedly began.

As Well was clearly out of the picture by this point and no solitary future on the summit seemed possible, James decided to

212

go over and find out.

Pulling his eyeholes flush with his sockets, he got up and shuffled over to it. He teetered, gripping the earth with his toes through his shoes while trying to imagine a scene from his film on the far side, some bright, populous event, fraught with meaning. He teetered inwardly as well as outwardly now, his secular side straining to predominate, whispering, *Don't do it… spend the night here and walk back down like a sane person in the morning,* but the combination of hive-pain and the desire to find out if the Edge was real overwhelmed him, and he leaned in, letting go of the ground. *Take me there*, he thought, ready to fall as far down as it went. *I'm ready to sacrifice myself.*

He blacked out, tumbling in freefall, cold air whooshing through him, endorphins making him jubilant.

The light behind his eyes went purple and his mind filled with the peace of Death, briefly, until he hit stagnant water with a gruesome splat. As he sank, bone-snakes brushed his skin and his hives warped inward, stuffing his body with pain. With his arms pinned to his sides, he sank as far down as his landing velocity would take him, then bobbed slowly to the surface.

When he broke back through, he floated, staring into a void too dark to be the night sky. The Psychogeography, stitching all salient locations together, was wide open. The Mountain was somewhere overhead, while down below, like a reflection made real, was the Blind Spot, the deepest point in the town.

He could feel it as a cauldron, roiling with both the frigidness of Death and the warmth of the Pornography, blending the two as it sucked him in. When he dipped his head under, he could hear his film struggling to take shape from within this liquid, constantly melting back into it.

Part of him wanted to push all thought of the film away,

as far into the past or the future as he could, but part of him knew that if he didn't resolve to return to the town for the sole purpose of seeing it through, he'd drown right here. *This could be it, right now… the End.*

He knew this was the only certainty he'd be given and, like a life raft, his survival depended on holding onto it. In the void overhead, he could see the two specks of the Mayor's headlights, parked on the edge, acknowledging his impotence for the thousandth or ten thousandth night in a row.

As James sculled the surface looking up at them, a hand grabbed his waist and pulled him down. He fought, spluttering, grabbing at water, kicking his feet to keep them from going over his head. His hives flexed and grew erect with fear, the pain now hot with arousal.

He ripped the thing off him and beheld it in the glow of the Mayor's headlights as it floated in the murk. It was white and thick-skinned, humanoid but twisted into a rougher mammalian shape, its mouth a black hole. It stared straight into him for a moment, and he stared back, accepting whatever message it meant to convey. It radiated an authority, in its simple lack of affect and pretension, that he knew better than to ignore.

My film isn't about the people we used to know, he understood, as it disappeared. *It's about those we will never know because they aren't knowable, or even people… it's about the people from inside the Blind Spot, waiting to surge up and overtake the town… not the Sub-Weird or the Dwellers or the Mayor or Ben or me… it's about the Blankheads.*

They live in water because they can't put down roots, he thought, trying to commit this moment to memory before it faded or scabbed over. *The Blind Spot is infested with demons. They make it more than a pit. They're what the Mayor fears so deeply.*

He paddled toward the edge, aware that there were

dozens, maybe hundreds of Blankheads clustered on the bottom, watching him go, promising they'd meet again.

I'll be ready, he thought in their direction.

When he reached the edge, he dug his hands and feet into the slippery rock and dirt and began to climb.

Sunday Morning

Outside the sheet, which had clung to his body throughout his submergence, James could see the sun starting to rise as he hoisted himself hand over hand up the edge of the Blind Spot. The walls were slick and crumbly, but he found enough hand- and footholds to make vertical progress. He was impressed with his ability, as if his entire journey up the Mountain had been training for this, the only real ascent. His hives roiling, he focused as hard as he could on the promise of a long soothing soak in the hot tub, which he saw now that he'd been saving for a time like this.

No, not a time like this, he thought. *This exact time.*

By midmorning, his arms were shaking from the exertion and his eyes were glazed over. He hoisted himself up by gripping long roots and digging his feet into the rock face, dislodging spectacular avalanches of dirt and pebbles, resting on outcroppings, until he landed on his belly on the Blind Spot's edge, where he remained until he could breathe evenly.

When he could, he pushed himself upright and set out past the lesser quarries toward the Mayor's house, drawing his arms around himself and wincing as bog water dripped from his hives. He leaned forward periodically and retched, remembering the particular combination of dizziness and dehydration that had marked his worst News City hangovers. Knowing it would agitate

215

his hives all the more, he tried to force through a memory of where and when the parties that had produced those News City hangovers had taken place: which apartments, with which people, under what circumstances?

By the time he'd given up trying, he was several quarries further along, in the deep woods now. He passed the parked tractors and backhoes, leaning against one to catch his breath, counting the ancient cigarette butts lined up on the driver's seat. There were seven. Then he continued, straining to glimpse the Mayor's house through the trees, wondering what he was doing in there now, given that he had no more Movies to lose himself in.

Cutting across the Mayor's lawn and down his driveway, James felt an unexpected pang of empathy, thinking, *Never again will I be able to tell myself that the Blind Spot isn't real.* He understood something of the totality of the Mayor's predicament for the first and possibly the only time. Almost crying, he hurried along the cul-de-sac and onto the Meadow-lined Road.

By the time he made it to the Gym, the Psychogeography felt far away, back in the barely-real state it resided in whenever it wasn't active. He pushed past the front desk, nodded to Janitor Pete who was dozing by the towel hamper, and sat down on the bench in the locker room to stretch.

Though he knew in the mythic part of his brain that he'd emerged here from the Blind Spot, his feet and legs were so tired it felt like he'd walked all the way down from the Mountain. *Back in town again*, he thought, massaging one hamstring and then the other.

Sunday Afternoon

James started his soak in the adult pool, observing protocol, then made a quick lap across to the children's pool, before progressing, finally, to the hot tub. He was naked now, enveloped in steam, stretching first one arm, then the other across his chest, trying to relax.

There was a droning underwater, which he could tell was a combination of the jets and the ear damage he'd sustained from the combined altitude and depth of his journey. He closed his eyes as he sat on the bottom, then surfaced, breathed, looked around in the green murk, and slipped back under, feeling his hives soften.

The longer he stayed under, the more he could feel the Pornography simmering. The bottom of the hot tub—several inches of plastic, a tile frame, some piping—was all that separated him from the tributaries of the Inland Sea.

He exhaled, accepting his place in all this, his tininess and the hubris of all effort to become more. Or at least he felt for a moment what it would be like to accept this, knowing that he never entirely would. If he did, that would be the end of his life. The moment at which he'd be unborn, returning to the broth he'd come from, ready to be made into someone else.

He surfaced again, breathed, and went back under. *I'm sorry,* he thought, sensing that something could hear him. *I'm sorry for how little I've done in twenty-nine years, and I'm sorry for how much I've wanted to do. More than anything, I'm sorry for having tried to escape. That was Well's journey to make, not mine. I was scared. It was wrong. I won't try it again.*

He sat on the bottom until he grew weary with relief. He gave in to it, tipping over, the purple glow filling his mind again, the warm light of ANGEL HOUSE beckoning from the far end of a tunnel. *The light at the end of the tunnel... is almost here*, he

217

thought, floating through it, delirious, losing consciousness...

A pair of strong hands hoisted him from the water and threw him onto the floor, pounding his back until he coughed. He rolled over, spluttering, half-blind with chlorine, to see Janitor Pete in a hooded sweatshirt staring down at him.

"You alright buddy?"

James couldn't respond except to hold his hand out.

Janitor Pete grabbed it and dragged him into the shower, helping him sit on the plastic stool before turning on the spray, letting go of him cautiously. James slumped against the wall but didn't slip off.

Once the hot water had shocked him back into consciousness, he reached up to fill one hand with soap from the wall dispenser and used the other to prod at his hives, not uprooting any but pulling each apart from the others so he could see what they actually looked like. Crusted with salt from the Blind Spot's water, they were whiter than he'd imagined, with the cauliflower-quality of warts and red veins on top. He soaped them up and cleaned them delicately, like he was their father and they were his fresh new brood.

When he was done, he reached his arm out again, letting Janitor Pete help him into the locker room, where he found a damp towel to dry off with.

"You up for a shot of something strong?"

Janitor Pete handed James a flask while he cut the lock on a nearby locker, pulling out an ancient pair of jeans and a hooded sweatshirt. When James had drunk his fill, he took the abandoned clothes and laboriously got into them.

"Lemme give you a lift," Janitor Pete said, taking the flask back and draining it before putting it away.

Drunk, exhausted, and dressed as a Sub-Weird, James finally made it home, crawling from Janitor Pete's car and across the threshold of his house like a pilgrim who'd almost died on the road to the Promised Land.

Sunday Night, Late November

The Mayor tasted hot chocolate on a wooden spoon as he stirred it in a saucepan on the stovetop in James' Dead House.

Over the past few weeks, he'd stocked both Dead Houses with hot chocolate supplies, though there'd be no more marshmallows. The rot of his Orchard had started creeping through his TV screen and into his basement, so he'd spent almost no time in his own house after dark since November 5th, figuring that the only way to get through whatever intermediate phase he was currently in was to keep his mind off it.

He licked more chocolate from the spoon and looked at the kitchen wall clock, as if the boy-James' appearance had been scheduled and he was about to be late.

There was a tentative plan to see the adult Ben and James tomorrow night, after the Town Council Meeting, but nothing had been confirmed. No one called him anymore. He sighed and shrugged, pushing these thoughts away, back into the daytime where they belonged. Nighttime consciousness was grim without Movies, but not as grim as being alone in his basement facing the cold glass of the screen, or upstairs waiting for the phone to ring.

He could feel his house growing haunted, the empty rooms filling in the night. It was better to be here, where the haunting was a given.

When the chocolate was hot, the Mayor found himself walking through the other rooms of the downstairs, supping from a giant mug with the remainder simmering on the stove.

It was exciting to pass back through the playroom, the dining room, the living room, where the three of them had burned off so many nighttime hours, feverish not to waste them even though they seemed infinite. He ran his fingers over the shelves, licking off the dust, touching the reams of printed and handwritten paper they had produced over the years, cutting ever closer to expressing the essential nature of the town, and thus of the universe. The shelves were covered in these, in lieu of books, and the Mayor knew that touching them had become a ritual, an act of devotion.

He turned and the boy-James was there, sipping from a mug of his own. "I helped myself."

The Mayor felt guilty for being caught exploring like this, but he suppressed it by remembering that he was the adult now. "There are no marshmallows," he said.

The boy-James shrugged. He sipped and made an as you were gesture with his eyebrows. So the Mayor continued rummaging, his mug forgotten on a shelf where it would soon become an artifact in its own right.

Voice low, like he was inventorying rather than expressing his thoughts, the boy-James started talking about the Desert behind the summit of the Mountain, the Oasis with its half-formed town like some organic entity growing in the sun, the beach of a distant shore, maybe the far side of the Inland Sea.

"Somehow," he said, talking fast, "the tunnels of *The Dream of Escape* will lead us there."

The Mayor let him talk.

"Steep, steep, steep, then flat... I saw myself climbing up

there, hand over hand, last night... I knew I was James, though he didn't look like me... he and I climbing together, as one, up and up, away from the town, beyond the Meadow"...

The Mayor chewed his knuckles, suppressing each wave of distraction as it washed through his head. *Just listen*, he told himself. Even this utterance felt like an interruption.

"And a tall man, very tall, thin, sad, blonde," the boy-James continued, "his own town dead because no one would go there anymore... his voice broken. He wouldn't guide them anymore, over the airwaves, above the telephone poles, in their dreams... they were dreaming other dreams now, dead dreams, with no town streets to walk down, the skin of their backs turning wet and dripping away, becoming wax, feeding an open mouth below."

The boy-James looked at the Mayor, waiting for him to say something. But the Mayor only nodded for him to continue.

"Once they reached the top, the tall man stayed. The Desert was there for him alone. Somewhere deep inside, further in than anyone's gone, lies his house, the one he grew up in, but he's afraid to go in there alone... he's afraid it's"...

The boy-James closed his eyes and fell silent, thinking.

"He's afraid the house all the way out there isn't real," he said. "He's afraid of having his heart broken twice.

"But, still, he stayed there after I left. I got to the edge and then I... I... I jumped. And I landed in a deep, deep pit. A nothingness. And it was full of"...

He closed his eyes again.

The Mayor decided it was time to go. These nine-year-olds often said things in the night that terrified him, but never before had they mentioned the Blind Spot. He didn't want to believe they knew what it was.

"I saw a man whose mouth was a void," the boy-James went on, his eyes fluttering behind half-closed lids, like they were struggling to fall back asleep. "A man who was nothing, a demon, sucking space into himself like he couldn't stop, like he had no belly, just a hole that"...

The Mayor could feel bears watching him through the outside windows, standing around his station wagon, sweating, chewing grass and spitting it out.

"Go back to bed."

Before he left, he almost added, as a question to the adult-James, *Will I be seeing you after the Town Council Meeting tomorrow night?*

When he was gone, the boy-James returned to the bed that the adult James had been a boy in, and synced back up with the boy-Ben across the park, dreaming of the word *Blankhead* carved into a thousand-foot high cliff of emerald, descending into a frothy lagoon at the edge of the world.

Driving up the Meadow-lined Road, past where Squimbop slept on his new mattress, the Mayor fell into a vision of all his children bobbing in the sky, their white scaly bellies starting to stink. By dawn, they would all have fallen to earth, piled up like locusts.

So Well was gone. The Radio Angel was no more. *There's no one to guide them safely up this road any longer.*

The realization was heavy, like he'd fallen from the sky along with them. He exhaled blood-flecked saliva as he pulled into the radio station parking lot, where he idled, looking at the spot where Well's car sat abandoned, remembering the night he had come out here and felt the disturbance in the children's parade while sitting in the station on a plastic chair, drinking two beers at once.

Lingering on the word parade, he looked over at the Meadow-lined Road and saw a line of Sub-Weird marching in, carrying pillows and teddy bears, hurrying like something was smoking the last of them out of their habitat. They looked extremely frail and exposed in the night, too fixated on the beacon of the Town's City to feel the cold.

The term *teddy bears* caused him to look back at the station, in front of which now pawed the real bears, glaring at him through the windshield. Their eyes, always slightly human, were blown out in his headlights. He nodded to them as he wiped his lips and shifted into neutral, clasping his hands over his belly as he began to drift to the Blind Spot.

Monday, December 1st, Evening

The Mayor slept off another day. In the evening, the first one fraught with the full darkness of winter, he woke up, showered, and did what he could to make himself presentable for the Town Council Meeting.

The Council Chambers sat atop a small hill.

The Mayor arrived winded from climbing it, after parking as close as he could. By the time he got inside, the pimply cameraman was already in the back booth setting up for the TV broadcast. Through the smeared glass, he appeared rail thin, lost under a tremendous head of hair, his shirt so loose it didn't even suggest the outline of a torso.

The Mayor took a seat in the audience. A few old-timers with walkers made their way in just as the Council Chambers were being sealed off, the atmosphere pressurized, the camera already rolling.

223

Everyone rose when John Lester Wind appeared, through a separate entrance, and only sat down after he was seated.

There were nights when the Mayor resented J.L. Wind's real-world power and his office in the Town Hall, which the Mayor had never entered and knew he never would, but not tonight. Tonight, he could not have taken on what J.L. Wind was about to take on. *I'm not that kind of Mayor*, he told himself. *It's not the doing of actual things that I excel at.* If anything, he admired the single-minded clarity and dexterity J.L. Wind brought to his job, though he also pitied him for the limitation of his vision, extending, as it did, only across the surface of things.

The door opened again. In came Janitor Pete carrying a vacuum cleaner on his back. He looked over at the Mayor and nodded, then went into the booth to see if the cameraman needed help patching through the mics.

There was a stir—it was low-grade sacrilege to enter after the Acting Mayor was seated—but J.L. Wind waved it off.

"Let us begin," came his gentle but commanding voice. "As you well know, I relish the days of ritual as much as anyone here. If I could extend the Reunion through the long nights of Hibernation, and make it so that we could all remain together in the past and never have to be alone in the present, you know I would. But Hibernation comes for all of us, every year, and we must descend into our long sleep alone, with the weedy tendrils of the past loosed from our wrists and ankles. This is the price we pay to awaken into summer, refreshed for next year's Reunion.

"So. This meeting is a ritual of sorts, but it must be the last of the year. After tonight, no more reenactment until spring. Whatever dreams come to us during Hibernation, we must each accept and face up to them separately, and with courage. My ritual presence before you tonight is required, as we teeter collectively on the edge of Hibernation. But, within this ritual, I will avoid all

224

ritualized speech by improvising all that you'll hear me say. I write nothing down, and encourage you to do likewise, on this of all nights of the year. Preserve nothing, fetishize nothing. Convert nothing to Scripture. Sad but true: the protracted afterglow of the Reunion is behind us, and all is darkness outside. If you come to the podium to address this Council this evening, I very much hope you will do so without notecards and with no formal petition. All of us together, as a community, must fight as hard as we can against ritual if we wish to have any hope of moving together into the exhilarating unknown of the future rather than sinking into a past whose nature we will never decode, leaving us only the feeling that yesterday was better than any possible tomorrow. Once sunk deep enough into this state, none of us will ever escape, nor manage to summon the will to want to."

The Mayor was absolutely still.

"Our business tonight," Wind continued, "is to seal our borders once again. Until now, the lines between town and Outskirts, and between Outskirts and Inland Sea, have stood partially open. Our town has seen an unprecedented influx of Outskirt-dwellers." He would not say Sub-Weird, but the groans around the chamber made it clear that his meaning had been received. "It is not my duty tonight to condone or condemn this development. It is, rather, my duty to seal those borders anew. To say, 'The town is the town and the Outskirts is the Outskirts, and the things that go to seed out there do not drift back in to sprout anew in here.' Let me make myself absolutely clear: the Reunion is over.

"As we speak, a work crew is on the Meadow-lined Road, seeing to it that a blockade between the town and the Outskirts is erected."

A collective moan, combining relief with deep, fearful regret, filled the Council Chambers.

225

"It is time to recalibrate the compass that shows us where we are. Tonight we seal all entrances to the town, and suffer Hibernation together as a fixed quantity, with no further influx. We are all together inside a sphere. We bear our neighbors in the world, whoever and wherever they may be, no ill will, but we must re-attain the conviction that we are at the center, indeed that we are the center, of all existence, not only of our own. Of all time and space: we are the yolk. There is no other way to live.

"The time has come for this year's Reunion to fade into that same history it has, until now, sought to recoup. So I am here to say," here J.L. Wind made a show of pausing to decide, on the spot, what he was here to say, "that anyone currently in town will stay until spring, and everyone else, all those sailing the frigid wastes of the Inland Sea or wandering the concrete byways of the outer Outskirts, squatting in the abandoned bus station or the rooms of what was once the Motel, shall remain where they are, perpetually circling if our town be their destination. From this moment forth, until all the snow that has not yet fallen has melted, our town is a sealed tomb."

When J.L. Wind sat back down, the Council observed a moment of silence.

The Mayor could hear snow in the high clouds, preparing to fall now that the Acting Mayor had said it could.

Wind continued, from where he sat, "I want us tonight to work to regain not only the belief but the brute creaturely certainty that our lives are our own, and that they are happening now, and for the first time, and for the last time. Whatever foreign elements have entered our borders this autumn, we are not to let them pry from us the conviction that our lives are genuinely happening here in the town, in our bodies and the bodies of our friends, and not in some other place or realm that uses this town merely as a screen

226

onto which to project them.

"No, I say to you all tonight, our town is not a remote location, any more than the Earth itself is a remote location."

Wind's words were sinking into the Mayor. He was starting to feel the planet's tilt through the night, the old ship feeling that only came when the seriousness of life as it really was rose up clarified from the haze of desire. *J.L. Wind wants what's best for the whole town*, thought the Mayor, amazed, as ever, and a little frightened, at the existence of this spirit of generosity, and its affront to his own solipsism, which felt, in moments like this, both absolute and extremely fragile.

"I want you all to be real and to be alive here with me during the course of Hibernation, though we must all bear it alone. We must creep alone down into the jagged winter crevices where nothing but existence itself, in all of its majesty and perverse longing, is there to oxygenate us."

"We accept our Hibernation nightmares as inextricable from the majesty of all dreaming," continued Wind. His voice now had the tone of approaching an end. "We do not grow into adulthood because we hate childhood, we grow into adulthood because that very growing-into is what childhood entails. It is a directional state and it has led us here. We are the arrows' heads, and we must keep going at the speed we have attained, no matter the vertigo. These arrows will not submit to our commands. We must submit to theirs."

There was mixed applause in the room. From Wind's point of view, the less the better, for applause was a ritual like any other, another sticky seaweed tendril glommed onto a ship that could tolerate no downward pull if it hoped to reach land.

One of the old-timers who had been sitting restively got up to speak. "The Acting Mayor is wrong," he began. "No

227

disrespect intended, but he is wrong. The borders of our town are not closing now. They are opening wider. People are spilling out of the Outskirts faster than ever. And only ritual will consolidate in us what we are, against what they will try to make of us. We must stay awake this Hibernation in order to prolong the Reunion, to remind ourselves yet again of who we are. So as not awaken in spring and believe we have been newly born."

He delivered the last sentence in a croon, grasping his walker as it shook beneath him. "Do not take comfort in believing that our borders are sealed. Do not Hibernate when they tell you to." He returned to his seat with his head down.

"Thank you for your input," said J.L. Wind. "As everyone here knows well, the next Reunion is already being planned, but it will not occur until we have undergone Hibernation and made it to the far side in good health."

This said, he announced a fifteen-minute recess, after which the Council would consider New Business.

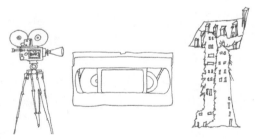

Monday Night

The Mayor went outside planning to come back in, but after the stuffiness of the Council Chambers, the pregnant winter air went to his head and he tripped down the hill to his car. As he opened the door and settled in behind the wheel, he decided he couldn't take anymore. He'd gotten what he could from the meeting; nothing else J.L. Wind could say would keep Hibernation from coming, or make it any easier to bear when it did.

He drove into the lot behind the Greek restaurant and called Ben at the Hotel, asking if he wanted to come over. He didn't want to be alone tonight, nor was he ready for another night in the Dead Houses. He had the feeling that if he didn't keep up a minimum of contact with the adult Ben and James, his contact with their boy-counterparts would veer from the obsessive to the insane, and he wasn't sure he wanted to know what lay on the far side of that.

Ben said that'd be fine, and suggested they invite James as well.

Soon thereafter, Ben and James were both in the Mayor's car, remarking on the redness of the night sky and the snow that was about to fall as they cruised up the Strip.

They were patient in the back seat, speaking a little just to warm up, not expecting to be heard by the Mayor. They knew it could take him a while to acclimate to no longer being alone, and weren't strangers to this condition themselves.

They stopped for beer. Inside the store, Saltwater watched as much of them as he could without moving his eyes or neck, tapping one finger in time to the anonymous background music that had come on the radio to cover Well's absence.

Incense burned from under the desk, where Saltwater probably also kept a gun. There were a few other people in the store, moving slowly and reeking of sweat. Ben, James, and the Mayor all recognized them as Sub-Weird, but only the Mayor knew they'd been sealed into the town, no longer on an open back-and-forth with the Outskirts, and only Ben knew they were loading up on beer to bring back to the Town's City, where by now they had

229

established a rudimentary culture.

They wore the same loose T-shirts and cargo pants they'd worn at the Reunion, impervious to the cold or willing to suffer it. While Ben and the Mayor regarded them, James loaded up on two bottles of vodka and a six-pack of beer, and took them to the register, where the Mayor eventually paid.

They pulled up the driveway and got out, carrying food along with their beer. It was in the thirties already, jacket and hat weather, but not yet too cold for a bonfire.

They carried everything straight to the backyard without going inside first.

Soon the fire was snarling at its meat and they all three had open beers, toasting their makeshift Sabbath. There was no discussion of the Town Council Meeting, but it was clear to all three that tonight was the last of something, tomorrow the first of something else.

"May the sanest man go crazy, may the craziest man survive!" the Mayor shouted, as usual. They raised their bottles and drained them.

When the meat was ready, they served themselves and stayed mostly quiet, eating and drinking, looking at the sky as it sagged so low it looked like a curtain. Their thoughts splayed out across it, away from one another, and then drifted back, syncing up for a moment before diverging again.

James rambled about his regimen at the Gym, how he'd let his body go but was now getting it back. "I do twelve reps of 160 on the bench, then eight curls with each arm with the 37.5 dumbbells, then another eight reps on the bench at 180, then"... He didn't mention the Mountain, or his hives, though both Ben and the Mayor could see him wincing as he tried to show off his new physique in the firelight.

Ben mentioned that he'd rented an office without any word about what he was doing there.

For the Mayor, it was a game to resist asking James about the Movie, which was all he wanted to talk about. He wanted to shout, *Speak in abstractions if you have nothing concrete to say*, but what came out when he opened his mouth was, "We should all do this more often."

No one answered. The sky was about to burst.

Looking at it, the Mayor felt sick, and scared, like he was about to be snowed in forever, cut off forever from... he had to admit it... Squimbop.

"Excuse me," he said, rolling his beer bottle against the rocks at the edge of the fire pit as Ben and James started on the vodka.

He went into the house and turned on all the lights. Then he warmed up the hot tub, removing the foam cover with one hand and his pants with the other.

He stood by the window, naked from the waist down, and looked out at them mute and motionless by the fire. Then he wiped burger grease on his thighs and thought about his Orchard rotting downstairs.

The water of this hot tub comes all the way from the Pornography, he reassured himself. It beeped when it reached 110 degrees.

The windows were fully fogged-over.

He took a deep chlorine breath and slipped in, affording himself a moment of relaxation before closing his eyes.

As soon as he closed them, in came a vision of Squimbop fucking him hard from behind as he knelt frozen on the mattress in ANGEL HOUSE, staring up at the children mashed against the ceiling, dripping tallow into his open mouth.

231

He hoisted himself out of the water just before Squimbop came and ANGEL HOUSE claimed him forever. His joints felt ready to crumble at the pressure of the floor against them, and he almost slipped forward and split the glass doors with his forehead.

Grabbing a towel and wrapping it around his waist, he ran barefoot across his backyard, yelling for help. "Get up! Help me get in my bed! Fuck the Blind Spot tonight!" he yelled, snot pouring from his nose.

But when he got to the fire pit, Ben and James were gone and a ring of bears had closed in.

They looked up as he approached, mouths glowing orange. It took him half a minute to realize they were eating the fire, swallowing whole burning coals to get at the meat drippings beneath. Their tan hides glowed like fine leather in the firelight and they looked right at the Mayor before turning back to the fire, chewing and swallowing in tremendous mouthfuls, sparks dripping down their chins. One held the last burning log in its mouth, flames pouring from its whole face as it bit the log in half and ate both before either hit the ground.

The Mayor let his towel drop and followed the bears to his car, his naked ass spreading out on the cold seat. He shifted into neutral and began to drift down the driveway, the sky pouring snow over him like a frozen hurricane.

He didn't bother turning his wipers on.

PART IV
Hibernation

Deep inside ANGEL HOUSE as the snow pounded down, Squimbop opened his laptop, checked the cameras (all of which showed only white), and composed an email.

Dear Master,

All motion, all endeavor, in this town has ceased. The period they refer to as Hibernation has arrived, immediately following a brief, manic hyperphagia, a desperate gorging on and consumption of all the food Ultra Max had to offer. The constant nervous energy of autumn has petered out, presumably to heat up again in spring, though I cannot say how long from now that will be.

The two children I referred to earlier are still at large. Without knowing precisely how, I can say that I feel them gaining power, much as I regret to inform you of this.

Given that school is closed and thus no consistent opportunity to deliver Lecture to them exists, I intend to don the giant fur coat you instructed me to use in emergencies and, thus cloaked, allow Death to manifest itself through me in the physical sense. Perhaps the sight of me in this gruesome aspect will be enough to unhinge their resistance.

All for now,

Prof. Sq.

He closed his laptop and lay down, hands behind his head, already aware that he wouldn't be sleeping tonight. Staring at the ceiling, basking in the scent of tallow, he felt as small and as lost as he'd ever felt.

He hated this point in the year, which seemed to always come, though he knew he couldn't trust his memory. Still, whatever the truth of his past was, he hated this moment, when it seemed he'd been in town as long as he could bear and yet no end was in sight. The school year—even if only two children remained—had to be seen to its end, despite feeling like he'd already said all there was to say.

And even if he did break the stragglers, he knew there was no guarantee he'd be let out. No guarantee, even, that there'd be anywhere to be let out to. All he had to go on were his memories of the Totally Other Place and these, already vague, were fading fast.

What does it look like there? he wondered. *Where did I live? With whom?*

He knew these questions were dangerous, blasphemous even, but each led to another, in a spiral he was now deep inside of: *How did I start doing this? Who roped me in? Was there some other life before it? Will there be any life after?*

It all hinged on one of his emails being returned, someone out there writing back.

He gagged on the meaty tallow in the air and felt Death closing in on ANGEL HOUSE, emanating from him, as ever, but no longer pointing solely outward.

Just keep it from warping in… he thought. *No matter what, keep it from turning on you…*

He was in a bath of sweat now, swimming on his mattress, half-lost in a dream of drowning in the Inland Sea, alone and shivering in the infinite dark expanse, the makings of a billion new towns strewn in the sand below.

He rolled out of bed, trembling, and took his laptop into the bathroom, locking the door as if otherwise someone might see him.

He opened it, spread it across his lap though it burned his thighs, and began to compose a new email.

Dear Master,

I was not entirely frank in my previous communication. I have not, I hate to say, been feeling as put together lately as I would like to. I know Death is within me, and that it is my duty to mete it out on the people of this town, but I can't suppress the fear that it will consume me as well. How can I be sure it won't? How can I be sure it hasn't already? I don't want to close my eyes, I don't want to be here anymore, I don't want to face these people anymore, I don't want to walk these streets anymore, I don't want to taunt the children that remain anymore.

Please help me,

Prof. Sq.

He took his hands off the keyboard, panting. After catching his breath, he highlighted everything he'd just written, looked away from the screen, and deleted it. Only when he was sure it was gone did he peel the laptop off his scalded thighs and place it on the ground beneath the toilet.

Then he got into the shower, relieved both at having written the email and at having found the presence of mind to delete it. Now, not only would he be spared the risk of accidentally sending it off, he'd be spared the calamity of accidentally rereading it, when he was more awake and once again determined to play the role he'd been assigned.

235

Stepping out of the shower, Squimbop put on the giant winter coat with a fur hood that resided in the backmost part of the ANGEL HOUSE Master Bedroom's walk-in closet. Then he stepped into his red leather boots and went outside.

He wandered through town in the red pre-dawn, in the direction of the Dead Neighborhood, stopping at a small, secondary park just before the hill grew steep. He spent the day, and all the early days of Hibernation, sitting beside a frozen pond full of goldfish in this park, sprinkling bread crumbs on the ice.

With the School closed, there were no constraints on his time except that the Totally Other Place still started its Lecture drip every night. Since he had no audience to deliver these Lectures to in the morning, he took to sitting by the pond and whispering into the bread he balled up and tossed to the fish, who came up from the water to stare at it on the other side of the ice, kissing the solid membrane with open mouths.

Though he'd skipped the Town Council Meeting, J.L. Wind's sealing of the town's borders was palpable in the air. It felt like a natural facet of Hibernation: things were close in now, dense, no longer sprawling. The snow had been falling without cease, piled higher than all of the buildings except the Town's City, which now jutted into the white sky like the only remnant of a swallowed metropolis.

All the houses had cut their doors out of the snowbanks, leaving the rest of their shapes covered. Squimbop pictured this snowbank settlement as a port on the coast of the Inland Sea, frozen solid during a rare Ice Age, so that a foreign population from the far side could cross on foot to this one, only to be stranded here once the ice melted.

He missed Well and sometimes even missed going to the School and imparting his Lecture to the duo. The rest of the

236

children were little more than bags by now, dripping tallow onto the carpet, which he scraped up with a spatula and used to season his beef, letting it numb his lips and tongue as he savored the taste of animal.

Under his fur hood, he was reverting to a more ancient version of himself, whatever he'd been before he was cast as a Professor.

As soon as it got dark and the Totally Other Place began to drip Lecture into his head, he closed his eyes on the bench by the pond to nap for a few hours before beginning the night's work.

When he woke up, in the aggressive pitch black, he trudged up the hill to the park in the heart of the Dead Neighborhood, climbed aboard the wooden ship and put his hands on the Wooden Wheel, in clear view of the camera he'd installed on his first day here.

He avoided looking into it. Instead, he looked from one Dead House to the other as the duo tried to sleep, their faces against the windows beside their beds, their eyelids beginning to flutter.

His body had thickened. Some of the fur from his hood melded with his head and neck, and his canines had lengthened into fangs.

This was a necessary defense against the Dead Houses, which exuded a coldness all their own, deeper than that of Hibernation. As he steered the Wooden Wheel, looking from one Dead House to the next, with the Mayor gulping hot chocolate downstairs in one of them, he imagined not only piloting ANGEL HOUSE across the Inland Sea but also piloting the night through the universe, toward the shores of the following day, moving fast enough to prevent ice from choking it in.

The Night's Rudder, he thought. *Sailing us one night*

closer to the thaw.

He knew the nine-year-olds could feel it moving, the whole vessel rocking in choppy surf, but the Mayor, sitting in those kitchens looking lonely enough to beg for oblivion, never once looked out the window in his direction. *He probably still believes the town's night moves through him,* Squimbop thought, feeling both disgust and pity for the man.

A couple of bears prowled through the park as Squimbop steered, rooting up frozen trash while they waited for the Mayor to come out.

Squimbop's alarm went off and he jolted up on his Mattress Store mattress, staring at the closet where his fur-hooded coat hung ready. It had grown so large the door wouldn't close, its arms swelling out like some creature beckoning him in.

He hit Snooze.

The Totally Other Place hadn't responded to any of his emails, so he was under no compulsion to put the coat back on, but he'd gone so far into becoming the Figure of Death that he would've felt naked in the night without it.

When the alarm went off again, he got up, scratching at the fur on his back as he pissed and looked at the shower, which, with no need to firm his Lecture into words anymore, he hadn't used in weeks. He pulled the coat over his naked body and put his boots on and left, nibbling a piece of tallow as he crossed the frozen Meadow, exhaling steam whose heat he couldn't feel.

He turned to look at the Mountain and saw a light shining from its summit. He waved, in case whoever was up there could see him.

In town, parked cars were furry with snow. The streets and sidewalks were no longer discernible; the only paths were the zigzags the plow had managed to cut between blizzards, widened by the feet of the denizens of the Town's City, who came down to wander in the deep nights, groping along the Strip to Ultra Max, which remained open on Ultra-Low-Maintenance Mode.

In the Dead Neighborhood, the snowbanks were lower due to the altitude and the cold was doubled. He could feel the wide, hollow bones of Death setting beneath his giant coat, crowding out the last of whatever in him had been human. Fringed in the fur of his hood, his face was so drained of color he could've seen his dripping Lecture in a mirror.

He climbed behind the Wooden Wheel and put his hands on either side of it. They froze solid, as did his legs and torso, and all the muscles of his face. Only his neck retained mobility, able to swivel from one Dead House to the other. He could see the Mayor sitting alone in one of the kitchens, looking longingly at the stairs in hopes one of the nine-year-olds would come down. And he could see the nine-year-olds in their windows, heads turned toward him, eyes closed, fighting their way into the Pretend Movie.

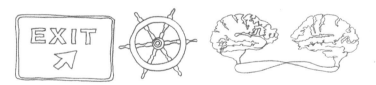

The duo slept by their respective windows, facing out across the Wooden Wheel, where the Figure of Death now stood steering the night, glowering up at them from his position at the helm.

They dipped in and out of the Pretend Movie, pushing their way down only to bounce back up. Over the weeks of Hibernation so far, whenever they'd gotten down deep enough to cross over, they found the nineteen-year-olds sluggish and indifferent.

Lying around in their hotel room, rationing their weed and idly contemplating James' offer of $50,000 apiece, the nineteen-year-olds felt no urgency to act. They did little but eat room service—Giant Chinese wouldn't deliver until spring, so they were stuck with whatever the Hotel had in its freezers—and pace back and forth on the orange carpeting, swearing and taking turns staring out the window at the buried Town Square and the eerie lights of the Town's City. A visit to the Night School might have held some appeal, but there was no way to get there except through the tunnels under the Hotel, and as soon as they reentered these, they'd be charged with resuming the duty of Escape. So they laid low.

The nine-year-olds did what they could, as Directors, to motivate the scene, but their influence was remote; as far as the nineteen-year-olds were concerned, they were the distant memories of their nine-year-old selves, now no more than a nagging sense of the ambitions they had ten years ago. *Fuck all that,* they thought, sprawled on the bed, staring at the dusty ceiling fan. *No one becomes what they dreamed of becoming. So fucking what?*

On many Hibernation days, it seemed to the nineteen-year-olds that there was little to do but wait around to die, which was fine by them. The only dispiriting thing was that it might take decades. *Life is short, but not short enough*, they thought.

What did they need with James' money anyway? There was nothing to buy in this town, and the effort of getting back in their car and making the trek to another seemed so difficult it bled into the impossible. *And even if we do get there,* they thought, *what's to say that the next town won't be the same as this one?*

So nothing happened until the Figure of Death took up his position behind the Wooden Wheel outside the nine-year-olds' windows.

Now they were writhing in bed, one of them dimly aware of the Mayor downstairs, the other lost in the silence of his Dead House, thinking about the Pretend Movie without making any progress on it. They pictured their Pine Hedge Office at school, empty and frozen-over, or populated by wolves, bedding down in the snow that had covered their sleeping bags, indifferent to the maps and charts that hung from the branches.

The night dragged on, exhausting but promising no rest, as they pulled their blankets up over their heads and tried to count to a million, getting lost around one hundred and fifty. Their heads filled with fog and static; they roiled. As a last resort, they tried to imagine the dawn, hoping that, if they worked hard enough, it would eventually come. Then, at least, they'd be able to go downstairs and face another day of sitting and pacing around and eating cereal at the kitchen table.

But after an hour or so they got confused and let the image of the rising sun slip their minds. Now they were in darkness again, on their feet, approaching their matching staircases. *We're back in the Pretend Movie!* they managed to think, before losing all sense of self and surrendering to the mission at hand.

They walked down the stairs, step by creaking step, seeking the buried tunnels, determined to resume their exploration, with or without the nineteen-year-olds. They pictured the entire *Dream of Escape* as a single tremendous staircase, leading down, past the warmth of their beds, past the warmth of their kitchens and the Mayor sitting, half asleep, at one of their tables, past the doorway that led into the snow, past the snow itself, down to the Earth, and under the Earth, down to where it melted into the Pornography and then the Inland Sea, oriented, as they could feel everything was, around the ANGEL HOUSE anchor.

They'd crossed the threshold. They felt snow and ice underfoot, creaking, breaking as they descended more steps, into a silent, ambient blackness tinged with purple.

They marched forward, unsure whether what they were seeing came from inside or outside their dream. They saw, dimly, a giant ship, an ark, bobbing in an almost-frozen brine, colossal, the largest floating structure there was or could ever be. It loomed in front of them, surrounded by purple darkness and gruesome cold, and they thought, *If we can only get aboard, maybe we can take the wheel and sail it through the tunnels… maybe that way lies Escape.*

Giddy, ignoring the pain that had spread from their feet to their ankles to their knees, they ran toward it, putting all the rest of what they had into the approach, thinking—in some pre-verbal, dinosaur part of their brains—that if they could only get aboard, the rest would take care of itself. They could be the Captains if they could only take the wheel.

So they ran faster, flapping their arms and almost swimming in the thickened air, hurling themselves at the flank of the ark as they got close, digging their nails in, climbing its frozen mass, until they landed, spent and numb on its deck, where they blacked out.

Sometime later, they came to.

Beneath them, the deck had turned to wood and they could hear, from behind, the creaking of the Wooden Wheel. The winter sun had started to rise. For one second, they were allowed to think, in peace: *We made this journey as us, not the nineteen-year-olds… we sleepwalked… somehow, we entered the Pretend Movie without losing ourselves in it.*

Then a pain like the full-fang bite of a bone-snake tore into their spines and they were on their feet, frozen solid, paralyzed and staring into the Face of Death.

The face, ringed in the copious fur of its hood and bearing its wolf fangs proudly, resembled Squimbop's only in its core malevolence and something about its cheekbones. And the mustache. Beyond that, the Figure of Death was its own being, more potent than their Professor had ever been. An entity that was Death, rather than one that merely knew about it.

They remained fixed in place when it put them down and returned to the Wooden Wheel, tilting it side-to-side, grinning at them. "Did you really expect to sail out of here just like that?" It smiled, adjusting its coat, flaunting the protection it had that they did not.

Then it put its face up to theirs again, close enough that they could smell its hot wolf breath, and said, "There's only one way out of here. ANGEL HOUSE. With all the others. You think you're better than them? You're not. Die out here or live in there. That's the only choice you have."

It smiled again and turned, climbing down from the ship and striding across the park, off into the Dead Neighborhood where it must have felt more at home than the duo ever would.

We are actually vulnerable, they thought, when they finally began to thaw and regain control of their nerves. They fell on their faces on the wooden deck, and lay there, spines soft as jelly.

We can die. The Pretend Movie can die. We have to get moving, with or without the nineteen-year-olds. We'll never outrun the Figure of Death, but that doesn't mean we have to crawl to ANGEL HOUSE on our knees.

When it got too cold to lie there any longer, they got to their feet, helping each other back across the park and into their separate Dead Houses, crossing the spot where the Mayor's station wagon had been.

Back inside, their minds detached now, they each found

243

themselves shivering so violently their lips bled. Their fingers could barely hold the cartons as they poured the last of their milk and stirred in hot cocoa mix, putting their mugs in the microwave for ninety seconds, closing their eyes and praying to live at least that much longer.

James pulled on his mesh shorts and laced up his sneakers. He jogged a few laps around his kitchen, downed a glass of water, and opened his front door onto a wall of snow. He stood before it, letting the fact that it was still Hibernation dawn on him. When it had, he went back inside and sat down on the stairs and took his shoes off.

This was the high point of his day. Another day without the Gym, another day when no film work except the endless accrual of notes would get done. He spent the afternoon and evening in Hibernation twilight, in the reclining chair in his office on the top floor, fingering his shrinking hives and looking out the windows at the walls of snow, thinking, *I'm in a small house inside a much bigger house made of snow, like my whole house is just one of its rooms and I'll never know who lives in the others.*

He hadn't seen or spoken with Ben or the Mayor since their night by the fire. Hibernation, so far, had been spent alone, eating the containers of Giant Chinese he'd been smart enough to freeze before they stopped delivering, and drinking more coffee than he ever had before, despite the threat of supplies running out. The house filled with anxiety during these sludgy, short Hibernation days and weary but restless nights, as he traipsed around licking his coffee-teeth and kicking Giant Chinese containers up and down the stairs, sometimes slipping on the grease and lying in it for an hour or two before getting up.

Whatever his film turned out to be, whether or not he found a means of processing his trip with Well and the appearance of the Blankheads—and whether or not the nineteen-year-olds ever got back in touch—it would only reach fruition at the Gym. From his current perspective, stranded in this rented house, that much was clear. The promise of the Gym, heated and institutionally lit and fraught with no one's homing stink, its air burned pure by chlorine, was the one solace during this interminable lull.

He was up in his office now, thinking in the dark with a blanket over his lap, beside a mug of cold coffee. Film notes were all around him in the dark, draped over surfaces, on the floor, on the windowsills. The film would bear no stamp of its place of origin. No gross half-limbs or vestigial tail, no sticky residue of the town and the years it'd given him and Ben, the cargo of undigested myth it'd left them with.

It might be filmed in the town, using the Mayor's money, but it would be about something else. It would prove that any and every place is just a place, and that anything can happen anywhere, anyone can come, do what they choose, and leave, go anywhere else, without being bound to it or even needing to remember having been there.

It would be a film about simple, pared-down beings, juxtaposed against landscapes that were nothing but backgrounds, or chalk outlines on the floor. It would expose the Psychogeography insofar as it would render explicit, through set design, the internal connections between the places and mental states in the town that he and Ben had discovered while making their Pretend Movie

245

twenty years ago.

The only difference will be its reality, James found himself thinking again, aware that he was losing his mind and that if he didn't get out soon, someone would have to bear him away in spring. He took out a notepad and wrote, *The film will be all of a piece, positing no clash between the natural and the supernatural, treating both realms or levels as equally real, the Blankheads as the true denizens of the town, which has always felt haunted, always felt like a place apart, riddled with demons that none of us could see until…*

His fingers were sweating as he pressed down: *All my actors will take on the life of a beast and the life of a man at once, to the point where the desire to posit any distinction between one state and the next will be laughably confounded. If you need to believe that humans are human, you'll have to leave, you will not be able to watch my film. It will not be for you.*

A moment later, he wrote Yep in pink highlighter over everything he'd just written, accepting that he'd never get to sleep without a long soak in the hot tub: *Time to go back to the Gym*, he wrote, rendering the whole page illegible.

Once again James pulled on his mesh shorts and laced up his sneakers. He jogged around the kitchen, downed a glass of water, and opened the front door into the snowbank.

Taking a series of increasingly deep breaths, he gathered his energy and plunged into the wall of white.

It burned his skin as he tore through, and the ice crystals cut into him like shards of glass, shredding his sneakers, but he got inside. He was running down in it now, eyes closed, summoning the ancient tunnel-knowledge he'd earned working on the Pretend Movie. He barreled along, veering left and right whenever it felt like time to, expanding the map of the town in his mind, zooming

246

in on it, fighting for clarity, begging the Psychogeography to stitch him together with the Gym as painlessly as possible.

He could taste blood on his upper lips and dripping down from his forehead, and he knew the soles of his feet would need a long, hot soak before he could walk on them again.

Please, he thought, invoking the Psychogeography again. This time he was begging. *You are the only map that matters. The mind-map of the town is the only map in my mind...*

This was what it took. The Psychogeography cracked open, sucked him through the tunnels of snow, and spat him out at the door of the Gym.

He panted on the mat for a moment, then shoved his way through, breaking one of the frozen-shut doors and landing in the lobby. He breathed in the sweat, concrete, and chlorine smell that he'd been looking forward to for weeks. It cleared his sinuses and dried his blood, returning him fully to the company of the living.

He limped to the front desk and was leaning against it when Janitor Pete came out, carrying a substantial pile of wires and cords.

They exchanged hellos and James apologized for showing up like this, saying only that he'd reached a breaking point in his house. "What about you, though?"

"What?"

"What are you doing here during Hibernation?"

Janitor Pete smiled, rubbing his thin grey goatee. "Where do you think I live?"

James had never thought about it. He shrugged. Changing the subject, he asked about the wires.

"Ripping out the Movie Room."

"The Movie Room?"

"Used to show things from the Movie Store to the children

247

after school when they were around. Not much point now."

James nodded, picturing the Mayor sauntering in alone with a bowl of brownie batter in the middle of the night.

"Gym's weird and empty without them." Janitor Pete caught a rolled wire that was about to whip out of his arms. "Always liked to see them trooping in to watch something just before sundown. It's like the whole reason we have Hibernation is because they're gone… like it'd be summer if they were still here."

James didn't reply. He stood there until his cut feet grew too slippery to balance on. Then he hobbled off to the hot tub.

"Lot of trash this all amounts to, huh?"

After dumping both armfuls of wires in a doorway off a corridor James had never seen before, Janitor Pete turned on the lights in a spacious white room he'd unlocked in the dark.

James had come to find him after emerging from the hot tub, wearing another Sub-Weird outfit he found in one of the lockers. This time, it was black jeans and a baggy sweatshirt embossed with the Ultra Max logo.

He followed Janitor Pete on several more trips around the basketball court and back and forth along this corridor, which ran up the far side of the racquetball courts. All the trappings of the Movie Room—more wires, screens, piles of hand-lettered tapes, speakers, and rolling carts—ended up in a pile in the center of this white room, which was possibly an old racquetball court. It had that shape and size.

In the middle of one of these trips, both of them panting, Janitor Pete stopped and said, "Hey, you want this space to work on your Movie in?"

Without stopping to think, James said that he did.

My Director's Hive, he thought, as Janitor Pete showed him two other doors that connected to this room. One led back

248

to the basketball court and the other opened onto a corridor that went all the way down to the basement and the sub-basement, which he and Ben had always imagined opening onto the network of tunnels underlying the town, yet another cusp point between the real streets and the Pretend Movie.

"It's where the heating and electrical equipment, gas meters, gauges, and the pumps that control the water level and temperature in the pools and hot tub are kept," Janitor Pete added, pulling James back from the brink of reverie.

After showing him all this, Janitor Pete dragged a long graphite folding table from the corridor into the room, opening its legs so that they straddled the wires and other equipment in the center, then pushing down on it until it settled flat.

"You'll be very quiet in here. No one will be able to hear you," he told James. It wasn't a question. "You'll only come to the Gym at night from now on."

James nodded, unable to picture himself ever leaving, as Janitor Pete pried a key from his ring and handed it over. "There you go. Now... make Movies!"

He seemed slightly nervous as he hurried out, back to wherever in the building he slept.

James sat behind the desk for a long time, wondering what being a real Director felt like. Someone with actual power, and a plan, in the real world.

The Gym was his now: Janitor Pete may as well have handed over the deed. He could swim and lift until he could barely move, then soak in the hot tub until his head got so heavy it almost drowned him with his feet sticking up into the room's cold air.

Then he could dry off, massaging his shrunken hives, and come to his desk to shuffle ideas around until dawn.

He could write them down or not. Either way, he felt sharp in a way he never had in his rented house.

And when the nineteen-year-olds showed up for work, if they ever did, the place would be ready for every scene they were in.

My film will have no exteriors, he reminded himself. *Nothing of the real town will penetrate.* James loved the Mayor, in a way, but not enough to make the kind of film he wanted now that the allure of abstraction had taken root. If he could put his man-hours toward burying his adolescence forever, rather than preserving it in amber for the Mayor's sake, perhaps he'd finally succeed in breaking through to the rest of his life.

Back in his Sub-Weird costume in the locker room, James realized he would need a Director's suit to wear in his new office. A few suits, for different moods. His mind was accelerating as the magnitude of Janitor Pete's gift sunk in.

Energized by the prospect of a shopping spree, he laced his shredded sneakers and visualized his route through Ultra Max, without which it was impossible to make it in and out in less than twenty-four hours: he'd need new clothes, and also more paper and pens, tapes, audio gear, and camera accessories.

And he'd wander through the Hometown—Ultra Max's fully-rendered model version of the town, where all the props and backgrounds were for sale—picking up whatever he needed to build an environment for the nineteen-year-olds to inhabit. Though Ben was the architect, James was determined not to involve him in the film's set design this time around. He had to believe that, at this point in their lives, they could achieve more alone than they ever had together.

He set out jogging through the utter cold, along the street where the mansions of the long-dead Town Fathers stood empty. They were so far behind their iron gates, and buried so deep in the snowbanks, that their driveways looked like roads to other towns.

Past this, running on the tops of the snowbanks as best he could, climbing out whenever he fell in, he cut through a frozen-over park and emerged onto the Strip, passing Saltwater's, the Night School, the Mattress Store, then a series of barely plowed yards, before turning into the open expanse of the Ultra Max lot, the wind tearing across it. Nothing was parked there tonight.

In the Ultra Max foyer, the fluorescent light bouncing off the white tiles, James felt time stand still. No one was present aside from a few guards and cashiers. The whole place was on Ultra-Low-Maintenance Mode—whole aisles were dark, and many of the shelves bore only tags stating what they used to contain.

Ultra Max wasn't a safe space, but it had always been a space apart, a backstage area where all the costumes and tools were stored, so that the true theater of the town couldn't occur within its massively distant walls. Everything here was on Pause. *Until I get what I need and carry it out of here, I will stand outside my life,* James thought, feeling his cold, wet hair warm at the prospect. *I will momentarily cease running out of time.*

The few people here were dead-eyed Hibernation sleepwalkers, Sub-Weird with untied shoelaces and no socks, their jackets hanging off their shoulders and halfway down their backs like the capes of a long-defeated army. Some had clearly been here all day and would be all night. Maybe some had been here since autumn and would remain until spring. He shivered at the thought, smelling the chlorine on his skin and in his hair. He probably looked enough like them at this point that he could easily be mistaken for one, so the smell of another place was a reassuring buffer.

251

He bought a tub of popcorn at the snack bar so big he needed two hands to hold it, and thus had to put down all the sundries he'd gathered so far.

Like so, he reentered the aisles, wandering past fishing rods, plastic pools, golf clubs, and row after row of guns, the toy guns and the real freely interspersed. He sat down in a foldout fishing chair set up before a demo flat-screen TV, eating his popcorn and watching the colors and shapes on the screen boil and fry.

Someone bought the TV from under his eyes, so he was left staring at dust on the shelf.

He ate from the tub with his face until the popcorn was too low to reach. Then he abandoned it where the TV had been and started gathering items again.

He bought matching jeans and sweatshirts and sneakers for the nineteen-year-olds, at first guessing their size and then deciding, *No... I'm the Director. I tell them what size to wear.* He pictured them as blow-up dolls he could inflate or deflate at will.

This accomplished, he started trying on suits. The options were cheap and poorly tailored, made of coarse grey fiber, but they would work. He stripped naked in the middle of the racks and pulled the pants on, then the jackets, without a shirt.

He looked at his belly in the mirror, flexing to maximum definition. Not bad, but there was still polishing to be done. In the coming weeks, he'd have to firm up to a level he'd never before reached.

He gathered three matching pairs of pants and jackets, deciding that his uniform would not involve a shirt underneath. Each suit would hang in its own locker now that the whole Gym was his.

Wearing the last suit he'd tried on, he stuffed his old costume into a tent in the Camping section and entered the HOMETOWN, beneath the slogan that read *Where We're From.*

Were he not trying to flatten his belly, he'd be drinking a 24oz beer as he walked, like he and Ben always had while wandering these pretend streets at this hour. You could take the cans right off the shelves with no one to ask your age, so from nine onward, he and Ben had availed themselves liberally.

He pulled out a rolling pallet from the stack by the Hometown entrance (the area marked *Outskirts*), and pushed it inside, piling his suits and other acquisitions on top.

Crossing from the main aisles of Ultra Max into the Hometown, the floor sloped downward so that the ceiling got higher and higher. Soon, he was deep enough in that he couldn't see over the cardboard walls. The lights overhead were dark, simulating night.

Each storefront and building was for sale. Piles of collapsed cardboard models were tucked under those that were set up, marked with ID numbers.

Plastic streetlights, also for sale, lit the way. .

He crossed the model Town Square, with the model Hotel and Greek restaurant on either side. He grabbed one of each, picturing them deployed on the basketball court. Then he grabbed a model Night School, a model Mattress Store, and a model Saltwater's liquor store. He even grabbed a model Ultra Max, which came in three connecting cardboard pieces and would require the whole basketball court to set up.

When he passed the Town's City, adorned with a sign that read NEW!!, he saw a gaggle of Sub-Weird on their knees, staring at the windows as if they believed they could see their relatives inside.

James peered in, looking for Ben, but the feeling of falling into a Sub-Weird Session made him recoil, so he set off in the other direction, dragging his pallet into the dark of the model of the Meadow-lined Road, toward the Meadow and, behind that, the Mountain.

In the center of the Meadow, where Well's Ghost Town used to be, was a sign that read OUT OF STOCK.

Behind that, the Mountain was pasted onto the cardboard wall that separated the Hometown from the rest of Ultra Max. James stared at it, trying to see Well on top, wondering if he was still alive up there.

Loaded up on all these items, he felt his denial deepen as he approached the register. "It's not that I want to model the town in my film," he told the checkout boy. "It's just that I want to model a town, any town, and this is all there is."

"Will that be credit or debit?" the checkout boy asked.

James floundered for a moment before he remembered how to answer. "Just put it on the Mayor's tab."

He dragged his pallet out into the snow and all the way back to the Gym with no intention of returning it.

Throughout these same hours, Ben sat in his office with his drafting paper and pen, looking out the window at the parade route, fallow now that the Outskirts had been sealed. Some days, if there was a breeze and the snow wasn't falling, he could open his window and smell the emptiness of the Outskirts, ashy, almost sulfurous in the frozen air.

He tried not to remember last year's Hibernation, when he'd been so deep in drafting the Town's City that he would look out his Hotel window and fail to recognize the town.

This year, his problem wasn't too little recognition of his surroundings, but too much. In the absence of a tangible project, the days went on and on, endlessly taking him past the same handful of places, rarely culminating in sleep. When he closed his eyes now, his thoughts looped back to the Motel he'd walked past during the Reunion. Without opening them, he drew a crude approximation of it on his drafting sheet, like an idea for a structure that didn't yet exist. He drew with the pen in his left hand and rubbed what he'd drawn with his right, after letting the ink dry for a second, pretending the fingers on that hand were people exploring the space that had just been created for them.

He continued like this for an hour, opening his eyes occasionally to orient his pen, but always drawing with them closed. When he stopped, he'd drawn the complete Motel with a face in every window. Looking at the image as a whole, he realized he'd drawn it starting in the middle of the sheet rather than the bottom, so that it appeared to be floating.

What is it floating on? he asked himself, already aware that the answer was, *the Town's City,* but enjoying these last moments of indeterminacy before the decision would be made and he'd be compelled to act on it.

When these moments were over, he accepted, with the resignation of a man finally conceding that fate is real, that the Motel would take its place on the streets of the Town's City, off to the side of the Square and the Greek restaurant, a thousand feet above the town. Inherent in this resignation, he knew, though he chose not to dwell on the knowledge for long, was the fact that he'd never return to News City. He wasn't ready to go so far as

255

to say that he'd never been there at all, but he knew now that building a Motel in the Town's City would mean building himself a permanent home, here in the town, or just above it.

He decided to walk back to the actual Motel to study its construction. As much as possible, his design would mimic the Motel that already existed, transposing it like a puzzle piece into a gap in the Town's City, drawing the whole work that much closer to perfection.

He sat at his desk a while longer, marveling at how much was doable in a good hour, but how rare these hours were. Picturing the abandoned street, the thought of going out there into it, into the zone he'd spent so long watching the Sub-Weird parade through, made him sad and tired, but he shook it off, knowing it wasn't a tiredness that would end in sleep.

Collecting his wallet and gun and big boots and heavy coat and hat and gloves, he walked out the window of his office and onto a snowbank he could follow all the way up the Meadow-lined Road.

It took him far less time to get to the Motel than it had during the Reunion, despite the instability of the snowbank beneath him. This time he went straight there, rather than circling until it drew him in. Even though the Reunion was less than six months ago, his sense of space and time back then seemed childish compared to now.

He felt his gun in his pants but no longer expected to use it, nor quite remembered why he thought he would ever have to. This time, he came in peace and expected the Outskirts to welcome him.

The old Prophet-feeling that the Outskirts used to stir in him was in remission now that the Reunion was supposedly over and the Outskirts closed, but he was starting to think that building himself a home within the Town's City might bring it back. *I'll live as a lodger among the neighborhoods of the Sub-Weird, and thereby find a place within my design, a room to inhabit that will not require me to join their culture, but will permit me to discover my prophecy and share it with them, from a position of power.*

If not for the NO CLEANING OF DEER OR OTHER GAME IN GUEST BATHTUBS sign, he would have missed the turn-off in the snow. The banks along this stretch of the Meadow-lined Road were twelve feet high, the result of a plow that must have passed this way, so that the sign looked as though it were prohibiting this activity within the snowbank itself, rather than in the Motel he knew to be somewhere beneath or behind it.

He climbed up and over the massive snowbank, emerging in the parking lot on the other side, kicking his feet in arcs to clear the snow in front of them, and pushing more of it down with his arms so he could see.

The Front Office was on his left, a two-story outdoor hallway of rooms to the right of that, along the back of the parking lot, and then another to the right again, framing him inside a U shape, his back to the road and the snowbank he'd just climbed over.

The sky was grey, the snow brownish white, and the concrete of the Motel greyish white. Everything Ben could see struck him as schematic, like it had been rendered partway in autumn and would be finished only once the snow cleared in spring.

He sat down in the parking lot. From here, the second-story rooms looked severed from the ground, floating above snowbanks that looked like dirty air.

When he lay down, the rooms rose higher. He imagined giant pulleys hoisting them up his Tower, into the neighborhood

257

that would contain the Motel.

His jacket was rucked up so that snow started to eat into his lower back, first itching, then hurting, then ceasing to register. He nodded off, picturing the faces of the Sub-Weird in the Motel windows. *When I wake up, my work here will be finished*, he thought, as night began to fall.

It had been freezing all day, but the temperature drop at sundown was enough to shock Ben awake.

Death touched his core and set off an emergency alarm. He found himself on his feet, snow-blind and woozy but alert. The Motel had receded entirely into the night, so that now he was standing in what looked and felt like an empty field of snow, darkness in every direction, all things possible.

The Mayor has given up on the Town's City. He'd known this for months, but never articulated it so clearly. *Which means it's time for me to stop living in the Hotel, on his tab, as his employee. If it's for anyone except the Sub-Weird, the Town's City is for me now.*

A quieter voice in his head whispered, *And James too...* but for now he didn't pull this strand any further. Before he'd fully come back to his senses, he looked at the Motel and thought it was already the realization of his vision of a home in the Town's City, and that all he had to do was go into one of the rooms and lie down and let the rest of his life begin to unfold.

But Death touched him again as he approached the freezing structure, and he began to run, tripping in the snow and falling several times but no longer feeling it, desperate to make it out of where he was and back to town before he was frozen forever, his skeleton never to be found, not even in spring.

His knees and elbows were locked, so he ran by throwing one leg in front of the other without bending it, milling his arms for extra speed and a little balance. His feet felt like bags of bloody ice about to crack off with each impact, but he made it past the Meadow and the purple glow of ANGEL HOUSE without collapsing.

Soon, the giant snowbanks of the almost-Outskirts were behind him and then he was back in town, teeth chattering like his jaw was a windup toy. Avoiding the Square, he verged onto the Strip, thawing a little under the streetlights without yet regaining any clarity of thought.

In this state, he dinged the bell on Saltwater's liquor store and collapsed in the gin aisle.

Saltwater sighed and set an egg timer behind his desk for five minutes. When the timer went off and Ben was still inert, he took out a whiskbroom and crept over to where Ben lay, scratching it across his nose and mouth until he sat up, batting at his face like a cat.

As soon as Saltwater took the brush away, Ben grabbed the nearest bottle and rasped, "I need this."

"Yes," said Saltwater, already on his way back to the counter. He rang it up, then, with another sigh, added it to Ben's ever-expanding tab.

Ben drank half of it before leaving the store. The fingers that held it to his mouth couldn't tell where they ended and the glass began. Only when seven huge gulps had settled in his gut did he start to revive. After ten, he was feeling good. After thirteen, he could tell this was going to be part of his life from now on. There was something in his center that would never quite thaw, so it would need to be regularly warmed.

"Okay," he said, in Saltwater's direction, stumbling backwards into the snow. "Okay," he said again, starting on the bottle's second half as he turned and resolved to make his way over to the Town's City.

As the contractors were all hibernating, the construction site was abandoned. Ben ducked under the fence, then shouldered through the plastic tarp hanging over the main doorway and started weaving up the unfinished staircase, feeling the dust on the new cement with his non-bottle hand, to which some feeling had returned.

He stepped on something on the stairwell and bent down to pick up a finger. It must've come off during construction. He carried it for a while, wondering which finger it was—*index*, he guessed, but couldn't decide if it seemed more right- or left-handed—thinking that perhaps it could be his talisman, but he dropped it after a few floors, sensing that its brand of luck would've been more bad than good.

The hallways extended now into a seedy quarter just below where the inner floors of the Tower opened onto the flat rooftop expanse of the Town's City. Sub-Weird Session noise surrounded him from the unfinished rooms: séances, bloodlettings, chants and belly-laughs, rough, perhaps nonconsensual attempts at intercourse.

Other Sub-Weird drifted by in twos, heads down, muttering, needles dangling from their arms. Ben wondered where they got their drugs. Perhaps they'd stocked up in the Outskirts, or else they'd found a way to make them here using Ultra Max chemicals. Neither seemed unlikely.

He climbed upwards, imagining that the Motel was already there, open and waiting for him. *Just a few more blocks,* he promised himself when he almost fell over from drunkenness and exhaustion. His thawed extremities felt used up, like meat no longer fit for consumption.

As he came out onto the roof and into what he decided would be the streets immediately surrounding the Motel, the crush of Sub-Weird got denser.

They were surrounding him now, making him look and feel like one of them, his head down at the same angle as theirs. Some crawled, others looked dead. He passed empty buildings, some full of bloody nests of people, some empty and emitting staggeringly foul air. Piles of drug paraphernalia, evidence of tattooing and amputation, even a few resting dogs.

When grouped this densely together, rather than dispersed across the Outskirts, the Sub-Weird emitted a collective buzz that confounded Ben's efforts to hear his own thoughts.

The whole expanse of the roof was framed by snowbanks, high enough that he couldn't see the edges. The night overhead met the night off to each side, and there was no sound except the buzz. Ben stopped in the middle and turned to see the Sub-Weird advancing toward him. He dug his ankles deep into the snow, bearing down on the gin bottle he only now remembered was still in his hand.

He fell to his knees and looked up at them, their buzz growing louder, filling the silence of the winter night. As he listened, he could tell it wasn't just the buzzing of the Sub-Weird; they were listening to some sound, picking up on it, as well as emitting a response.

Radio waves, he thought, looking around for their source, his brain bobbing around in its casing. In one section of the black night, he thought he saw the outline of the Mountain and a tiny blinking beacon on its summit.

When he looked back at the roof, the outlines of a one-story structure he'd never seen before came into view, materializing from the night. He recognized the radio station for what it was, and could tell that if he went inside now, he'd find a mic and a monitor and everything else Well had used to make his broadcasts.

As below, so above, he thought, realizing that, like everything else in the town, he'd designed an exact replica of the radio station to take its place in the Town's City. The contractors must have finished building it just before Hibernation. For now it was just broadcasting static, but apparently this was enough to draw the Sub-Weird out.

The Mayor slouched behind the boy-James' kitchen table, sipping his cocoa and pretending that everything was okay. But every few minutes, he looked out at the Wooden Wheel and the Figure of Death behind it, and found this pretense impossible to maintain.

The boy-James was upstairs, trying to sleep. There were many nights when the Mayor came and the boy-James or the boy-Ben never appeared at the kitchen table, but last night had been different: the boy-James had sleepwalked right past him, meeting the boy-Ben in the park, where the two of them had climbed onto the ship and confronted the Figure of Death head-on.

The Hibernation routine had been broken by the sleepwalking episode, so that now felt like the first night of something new. For hours, the Mayor meditated on what this might be, dreading the moment when he'd have to find out.

Finally, deep in the night's stillness, near the point where he'd have to visit the Blind Spot, the Figure turned to face him. He turned the Wheel as well, so that the whole night tipped and the Mayor recognized Squimbop under that fur hood, wolfishness only magnifying his innate beauty.

He was locked in this recognition until Squimbop released him with a grin, beckoning him out of the Dead House and into the snow.

Squimbop anchored the ship and stepped off, striding in his giant coat right up to where the Mayor stood, holding his cocoa mug. He froze as Squimbop loomed in his face, mustache caked with bluish ice, eyes hollow and veiny and visibly filling with Lecture. He reached up to wipe a drop from his left eye, like a creamy tear, as a bear strode from behind the Mayor's station wagon into their midst.

It looked at the Mayor with its almost-human face, pleading with him to hurry to the Blind Spot.

Squimbop calmly took one hand from his coat and reached under the bear to remove its heart.

Hot blood sprayed onto the Mayor's feet and the bear tipped dead against his belly as Squimbop bit into the heart, tearing off more than half on the first bite and finishing it on the second.

Then he leaned in and, with bear-blood pouring from his lips, kissed the Mayor on the mouth, holding him riveted with the hand that had torn out the heart.

Then he returned to the Wooden Wheel whispering, "Go home and get some sleep. Freshen up. See you at the Greek restaurant at six tomorrow evening."

Stunned, the Mayor couldn't walk until the dead bear leaning against him toppled over. Then he staggered back to his station wagon, got in, turned up the heat, and put it in neutral.

At five p.m. the next evening, the Mayor was dressed, perfumed, and in his best shoes. He got in his car and ran it in the garage for a full minute, in the familiar pose of a man sizing up suicide on a slow Sunday afternoon. But, tonight, giddiness was stronger than

263

despair. He felt a kind of excitement, arousal even, which, though frightening, compelled him out of the garage, down the driveway, through the treacherous streets and into town.

Idling in front of the Greek restaurant, in the small patch of the Square that had been plowed enough to fit a car, the Mayor was covered in sweat, his chest steaming. He tried to unbutton his shirt, but his fingers were too nervous, bunching up the cloth without getting ahold of it. So, after a long exhale, he smoothed it down, got out of the station wagon, and went into the restaurant, where Squimbop was waiting under the only light the management had left on.

He had hoped for the Professor in a matching suit and shaved face but found him in shabby corduroys and a thick wool sweater with shoulder and elbow patches, his mustache growing out of a week's stubble around his mouth, his fangs still stained with bear blood. His coat with the giant fur hood sat on the booth beside him, like a silent partner.

Trying not to stammer, the Mayor said, "Tonight we eat in my Private Booth."

The waiter, who was standing behind him, nodded and said, "Right this way, sirs."

He led them across the empty dining area, all the chairs on the tables and the menus stacked by the cash register, then through a back door that led past the kitchen and the bathroom. He took a key from a ring under his apron and opened another door. Then he led them down a hall, past a stack of soup cracker boxes, and into another room, opened with another key.

Here they were seated in matching green leather booths, with curtains hanging all around and big cushions on all sides, rugs and a bubbling fountain, which the waiter turned on along with the lights by plugging in an extension cord.

Squimbop seemed indifferent, so the Mayor had to console himself with the night's menu, which the waiter was now opening for them.

Before looking at it, the Mayor imagined a feast of caviar, shark fin, pink champagne, items so intimate and sensitive they could only be ordered by writing them down on a card and handing it to the waiter under the table. He'd order it all and have it laid out before them, grapes hanging from the ceiling, swollen udders dripping sweet milk, mollusks crawling hypnotized out of their shells.

Squimbop arranged his coat beside where he sat and rolled his sweater sleeves up to his elbows. His arms were thin and very white with a few long hairs, like those on a turnip, and he was solemn and evasive as he watched the Mayor run his fingers over the menu, which was bound in green leather and printed on cardstock.

The waiter leaned in and lit a candle and the Mayor said they'd have all the specials.

He saw the night ahead as a long thread on a spool, already beginning to come unwound. In the next hours, he'd grope his way along until touching the spool itself: the point at which he'd risk getting too close to the Professor if he didn't pull back. By then, both string and spool would be trash and he'd have to part ways with him at the edge of the Meadow and return to the Blind Spot alone.

The waiter appeared with a platter of fish, long-frozen but still attractive, laid out on a bed of ice and lemons. They were examples of the kinds of fish that were available tonight, and also the fish themselves, the ones that, once chosen, would be taken to the kitchen, cooked, and brought back.

Squimbop pointed to the grouper, the Mayor to the sea

265

bass.

The waiter nodded and returned ten silent minutes later with two giant platters, a whole fish on each surrounded by lemons and potato wedges and wilted greens. He put one in front of Squimbop and the other in front of the Mayor, then stood back from the table, looked at both, apologized for the mix-up, and switched them.

Then he brought wine in tall glasses.

The Mayor was calm now, in his element, wholly focused on eating as more courses came: a lamb roast, stuffed quail, creamy squash soup, a bowl of lobsters too tangled to count at first glance.

Walnut and pear salad came last, then dessert, great hulking tortes with barely whipped cream and a pitcher of coffee and hot milk, and a bottle of sherry in a burlap sack that matched Squimbop's sweater.

The more he ate, the more anchored the Mayor became. He started to feel like Squimbop held no sway over him, that he was the predator and the Professor the prey. He relished this feeling even more than the dessert.

When they'd eaten all they could and then several portions beyond that, they made their way out through the Private Booth's side door. It would have spoiled the mood if they'd had to go back through the main restaurant, past the revolving pie cases and the empty orders rack, the morose fry cook staring at the grill.

"Take me to the Night School," Squimbop commanded.

Coming around to his car, the Mayor drove them up the Strip, struggling to stay above five miles an hour in the snow.

The interior of the Night School was a grinding Carnival. Squishing together and shimmering with a visible heartbeat, the Sub-Weird were out in force. They pushed up against each other, drugged and restless, devouring chicken wings and gulping beer. The window shades were held fast by sweat and cologne, and their numbers kept growing, like they were generating one another through their ceaseless contact.

The Mayor was confused and fearful, his sense of power over Squimbop shriveling now that his Private Booth could no longer contain them. He sucked down bad whiskey and held onto the bar.

Squimbop drank less, but lost more and more of his presence as the Totally Other Place worked its way up in him. The liquor froze in his stomach, sucking life out of his core and into his extremities, which tingled as he looped around the room, bumping into naked men and half-deflated sex dolls, carried over from the Mattress Store and abandoned on the floor and under the tables.

Without checking if the Mayor was following, Squimbop forced his way through the Birth Canal and into the Mattress Store, past the mattresses in the first room and into the second, where the Sub-Weird were all over each other and entwined with the dolls, fucking them in several holes at once, crushing them and one another into a mass that was half-human and half-rubber, nameless and unconstrained.

They proceeded through this crush and into the third room, where the Mayor had bought Squimbop his mattress in autumn. The Mayor, though he stepped in vomit, followed as best he could, shaking his shoes to both sides, determined to keep up without clinging to the Professor's fur coat like a child. He fought his way through, panting into his collar so as not to gag on the ripe air.

The third room was empty except for the mattresses, some tipped off their box-springs, others piled on top of each other

267

on the floor and against the wall.

Squimbop vanished across the threshold to the fourth room with no regard for ritual.

The room he wouldn't even know existed if I hadn't taken him there last time, the Mayor thought, with some pride, though he couldn't be sure this was true. It was possible, he accepted, that Squimbop knew more about the town's inner workings than he ever would. He sat on one of the mattresses in the third room, panting and wiping his shoes on the carpet, coming to terms with the fact that, if he followed Squimbop into the fourth room, there'd be no way to keep him out of the Psychogeography.

Ok, he thought, ready to go where it took him.

The Mayor emerged through a curtain into the fourth room, which had only the one gigantic mattress in the center, twenty feet high, with a ladder climbing its side. The thermostat, as ever, was set at 110.

At first it was silent, but then he heard a low groaning and scratching from overhead. The Mayor looked up into the dark and pictured Squimbop climbing it on the non-ladder side like a giant crab on a cliff high above the Inland Sea. He stopped again to catch his breath, feeling his dinner threaten to pour up his throat.

He swallowed it down and grabbed the ladder.

It was an immense effort to hoist his weight from rung to rung, but after he made it a few feet off the ground, he knew he couldn't stop. So he kept dragging upward, wiping more vomit from his shoes as he scraped them along the rungs, the scratching of Squimbop above growing louder the closer he came to the top.

He didn't look down. The darkness of the lower room fell away as he neared the top, where a weird light was shining from a source other than the ceiling.

He's already opened the Psychogeography, thought the

Mayor, smelling his Orchard so strongly he couldn't tell if he was already inside it.

Emerging onto the top of the mattress, he dug his feet into the semi-firm material and surveyed his surroundings, as vast and high as the top of the Mountain. He swooned and almost fell off. Only by sitting down and then rolling onto his belly could he quiet the vertigo.

There was neither a ceiling overhead, nor any sky, only a thin membrane that Squimbop had already penetrated. A vine dangled down, thin but sturdy. The Mayor knew that if he grabbed it and held tightly enough, it would pull him out of the Mattress Store and into his Orchard, across a line he could never uncross.

Swallowing his dinner for the third time, he committed himself, wrapping the vine around his wrists and forearms as it began to pull him upward, out of the public night and into the private.

As the Mayor surfaced, the hole in the Psychogeography closed beneath him and a layer of soft dirt settled over it, so that the vine appeared to be growing out of the ground, culminating in one of his old vaginas.

He stood in his neglected Orchard now, on solid but soft ground. The muddy soil reeked of wine turning to vinegar, and deep, old sex, like Hotel sheets that had never been washed.

The Mayor surveyed the grounds, bounded by sloping hills on all sides, the vagina plants drooping over and dripping lubricant that had congealed into a cold jelly. Squimbop stood in the distance, proud and scarecrow-stiff, watching the Mayor get his bearings. His face, under his fur hood, was coated in a layer of fuzzy blue mold, though his mustache remained black. His body was wet with Lecture-runoff, as the Totally Other Place continued to spill into him.

269

He bared his fangs and waited for the Mayor to approach.

The Mayor moved slowly, exhausted from the climb and partially anesthetized from the passage through the Psychogeography. His ankles sank into the wine-mud as he waded, closing the hundred feet between himself and the Professor in the time it would've taken an able-bodied person to walk a mile.

When they were face-to-face, Squimbop loomed, taking on giant proportions, and the Mayor shrunk down to the level of his vaginas, which drooped toward him, reeking of a past he knew he would never reclaim.

Watching the Mayor cower in awe, Squimbop held out his hands, gripped the Mayor's shoulders, and pulled him to his feet. The Mayor sunk a few inches into the mud before stabilizing.

"Shh," whispered Squimbop, kneeling to ease the Mayor's pants down. Keeping one hand on his shoulders, he pushed the other under his belly, cupping his genitals, holding them tenderly for a moment.

Then he leaned in, clamped his fangs around the Mayor's penis and, in a single fluid motion, bit down.

When the Mayor came to, he felt the torn flesh of his crotch sealing itself shut, a smooth flap growing to cover it. He tried to remain on his belly, but felt Squimbop grip him by the neck and roll him over onto his back.

Lying on his back, on the verge of passing out again, he had a vision of all his children buried under the mud, white and cylindrical like giant maggots, wriggling even when dead, flaking off into tallow which Squimbop scooped up from the ground and shared with him.

Then he passed out again.

The next time he came to, he was on his knees holding out his partly chewed penis with the testicles attached.

Grinning with his beard of blue mold under his fur hood, Squimbop bit into it again, chewing slowly and, this time, swallowing.

When he'd swallowed it all, he bent down to kiss the Mayor, letting him taste his breath, and then walked off, disappearing at the far edge of the Orchard.

After he vanished, the Mayor crawled through the mud until he found another hole in the Psychogeography, emerging through his TV back into his basement, where he settled onto his couch alone, still bleeding from his flap and staring at his reflection in the screen.

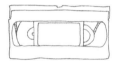

The Mayor lay on his couch in the basement, stunned, still staring at the screen, which reflected him where he lay, dark and egg-like.

In a semi-conscious murk, he understood that James' Movie, if it ever got made, could no longer save him from the Blind Spot. That was now the thinking of a lost era, as naïve as expecting the Town's City to render the town impervious to the outside world. *Another decade of childish thinking gone by*, he thought. It seemed never to be true that he'd grown up all the way, much as he often felt he had, and mourned the fact, bitterly.

He sat on the couch and cried.

When all the tears were gone, he crawled across the basement floor and up the stairs. Back in his kitchen, he crawled to the fridge and found the two remaining sticks of butter, slightly rancid, like they'd been spiked with chili powder. With these cupped in his forearms, he crawled on his knees and elbows to the hot tub, and pushed off the foam covering with his face.

Closing his eyes to summon the very last of his energy, he rose to his feet and got in, dropping in the butter as well.

It began to melt, forming a soothing scum around his body as he sank down. He closed his eyes for ten minutes before gingerly reaching down to feel his crotch.

When he finally did, probing with his two index fingers, he felt a smooth expanse of skin where his testicles had been. There was no opening there, only a lack of protrusion. Reaching further up, toward the base of what used to be his penis, he felt a small, sensitive knob.

Sighing, he massaged this gently with the two fingers, lingering on the memory of Squimbop eating his penis and testicles, mentally extending the interval between one bite and the next as far as he could. After a few minutes, he felt a small release as a jet of semen trickled from the knob, mixing with the butter scum swirling around him.

He sighed and put his head back.

A scratching on the glass startled him, and he looked over to see the faces of three bears staring in through the fog, mouthing "Blind Spot... Blind Spot... Blind Spot."

He slipped deeper into the brine, shaking his head. His whole system refused to consider the prospect of getting out now and putting his station wagon in neutral. If his refusal to go meant the town would be plunged into eternal night, so be it.

He propped himself on his elbows and shook his head at the bears.

No, he mouthed. *Not tonight. Not ever again. Let the Blind Spot come to me if it has to. If I am the custodian of the town's night, and the dawn comes only after I've humiliated myself, then may the dawn never come. May we all plunge together into the perma-dusk.*

The bears could tell he was serious, in a way he never had been before. They growled and pawed at the glass, shaking with fury.

As the Mayor closed his eyes and acknowledged that his life had just been changed for good, the faces of the bears, already partly-human, changed the rest of the way, shedding everything that had let them pass as animals.

Now they had human features, pale and emotionless, with cruel snub noses and voids for mouths. Though the Mayor wouldn't open his eyes to look, a posse of Blankheads stood less than ten feet away, whispering that more were coming.

Back in ANGEL HOUSE, licking the last of the Mayor's flesh from his molars, Squimbop sat on his mattress and opened his laptop to compose an email.

Dear Master,

Hibernation has been uneventful, boring even. Continued friction with the Mayor, whom I'd describe as a problem person, but nothing of especial note.

All for now,

Prof. Sq.

He sent off this email, then began to compose another.

Dear Master,

Where the fuck am I? What am I doing here? I hope you're benefiting in some way from my suffering. I did something awful tonight, and I don't know why. There was a man I wanted to be close to. He seems to love me, he seems to need me, to see me as I wish I could see myself. But I went too far, perhaps—what are the rules? Are there any? Am I bound by anything? Does anyone care what I do? Does anyone know? Should I offer some form of love to this man, who clearly needs it? Am I capable of that? Will I destroy him if I try? Will he destroy me?

Please help me,

Prof. Sq.

He yawned, wiped sweat from his eyes, and deleted what he'd just written. *I haven't slept in weeks*, he thought, as he went to lie down on his mattress until, inevitably, he got up and wrote another email and then deleted it again, sometime in the long hours ahead.

PART V
The Duo Entangled

Acting Mayor John Lester Wind came on the radio the next morning to announce that Hibernation was over. It had to end. No one could sleep; people were losing their minds. They were causing scenes at Ultra Max and Saltwater's and especially the Night School, where ten rapes had been reported in as many days.

So much for the deep freeze.

"Since you're all so eager to be awake," said the Acting Mayor, his voice slow and heavy like he'd been the only one truly asleep, "have at it. The town is now open for business again." He put the mic down without turning it off, so everyone could hear him sighing until he finally got up and walked away, permitting the airwaves to revert to static.

There was a lushness around town, as the snow began to melt ahead of schedule. The smell of fresh roughage came through windows and wings tapped hesitantly against them. Premature green shoots grew through cracks in the sidewalk, unable to tell that they'd likely freeze through again before the time came to flower. Snowmelt flooded the Meadow-lined Road, along which the Sub-Weird had processed into the Town's City, where they now lived as if that's where they'd been born.

What no one yet knew was that the pressure they felt in their sinuses came not from how poorly they'd hibernated, but from the atmospheric disturbance caused by the Mayor's decision to stop visiting the Blind Spot. This would eventually become clear.

School resumed as soon as J.L. Wind's announcement went into effect. The duo trudged to the Chamber where Squimbop awaited them, his head mealy white after so long under the fur hood. He still had wolf fangs and a patch of grey fur under his chin, but these receded along with the blue mold as he became their Professor once again.

Helplessly, the duo went back to absorbing his Lectures, staggering alone onto the playground at recess, climbing the hill to the Pine Hedge Office, mouths heaving with nausea as they crawled into their sleeping bags, clammy with slush.

Ben's Motel blueprints had been finished since the end of Hibernation, but it took a week for the contractors to get back to work. Every morning, he went to the bakery next to his office, bought more coffee and donuts than he could comfortably consume, and took them upstairs, where he sat brooding over his drawing desk until, one morning, he caught sight of the contractors marching down the parade route and back to work.

Swallowing what was in his mouth, he rolled up the Motel blueprints and carried them to the edge of the construction site, where the contractors had just arrived, eating donuts from the same bakery.

They unlocked the gazebo with what looked like a five-digit code, put down their toolboxes, and picked up where they'd left off however long ago their last day here had been. Their first task seemed to be removing the house wrap that covered the first few stories, and fitting windows into the frames.

Ben watched them work throughout the morning, crouching behind a car next to the fence, until they wandered off at lunchtime to pick up their Giant Chinese delivery on the corner. They saw him on the way out, but didn't react. *For them*, he thought, *there's nothing but work here. No context, no situation… they're made to execute concrete processes. That is all.*

This was so intriguing to consider that he almost missed his chance to sneak into the gazebo, which they left open with the same indifference they'd shown in passing him by. Only a loud moan from the Sub-Weird above woke him back to where he was. He shook himself, tightened his grip on the blueprints, and hurried under the fence, shoving his way into the gazebo just as the contractors were coming back down the street, carrying takeout containers and laughing loudly.

Inside, his original blueprints sat on a wooden shelf built especially for them, weighted down with rocks in the four corners. It was the most official capacity Ben had ever seen his work displayed in, and thus the closest he'd come to feeling like a real architect. He blushed with pride as he studied his draftsmanship, until another moan jolted him back to the task at hand. He quickly unrolled the Motel plans and spread them on top of those for the Town's City, just as the contractors crossed the fenceline and put their hardhats back on.

He heard them entering the gazebo and then it was too late: they were in here with him, eating dumplings and continuing to laugh. His throat tightened as he thought, *Something is finally about to happen to me…*

But the contractors just bustled around him, lighting cigarettes and looking over the Motel plans like there was nothing even remotely surprising about them. After they bumped into Ben several times, one of the contractors grabbed his shoulders and barked, "Do you mind? We're working here."

Before he could think of a response, Ben let them elbow him outside, into the mud and strewn nails. Head down, he made his way back under the fence and straight to Saltwater's, where he put a six-pack on his tab and drank five in the parking lot, trying, for what felt like the trillionth time, to tell himself he was just a drifter here, in need of nothing but a Motel to pass the night in.

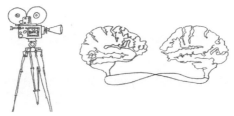

The nineteen-year-olds still hadn't gotten in touch, though James had been by the Hotel several times looking for them.

Since returning to the Gym on the cusp of Hibernation-madness, James had locked into the habit of spending every night lifting, then soaking in the two pools and the hot tub, trying to think without stewing. Then he'd put on one of his new outfits and sit in his office, staring at the wall or at his hands on the table.

His hives were no more than scars now, but he knew they could erupt again at any moment. The fundamental thing was clear: without the nine-year-olds dreaming inside the Gym itself, the nineteen-year-olds wouldn't show up. And without the nineteen-year-olds, Blankheads would swarm the film, filling it with nothingness, stuffing the screen to bursting with their aggressive refusal to stand for anything at all.

Every time he went underwater in the hot tub, he could see them coming, up from the Blind Spot and into the Gym parking lot, pushing in an evil mass toward the front doors, shoving their way in, clotting in front of his lens, to the point where all narrative would be moot. Much as he yearned to embrace this possibility, he wasn't sure if he could.

He surfaced and thought, *The nine-year-olds will be the embryos in the larger organism of the project, the homunculi in the boiler room. The kernel of meaning in the maelstrom of my film.*

In this way, they could go on directing their Pretend Movie while at the same time acting as the nineteen-year-olds in his real one. This seemed a feasible compromise, and—he told himself—an ethical one too. A means of achieving both things at once.

As he sat in the hot tub mulling all this over, he watched a succession of Desert images pass by: another hot tub, a Tower, more buildings shooting out of an Oasis. The more he thought about the Desert, the more his thoughts drifted back up the Mountain, along the route he'd taken with Well, to the summit and then beyond it. Whenever Well entered his mind, he felt his hive-scars throb. Often, they grew so itchy, he had to reverse the natural order and dive back into the adult pool after the hot tub just to ice them down.

More immediately disturbing was the call from the Mayor a few days after Hibernation's end.

James was in his house, in a snarl of blankets on the couch, listening to the snowbanks melt when the phone rang. He tipped the receiver onto his ear and grunted.

"Morning, James," said the Mayor, grave and determined. "Listen, change of plans. I can't wait for your Movie anymore. Last night, I didn't go to the Blind Spot, and I'm not going tonight either. I don't know what's going to happen to me, or to the town for that matter, but I'm going to let it. No more children, no more Orchard... I'm living a new life now."

James tried to check if he was dreaming, but couldn't remember how. "So... what does that mean about my money?"

The Mayor paused, like he was thinking about it for the first time, barely capable of remembering what money was. "Any debts you've racked up so far, I'll pay," he began. "And any living expenses going forward, for as long as you want to stay, I'll pay those too. I like having you here. I hope you'll stick around. But, in terms of production expenses... that's over. Squimbop invaded my Orchard; he ate my, um... I'm off Movies for good now. I don't need them anymore."

He hung up, crying what sounded like tears of joy.

With the receiver still on his ear, James thought, *Now, the nineteen-year-olds will have to work for free. They'll be prisoners of a film without a budget. They should've signed the contract when they had the chance.*

This was objectively bad news but there was pleasure in accepting it.

After a long shower, he zipped himself into an Ultra Max tracksuit and ran to the Gym, blowing past Janitor Pete without a nod.

He did bench press repetitions until his mind shut down, then sat on the bench slurping water and panting. When his mind turned back on, he picked up a 42.5-pound dumbbell and screamed into it until his vision went white. When color returned, he flexed in the mirror and marched downstairs, under the basketball court and into the boiler room to build a new home for the nine-year-olds.

As he worked—breaking down boxes, sweeping fallen insulation, taping over cracks in the ductwork overhead—he ranged over possible names for this chamber. He settled on the

Crawl Space. It was a little sexy, a little ominous, cryptic in its particular meaning but not in its general resonance.

It was the kind of headquarters he wished someone had built for him and Ben, had any adult taken their Pretend Movie as seriously as he was prepared to take the duo's.

His film, he was now certain, could not grow without their Pretend Movie. It was the living core, and no film could be made solely by suturing together the inert detritus of adult thought.

He ran to Ultra Max, bought as much bedding as he could hold—still on the Mayor's tab, which hadn't been closed yet—and ran it back to the Crawl Space. When he'd finished setting up, there were two identical mattresses fitted with blue dinosaur sheets and pillows, side by side with just enough space to stand between them.

After another quick shower, he ran outside at ten p.m. to find the sky a watery whitish-blue, the same as it had been when he ran to Ultra Max at five. He unzipped his sweatshirt and walked back to his house without yet wondering what it meant.

James woke up in the same dusk he'd gone to sleep in and called the town's lone taxi to take him to the School, where he would confront the nine-year-olds about moving into the Crawl Space.

After sliding through the snowmelt along the Meadow-lined Road, the taxi dropped him off in the traffic circle in front of the School, where an empty bag of chips blew in the wind. The driver watched its progress while James stepped out, setting foot on the School grounds for the first time since the Reunion, which already felt as distant as childhood, claimed by the same past it longed to commune with.

He stood there, hoping the driver wasn't watching him. The taxi was parked facing the opposite direction, but he still felt uneasy as he began to tear up, fighting the urge to put his face to

281

the portico and kiss the cement, whispering, *You were the cement beneath all the time I was given to simply be a person in the world, and not a filmmaker whose gamble to be worth anything at all relies wholly upon my making a film I cannot make.*

Out of sight of the taxi, he put his face against a tree and wept, preserving his sense of being a man by imagining the colossal violence he'd unleash on the driver if he turned out to be watching. He could not defeat the feeling of lost time, of the past as a promise he was guilty of breaking, his only home a flooded Movie Store, empty because of all the Movies he never made and never would…

He pressed his teeth into the bark and felt tears run off his nose. His hives flared up along his lower back and in his armpits, so painful that they made him whistle.

Beneath this sound, James became aware of the synced footsteps of the duo as they were released onto the playground for recess, Squimbop following behind them.

He crept further into the pines, ankle-deep in snowmelt, and wiped his face as he watched them approach, climbing the hill toward the Pine Hedge Office.

For a glorious un-self-conscious second, he allowed himself to imagine that they were a form he would one day grow into, and that all he had to do was wait. Then he sobered up, remembered his age and purpose, and began to creep through the pines into their Office, where memory told him he'd find them trying to dream.

At the bottom of the playground, he saw Squimbop sitting on a bench, staring up at him, radiating Death. James shivered, closed his eyes, and hurried onward, letting the pine branches scrape his face, the pain sharpening his senses against Squimbop's silent entreaty to *give up now.*

In this way, he made it into the Pine Hedge Office without realizing it, and only opened his eyes when he stepped on the duo. He looked down at them, and they up at him, before closing their eyes again, determined to make it into the Pretend Movie before recess was over, desperate to overcome the friction they felt growing between themselves and the nineteen-year-olds.

James knelt down and shook the two cans of beer left open by their heads, hoping that one would have a sip left, but both were empty. Putting them down, he leaned over the duo's ears, peering inside as if through the peephole of a nickelodeon with the Pretend Movie on loop.

Run from me, part of him thought. *Guard the Pretend Movie against my influence with everything you have.*

He closed his eyes, picturing the nineteen-year-olds on the basketball court in front of his camera, ready to do whatever he told them, even as the Blankheads rattled the doors of the Gym.

Fixating on this image, he leaned over the sleeping nine-year-olds and whispered, "Your new home is the Crawl Space. Leave the Dead Neighborhood tonight and come to the Gym... I'll be waiting for you... the next scene in the Pretend Movie takes place in the Gym... your beds are waiting for you there."

Then he sat back, winded from the exertion, dizzy, trying to imagine the course his words were on, through the nine-year-olds and into the nineteen-year-olds.

He sat under the overhanging pines until the Recess Aides blew the whistle, and scrambled away just as the duo yawned and rubbed their eyes. Driving off in the taxi, he envied them their faith in the efficacy of the Pretend Movie, but not the afternoon with Squimbop ahead.

As soon as he passed the front desk, James ran into the locker room with a leaking bag of Giant Chinese, tearing his clothes off as he went, so that he was naked in the shower before he'd managed to untie his shoes.

The hot water sent up a meaty smell as it hit his cold skin. He unpacked the bag and ate it under the shower, picking up handfuls of noodles and biting them off his palm.

When the container was empty, he threw it into the drain with the hair and the scabs. Then he reached into his armpit, clamped his teeth together, and tore out a hive. He couldn't tell if it had grown back or remained there, a relic evading his attention last time he checked.

The timed shower ran out.

He slammed it back on, and the water came out harder and hotter than before. He ducked under it with the bloody hive outheld on his palm, waiting for the water to turn it into an unremarkable flap of skin. Then he threw it away.

It was his offering to the film, his prayer for clarity and good luck now that he was beyond the Mayor's support, pursuing a vision that no one had sanctioned.

The duo would be here any minute, if ever.

After drying off, James decided to shave his head, in further offering to the God he'd just fed the hive to. *The Director is, in a sense, the prime actor in any film,* he thought, uncertain whether this line had come from film school or was his own invention. *If he doesn't look the part—which is to say, if he doesn't embody the essence of the film he intends to make—no one in the cast can be expected to either.*

He found an electric shaver in one of the lockers and turned it on. He held one arm tight again his bloody side, caked and sticky, and, with the other, went to work. The blades bit into his scalp and the hair began to fall. It rained over his shoulders and landed on his feet. Soon the ground was moss-covered, the hairs soft but sharp, puncturing the tender skin between his toes.

When it was over, he got back in the shower and turned the water hot enough to cauterize his scalp, which felt like a brand new covering for a brand new head, atop a body whose musculature finally reflected the hours of work he'd put into it. It was, for the first time in his life, the true Body of the Director.

James had the same name but he felt like a new man. The man in the pines this afternoon had been a coward. Now he felt total, capable of regulating all flow in and out of his film, repressing all forces that could come between him and its completion and canonization in the Movie Store.

Two big hands passed over his new, smooth skull, declaring it worthy. Then he put on a pair of boxer-briefs and bought a bag of almonds from the vending machine in the lobby. He paced and ate them, curling his bare toes into the carpeting, trying to uproot it.

He had an impulse to go to the basement and get out the aluminum siding he'd been stockpiling from Ultra Max and nail it over the windows, door, and the glass wall that made up the Gym's front faç de. Barricade himself inside before anyone came for him. *Independent film is, by definition, a sort of insurgency,* he thought.

Now that he'd admitted this, he had to admit that he felt presences surrounding the Gym, peering in through the windows to watch him. Like he'd announced an open casting call and now all the extras were here. Faceless bodies ready to take up space.

Walking to the lobby and looking out at the parking lot, he saw them there, massing in the black expanse, standing so tightly together he couldn't tell where one ended and the next began. They looked like many arms and heads growing from a central node, their void-mouths conjoining into a convincing facsimile of the Blind Spot. Whatever his previous vision of them had been, they were meaner and more numerous now.

He knew the Gym basement was full of supplies, so he tried to think if there was anything down there he could use as a weapon, but he'd been so focused on building the Crawl Space all he could picture were blankets and pillows.

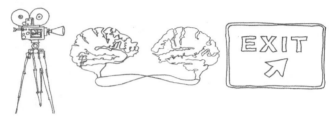

Retreating to the locker room, he pulled his shoes back on and punched the wall with each fist. Then he leaned in and rubbed his smooth scalp against the wall, sourcing energy from the wires behind it.

He drank from the water fountain until he felt his stomach balloon out, then, having declared a state of inner emergency, he put his head forward and charged through the front doors, running hard across the parking lot, through the swarm of Blankheads in the bluish dusk.

He ran up the street, past the mansions, and all the way through downtown, until he reached the hill that led to the Dead Neighborhood. Its steepness slowed his pace to a jog, but he didn't stop to think or pant or spit out the bloody saliva that was filling his mouth. He just sucked it down, pretending it was the blood of his enemy, the living manifestation of all the forces that, over twenty-nine years, had kept him from making a single film.

He kicked down the door of the Dead House that had been his and, without stopping to pay his respects to the threshold, clambered through the kitchen—where the Mayor sat stunned behind his mug of cocoa—and up the stairs he'd crawled down, on his belly, in the midst of so many thousands of nightmares before he turned nine.

Feeling thirty feet tall, he tore the boy-James from the same bed he'd had those nightmares in and dragged him out, across the park, and into the Dead House of the boy-Ben, whom he grabbed with the other hand. He bit his lip and sucked down pain, gasping as he led the boy-Ben down the stairs.

He charged back to the Gym with the duo sleepwalking beside him, still inside the Pretend Movie, shaking with terror as the waters in the tunnels the nineteen-year-olds were exploring turned septic, bone-snakes swarming so thickly together they couldn't see.

James dragged them through the swarm of Blankheads in the parking lot, past the front desk where Janitor Pete looked the other way, and into the locker room, where he placed them on the floor under the showers and turned on the water, like they were concentrated versions of people he meant to reconstitute.

Then he retreated to the water fountain and drank until his stomach ballooned out again, deciding that tonight he would walk the nine-year-olds around the basketball court and the two racquetball courts, to familiarize their bodies with the main parameters of the film set before putting them to sleep in the Crawl Space to wait for the nineteen-year-olds to show up to rehearse the first scene, which would be called *Arrival in Town*.

He knew that the giddy, defiant energy he'd been filled with ever since the Mayor cancelled the Movie commission would soon wear off, so he was eager to get to work.

When he came back to the shower area, the duo was asleep in the drain trough. He found a bag of candy in an otherwise empty locker and tore it open, throwing pieces at them and shouting until they stirred.

They ate the candy with their faces still on the ground, tipped to the side just enough to open their mouths.

When they were done, he picked them up, one in each hand, and carried them onto the basketball court, their soaked pajamas dripping the whole way. He put them on the waxed floor and turned on the lights, forcing them to squint and yawn.

"This here is the downtown," he said, pointing at the cardboard Ultra Max sets. "This is where the primary outdoor action will take place. The racquetball courts we'll use for interiors. Like your pretend bedrooms. Now, for your actual bedroom, follow me."

He knew that when he led them down to the Crawl Space, their dreaming minds would edit the corridor out of the Gym and into the Pretend Movie, but as long as it yielded up the nineteen-year-olds, it didn't matter. All that mattered was that the nineteen-year-olds, when they arrived, consented to enact a pretend arrival in town instead of trying genuinely to escape.

Ten minutes later, they were both burrowed deep in the Ultra Max bedding that James had laid out for them in the Crawl Space, cooing like they thought they were in the Pine Hedge Office at recess and all was well. The shock made any other response impossible. The ceiling was barely a foot above their noses as they lay on their backs, and the heating system blew hot, dusty air into their mouths. Rocking on his haunches in the gap between mattresses, James leaned over them, as he had in the Pine Hedge Office, and spoke to the nineteen-year-olds through their ears.

Inside the Pretend Movie, the nineteen-year-olds awoke in the Hotel, where, with Ben out most nights and Well gone for good, they were now the only guests.

Bottles, cigarette butts, weed stems and a hand-drawn map of the tunnel entrances and confluences covered them where they lay. Out the window, the Town's City glowed under the dusky blue sky, the streets on its roof seething with bodies. Crumpled beneath the window was one of the sex dolls from the Mattress Store, which they'd stolen during Hibernation and used to the point of deflation.

Now, driven by the nine-year-olds in the Crawl Space, their only thought was of returning to *The Dream of Escape* with redoubled intensity. *The only external world we'll ever succeed in escaping into is the one we succeed in making up,* they recited inwardly, stretching and yawning.

But by the time they had their shoes and coats on, and money in their pockets for Greek restaurant coffee on their way up to the Meadow, determined to resume investigating the tunnels under the town, a new calling took hold of their shared mind and they set off for the Gym instead, James' Director voice overriding that of the nine-year-olds in their ears, hijacking thought processes that, even at the best of times, had little or no autonomy.

They crossed the Gym parking lot, full of faceless figures lapping up the dim air, and banged on the locked front doors for a long time before James, huge in his gray suit and shaved head, ran to open it and said, "Come in. Let's get started before they wake up."

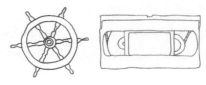

The Mayor finished his third mug of cocoa at the kitchen table.

He was in shock, therefore calm. He felt like he'd already processed the abduction, shoving it deep into his past without first letting it force him to suffer. He had watched James abduct the boy-James in slow motion, like something that had to happen and was thus as innocuous as something that already had.

Now he sat alone under a dying bulb, running his finger along the chocolate-smeared edge of his mug, watching the dusk swell out and out and out, now that the Blind Spot offered no means of delineating day from night.

The perma-dusk is here to stay, he admitted to the empty Dead House. *Thanks to me.* The irony of this power reversal wasn't lost on him.

He didn't even reassure himself that he wasn't about to go back to the Blind Spot tonight. His decision felt absolute, like he had mailed a signed declaration to a higher power.

Resigned to life in the perma-dusk, he left the kitchen table and tried to pee standing up in the downstairs bathroom, squirting the wall with his clitoral protrusion. Then he dabbed himself with a square of toilet paper, zipped up, and left James' Dead House for the last time.

Walking down the front steps, Blankheads eyed him indifferently.

"*If you won't go to the Blind Spot, the Blind Spot will come to you*," they rasped in such a way that the Mayor couldn't tell if they were speaking inside his head or through his mouth.

He looked past them, to where Squimbop sat on a swing, grinning, beckoning him again into the park. He crossed the street, uneasy with the sense that Squimbop had stopped steering the night before returning it to the safe harbor of day, and that this is how it would be from now on, the town bobbing in the dead center of the Inland Sea.

More frightening than the Professor's attention as he approached was the lack of attention from the bedroom windows of the boy-James and the boy-Ben on either side of the park. Without their dreaming surveillance, he would meet Squimbop in an arena outside of all dramatic cohesion, a set without a Director, where anything could happen and its meaning would never resolve into Movies.

Squimbop stood, kicking a swing hard enough to make it fly in an arc over the bar it hung from.

When the Mayor made it over to him, he realized it was the first time he'd stood face-to-face with the Professor since the Mattress Store. He felt the place where his penis and testicles had been vibrate, wondering if it was going to be the subject of further attention.

"Can we walk?" he eventually managed to ask.

Squimbop spat out a white mouthful of Lecture and nodded.

As they left the Wooden Wheel, Blankheads seeped in from the edges and sat on the swings, rocking back and forth and watching them leave, their mouths emitting the frigidity of the void. They, at last, were the rightful residents of the Dead Neighborhood, those who belonged there most of all.

But soon the Dead Houses were out of view and the sense of Death that surrounded them was universal, tied to nothing, emanating from nowhere in particular. As the Figure of Death, Squimbop knew that his work in this area, for better or worse, was done. He was hungry for a breakfast of ground meat from the ANGEL HOUSE basement and a few hours' sleep, his dry mouth open to the tallow dripping from the ceiling.

The Mayor looked up at the perma-dusk, then down at his belly, obscuring his feet. His mind was lost in superimposing this instance of leaving the Dead Neighborhood onto the last time he'd left it, a decade ago, when Ben and James had dragged their suitcases down this hill and all the way out to the bus station and on to News City.

The lights of the Town's City came into view once they were off the hill and back on the flat streets of outermost downtown. Having resolved never to visit the Dead Neighborhood again, it only now truly died to the Mayor. He felt the whole town shrink, inching closer to the moment when it would close in for good.

After a mile of sparse buildings and grassy lots, they came to the edge of the construction site and looked up.

The whole structure hummed with Sub-Weird Sessions, somewhere between sex and sacrifice, as radio waves coursed through the perma-dusk, gathering on the roof.

Staring up, the Mayor could see the naked edges of the Psychogeography: without the blackness of night to obscure it, the whole architecture was laid bare. He could see the doors and tunnels and wormholes that stitched together the otherwise invisible town within the town, which, until now, only Movies had made manifest.

The Orchard, the Blind Spot, the Ghost Town, the Desert, and all the tunnels of the Pretend Movie... all were real, connected through the Psychogeography, etched into the sky like constellations.

If only one could keep it all in mind, he thought. *And forget the static in between.* Tilting his head too far back, he fell over and lay on the ground, taking it in, feeling the immensity of time ahead now that day and night had merged and the ritual of the Blind Spot was behind him, lost in the layer of myth that, over centuries or

292

millennia, had broken down and rotted to feed the aquifer of the Pornography.

"Too much, it's too much for me," he moaned, extending his hand for Squimbop to help him up.

But the Professor was long gone.

The Lecture pooling in Squimbop's throat and chest was heavy. He could tell the time to let it out had come, well in advance of the school day. So he climbed under the fence, past the locked gazebo, and through a tarp into the Tower lobby. Without stopping, he ascended the stairs, then the ladders.

On the uppermost floors, a cold wind indicated that he was no longer in an enclosed space. He came out onto what looked like the external hallway of a Motel, past rows of concrete shells that might, in time, become rooms.

In one of them lay Ben, surrounded by beer bottles.

Squimbop knocked loudly on the cement. Ben bolted up and took a wild shot with his gun. The click of the empty barrel hung in the air.

Smiling, Squimbop pressed his finger to his cheek, then to his lips, and pretended to taste blood.

Ben sat up, wincing, and put the gun away.

"The famous architect," said the Professor. "What's all this?"

He indicated the row of rooms.

"Part of the Town's City," said Ben, opening a fresh beer after knocking two open ones over. "Every city needs a Motel.

Paradise of drifters."

Squimbop nodded and made his way into the recreated downtown. The streets of the Town's City extended away from the Square in the center, the Hotel on one side, the Greek restaurant on the other. It was identical to the town below but for the nearness of the Motel, just behind him, and, just ahead, a smaller replica of the radio station Well used to work in.

Lecture bubbling over what was left of his fangs, he hurried toward it, letting himself in through the unlocked side door and taking his position behind the desk. He turned on the equipment and tapped the mic, putting on headphones so he could hear himself clear his throat.

Tuning in to the night's frequency, a burst of static gave way to Well's voice in his ear.

"And I would hide in Dust House until it got dark, inventing codes, organizing my data to better reflect the devil's hand in everything that kept me from becoming... that kept there from being actual magic in the world. That made me have to work for it, whatever it was... to forge the impression of magic after the fact, concealing the dreary labor that actually goes into things"...

Well's voice got clearer the more Squimbop focused on it.

"Hello Well," he said, slowly and clearly. "Good to hear from you. Where are you coming to us from?"

A pause.

Then, tentatively, "Hello? Hello? Are you coming from inside Dust House?"

"No," said Squimbop. "I'm still down below. Relatively speaking. In something like your old office. Where are you?"

Another pause. Then, more assertively, "The Mountain. I'm on the Mountain. There are wires up here. A mic."

"Here too," said Squimbop. He could hear the footsteps of Sub-Weird beginning to congregate outside.

"This endless night is a ship," he continued. "And the ocean that ship is crossing is the Inland Sea. We are its crew, Well. You and I. I've crossed an ocean to be here. Have you?"

Silence.

Squimbop felt his throat growing huge with Lecture. "Then you will be my first mate aboard this vessel. I am the captain. There is no morning anymore. No far shore of dawn. But I will keep us from capsizing. Understood?"

Silence. Then the sound of Well nodding, mumbling, "Just protect my Dust House. See that it isn't flooded. It's all that's left after you destroyed my Ghost Town. Dust House is in the deep Desert and I can't get there yet, but I know it's real. It's my home. My only home. The last one I have left."

More Sub-Weird crept in, clustering around the station, desperate for a strong voice to tell them what to think, what to do, how to feel. They sat in rapt attention, hanging on Squimbop's every word just as the children had at the beginning of the year, though there would be no place for the Sub-Weird on the ANGEL HOUSE ceiling.

"I will. If you sail with me, I'll load your Dust House aboard this ark and keep it from tipping into the freezing, evil waves. I will shepherd you into Death seamlessly, painlessly, without ripping." Squimbop could hear Well begin to cry.

Lecture poured into his head and he opened his throat and let it out, unprocessed, into the mic and across the roof, across the town, and up the Mountain.

More Sub-Weird had congregated outside, massed on carpet squares, riveted as the Lecture infused their Reunion-addled brains with a jolt of the genuinely new.

"There are things under these waves, Well. Giant creatures, without arms or legs or hearts, but full of thoughts, and anger, misery, sad things that don't want us to stay on the surface.

295

That miss us and want us to join them down where it's so deep there is no bottom and no sides and no top, just down, down, down... and we will oppose the pull of these things by talking, and by being listened to."

He could hear the Sub-Weird groaning in eagerness to hear more, and decided to save none of his Lecture for school tomorrow. When he and the duo were sealed into the Chamber, he would stare at them in silence until recess, and then again until dismissal.

There was nothing more he needed to tell them. They knew what the Figure of Death looked like, and that it was as real as they were, and would go where they went. That was enough.

"Listen, Well, I'm going to tell you everything," he said, Lecture rushing up his throat and into the porous heads of the Sub-Weird, clustered on their carpet squares under the perma-dusk, losing themselves in the feeling of sitting in school, hearing about life for the very first time, cocooned in a space that Death could never penetrate.

It was a long grunting slog through the hours that used to correspond to the night.

When he'd spit out all the Lecture in his head, Squimbop left the station.

The Sub-Weird dispersed, back to their Session rooms in the backstreets of the Town's City. Only Ben remained, drooling against the stairwell, watching Squimbop approach.

"This your pulpit now?" he slurred.

"That's right. I'll be here every night. If the heads of these people explode, I'll pump my Lecture down their necks. I'm their Prophet now. The End is coming. They may as well know it."

He shoved his way down the ladders and then the stairs to the lobby and across the construction site that the contractors were starting to fill up, having decided it was morning despite the sky's inability to show it.

There was now the problem of where to shower. Though he'd already expelled his Lecture and thus had no liquid to firm up inside him, his body was coated in Death, which caked in his groin and armpits and would itch painfully if he didn't scrub it off.

Hurrying through the side streets, he turned toward the Gym.

The parking lot was full of Blankheads, as was the basketball court, lingering motionlessly, watching him with faces that radiated neither love of life nor fear of Death. He could tell that, unlike the Sub-Weird, his Lecture would have no effect on them, and thrilled at the rare prospect of being ignored as he threw his shoulder into the locked front door, breaking it clean off its hinges. It tipped inward and he stepped over it, past the unattended front desk and into the locker room.

He didn't carry a wallet or keys, so he simply pulled off his clothes, slung them over a bench, and walked into the shower.

Under the jets, he experienced the extremely unusual sensation of nothing firming up. His inner machinery came alive but, without fodder, the gears ground. His head filled with sparks and white heat, which created a stomach-sick sensation and a groaning in his ears. He slammed the shower jet back on and rubbed soap from the dispenser all over his body, up his face, and into his hair, peeling off handfuls of Death and throwing them in the drain trough, where they congealed and refused to go down.

He opened his eyes and stuffed them full of soap.

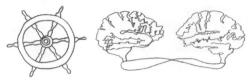

While Squimbop was showering on the ground floor, the duo was waking up in the Crawl Space below. They rubbed their eyes under the low ceiling, aware that they'd barely slept and that it was not a normal day outside.

They yawned and then, still in pajamas, wriggled on their sides and into the tunnel where they could stand. *This tunnel is part of* The Dream of Escape, was their first shared waking thought. *The time to stop exploring and begin the final journey is almost here*, was their second.

They climbed to the ground floor eating the candy bars that James had slipped under their pillows, and set out across the parking lot into the perma-dusk, elbowing their way past Blankheads without stopping to look them in the face.

Squimbop and the duo exited the Gym at the same time and found themselves walking in an uneasy procession up the streets to the School. Just before the traffic circle came into view, Squimbop stopped short and said, "I know where you're going."

The duo didn't respond.

When they arrived in the Chamber, the day followed its usual form, breaking for recess, with Squimbop sitting on his bench and the duo crawling into the Pine Hedge Office.

They didn't get much work done. Instead, they lay there stunned from the night in the Gym, fighting to enter the nineteen-year-olds, who were also stunned, lying on their bed in the Hotel, once again beyond coaxing into action.

Squimbop was silent all day, staring at them with a snarl that never changed. During these long dead hours, they came to understand that the Pretend Movie was under threat. They could envision it ending right here in town, all Escape routes blocked off by the leering grins of scarecrows. A sad, awful ending. A botched delivery.

So, for the rest of recess, instead of dreaming, they lay in the slush and thought: *The tunnel in the Gym is the beginning of true Escape, again and again*, as clearly and meaningfully as they could. *The Crawl Space is the doorway.*

Denying themselves the potential pleasure of achieving anything more, they dedicated the rest of the day to remembering this fact.

Back in ANGEL HOUSE, Squimbop put down his briefcase and booted up his laptop, munching tallow as he began to compose an email.

Dear Master,

With Hibernation over, I am required to resume my duties at the School, ministering to the two remaining children despite the apparent ineffectuality of my Lectures at this point.

Nevertheless, of course, I will continue in good faith.

All for now,
Prof. Sq.

He sent it off and then continued writing.

Dear Master,

I have grown so aimless and anxious in this town that I have resorted to talking through the nights, over the airwaves to the old radio host, surrounded by a gaggle of pathetic adults desperate to regress to a sort of babyish story-time. They are, let it be said, far easier to impress than the two remaining children in my classroom.

299

I wish you would write back, if only once. To remind me that I am not here alone. To reassure me that this year will end, and this town will go under, and I will be let loose back upon the Inland Sea, not only to drift but to return to where I belong... there are nights, I'll confess, when these notions seem like fantasies to me.

Are they? Is there nothing else? Am I just one of them, equally mortal, equally past-hungry, equally immersed in this miniscule fishtank of a town against the freakish immensity of the nothingness beyond its borders?

Please help me,

Prof. Sq.

He deleted what he'd just written, closed his laptop, and went to bed.

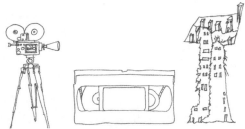

Ben was back in the Hotel for the first time in several days, to shower, change his clothes, and get ready to move into the Motel for good.

Inevitably, he found himself in the hot tub. This was what he'd miss most when he moved out. He'd considered designing one for the Motel, but the actual process of drafting it had eluded him: there was a holiness to hot tubs that exceeded whatever skill he had developed as an architect.

Though the tub was only lightly chlorinated, he felt clean in it now, smudged only with ex-versions of himself. He slipped off his bathing suit and let it float up to the surface, which he imagined was miles overhead.

Lying on the bottom with his hands on his belly, he could see the Psychogeography straining for definition in the greenish murk. Outlines of all the old salient places, from Ultra Max to the bus station, all the sets that had sparked the Pretend Movie in him and James, came visible under the water. He could feel the Pornography opening just beneath the hot tub, and believed that if he could only break the plastic bottom, he could swim down into it and stay there forever.

Bobbing with him on this cusp were the heads of James and the Mayor, deep in their own hot tubs, one at the Gym and the other at home, looking across a chlorine ocean at one another, making a form of closed-eye-contact that Ben understood to mean, *There is still something that unites us.*

Now came the moment where he had to decide whether to drown. The hump of air in his belly had deflated and he could hear his brain begging his mouth to open.

There is no more work to be done… there is no more work to be done… His mind started chanting this in mockery of his brain's furious need for air.

He could see the faces of James and the Mayor turning toward him, grinning and spitting bubbles, all three ready to die together and sink into whatever heaven awaited the Heads in the Brew.

The old term the *Heads in the Brew* pulled Ben out of the reality in which he needed to breathe and inducted him into a warm, airless dreamspace. *The original three Godheads,* he thought. *The trinity that dreamed this town up, out of nothing but the hot Inland Sea. The Heads that set the tractors behind the Mayor's house in motion, dragging the gravel from the quarries. Before the waters turned cold and buoyant enough for ANGEL*

HOUSE to sail across.

The Heads were gibbering underwater, swallowing chlorine and turning it to DNA, as if the Age of Generation were not yet over, the Mayor's Orchard more fertile than ever.

The Pornography, added the Mayor's Head. *The Movie beneath all Movies.*

All things are connected through water... warm water, deep water, all thought and ambition melting down, running away from the center, through the Outskirts... back to the Inland Sea, from which we too emerged and to which we will in time return.

There was something comforting in the finality of this, the way in which everything would come to nothing in the end, and, as nothing, transcend judgment. His thoughts bubbled up and away from him, infusing the water with the marrowy thickness of lamb stew.

The three Heads merged into One and it was as though the entire town had not yet been created and condemned. As if everything that had ever happened were only a draft of what could.

The time to make something out of nothing is now, thought the lone remaining Head, as it began to dream up a town with one street, one restaurant, one Meadow, one Mountain, and three inhabitants.

Ben came howling back to the surface, alone again. The reality of Death had found a way in, tainting the reverie. He leaned up on the side of the tub, panting, shocked to be human again, subject to forces outside his will.

Through the steamy Hotel window, he could see the lights of the Town's City. It sickened him to think that Squimbop was on the roof now, preaching with Well as his co-pilot and all the Sub-Weird clustered around him on their carpet squares.

Ben didn't even bother thinking, *That should be me.* Squeezing his bowels to release as much gas as he could, all he thought was, *I need a drink.*

He dragged a duffel bag full of beer through the streets, beneath a sky that was the color of an unripe fruit whose name he couldn't remember.

He cut through the alley behind the Greek restaurant and peed on the section of wall that corresponded to the exit from the Mayor's Private Booth, which only opened from the inside.

With his penis between his index finger and thumb, he turned and saw two figures stalk by. They weren't Sub-Weird, and definitely weren't anyone he knew. The total nothingness of their faces froze the urine in his bladder. He zipped up and walked quickly past them.

He drank three more beers on his way to the Town's City, desperate to get his bladder moving again and thereby, he hoped, forget what he'd just seen.

When he came to the edge of the construction site, he had to sit down under the force of Squimbop's broadcast. The roof was vibrating, causing the entire Town's City to take on the rocking motion of a ship chugging through a nighttime sea.

"There is marine life under us of such complexity that our entire bodies amount to less than a single cell of theirs," Squimbop was saying. On the other end, Well moaned, "Just let me rest in my own bed, dear lord, my own bed for one single second before

303

the blackness. Let Dust House be a home for an instant before it turns back to dust. Bring me the duo and I'll never ask for anything again."

Surrounding the two voices was a buzz of Sub-Weird, which Ben could see clustered on the roof. They sounded like appliances plugged into faulty sockets, regressing out of functionality.

They're my guests, he consoled himself, as he climbed the stairs and then the ladders, *even if they're his congregation. I don't have to be a Prophet so long as I can be a Motel Manager.*

Drinking another beer and beginning to pee down his left leg for fear of removing his penis again and seeing more of those figures, he thought, *Soon the Motel will be finished, and I will give myself a room above the Front Office, and never again be anyone's guest but my own.*

"There is a snake beneath the Inland Sea so long its head has never been found," boomed Squimbop's voice, and Ben fell to his knees, his gun clattering out of his pants as the call to worship overwhelmed him.

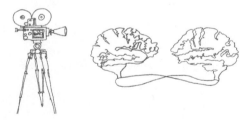

James walked onto the basketball court just as the nineteen-year-olds pushed past the front desk and into the Gym.

He sat on the bleachers and watched as they strode onto the court, yawning, looking uncertain as to why they were here. They asked where to stand, and he told them, "Over there, in front of the cardboard Hotel. Let's rehearse your arrival scene."

He had spent all day making sure the Ultra Max sets on the basketball court were in order, setting up the models of the Greek restaurant, the Hotel, Saltwater's liquor store, and the chalk outline that corresponded to the Meadow-lined Road. One racquetball court would serve as the Movie Store and the other as the Mayor's house, when the time to shoot scenes there came.

His head was already throbbing, drifting away from the scene in front of him toward the parking lot outside the Gym, where he could picture the swarming Blankheads so vividly he felt like he was among them.

He tried to regroup by picturing the nineteen-year-olds walking off and never coming back, leaving him to film the model town with himself as its only inhabitant.

Get them in hand before you lose them. Convince yourself you're a real Director, even if you don't fully believe it. If you want to keep your film from becoming a self-portrait, keep hold of them at all costs.

He felt their attention on him, cocky and judgmental, as he warmed up his video camera and said, "Okay, I'm going to shoot some tests. For this scene, you're exhausted from months on the road. You've finally found a town where you can stop. An exit has appeared, though only briefly, allowing you to get off the highway. The crucial thing to convey here is that you've developed a prophecy from a combination of dreaming and living in the giant open swaths of land outside the town, and you've decided to come here to deliver it. And by delivering it, you'll hear what it is for the first time. Only by speaking it aloud, to those primed to believe it, will it turn into something tangible, beyond the set of inklings currently hovering inside you. So your trajectory is toward the town, ever deeper into it... this is where you've come to seek your future and make your mark as men in the world. Understood?"

305

The nineteen-year-olds nodded, blowing bubbles with gum that James hadn't noticed them chewing. He pictured the nine-year-olds asleep underfoot, their teeth grinding in the Crawl Space, fighting for control of their actors.

He started rolling the camera, watching as they walked around the court, trampling the cardboard models without appearing to understand what they represented.

They looked partially asleep, their heads lolling so idiotically that James wondered if perhaps the nine-year-olds had found a way to go on directingthem, subverting the power he'd hoped the Crawl Space would exercise over their dreaming minds. The nineteen-year-olds looked longingly at the door, but whether their minds were refilling with *The Dream of Escape,* or they were just losing interest, was impossible to determine.

"Cut!" he shouted. "Look, guys, you've just gotten to town, okay? You've been on the road for close to a year, out in a part of the country that no one here has ever seen, or will ever see. A country that exists for you two that doesn't exist for anyone else. A private country. Okay? A landmass that everyone else dismisses as the Inland Sea. And in this private country, you've become aware of a transcendent truth, a key to eternal life. And you've hurried across giant salt flats and through carnivorous peat bogs to deliver your prophecy here, in the town, before it goes bad. This town is the end of the line, the terminus at the end of the dead-end street of your whole lives up to this point. That's what the film's about. Alright?"

The nineteen-year-olds nodded again, but their eyes were glazed over and they looked unsteady on their feet.

James resumed filming, knowing he wouldn't get any usable footage no matter how many nights he spent like this. He could feel the blood under his shaved scalp throbbing, and he could hear the nine-year-olds stirring in the Crawl Space underfoot, fighting toward the Pretend Movie through waves of static. He closed his eyes against the viewfinder and pictured *The Dream of Escape* in its full splendor, featuring himself and Ben in a truly new world, a place free of the town, and of art, ambition, time, the Mayor, reproduction and limitation of every kind, money, News City, Death... beyond even the deepest Desert, where dreaming and waking were one, and neither of them had to be embodied, and there was no work to be done because everything was already...

He fell over while trying to hold the camera still. Sitting on the ground, he heard banging on the cracked remnants of the front door, and knew the Blankheads would be here soon, and though he considered shooting another take with the nineteen-year-olds, he saw the full futility of his film laid out before him like an ancient artifact recently unearthed, dirt falling away to reveal what was written, which was *RELINQUISH THE NINETEEN-YEAR-OLDS.*

The Age of Denial is at an end. He couldn't suppress the thought. *You're no filmmaker and you never were. If it takes an army of demons to get you to see this, well here they are.*

By the time he was back on his feet, all he could say was, "Look, guys, take the night off. Go back to the Hotel. Think about whether acting is right for you. We'll try this another time."

He put down the camera and began disassembling the model of the Mattress Store, where he'd planned a sex scene with one of the life-sized sex dolls it came with. Under the floorboards, he could hear the nine-year-olds revving up where they slept in the Crawl Space, reclaiming control of their stars, throwing their minds into the nineteen-year-old bodies that were no longer occupied by the trivialities of a twenty-nine-year-old's notion of an art film.

James left the nineteen-year-olds with the camera in his hand,

307

hurrying so as not to see them slipping back into the Pretend Movie.

He stomped through the locker room and into the corridor that led to the steam room, which he'd avoided all year in order to keep one location in reserve for a moment like this.

Now he let himself in, relieved to find it full of steam and eucalyptus. The heat drew oil through his pores until his skin turned as thick and slippery as that of a seal. He stripped off his Director's suit and sat against the tiles of the back wall, holding his camera in his lap, staring at himself in the side monitor as the steam appeared to conjure his face.

When he almost lost consciousness against the back wall, his mouth open and dripping, he rolled onto his knees and pushed himself up, back to his feet, holding the camera by his side and stalking in circles, so dizzy he wouldn't know he was falling until his head hit the ground.

He stalked the floor like this, sucking moisture into his lungs, allowing himself to imagine the Movie Store packed full of the devout, fighting one another for the privilege of renting his Movie, killing one another if need be.

It felt sick to continue this reverie, but the sick part of him was powerful. It suckled at his skin, drawing the hives back out with its poison tongue. "They'll have to build a second Movie Store to hold everything I'm about to unleash," he barked into the camera he was still holding, imagining the Mayor's tears of apology for having ever doubted him.

He reached up to the steam vent and flicked the switch to send more in, clouding the lens and raising the temperature above what an ordinary man could tolerate. Swinging the camera in time, he began to march in wide circles around the steam room, pounding his chest with his other hand, chanting, "Everything that matters is right here in the Gym. The Pornography is exploding

308

from within me. I am the Godhead. I am the source of all Movies!" In the middle of this ecstasy, he opened his eyes onto those of a Blankhead. He hadn't heard the door open, but now he heard it close. His first thought was, *They were waiting for me to dismiss the nineteen-year-olds. Now it's open season.*

The Blankhead did not try to stop James from what he was doing. Rather, it fell into step with him. Clouds of steam like pillow stuffing clung to its skin, as it and James marched mirroring one another. James' eyes were narrowed to a crack, and, through this crack, under the steam, he saw the hulking outline of this new being, its thick white skin mottled with blue veins, its mouth an abject darkness.

Without trying to claw through the steam, he turned the camera around, recording the Blankhead's mouth as it opened and closed like a lizard's.

It mimicked James' movements, holding up an imaginary camera, and scratching its skin when James reached down to soothe his hives. When he sat back down, swooning, the Blankhead sat beside him, emitting breath so cold it chilled the entire space until a new gust of steam blew in.

Sitting beside it, James could tell this thing was not thinking, or even forming impressions. It emanated not stupidity but an awful purity, true blankness in the sense of wanting nothing, knowing nothing, and, in some way beyond his imagining, being nothing.

When he stretched, the Blankhead stretched. When he yawned, it yawned, revealing the void, black and enticing in the white steam, devouring whatever megalomania he'd succeeded in drumming up in himself just before it arrived.

He pointed his camera at it, surveying its bearish jawline and neck.

Eventually the steam system shuddered and turned off, and the steam that was floating in the air started to settle. James could feel it turning to water and running over his feet and down the drain, dripping from the camera lens and into his lap.

The Blankhead yawned in a way that sounded like a growl, and James shivered, mustering all his inner resources to keep from putting his head inside that mouth right now and whispering, *Relief, here I come.*

Staring into the void-mouth through his viewfinder, recording that blackness in lieu of the scene he'd planned with the nineteen-year-olds, he'd never been more aware that he was not a God, and would never in his life express a totalizing, Godlike vision, neither in cinema nor in any other medium.

Hives exploded in his groin and armpits as the steam room turned into a freezer. He reached the edge of consciousness. Just before shutting off, his brain filled with a single, luminous thought: *Only the nine-year-olds are the real thing. That's the way it's always been. Whatever it takes to help them see the Pretend Movie through, that's the only good that can come from any of this.*

Back in his house, images of Blankheads swarmed James' center, where his main self dwelled.

They pressed in from the Gym's lobby and the racquetball courts and the corridors, congregating along the three-point line of the basketball court, crushing the cardboard town he'd set up. James could hear his heartbeat transformed into the chugging of a video camera, taking in what it could through the blankness thickening its lens, and he knew that if he played the tape in his actual camera right now, the footage would show the Blankheads mushed together, breathing out more smoke until they became a single mass, no longer discernible as individuals. He could see hundreds of arms protruding, waving crushed fistfuls of cardboard, and he could see that this act corresponded, voodoo-like, to the real town. The Blankheads would turn everything into nothing, the town into nowhere, farther out than the absolute outermost Outskirts, less habitable than the bottom of the deepest trench in the Inland Sea.

He saw them thousands thick on the basketball court, writhing and squirming up and over each other, their white skin merging with the whiteness of the smoke they exuded, so their outlines only came into definition through the profound blackness of their void-mouths.

The more they writhed, the more they replicated themselves, until the cloud of white smoke surrounding them thickened into a cream, smearing the lens with more and more layers until, finally, the Movie was nothing but butter disturbed by long fingers that bore no prints.

Waking in his office chair to itch a hive under his armpit, he permitted himself a single pleasant thought:

Perhaps only the Gym will remain, an ark housing the Director and my troupe of actors, making the last Movie that will ever exist, to be seen by no one except everyone in it. When I get thirsty, I'll leave the camera running and drink straight from the adult pool, its water fresh and clean, nutritive, amniotic, constantly birthing new forms, all of them beautiful and ready to take their places onscreen...

The nine-year-olds woke up in the Crawl Space, disoriented but happy. As they yawned and rubbed their eyes and collected their thoughts, a sense of freedom emerged. A weight had been lifted, palpably enough that the ceiling seemed further from their faces than it had when they fell asleep.

We don't have to stay here anymore, they thought. *Whatever spell James tried to cast over us has broken, or never took in the first place. He's weaker than he seemed. Or we're stronger.*

Before the feeling wore off, they wriggled out of the Crawl Space, up the stairs, through the crowd of Blankheads on the basketball court, and out of the Gym, breaking into a run as they crossed the parking lot.

They flapped their arms, so happy they wondered if they could fly. They found that they could not, but another, equally gratifying power had grown in them: without stopping to decide to skip school, they ran straight past the traffic circle and all the way downtown, feeling invincible, determined to outrun Squimbop if he came looking for them.

Catching their breath outside the ice cream parlor, they felt totally liberated, like they'd never have to go to school again. The doorway between them and the fruition of the Pretend Movie was open. All they had to do was tire themselves out enough to fall asleep, back in their Dead Houses tonight.

But the perma-dusk was disorienting and they felt revved up, too manic to close their eyes. If they didn't go to school, they'd have to spend the day somewhere else.

They decided on the Movie Store.

Saltwater eyed them from behind the checkout counter as the bell clinked when they came in. He sat on a high stool, wearing a denim vest. The screen near the ceiling played a sample Movie, which radiated static onto the back of his head, filling his long gray hair with white flecks, like pockets of dandruff or lice eggs.

The New Releases shelf was bare and every other shelf, including the Shrine of Great Directors, was full of empty boxes. There was a laminated sheet of Hibernation Specials on top of a pile of other sheets describing rental packages (2-for-1 Tuesdays, $1 Movie day, All Late Fees Waived, etc.), a wry joke since, as everyone knew, the Mayor had used everything up, leaving nothing for anyone else. The ashes of his spent tapes sat in a bin under the Returns slot, melted shut.

The nine-year-olds had never seen other customers in here, so they assumed that the New Releases shelf was empty not because everything had been checked out, but because nothing here was new.

They took the stairs down to the lower level, where the complete model town was laid out. There was a curtain at the bottom, as there so often was in the places that mattered. They paused to adjust to the coolness and the increased pressure; then they pushed the curtain aside and went through.

Now they were in the model town, the shelves arranged according to their correspondence to the town's geography: Movies about or set at the Greek restaurant were arranged inside a full-size model of the Greek restaurant, same as the Meadow, the Hotel, and the Strip.

In this way, the basement of the Movie Store took up the entire underside of the town, opening into the foundations of the buildings whose representations it featured.

The only site not to scale was the Movie Store itself, about which at least a hundred Movies had been made over the course of the town's history. This was represented as a small kiosk, with a dummy model of Saltwater sitting on a stool and staring out, surrounded by a pile of boxes.

At the edges, where the Outskirts began, were signs reading ZONE OF ABSTRACTION. Here were the strangest Movies, the most occult and experimental, those that departed most from the immense boredom of life in the town to approach the totalizing grandeur that the duo envisioned for the Pretend Movie, though theirs would go farther than any real Movie could, by dint of the fact that a real Movie could depart from reality but then had to veer back into it, in order to market itself and earn its accolades, whereas the Pretend Movie—they reminded themselves—was designed to depart from reality and never return.

The Movie Store, they thought, pausing in their procession across the downstairs, *formative as it's been and much as we love it, is ultimately a Hall of False Idols. We will not look back once we've left it behind.*

So this would be their goodbye. They could feel the tunnels groaning and opening up just inside the walls, the Psychogeography alive directly behind the thousands of Movies it had inspired.

They roamed out to the Welcome Center section, exhausting themselves as they traced the underground analogue of the Meadow-lined Road, lined here not by the Meadow but by thousands of Movies about it.

Up past the Welcome Center, they verged further, toward the sign that read EDGE OF ALL MOVIES: NOTHING BEYOND.

The Pretend Movie vibrated inside them as they approached this Edge, beyond which lapped the Inland Sea. They pretended it was a bath of molten celluloid. The Dream of Escape *lies further in this direction, not in retreating from it,* they thought,

314

nodding off slightly as they walked, their mind shuddering with flashes of the nineteen-year-olds, lying passed out in the Hotel. When they lost their balance and tipped forward into another curtain, they fell deeper into the Movie Store than they'd ever been before.

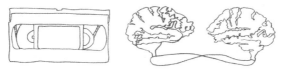

The Mayor was on the other side, trying to kill another lonely afternoon.

Since James had taken the nine-year-olds from their Dead Houses, he had nowhere to go. The smell of his rotting Orchard still filled his house, and the light of the perma-dusk through his windows menaced him in every room, whispering, *Soon the Blind Spot's going to eat you.*

He spent a few days stroking his clitoris in the hot tub until it grew sore and the chlorinated water burned it, and then he ate all the sugar and butter he had in storage, and then he had no option but to come to the Movie Store and revisit the boxes of all the Movies he'd bred with and never would again, experiencing now only the degraded memory of having once been aroused by them.

Like his Private Booth at the Greek restaurant, the Back Room was part of the Psychogeography. Home to the most potent Movies, which he'd bred with first, as soon as Ben and James had left for News City and his long, unmarked future alone in the town had spread out before him.

If there was anywhere left in town where he might forget what Squimbop had done to him—and what he wished Squimbop might still do—and forget that he'd canceled James' production and lost faith in Ben's building, this was the Room. Here, the future was unwritten and denial was unnecessary.

So he was on his knees, pressing the boxes to his face and crying, when the fingers of the duo agitated the curtain from the other side.

Their fingers remained against the curtain, in the middle zone between the Movie Store and the Back Room, sprouting joints as he reached his own fingers out, still kneeling, and began to pull. Desperate to put the thought of Squimbop out of mind, he enveloped their fingers in his fists and pulled with everything he had left.

The duo's feet strained to stay planted in the Movie Store, even as their minds thrilled at the prospect of breaking through, onto the other side at last. As they hovered in the middle space, the Mayor closed his eyes and dug his knees into the carpet, squeezing his clitoris between his thighs as he hauled, focusing his entire being on the task at hand, for once in his life thinking of nothing except the scene he was currently in.

The nine-year-olds left their feet and flew, the air turning cold and wet like the mist that hovered over the Ghost Town. In this middle air they could hear the crackle of Well's voice, reaching them from a distance that used to be very far away but that now, within the Psychogeography, was suddenly very near.

"You are free of the town... come to me... leave the Mayor and come to me"... rasped Well, through the radio station atop the Mountain.

Remember the Pretend Movie... Remember the Pretend Movie, they chanted in their shared mind, clamping down on this as the lone truth in a universe that was otherwise warping out of all recognition.

They flew through the curtain, pulled by their fingers

316

toward the light of the Back Room, where the Mayor was waiting for them, sobbing with anticipation.

He fell onto his back in the final instant, swooning as he lay there and felt them land on top of him.

Then all three were together in the Back Room, where no one but the Mayor had ever been. They sat up and inhaled the hot, still air, catching their breath as empty Movie boxes fell off the shelves and landed on top of them, sticking to their skin.

The Mayor's clitoris trembled and leaked into his underwear, and he felt blessed beyond any gratitude he could show. *Ben and James are trash-people, Sub-Weird... worth nothing. Through the nine-year-olds, they will be subsumed in the shrine I'll build to the three of us at nine, when we were the budding Redeemers of the town, growing stronger by the day... strong enough to defend it against all incursion.*

Every time he closed his eyes the image of Squimbop pounding him into submission returned, so he kept them open, fighting not to blink.

The Mayor realized he was famished as an alluring image of the duo fattened to bursting entered his mind and refused to leave.

He decided to take them to dinner.

The Mayor parted the curtain onto a padded tunnel that led away from the Movie Store and into his Private Booth in the Greek restaurant.

"You're about to have a feast like you've never had before. You'll see things you never would've thought existed," he announced to the duo as he settled onto the massive leather seat across from them in his Private Booth and motioned to the waiter to light the candle in the center of the table and turn off the overhead lights. He obliged, then handed the Mayor the green leather menu in the semi-dark.

The Mayor was so hungry and worked up that, for a few moments, he could neither read the menu nor remember what was on it. He wanted the food to be here already, to be already in his mouth.

The duo watched him, seated where Squimbop had sat, working in tandem to perceive his immensity.

When he'd gotten it together to order, the struggle became to wait. He chewed his knuckles and slurped water, jiggling on the leather seat, completely unsure what to say.

Part of him prayed they would tell or ask him something, while the rest of him seethed with horror at the thought of trying to respond. He'd never been this close to them outside of their Dead Houses; their attention, now that they were awake and fully themselves, felt like sunshine through two magnifying glasses.

The food finally arrived, on three carts draped with tablecloths. The waiter unveiled platters of grilled pork with cinnamon glaze, salmon and tuna, roast chicken and turkey with anise and rosemary, couscous and saffron rice, honey polenta with diced chilies, a whole suckling pig, a pot of beef stew, and another cart of desserts, waiting to be unveiled.

The Mayor parceled out the feast onto their plates, saying, "You will eat when I tell you to," then laughed, saying, "Now! Now! Eat now!"

They ate.

He watched them through eyes sweating from the ordeal of his own eating. The more he shoveled in, the less he had to worry about this moment ending. As he focused on keeping his mouth full at all times, shoving entire chicken legs and buttery dumplings down his throat, he could feel his heart straining not to break.

When it came time for dessert, the waiter unveiled the final cart, crammed with chocolate mousses and tortes, raspberry and cherry and lemon curd pies and cinnamon and egg and pistachio custards.

Then the waiter stepped back and asked what they wanted to drink, and the Mayor said, "Vin Santo," and the duo, without hesitation or conference, said, "Hot cocoa," and the Mayor fell out of his seat, onto his belly on the floor, writhing in panic as those nights in the Dead Houses caught up with him and Squimbop as the Figure of Death filled his mind, grinning under his fur hood, pushing him face down onto the Mattress Store mattress, and he knew he would never be free of the past, nor of the future that past had foretold, no matter how hard he tried or how much he ate.

They left without finishing dessert.

On their way out, they plowed into the waiter carrying a bowl of rosewater with three warm towels; it flew into their faces, ensuring they'd reek pleasantly the rest of the time they knew one another.

As soon as they got outside, Well's voice filled the air, swimming upward like steam to seep into the Sub-Weird massed in the Town's City, high overhead.

"I'm waiting for you on the Mountain," he whispered, modulating his voice to the frequency only children could hear. "Come up here, far from the town, and we'll live together in Dust House forever."

On their way to the Mayor's station wagon, they passed Ben, drunk and whispering as he pissed on a fence. He turned but wouldn't look at them, ascertaining only obliquely that the Mayor and the duo were getting into a car together.

The Mayor got in the driver's seat and started the engine, awash

319

in the relief of putting it into drive rather than neutral. The duo recognized the car from where it had sat all those nights outside their bedroom windows, tipping gently side to side as Squimbop steered the Wooden Wheel.

When the Mayor floored the accelerator on the way out of town, the nine-year-olds got sucked against their leather seats in the back, breathing through mouths that were fixed open as the Meadow-lined Road whipped by in a queasy blur of grass and manure, silos and parked tractors and resting dogs unable to sleep in the perma-dusk.

When the Mayor parked the station wagon inside his garage, he came around to the backseat and helped the duo out like cargo he'd picked up at a dock in the black market district of the Town's City, as he'd imagined it before Ben had tried to make it real.

They let themselves be carried into the kitchen, weary from the dinner and Well's voice, droning the same message again and again. The Mayor turned on the hot tub and told them to relax in there while he went upstairs to make up their room.

Climbing the stairs, he knew his first task was to tell the ghosts who'd filled his house that he wasn't available tonight. They'd materialized out of the perma-dusk to moan in his ears, demanding that he reckon with them, turning this house, too, into a Dead House. But tonight it would be filled with life.

"I can't see you tonight," he practiced saying, relishing the ambiguity of the phrase as it related to ghosts. They wouldn't take the news easily, since they'd been waiting for him all day, alone in those many rooms with nothing else to look forward to. The rooms would grow hot and stuffy as they lingered without his company, the ghosts burping unused energy that, on any other night, would have been absorbed by the Mayor's greasy, naked hulk.

Entering the first of the many upstairs offices where he did no work, he whispered, "I can't see you tonight."

Nothing happened except that his unease grew. It unfurled in him, racing through his blood. He felt his fingertips pulsating, desperate to fly off of his body.

He shouted, throwing more authority into his voice than he thought he could muster: "I said, I can't see you tonight!!"

The walls shook and groaned, angry, finally aware that the Mayor was serious.

"I have company! I'm not alone in my house anymore!" he shouted, rubbing his sweaty forehead with his arms.

"My sons are home!!"

He lay down on his back in the hallway after he'd made this announcement in all of the upstairs rooms, kicking his arms and legs like a nine-year-old making a snow angel.

"You can't touch me anymore!" He rolled up his pant legs as high as they would go, shocked by the girth of his calves. Ghost-heads peeped from all the doorways.

"Come to bed, honey," they whispered, but defeatedly, having accepted that tonight he would not come.

"And that was the night it all changed," he declared, imitating J.L. Wind addressing the Town Council. He closed his eyes on the hallway floorboards and blew hard into his hands, inflating a bag around him and the nine-year-olds, encasing them in a balloon so big that no one would find them until all the air was used up and they'd died peacefully in each other's arms.

The linen closet was open and spilling forth as the Mayor jogged up and down the hallway that led to the bedroom, smelling each sheet and pillowcase and comforter as he took it out, pushing it into his nose and mouth, chewing the cotton and wool, inhaling the deep past. He smoothed the wadded-up sheets, unwashed since his childhood, then tied them around his neck like an emperor's robes.

He could still smell the rosewater in his sweat, but it was losing out to the detergent and dust on the sheets, and the musk in the wool. *This is what my life has come to*, he thought. *I'm making a home for them, and they are here, downstairs, in my house, waiting for their bed, which will be their new habitat, because James and Squimbop destroyed their old ones, and Ben built a place in which no one with any integrity can live.*

He threw sheet after sheet onto the bed, bouncing on the mattress, huffing, trying to feel strong and sure of himself. "I am the Father," he chanted, smelling and tasting the sheets, gagging when they went down his throat. "Despite the Blind Spot, I have living sons, and they are here."

That's more than Ben or James will ever be able to say.

With everything laid out, he set about piling the sheets and pillows in an exact replica of the Fortresses he'd rutted in when he was their age, rubbing his nascent boner against the smooth sheet-covered mattress while imagining himself as the God-emperor of a tribe of fearless warriors whose exploits would end up in epic Movies.

These warriors saved the town from entropy and mediocrity with a savagery that had never been equaled in human history, sawing and eating and raping their way through everything that was disappointing about the human race until the nine-year-old Mayor had so thoroughly redeemed the species he was the only one left.

The blankets and sheets on the bed were falling into place, fleshing out the stronghold's rough architecture. It wasn't time yet, but before long he would reward himself by tilting his head back and letting out a War Whoop, his first in twenty years.

This would consecrate the Fortress, elevating it above the state of being a replica. *I will be the ur-warrior and they will be the young braves*, he decided. *They'll save the town from Death, which has come here merely to test them.*

It's okay that the town's redemption didn't manifest through me, as long as it manifests through them.

In a sense, the credit will still be mine.

The War Whoop would summon them up here from wherever in the house they were, and then the three of them would explore the Fortress together. He would show them how to worship in the right way, inducting them into the secret rituals he'd kept to himself throughout his twenty-nine years. He hoisted a beanbag onto the bed, and stood on top of it to survey the countryside.

The rhapsody passed quickly and the hangover began right away. Reality renewed its vow to oppress him forever, having absorbed the War Whoop as soon as he let it out, so thoroughly that he couldn't be sure he really had. There was no echo, nor any sense that he could try again.

His thoughts thus turned to the nine-year-olds, whom he prayed were still downstairs. He got to his feet and pulled his pants back on, walking away from the Fortress without looking at it again. He didn't want to see what it looked like now that the reverie of making it had worn off.

He coughed into his fist and it came out as a second, miniature War Whoop, meek and childish as he closed the bedroom door. On the way to the indoor porch that housed the hot tub, he picked up a crate of warm beer from a stack near the fridge, and an opener. In the doorway, he peered through the steam at the nine-year-olds, fully clothed, their heads barely above water level.

He stripped but left his underwear on so as not to reveal his clitoris.

Then, opening the crate with the sharp corner of the corkscrew, he took out three bottles and cracked them, slipping down into the water and pushing two into the duo's faces, holding them like that until they opened their eyes and accepted the bottles.

"Cheers," he sighed, downing his bottle in one slug and letting it float in the brine while he opened another.

"Your Fortress is ready upstairs."

The duo nodded. They had no intention of going up there. The beer only accelerated the effects of the hot tub, in conjunction with Well's voice, still streaming over the airwaves toward them. Their bodies were turning spongy and swelling up, gaining volume without gaining mass.

So as not to fixate too obsessively, the Mayor kept drinking and looking away.

Still, it was undeniable: Ben and James were growing out of the nine-year-olds. Or, rather, spongy, soggy bread effigies of Ben and James, the intervening twenty years seeping into them as used and reused hot tub water.

There was still life at their centers, but their eyes were becoming raisins.

Inside the effigies, the nine-year-olds were roiling hard.

They could feel the tunnels opening under the hot tub, the Psychogeography becoming accessible through the drain as Well's voice hummed in the sound of the jets, bidding them, for the thousandth time tonight, to come to the Desert.

Do not fall asleep in this house. The Mayor will never let you leave if you do, it said. *I will guide you through the Psychogeography... just dive under and follow my voice.*

324

As they closed their eyes, the nineteen-year-olds stirred on their Hotel bed, but the nine-year-olds knew this was a mission they had to make on their own. *This is where we take charge of the Pretend Movie,* they thought, in a confident, directorial inner voice. *We make this journey as us, not as them. Tonight, we begin to live our own lives, in the Desert, far beyond the town.*

It certainly seemed the better option, as compared to whatever life in the Mayor's house might hold in store. In the far, far distance of the Oasis, the Comedy Troupe laughed in hearty assent.

The effigies kept growing, getting limper the more water they absorbed. Soon they were more than life-size, slumping down toward the Mayor, their spongy raisin eyes level with his.

When they were about to crumble, the nine-year-olds heaved in a last breath, took a last look at the sorry hulk of the Mayor, who was maybe their father but would never have a role in the Pretend Movie, and plunged out of the effigies and down the drain. They went all the way down, through a slimy, sewage-choked valve, into the tunnel, where, immersed in the Psychogeography, they found they could stand.

The Mayor sat in the hot tub, watching the Ben and James effigies topple onto him. He could tell their spirit was gone. They were nothing but toys now.

In this constellation, he was the only living Head in the Brew, a lone God that had outlived its trinity.

Too frightened to close his eyes, he nevertheless tried to summon a little of the universe-creating power of the Heads in the Brew, pretending that the town didn't yet exist and that all his memories were only sketches for the far future, too distant to be reached in his lifetime.

The effigies smothered him, so that he could only breathe

by biting into them and sucking bread down his throat.

When the misery of lying like this reached its apex, the Mayor pushed them back and rose, feeling lukewarm water stream from his hair. He looked at the foggy glass windows of his porch, leading onto his lawn in the perma-dusk, and then to the ash-filled fire pit, and, beyond that, to the gravel quarry where his grave awaited.

Yawning and refusing to stand still above the drain the duo had escaped through, he grabbed the effigies, one in each hand, and heaved them out of the hot tub, spilling all over the mat and tiles as he eased open the door onto the backyard and began the long walk to the quarry.

Only once did he make the mistake of looking down at Ben and James' faces, slack and stretched as the water squished out of them onto the roots and pine needles.

Past the parked tractors, he heaved what was left of the effigies over the quarry edge, watching them careen down to cover his grave, though he knew they'd be gone by the time his turn to lie there came.

Then he lay down on his back at the edge of the pit and closed his eyes, listening to the hot tub water seep out of his ears. When he sat back up, the pine trees around the peripheries had come to life in the form of hundreds of Blankheads streaming in, forming a circle around him.

They looked up at the sky, then down at the Mayor. Then surveyed the quarry, oblivious to the two bodies that had been thrown in. Watching them open and close their mouths, revealing voids far darker than the perma-dusk, the Mayor's only thought was, *The next Reunion will take place here, and these will be its participants. When they told me they'd bring the Blind Spot to my house, this is what they meant.*

He watched as they processed back along the row of quarries, past the parked tractors and toward the Blind Spot, which, although they were no longer bears, they perhaps still intended to sleep in.

PART VI
The Desert

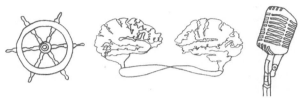

The Desert was vast and frigid in the dark behind the summit where Well had restarted his life. The perma-dusk formed a skin over the town at a height of several thousand feet, above which night and day persisted unchanged.

The duo emerged from the Psychogeography into a cave in the side of the Mountain just beneath the summit. Still wet from the Mayor's hot tub, they shivered, grasping their knees and leaning against the rock wall. The night was cold, as if Hibernation hadn't ended at this elevation, though they could smell spring in the wind that tore past the cave mouth. It smelled fresh and hearty, new in a way they'd never smelled before, like the whole town was a locked room and now, finally, they'd made it out, into the world.

Lying on their backs, they wanted to set out for the Desert right away, but hunger and disorientation held them in place. They were stunned from their journey, brief as it'd been. So they lay on the rock floor, murmuring, stuck in indecision.

They were still murmuring when they heard voices. Someone was nearby, maybe several people. As they fell silent and tried to glean whose realm they'd stumbled into, a pair of Dwellers in overalls and baseball caps perched behind a boulder just outside the mouth, deciding what news to present to Well. They briefed him every evening, when he returned from his long day in the deep Desert, where he disappeared early every morning carrying a backpack with a gallon of water and a pound of walnuts, returning just in time for dinner and a short nap before his nightly broadcast with Squimbop began.

Aware that he'd be back within the hour, the Dwellers peered out from behind the boulder and took the duo in, whispering, "They're here. The ones he's been calling to, from down there... they're up here now."

Glad to be the bearers of good news, they climbed back to the summit, where others like them were emerging from their tents to start a cooking fire, hauling sides of meat from the coolers they kept them in.

Well was just returning from his day in the Desert, taciturn and obsessed as ever. One Dweller poured him a plastic cup of vodka while another continued stirring a pot of beans and prodding at the meat on the fire.

The two who had discovered the duo in the cave waited nearby as Well drank and washed his face in a basin of water he'd washed with several times before. They watched him, biding their time, wary of rushing the announcement. He rubbed his throat, preparing for the long hours ahead, and accepted the towel that another Dweller held out to him, signaling for more vodka as he sat in his plastic chair, waiting for the meat to be done.

Dust House was full of sand and broken glass and half the floorboards were loose, but it was dim and cool and had working plumbing, and, more and more, Well found he was able to sit in there with his eyes closed and not only think but feel that it was where he was about to relive the formative years of his life, the good years before the ghosts had come to the Ghost Town.

The line between the Desert and Dust Street was sharp: the path to it was winding and variable, but when he reached it, it was the only thing there. Before this point, the journey took him past endless dunes and low hot sky, drifting sand and sparse cacti and scrub brush, and then, like stepping onto a set, he was walking down Dust Street toward a house at the far end, the Desert nothing but a shaken-off daze behind him.

He didn't have to ring the doorbell when he got to Dust House. The key was hidden in a flower pot hanging from the window to the right of the porch. He found it there every day when he let himself in, and returned it every day on his way out.

At the crack of the door the glaring sun vanished. Inside it was always cool and dim. He stole in quickly so as not to let this sacred air out.

He took his shoes off as soon as he crossed the threshold and closed the door, and walked in his socks across the living room and dining room and parlor into the kitchen, where he filled a glass that he kept upside-down beside the sink, marveling every time at the running water.

When the brownish water had gone clear, he brought it back across the same set of rooms in reverse, and sat on the couch to drink it, holding it with both hands like a chalice, savoring the sand on the rim. Drifting into memories of a childhood spent sipping from this same glass, drowsing on this same couch, he felt time break into shards and slice his fingers. He only looked down after several minutes of bleeding to see that he'd crushed the glass in his fist.

Back on the summit, in his chair by the fire with his vodka in his hand, he looked up as two Dwellers approached him and announced, after asking if they could make an announcement, that two children from the town had been spotted bedding down in a nearby cave.

"They are in there, on their backs, stunned," the Dwellers

announced in tandem.

"Thanks," Well gasped, trying to downplay the impact of the news. "Stand guard at the cave mouth until morning. Have them ready to go by then."

The Dwellers nodded and departed.

When they had, his guts, already burning from the vodka, opened and sucked him into a vortex of images of ensconcing the duo in Dust House, tucking them into the upstairs bedroom in which he had spent so many years, shivering in terror of growing old and hoarding the candy that... who had given it to him? He couldn't remember.

Before this fact became oppressive, he forced himself to his feet and into the broadcast cabin without having eaten.

Since he'd succeeded in summoning the duo and thus had no reason to go on speaking with the town, he considered skipping tonight's broadcast, but decided against it. Entering Dust House with the duo without having first made peace with Squimbop and all those who gathered around him to listen felt dangerous.

So he made a cup of tea and sat down in front of the mic, licking his lips and picturing Squimbop way down below, beneath the perma-dusk in the heart of the Town's City, the Sub-Weird pressed around him as close as they could bear.

He unfolded his voice from his body like an heirloom violin from its crude carrying case. He was cagy and evasive as the broadcast got going, giving up control over his throat only a little at a time in an effort not to blurt "Dust House" and "nine-year-olds" and "live forever" in one gushy breath.

"You have enough children already," he said into the mic, and Squimbop laughed long and slow inside the radio station in the Town's City. "These two are mine."

"The ones I have are not mine, but I will use them up until

they're no one's," Squimbop replied, and the broadcast's rhythm was established. "This is my job. It's what I do."

Just as the Town's City was clogged with Sub-Weird, skinny and shivering as the broadcast took them higher than heroin could, the plateau around Well was clogged with Dwellers, lying with their shirts pulled up and bellies open to the sky, like lizards sunning themselves in sound.

"You can take them there, but you cannot keep them," Squimbop cooed. "Wherever you end up, we will meet again. Plan on it."

Well heard these words, but he was too lost in fantasy to hear them ring true. He put the mic down and felt the summit night re-sealing around him. The ringing in his ears sounded like the town sinking even farther below than it already was, until it felt like the only habitable land was right here, all around him, the summit an island in the Inland Sea.

He tipped his teacup on its side and felt the wet tea bag plop onto his lap. It was too dark to see, but he looked down in its direction as it began soaking through his pants and underwear, motionless as a beached tadpole.

He stretched his hands behind his head, closed his eyes, and immediately felt his gut fill with an urge, somewhere between strength and sickness, to spring up and storm the cave where the nine-year-olds slept, stuff them into his backpack and hurtle into the Desert right now, before sunrise, tucking them into bed in Dust House so they'd wake up there, returning from wherever they went in their dreams, and never have material proof that they'd ever lived anywhere else.

Obviate their whole previous lives in one fell swoop...

He was panting so fast he feared for his heart.

Closing his eyes and forcing his breath into a mellower

333

rhythm, he resolved to gather them up first thing in the morning. If he couldn't wait that long, he thought, he wasn't in a stable enough condition to attempt the journey in the first place.

Well woke early, dismissing dreams of Squimbop tying him up like a gutted pig in the Dust House kitchen, after having somehow found a way to light the extinct oven.

He stumbled from the broadcast shack and looked out from the summit as the sun rose, hot pink and orange, over the bowl of the perma-dusk below, and felt himself to be inside the sky.

He knew that the town below would not exist much longer. He couldn't conceive of how Squimbop's departure would spell the End, but he knew that it would. All he could do up here was strive to inhabit Dust House as completely as possible before that occurred in the hopes that, at this altitude, life would go on.

If not in the Desert, then nowhere. There will be nowhere else as soon as this year's Reunion is over. Picturing this grim ending, he felt equal parts relief at having extricated himself in time, and guilt at having abandoned the only real community he'd ever known. He wondered how much he'd miss the Mayor and the few other faces he'd once considered familiar when he knew for sure that they were gone.

He jolted to attention when a Dweller pressed a mug of coffee against his open palm, then a hock of bread against the other. "Leave me," he said, getting a grip on his food and drink and, as soon as the Dweller left, regretting that he hadn't been kinder.

He drank half the mug and shoved the bread into his mouth before he'd swallowed, indulging in a fantasy of Squimbop jilted alone at the mic tonight, the radio station lost amidst the desecrated acropolis of the Town's City. Squinting through the

334

perma-dusk, the Professor would walk out into the crowd of expectant Sub-Weird and say, "Sorry everyone, no more stories. My conversation partner has left us. Your lives will henceforward return to vagueness and boredom, in those dank unfinished rooms of yours, for what little time you have left."

When he'd finished his breakfast, Well went back to his cabin to put on the pair of Ultra Max jeans and the plaid shirt the Dwellers had brought him from their last supply run, tearing off the price tags and the stickers that said the size.

Then he pulled on his leather boots and filled a few canteens in the cabin's miniature sink, its basin flecked with dots of beard from the last time he'd shaved. Gathering his hat and sunglasses, he took a pound bag of walnuts from his cooler and declared himself ready to go.

As he walked through the encampment, past all the Dwellers who did not yet know he was abandoning them, he felt slim and strong through the shoulders, grown up but not yet old.

A Dweller approached, ready to debrief him on the state of the duo in the cave, but he shooed him away with a simple, "Get them out and ready to go."

The Dweller nodded.

Well paced the summit as he waited for the duo to get dressed, use the outhouse, have breakfast—they drank even more coffee than he did—and present themselves ready to go with their shoes tied and pockets full of Ultra Max sandwich cookies, which someone had given them. He'd entrusted the Dwellers to convince them to follow him into the Desert, using any means necessary, but now his own conviction wavered.

Maybe we'll go tomorrow, he started thinking. *Maybe I'll discuss it with Squimbop first… Surely it's better to ask permission than forgiveness from one such as him?*

Like the Mayor's War Whoop, he opened his throat and prepared to scream to rally his resolve. But the duo, staring right at him and ready to go, pulled him out of himself first. "We have as much reason to flee the town as you do. If we're going, let's go," they said, their voices much calmer than his would've been if he'd spoken just then.

He nodded, shouldered his pack, and turned, for what he hoped was the last time, away from the Dwellers and their settlement, toward the deep Desert. Believing the Oasis at the heart of the Pretend Movie awaited them in this direction, the duo followed without regret, though they knew they'd missed their chance to make the journey on their own by lying stunned in the cave last night.

Soon the summit encampment was invisible behind them and the landscape they were passing through was pure and unrendered, the dunes like sketches of planes, slopes, and curves in a calculus textbook.

The air was a motionless dry heat, lying over simmering yellow sand, firm enough that they didn't have to wade through it, light enough that it drifted slowly around them without being blown.

No one spoke.

The duo was memorizing the route, committing it to memory.

Less than a foot away, a handsome blue lizard took the three trespassers in, lodging their presence in the cold empty chamber behind its eyes.

When it moved on, so did they.

The landscape changed as the light dimmed.

They'd consumed half of their walnuts and water and were starting to feel the heat building up in their guts, burning off their sense of time and ability to walk upright.

They were slouching at diagonals now, trying to resist the temptation to sit down for fear of passing out. Well knew they were getting close. He'd made this journey enough times to have a feel for its stages, even before the first landmarks appeared. *The Outskirts of Dust Street, the threshold between wasteland and home.*

"Just keep with me a little longer," he told the duo, unsure why he was still so afraid they'd abandon him. *If you hear Squimbop's voice in the air, don't listen,* he thought.

There started to be bare telephone poles and ruts in the ground, as it transitioned from sand to loose dust to tighter-packed dust with stone beneath.

The yellows were becoming ochers, partly due to the sunset, partly to the change in geography.

Well tried to picture the bed in Dust House, upstairs where he hadn't been in thirty years. His mind kept gnawing at the possibility that there wouldn't be sheets or pillows, that the duo would have to sleep on a bare mattress, or even a bare box spring, or even that there wouldn't be a bed up there at all, and thus, somehow, the transplant wouldn't take.

Then he'd be nothing but a kidnapper, a desperate man alone in the Desert with two children he couldn't keep, and had no right to.

He exhaled in a rasp and said, "Let's stop here a moment."

The duo stopped and he turned into the distance so they wouldn't see him cry.

When they started moving again, it was dusk, the Desert glowing

337

with the last of the light it'd absorbed. The rest of their water and walnuts and sandwich cookies were gone by the time they reached the edge of Dust Street and began to walk down it, past the hollow facades of other houses and the few warped telephone poles and blank signs that gave the street the feeling of having once been part of a town.

Well could see Dust House up ahead, and he could tell it was time to run, before doubt overwhelmed him again. The dead-end awaits us, he thought, picking up the pace and swallowing his fear that the duo wouldn't follow suit.

He ran the rest of the way, not looking back, as a breeze whipped up. It carried a faint undertone of salt water, like there was an ocean in the near distance, behind Dust House, despite Well's conviction that the Desert ended there.

The thought speared him with new loneliness, and then he looked down and it was so dark he couldn't see the duo at all. For a moment, he felt certain they'd vanished back into the Psychogeography and were right now being fondled by the Mayor in the locked Back Room of the Movie Store.

"C'mon!" he shouted. "We're home!"

He swept his hands desperately through the air until he felt the duo's warm backs, and pushed them with all the strength he had left up the steps and onto the porch, only letting them go for the time it took to find the key in the flowerpot and open the door.

Dust whipped up outside as Well sealed them in.

He leaned against the door, the duo a few steps into the living room, and relished the feeling of pure arrival. *I am at last where I've always been going*, he thought, his relief mixed with melancholy as he pictured the dust pouring in through the windows and the mail slot and down the chimney, burying them,

338

three statues lost forever in the sands of time.

He cleared his throat and led the way into the kitchen, where a bare bulb hung from the ceiling, swaying in the wind that came through the loose wood of the walls.

Turning it on, he had to look away from the duo, whose faces were suddenly too individuated, too far outside the roles he needed them to play. Too unlike the boy he'd been at nine. If he let himself think, *But they don't look like me...* he'd never make it through the night. "I'll".. he muttered, covering his own face with the shame of being seen this clearly.

They watched him roam the cupboards like a crazy man who'd lived in this house alone for years, following a regimen that had grown both more precise and more deranged with repetition.

He rustled up two potatoes, a few handfuls of oats, and some salt in a bag, all of which he mixed together in a pot of water he put on the stove. He wished there was liquor, even beer, in the fridge, but there wasn't even a fridge.

When it was ready, they all ate from the pot with two spoons, one for Well and one for the duo, stabbing at the potatoes that had barely softened.

The dust that settled over everything tasted like stale cinnamon.

Dinner gave way to pre-sleep wandering, equivalent to the hour Well used to spend picking up Giant Chinese and making his way to the radio station before broadcast time.

And the dead shot up into the sky like bubbles loosed from under a rock on the floor of a rushing river, seeking the surface. He recalled the sentence he'd used to begin a process in what felt now like a vestigial stage of his evolution.

Then he purged the sentence from his head, along with all those like it, never to be repeated. He pictured the notecards blackening and curling as they went up in flames.

The downstairs had only the kitchen, the living room, and a small study in back, but he and the duo still managed to diverge in their wanderings, careful not to crowd each other as they digested the first of what Well prayed would be an eternity of meals together, though he couldn't quite imagine where the food would come from, nor whether this would remain a relevant question in the future they were moving toward.

As they traced these loops, the house filled with dust, and with the dust came an atmosphere of swimmy unease, making both Well and the duo unstable on their feet.

When it got late enough that sleep was the only way forward, Well forced his mind into a more solid shape and said, "Okay, your room's upstairs. I'll be here on the couch if you need me."

One night he'd follow them up and see their room, and thereby, at last, remember his own, replacing the vague memory with a vivid image. But not tonight. Tonight was only about arrival. He knew enough about the liminal states of children to resist pushing too hard.

"Go!" he repeated.

The duo was covered in dust, still coughing and rubbing their eyes, making no sign that they'd heard.

He turned his back on them and went to lie down on the couch, burying his face in the cushions. The house shook and dust poured in through the front windows, which didn't close at the top or the bottom.

It's not true that I've taken something I shouldn't have, he pleaded with the cushion, as if the coming storm were still up for debate, waiting to hear both sides.

I can keep them. I can. Why should I have to grow old and die while others live forever?

The House shook and he heard the duo scurry away.

Please don't let them already be gone, he begged the cushion, choking on the dust that seeped out when the first crashing jolt arrived.

All of Dust House shook.

The roof buckled and the wooden walls groaned, and Well could feel the pressure rising like they were being plunged underwater. The cement of the foundation was cracking, chunks falling out, its integrity breaking down.

Face down on the couch, his lips buzzed, forming words his mind had no grasp on, desperate to make it through tonight, as he had so many nights before, by talking.

He pictured himself flying upwards toward the ceiling, then through it, through the second floor where the duo had gone, through the roof, through the sky. The only limit to his altitude would be his store of things to say.

Then the floor tipped at a harsh diagonal and a whole edge of Dust House came off the ground. The windows broke, glass raining in on him, and he apologized, with true contrition, for having had the hubris to believe he could make this house his home. Eyes closed against the shards, he gripped the couch like a life raft and felt the house lurch into the air, hanging suspended for a moment before spinning end over end, out of the Desert and back into the Psychogeography, Squimbop's laugh echoing over the sounds of splintering wood and crashing china.

The storm opened its eye.

After a series of violent jolts, the house hovered in a gentle sea. Well crawled up from the couch to look through the broken window, as if expecting to see the town on the far shore, but it was only blackness.

He turned from the hole and looked up, saw the duo hovering against the ceiling, lit by the bulb from the kitchen, which was broken but still bright. They jerked like ropes were around their necks, torn between clinging to the ceiling for fear of falling, and fighting their way to the floor for fear of strangling.

Then Well heard a crack and the ceiling caved in, dropping the duo to the floor, amidst the rubble. Dust swirled around their heads and their hair stood straight up.

Wood splintered; nails flew.

Chaos returned.

The duo crawled from the rubble, grabbing Well's outstretched hand on the couch, brushing away the broken glass and settling into the cushions as the house sailed through oceanic space.

The glass rolled off the duo and into Well's face, cutting his cheeks and chin and the smooth patches under his ears.

He wanted to press his hands against the blood to hold some of it in, but they were clutching the duo too tightly. He knew that if he let go, they'd be gone and Dust House would sink under the waves it was sailing on, and that would be the End.

So he let his cuts bleed, his body temperature sinking as old images of the town flooded back into the places in his mind he'd emptied in preparation for a new life.

His breathing slowed and evened out, and he felt old airwaves streaming through the broken window, wrapping around his neck and stanching his wounds. When he closed his eyes, he was back in the radio station, sending the children into the Ghost Town like it was autumn again and none of this had ever happened.

He kept breathing, sucking the old airwaves in, feeling them smooth Dust House's passage down from the Mountain and back to the town, which he now knew he would never leave. He knew, having accepted this, that they would get there safely. Dust House could now float rather than fly.

He dozed off, safe and sad, dreaming of autumn and normalcy, the duo's hands loosely balanced in his.

His blood dried and his lips bubbled with old broadcast.

The purple glow streamed through the broken window and woke him gradually, gently. He leaned onto his elbows and looked out, seeing clean into ANGEL HOUSE, feeling his legs lock into scarecrow-legs where he lay. The duo shivered and closed their eyes tightly without being told to, fighting to preserve the Pretend Movie against the glow's promise of relief.

Well knew it was too late to do likewise, so he opened his eyes all the wider, staring straight into the purple glow, past the dripping children on the ceiling, making eye contact with Squimbop, who knelt in a corner on ANGEL HOUSE's far side, bunching up the skin over his heart and whispering, "I told you I'd bring them back... I told you"...

A chunk of tallow drifted in through the broken window and landed on Well's lips as Dust House lurched on, up the Meadow-lined Road and into the town.

Well sat up as his mouth went numb with tallow and Dust House came to rest in the Dead Neighborhood.

The center of the living room floor split open as the Wooden Wheel burst through. It creaked, tilting a few degrees, and the house turned, already synced up to the Wheel's rotation.

The tallow melted in his mouth with a syrupy sweetness that numbed his throat as he leaned up to peer out the window into the Dead Neighborhood, the duo's Dead Houses clearly visible on both sides.

343

After a minute, he forced himself off the couch, past the stunned duo, and into the kitchen. Catching his breath, he ran his fingers over the cuts on his head as he filled the glass he'd used last night, sucking down water that tasted spermy, coming, as the town's water always had, straight from the Pornography.

PART VII
In The Perma-Dusk

The perma-dusk dripped through the windows, sickly and damp.

When he couldn't stand in the kitchen drinking water anymore, waiting for the duo to wake up, Well decided to go out for breakfast.

He tried to shower, but there was only cold water, so, naked and damp, he put his clothes back on. Stepping into his boots, he glanced at the duo, still dazed on the couch like they were staring hard at something only they could see, fighting their way toward it. He wanted to hide them in a closet, but knew that whatever power he'd held over them in the Desert didn't apply down here. In this regard, as perhaps in all others, Squimbop had won.

He tiptoed around the Wooden Wheel, careful not to tilt it, and heaved open the front door, unsure if there'd be wreckage. There wasn't, beyond the usual decay of the Dead Neighborhood.

The streets were the same as ever, the asphalt cracked and weedy, but the perma-dusk made everything feel partially illusory, its resolution turned down to seventy-five percent. Well appreciated this: it smoothed the transition away from Dust Street, lending the town an air of slight difference, as if it weren't quite the place he'd left behind. He hoped the feeling would last.

As he walked into the main streets of downtown, approaching the

Greek restaurant, the few people he saw unsettled him.

There was something wrong with their faces and posture, the way they neither ignored nor responded to him as he passed by. They didn't have the past-reek of the Sub-Weird, the desperation to prolong the Reunion past its ordained finale, and they didn't seem to have lost what was most important to them. As their mouths flapped open and closed, Well could see a yawning blackness that made him cringe.

He wanted to hurry past them into the Greek restaurant, but a quick glimpse through the windows revealed that all the booths were full of them, eating pancakes without enjoyment, sucking them clean out of existence.

So you're what it's come to, he thought, blanching at their indifference as he headed toward the bakery to pick up coffee and donuts to go.

Back in Dust House, the duo remained posed on the couch.

The Wooden Wheel creaked.

They held their eyes closed but remained awake, fighting to hold onto a vision that wanted to dissipate. Dusty light was blowing over the vision's edges, like a photograph being buried in the sand, but they could still see the outlines of the open Desert beyond Dust Street, which had shown itself to them through the windows of Dust House just as the storm lifted it off the ground.

The Oasis was beyond what Well could conceive, deeper in than his longing could burrow. *He only got part way*, they thought, conjuring vague but potent memories: a hint of buildings, some of them very tall but obscured by sand and haze, the slightest implication that the sets had been built, the site upon which the Pretend Movie would finally attain realization, if they could only make it back there, on their own terms, unsupervised, no one's prisoner, no one's fantasy, the nineteen-year-olds cast off, the lure of ANGEL HOUSE cast off, the regrets of Ben and James cast off...

How much failure must we endure? They wondered. *James, the Mayor, Well... Does nothing work? Is that what life ends up being?*

Their energy was starting to flag, so they used the last of what they had to get themselves together, bearing down on the future, blotting out the past.

We are not them! They thought, several times in a row. *The ruin of their lives is not the ruin of ours.*

The thought rang so true it set them to laughing, first just chuckling, then rocking and bellowing, falling off the couch to roll on the floor, breaking a sweat with the hilarity of how close their freedom was, and the Comedy Troupe joined in, singing and gibbering in the duo's ears, the bones of their cart clacking merrily, summoning them back to the Desert, shouting *Yes! Yes! The sets are ready and waiting in the Oasis, and now you know the way!*

Reeling from the effort of summoning Dust House out of the Desert and back through the Psychogeography, Squimbop nevertheless forced himself out of bed and onto his laptop, where he checked the cameras and composed an email.

Dear Master,

The two remaining children nearly escaped. They got quite far, abetted by the man I mentioned to you earlier—the one who used to host the radio show. He remade himself far away, and called the children to him.

But I am happy to report they did not break free. I summoned them back by means of a dust storm. It cost me a substantial reserve of energy to do this, and I am not sure I could do it again, but I was glad to this time. I hope you are proud.

All for now,

Prof. Sq.

As had become his habit—a habit he knew it was time to break— he composed a new email immediately after sending this one.

Dear Master,

How much longer must I remain in this town? I am here to do your bidding, of course, but still… how much longer? I am losing track of time and cannot say I enjoy the sensation.

There are times when I think I'd be better off in communion with the Mayor, making a sort of life with him, far from you, far from ANGEL HOUSE. Imagine it sitting empty outside of town, a haunted house that nobody lives in! Children creeping up to the windows to look in…

Why not?

All I ask is one email from you, one single email that reads, 'good work… keep going.'

This is too much to ask for?

Apparently. Apparently. Apparently.

But we all have our limits, and I feel mine encroaching.

Fuck you,

Prof. Sq.

He sat with his fingers on the SEND button for a full minute, heart pounding. Then he deleted what he'd written and closed his laptop, vowing to never write another email of this nature again.

Sitting cross-legged on his bed in the Hotel, where he hadn't felt at home since Hibernation at the latest, Ben looked out at the Town's City and decided that today was the day to make the move. It could have been any day this week, any day this month even—if such units still applied in the perma-dusk—but just now he'd woken with a start, his disorientation sharper than it had ever been, and he thought, *If I stay here another hour, I'll find a way to kill myself even if my gun's just a toy.*

Though the perma-dusk looked the same as ever, he could feel heat curling in through the poorly sealed windows, and knew that soon his room would be an oven. He could picture himself writhing on the bed, sheets soaked and twisted around his ankles, arms spread to the far sides of the mattress to maximize his surface area, not that it mattered since there was no fan and opening the windows would only let in more boiling air.

He extended these images further, until he was truly boiling in his bed, his skin puckering and coming off, his bones blackening, leaving him nothing but a husk, a locust-man without name or resume, whose time in the town added up to no more than that of a plant. He forced himself out of bed and into the shower, the water as cold as he could make it, his skin shivering and tightening, cleaving to his bones now rather than sloughing off.

He used up the last of his soap and shampoo, then he got dressed, rolling his dirty clothes into his duffel bag, and walked out, gun tucked into his jeans. He took the stairs down to the lobby, head down, prepared to insist the bill be put on the Mayor's tab if the clerk hassled him, but no one said anything. By the time he looked up, he was in the Square, watching the old-timers ask each other how they were doing.

The air chewed into his neck as he walked, head down again like there was something fundamentally shameful about him, no matter where he went. He hurried up the street, through the fence, past the gazebo, and into the Tower, slinging his duffel bag over his shoulder as he took the stairs, then the ladders up through all the levels of Sub-Weird housing and out to the Town's City on the roof.

As he emerged in the center, he passed the Sub-Weird sitting on benches between the Town's City's version of the Hotel and the Greek restaurant, asking each other how they were doing. A few asked each other when Squimbop was coming back on the air. They looked awful, their skin loose and yellowed, their old air of semi-familiarity smudged by what heroin and radio waves had turned them into.

None of them looked up as Ben made his way past, entering the Motel. He tossed his duffel bag on a chair in the Front Office and exhaled as he sat down across from it.

Then he opened his duffel bag, took out a hammock he'd picked up at Ultra Max, and laid it on the desk, after which he took out his last two beers and stood them on either side of it, like posts between which it might be stretched. He studied this array, drinking one can and then the other and putting the empties back into position after apologizing to the hammock for the interruption.

Now it was time to take the crucial step: he walked to the back of the Front Office and flicked a switch. Outside, the huge neon VACANCY sign buzzed on, burning orange through the perma-dusk.

He closed his eyes, picturing a long line of drifters at the door, drawn inward from the Strip and the bus station, duffel bags over their shoulders, waiting to be shown to their rooms. He would accept only cash, he decided, and no personal information upon check-in. *John Doe,* he thought. *That's everyone's name up here. In this way, and this way alone, the Town's City will retain something that sets it apart from the town. Down there, everyone has to be someone. Not up here.*

His last thought before drifting off was, *The Sub-Weird are doomed. They should have stayed in the Outskirts.*

A loud knocking woke him up in the room he'd dubbed the Manager's Suite.

Yawning and smoothing his hair, he trudged out, carrying the master key ring in front of him like a torch as he shuffled past his first guest, who was pounding on the door of the Front Office. He shoved his way past him and opened the door, so that both of them could go in together. Then he sat down behind the desk, studying his limp hammock and affecting a pose like he'd been there all along.

"Welcome," he managed, before looking up, into the Blankhead's expressionless face. It opened its void-mouth and

351

Ben swooned, trying to close his eyes and finding he couldn't.

"H... h... how may I help you?" he asked.

The Blankhead stood there, hands slack at its sides. There was no solidarity, no fellowship of drifters.

"Right." Ben tried to imagine how he'd sound if he weren't so scared, and to speak with that voice. "Let me show you to your room. It's $60 per night, cash, but we can worry about that later."

Wishing he were the kind of person who could demand to be paid upfront, he took the key ring and walked out, past the Blankhead and all the way to the end of the corridor, opening the furthest door on the left.

"Here you are then," he gestured to the room's interior. It still smelled of new paint and flooring chemicals.

The Blankhead pushed past him and lay down on the bed. Ben closed the door, leaving the key just inside, and wandered away from the Motel, through the streets of the Town's City to the edge.

Looking over the town, tiny and forlorn below, he felt an upsurge of the sadness he'd built this whole structure to escape from. He sat on the edge, playing with the key ring and dangling his feet over, and thought, his voice childish in his head, *Scary as it is to know people too well, it's perhaps even scarier not to know them at all.*

He closed his eyes and pictured the Blankheads as a wave, washing the town clean, leaving nothing but a shiny, lemon-scented floor in their wake.

Ben's lonely spell on the edge of the Town's City—he wasn't quite contemplating jumping, but the thought was in his head—came to an end with the noise of more Blankheads behind him.

He could hear them pounding on the door of the Front Office, and longed to hide in the lower floors of the Tower, among the Sub-Weird, but he forced himself to his feet. *I'm the Manager*, he thought, wondering if this guise was any more legitimate than when he'd called himself the Prophet.

Walking back to the Front Office with his key ring out, he tried to keep his head down so as to avoid eye contact. He got most of the way, but faltered and looked up when he reached the door. Standing right in front of him, at the head of the procession, were the nineteen-year-olds.

Knocking on the door with mechanical regularity, they looked enervated, dead-eyed, their heads no more than covered skulls. "Hey guys".. Ben fumbled with the key, pushing past them to open the door.

"Looking for a room?"

The nineteen-year-olds nodded, automatically. "Hotel's empty, and we're out of work, kinda stuck here until we figure something else out, so"..

"Yeah," Ben agreed, wondering if he should treat them as Blankheads now. They certainly looked the part. He tried to picture himself and James arriving in News City at that age, looking for a room to pass the first few nights in, while they got their act together. These nineteen-year-olds seemed a horrible mockery of that. He wanted to hate them, but they were too hollow. There was nothing there to hate.

"Well, rooms are $60 a night. You two are sharing, I imagine?"

They nodded, but made no effort to produce any cash. This time, Ben stood his ground. "Guys, you gotta pay."

They waited a minute, then, sighing, took out their wallets and found, between them, nineteen one-dollar bills and three quarters. Ben took these, proud of himself for having asked, and peeled a key off the ring. They took it and shuffled off as the next Blankheads made their way in behind them.

After processing sixty more guests in the orange glow of the VACANCY sign, all the keys were gone. There were only twenty-two rooms, so the Blankheads would have to bunk together. Ben didn't bother trying to explain this; he simply turned on the NO part of the sign and left it at that.

With all of his guests filed away, the nineteen-year-olds somewhere among them, Ben wandered back into the Town's City, making his way, without thinking about it, to the station that Squimbop had broadcast from. The Sub-Weird's carpet squares were still strewn outside, a few of them with needles sticking out, like pincushions.

He took a deep breath and, with the thrill of sacrilege, shouldered open the door and found himself inside a holy site, for the first time since he'd stopped visiting the Movie Store with James. A place from which genuine prophecy had emanated. The air in here was thick and still, rich with the smell of burned meat.

Shoulders hunched in fear that something might shock or bite him, he went deeper in, up to the desk that Squimbop had sat behind. He leaned up to the mic, touching it with his lips, the metal cold and useless now. Curling his fingers around its base, he found that it wasn't impossible to make the leap to taking it with him, so he clutched it and ran, bruising his shoulder from the force with which he barreled through the door, suddenly terrified that someone was following him.

When he caught his breath, he found himself back at the Town's City's edge, again looking over the town, imagining it to be evening despite the sameness of the perma-dusk. Haltingly, he put the mic to his lips, tasting Squimbop's dried spittle, the sour richness of Death. He licked at it like a spoiled ice cream cone, eyes closed, feeling the spittle sink down his throat and into his core, annihilating whatever he'd been about to think.

He might have sunk to his knees and slept right there on the edge, or fallen off, had a scuffling from behind not cut through. He turned, mic to his lips, to see three Sub-Weird, hand in hand, gazing through wet, imploring eyes. For a moment he thought they'd come to hear what he had to say, before realizing they must have mistaken him for Squimbop, back for another night's broadcast, to tell them more about other places and other times, reassuring them that, somewhere, somehow, life would go on.

His eyes grew wet too as he put the mic back to his lips. "I have no good news," he whispered into it. "The Inland Sea wins in the end. All towns go under. All I can say, if it's any consolation, is that I'm the same as you are. I'm no Prophet. We're all in this together. I'm sorry I couldn't admit that at last year's Reunion."

His eyes grew so watery he had to close them. When he opened them again, the Sub-Weird were gone and the mic had fallen out of his hand and over the edge.

With Well off the radio and the duo missing from school, Squimbop had no obligations. His time had lately been spent in solitude inside ANGEL HOUSE, the windows blacked out against the perma-dusk, the floors ankle-deep in tallow, which he had to ration now since there wasn't much left of the children.

While he scrubbed through the footage his cameras had recorded so far, wondering what purpose it would ultimately serve, his head grew savagely full of unprocessed Lecture, making him drunk and half-blind with what the Totally Other Place couldn't stop sending. He kept his closet doors open to admire the massive fur coat he'd worn all through Hibernation, missing the wolfish power he'd had then. Today, he resolved to shower and firm up the Lecture in his head, to keep it from turning rancid.

Afterwards, he dried off, shaved around his mustache, put on a blazer, and set out for town.

He got a cup of coffee at the Greek restaurant and sat with it in the Square, sharing a bench with the old-timers, who still circulated, asking one another how they were doing, oblivious to his presence. He closed his eyes and relaxed, warm in the weird semi-darkness.

When he opened his eyes again, a procession of humanoid shapes was passing by, unhurried but deliberate. They lumbered like bears, balanced uneasily on two legs, their skin thick and white, their aura cold. He finished his coffee and stood to walk among them for a moment, observing their indifference and the icy black holes that opened in their faces whenever they yawned. He could see the void in their mouths and was comforted by it.

Turning to face the direction they were facing, he looked with them through the perma-dusk at a glowing orange NO VACANCY sign, so high above the town it appeared to be floating in the sky, like a portal to heaven.

He then took his leave of them, confident that the End was near. *This year's Reunion,* he thought, *will be a convocation of these things.*

It was almost as if the Totally Other Place had finally sent him a response. Buoyed by this feeling, he set out toward the Movie Store to look for the Mayor, planning to begin the process, in whatever form it would ultimately take, of saying goodbye.

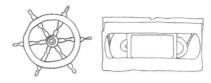

The Returns slot clacked on a loose hinge as the door swung open. Behind the checkout counter, Saltwater jerked awake to watch the Professor glide down the empty New Releases aisle and over to the carpeted staircase.

Behind the curtain, the downstairs was wild. Overgrown, imposed upon by forces of nature, thick with the boxes of deep old Movies that had never seen the New Releases aisle. His knees weakened, bowing him forward in reverence before the dim shelves. This felt natural, so he didn't fight it, though it didn't correspond to any emotion in his heart. He had to lean against the wall to remain standing, and brushed against the light switch.

This turned the space black.

The whole Back Room was coated in steam and fungus, the boxes wet and reeking. Matter was growing everywhere, little fleshy packets sprouting on the boxes, stripes and slices of tissue and bone.

The Mayor was huddled in here, sweaty and sobbing, arms full of empty boxes. Since the duo had left, there'd been nowhere to go except back to where he'd found them, to pray they'd appear again.

He exuded sweat and unspent sperm, rubbing the boxes over himself, looking at the pictures on the back and trying to remember the children he'd had with each one, muttering warrior phrases that felt like sacrilege now. He was fondling his clitoris in despair, mouth-breathing in the reek, when the sound of approaching footsteps grew loud enough to make him stop. He searched his ankles for his pants, thinking, as if he'd been expecting this all along, *He's here.*

Squimbop had to piss very, very badly.

He didn't even consider holding it until later.

When the Mayor came through the curtain, out of the Back Room and into the main concourse of the downstairs, he found the Professor with his back turned, pissing in the face of a giant stuffed gorilla.

He turned, regarded the Mayor, and resumed. By the time he was done, the gorilla's head lolled to one side and then tipped over, coming to rest with one ear to the ground and one leathery stuffed foot in the air.

Then he turned, zipped his fly, and listened to the Mayor try to control his breathing. Smiling, he took up the nearest Movie box, from the School section where the stuffed animals were, and bit into it, tearing the cardboard apart with his canines.

This desecration was enough to start the Mayor sobbing.

Squimbop didn't stop until the box was gone. He burped as the Mayor dried his eyes. Then he began to wander.

They walked in mirror image of one another, out of the Children's section, past the Hotel, the Strip, the Meadow-lined Road, and finally into the section labeled "Meadow."

The Mayor pictured dragging Squimbop upstairs to the Returns bin, stuffing him inside and muttering to Saltwater, "He's ready to go back where he came from." Then he'd walk out into a redeemed town, every street dead-ending in his Orchard.

"Can you be hurt?" he whispered.

Squimbop didn't reply, though he'd come here wondering the same thing.

"Because if you can be," said the Mayor, "now's the time. Nowhere am I more powerful than I am down here."

Squimbop yawned, his eyes watering. He was spent, ready for this year to be over. Why not let the Mayor do what he wanted, this one time? The End was close enough. So he exhaled, letting the strength out of his body, leaning forward against the Mayor, whispering, "Let's find out."

The Mayor got an immediate Orchard-high, shivering against the body that was now his to use, in real time and space. His mouth heaved with the desire for brownie batter... the silver bowl, the scuffed plastic spatula, the sugar crystals that never dissolved...

He grabbed the Professor and pulled him down. The carpet was soft as foam rubber, and he could see the glistening eyes of the piss-soaked gorilla as he brewed a fresh War Whoop in the center of his gut.

The Mayor buried his nose in Squimbop's hair and smelled the mud and sex of his Orchard. He groaned, hearing his hot tub bubbling like it was just behind the wall, thin as a paper screen.

Then he climbed on top and undid his belt and pants button to accommodate the swelling of his clitoris. "I'm gonna come all over you," he whispered in the Professor's ear, sinking his fingers into the carpet, feeling Movie boxes rain down on his back as he bucked back and forth atop the man who'd bitten off his penis and testicles and eaten them in two bites.

He rubbed and jerked, seething with hatred and jealousy, remembering how it felt to sink into the vaginas in his Orchard when there were still children to be sired.

His clitoris expanded, fanning out, growing porous as it filled with liquid.

The knowledge that this would be his only chance to dominate the Professor welled up in the Mayor's body like the thing it was preparing to spew out.

It felt like the lead-up to Death. Species extinction was near.

359

He dug in, felt the Professor going soft and recessive beneath him, his body hollowing out.

Enjoy it, chanted the reptile layer of the Mayor's brain. *Make it last. The chance won't come again.*

He reached between them and pulled his pants all the way down so his clitoris pressed against Squimbop's belly, which was soft but not warm.

Squimbop remained fully clothed and had no orifice, but as the Mayor hurled himself against his belly, he found purchase. The sheen of the Totally Other Place coated Squimbop's whole body now, lubing the Mayor as he rutted.

When the Mayor finally came, letting go of the power that had pooled inside him, the force of it pushed him backwards, onto his feet. His eyes, mouth, and nose went completely dry, and the bones in his fingers and toes turned to string.

The liquid spurting through his clitoris pulped-up Squimbop's skin like a roll of paper dropped in the toilet.

Crying and knocking Meadow Movies off the shelf, the Mayor's come covered Squimbop's body and seeped into his churned-up skin, peeling it back to reveal workings that looked nothing like human tissue.

He blacked out on the soaked and partly eroded carpet, dreaming that all the Movies surrounding them had come back to life and merged into one, robust enough to contain him forever.

Hours later, he came to, squeezing his crotch so hard it looked like he was finger-painting it purple. Looking around, he saw that Squimbop was little more than a skeleton.

He stared, wondering what had happened, and what to do now. He knew the Professor wasn't dead, but he didn't know what state he was in. He lay back down, stretching out on the carpet, until he resolved to bring Squimbop back to his house. He had a bad feeling about what would happen if he left him here alone with the Movies. Even if they were just boxes now, the shrine still deserved protection.

So, painfully, he rocked to his knees and stood up, trying to pull his pants over his sticky thighs without touching them. The skin was raw and tender, the top layers sheared away.

He leaned forward to grab hold of the carcass before his resolve wavered. The sharp bones bit into his fingers, breaking his skin and binding with his own bones inside. He couldn't pull his hands away, so he ran upstairs with the carcass bound to him like a dead twin, past Saltwater, who had put on a sleep-mask and earplugs, and out the door, through the streets, and finally onto the Meadow-lined Road.

The Mayor had never run like this before. He rarely even walked all the way to his house from town. But he was running now, past the Meadow, with the Squimbop-carcass in his arms.

He considered dumping it on the ANGEL HOUSE lawn, but feared what would happen if he became a scarecrow with it still attached to him, so he ran past it, his mouth filling with salt and iron, his lungs bubbling into his armpits.

For the last half mile, he closed his eyes and imagined himself and the carcass plunging together through the bottom of the hot tub, down the drain and into the Pornography, which would flow into the Inland Sea, where, on the hot bottom, they'd be melted together and reborn as one, a single entity ready to live a new life.

He panted up his driveway, kicked open his door, carried the still-conjoined carcass through his house without taking his shoes off, knocked the foam cover off his hot tub with his hip, and threw it in, letting it pull him in on top of it, still dressed, ready to

361

sink down and experience in reality the union his fantasy had just fleshed out.

The water went quickly septic, and the Mayor felt it stinging his skin through his clothes and burning the hair on his arms and legs as the carcass finally slipped off.

He closed his eyes.

When he opened them, Squimbop's seams had begun to zip back together. His carcass was filling back out.

The Mayor had the sickening sense that a new Squimbop was being made, like a casing filling with fresh sausage grounds, indistinguishable from the old but somehow more potent. He closed his eyes again and let the process go where it would.

In his next conscious moment, he saw the Professor standing naked beside the tub, dripping on the tiles.

"Where's my towel?" he asked, gruff and distant.

The Mayor told him.

Soon he was dry and wearing one of the Mayor's shirts, which came down to his knees.

As he walked barefoot to the door, he said, without turning around, "I hope you enjoyed that. Next time, I'm going to do it to you."

Back in ANGEL HOUSE, glad to be alive, Squimbop seriously considered skipping today's email, but got ahold of himself after an aborted attempt to nap. He opened his laptop, checked the cameras, and began to type.

Dear Master,

An exhausting run of days. Little accomplished.

Some demonic presences are now at large—horrible bear-like men with deep holes for mouths. I do not believe, to put it mildly, that they mean well. Have decided to read their emergence as a sign from you... a sign that the end, at long last, is nigh. The second Reunion is nearly upon us, and not a day too soon.

Other than that, nothing to report.

All for now,

Prof. Sq.

After he sent it, he prepared to type another. I think I love the Mayor, he intended to write, but remembered his vow to never to write another email he didn't send. That font of relief, such as it had been, was now dry.

Ben lay in his hammock in the Front Office—stretched now between the doorknob and a hook on the far wall—where he'd been spending every day since the Blankheads first started filling the Motel. They hadn't stopped coming, despite the NO VACANCY sign, piling into the rooms until they were twenty or thirty thick.

Now, he looked up to see them massing outside their doors, freshly showered, their white skin gleaming as they stood assembled like some signal had been given.

He went to the window to watch as they strode in slow motion into the main Square of the Town's City, the Greek restaurant on one side, the Hotel across from it, congregating in the center, facing outward.

In unison, they joined hands, closed their eyes, and opened their mouths. The void inside them grew, taking up more and more of their heads. When it had opened as wide as it could, a sound began to emerge. A low, constant bellow, as seductive as the broadcast crackle but no longer past-tending, and in no way benign. This was the sound of nothingness beckoning, the warm hole of non-being opening up and declaring itself ready for fresh meat.

Hypnotized, the Sub-Weird emerged from their squalid rooms below, carrying nothing. Some of them were naked, others in the middle of shooting up. Whatever they'd been doing was over now. They streamed forth from the sketchy network of their new homes just as they'd streamed forth from the Outskirts in autumn, massing in the Square, forming an outer layer around the Blankheads. Their numbers appeared roughly equal, each group mirroring the other.

Ben stared as the Sub-Weird presented themselves for annihilation, giddy and mindless as the children on the first day of school, marching with their lunches into the Chamber.

He didn't even bother wishing they'd turn back before it was too late.

Now their faces were in the Blankheads' mouths and what little personality and intelligence they had left was pouring out of them in fart-smelling gusts. They were pulled off their feet as the Blankheads sucked them down their throats, their shoulders and torsos wriggling in the air, their bodies going slack and flaky.

The Town's City was silent, all moving pieces frozen until the Blankheads had sucked their fill.

Then, with the Sub-Weird still dangling from their mouths, they waddled up the street to where the Town's City ended.

Leaning way over the edge, they released their victims, spitting the drained bodies back into the town they'd risen from.

Though he couldn't see, Ben imagined them falling, spent, so light they fluttered in the air, twirling down like seed pods. He thought, for the last time, of the Outskirts Prophecy he'd nurtured all autumn. *What could I have said that might have saved your lives?* He wondered, his attention drifting back to the hulking, sated Blankheads as they retreated toward their rooms to rest.

He cradled his gun in his lap, clicking its trigger like a metronome, trying to force his erratic thinking into some kind of rhythm. *If I could have told you one thing before it was too late, what would it have been?*

There was nothing.

The Blankheads were back in their rooms now. Perhaps they'd vomit up what they'd just sucked out of the Sub-Weird, all the sadness and need for belonging and orientation in time, flushing it down their toilets so as to keep the voids inside them clean. Perhaps the Motel's plumbing would never work again.

If I'd known what to tell you, you wouldn't have ended up like this, he thought. Neither would I. Neither would James. He pictured them piled in the Square below, to be found by the Mayor or whomever else passed by. He put his gun in his mouth to quiet any mental elaboration of the scene.

Don't end up like me, he thought, his inner voice muffled around the barrel. *Don't listen to anyone but yourselves. All Prophets are false.* Just before he pulled the trigger, he realized that his thoughts were no longer directed at the Sub-Weird: they were directed at the duo.

Cowering from the violence he'd just witnessed, Ben called Giant Chinese and asked Sam Ren to come as quickly as possible, after

365

picking up beer from Saltwater's on the way.

Then he tucked his gun into his pants and ran from the Front Office, like the Motel was on fire. He ran down the ladders, down the stairs, past all the rooms the Sub-Weird had tried to make a life in, then through the lobby where he'd met Squimbop at the start of the year, and across the still-muddy construction site to the fenceline, where he awaited the Giant Chinese van.

It came twenty minutes later. Of the twelve beers in the pack he'd purchased from Saltwater, Sam Ren had polished off three on the drive over. He opened one of the remaining nine for Ben, and another for himself, not mentioning the food.

As Ben drank, sighing gratefully through his nose, he could tell that Sam Ren was going to say something as soon as the beer was empty. Though he didn't want to hear what it was, he couldn't slow down.

"John Lester Wind is making a speech at the Gym," said Sam Ren, as soon as Ben pulled the can from his lips. "Emergency Town Council Meeting. You need to be there."

"Okay. How about I drink one more of these, then you drive me over?"

Sam Ren nodded and cracked another for himself, as well.

They drove fast, veering around the pile of Sub-Weird in the Square without remarking on it, careening onto curbs and down into the potholes that Hibernation had left in its wake.

Ben closed his eyes and felt like the Giant Chinese delivery van was squeezing through a tunnel, cutting between sites in the Psychogeography like a dissolve between one Pretend Movie scene and the next.

As they got out in the Gym parking lot, surrounded by parked vehicles and straggling Blankheads, Ben looked up at the perma-dusk and pictured it as a sheet stretched so hard over a mattress it was about to snap off and reveal the stained corners underneath and the hairs of the horrible head that had slept there.

He turned to watch Sam Ren drive away and felt two Blankheads standing behind him, their breath freezing his neck. Wincing, he teetered past the front desk, tasting spit-up in the back of his throat. As he swallowed and realized that he'd left his food in the van, James appeared, regal and bald in a tight sleeveless workout shirt. The Mayor stood beside him, sweaty and panting in a ruffled suit without a tie.

"Gentlemen," said a voice over the intercom, echoing down the tiled hallways. "Gentlemen. We have no time to waste. No time at all."

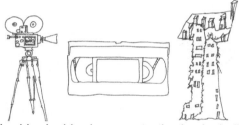

Through the big double doors, onto the basketball court, Ben, James, and the Mayor walked as a unit. The floor was so covered with Blankheads that only splinters of the Ultra Max models were visible between them.

Still, J.L. Wind made an effort to stand inside the model of the Council Chambers, preserving as much dignity as he could.

James had lost count of how many nights he'd spent in here filming these sets, first with the nineteen-year-olds and then with the Blankheads, filling his frame with their non-town-ness, their reminiscent-of-nothing-ness. He had thousands of hours of footage at this point, tapes piled on tapes on the desk in his Director's Hive, unwatched, unlabeled, in no order.

The Blankheads didn't give any sign that they knew J.L. Wind was speaking, just as they'd never given any sign that they knew James was filming them. They wandered into and out of his shots in no pattern, at no predictable rate, mesmerizing him until he lost hold of whatever story he'd once imagined he could direct them to tell.

Some of them wandered out of the basketball court and into the adult pool, which was also full of them now, while others wandered in from the pool, dripping, sometimes slipping, falling over, and getting back up only to fall again.

Ben was transfixed. He wanted to tell James, *Both our lives have coalesced around these things*, but he assumed James already knew.

J.L. Wind, in sturdy sneakers, a pair of a track pants, and a zipped-up windbreaker, spoke through the old sound system used for announcing basketball games. He stood with the mic against his lips, trying to speak as Blankheads pressed into his face, sucking out his life force. Unflappable as ever, he stood on tiptoe and continued.

"Gentlemen," he said. "Glad to have you here. Take a seat."

The three of them filed into the bleachers, where assorted townspeople already sat. A Blankhead tripped over a flat basketball, sending it wobbling across the floor, where it tripped another, who landed on it.

"Gentlemen. We are here to discuss a number of emergency developments. We are here to wonder aloud what—and it must not be nothing—is to be done. To wonder what is to be thought, and, by thinking, to arrive at what is to be done. A pile of our former neighbors from the Outskirts has tragically been found in the Town Square, and the stench of Death has drifted all through the center. Our normal Council Chambers are unusable.

Thus, here we are.

"We have fallen off the scale of normal seasons, so who's to say if we are now in spring, or summer, or even late summer? There is no change in the light, and the air has retained the same temperature for as long as I can remember. And there is no longer any school year by which to mark our progress, for reasons I can hardly bear to bring up. Regardless, the time has come to face this year's Reunion, which must remain our one constant, however much else slips from our grasp. This is our last bulwark against irrevocable collective madness."

He stopped as two Blankheads leaned against him, their backs crushing his nose. When they'd moved on, he continued, "There are not enough fingers in the whole town to point to what's happening to us."

The Mayor, indulging in soft thoughts of screens and curtains, satin and cream, squeezed his clitoris through his pocket, just enough to feel slightly better about the fact that whatever had descended on the town was partially his fault.

"The children are gone. Well Broadbeam is gone. Janitor Pete is gone. ANGEL HOUSE is thriving. The Town's City is a ruin on a superhuman scale. The Gym—and not only the Gym—is swarmed with Blankheads, which, to the best of my understanding, have emerged as a sort of human embodiment of the Blind Spot, which has grown wrathful. These Blankheads are the first bonafide strangers our town has ever been infested with. Not Outskirts dwellers, but true strangers. Entities who have managed to enter the town without in any way being of it. A phenomenon I have never witnessed in all my years as Acting Mayor. And one I hope never to witness again."

"Our Movie industry," continued J.L. Wind, after a silence long enough to serve as an intermission, "has ground to a halt and I fear it may never find its footing again."

James was braced for this, but it still hurt. He looked over at Ben and the Mayor to see their reactions, but neither appeared lucid enough to take it in.

"I hate to stop any production in mid-course," J.L. Wind continued, "especially since, as we all know, the New Releases shelf at the Movie Store stands empty, and has for far too long. But, in this case, in the interest of reinstating sanity as our common goal, I have no other choice. These... things," his lips were on the neck of a Blankhead as he spoke, "have no business being preserved for eternity on the shelves of our Movie Store.

"Once production has ceased, it is my great hope that the Blankhead population in the Gym, as in the town at large, will dwindle, ideally to nothing. At the very least, we will discourage their presence by no longer consenting to canonize it. Whether or not they abate, it is time to prepare for this year's Reunion. Last year's is far, far behind us. The School is contaminated, no longer a safe place for us to expose ourselves in the way we at Reunions must. So, this year, I propose holding the Reunion on the lip of the Blind Spot, at the far back quarry behind the Mayor's house."

Groans from the audience. J.L. Wind ignored them.

"The time has come to return to our roots. The quarries from which the foundation stones of this town emerged. And it is time that we face the Blind Spot as a community. No longer, I am sorry to say, can we trust the Mayor to face this abomination for us. This is a conclusion we should have arrived at long ago, but better now than never. It is my great hope that this year's Reunion, held on the lip of the Blind Spot itself, will restore equilibrium to our town's sky, and thereby also to the hearts of its citizens. Ritual, as we well know, is our sole means of wringing order from chaos. All of you," he turned to face the Blankheads, speaking to them directly with his back to the bleachers, "are requested to attend.

It is my hope that you will, after this year's Reunion, find it in your hearts to return to the Blind Spot from whence you came, provided we, as a community, pledge to never again neglect our ritual humbling before you."

He concluded by looking at the Mayor with an expression of combined benevolence and scorn. Though he couldn't overcome his compassion, he was disgusted by the unchecked selfishness of the Mayor's decision to turn his back on the Blind Spot. The Mayor had never had the town's best interests in mind, but this was a failing on an unprecedented level.

James had tuned out most of the speech in order to fixate on the Crawl Space, directly below. He closed his eyes and forced his mind downward, through the floor, into the nest of sleeping bags he'd set out for the nine-year-olds back when he still believed himself capable of art in the adult sense of the word.

When J.L. Wind had turned off the sound system, James leaned over and whispered in Ben's ear: "Come with me. There's something I have to show you."

Blinking and yawning, Ben found his feet and allowed James to lead him out, past the Blankheads by the door, past the racquetball courts behind the basketball court, and down the back staircase.

At the bottom of the stairs, they entered the tunnel under the Gym, which, twenty years ago, had synced up for them through the Psychogeography to the network of tunnels underlying the town. They'd dreamed their way from their Dead Houses, under the streets, through this tunnel, and up onto the basketball court, wandering its tan expanse in the middle of the night, a mock Desert, as they trained for the real act of Escape.

Now, turning off the tunnel to enter the Crawl Space, James mustered all the optimism he had left to formulate the faith that, if they were willing to sacrifice their twenty-nine-year-old selves, they'd find it wasn't too late to give the nine-year-olds what they needed in order to achieve Escape for real this time.

The Dream of Escape, he thought, as he stooped over to help Ben take his shoes off in the Crawl Space and they both bedded down in the sleeping bags, *was and still is the only Movie worth making.*

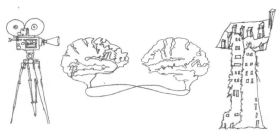

Ben and James lay side by side, overflowing their child-sized sleeping bags like insects that had grown too large for their chrysalises without yet beginning to hatch. The ceiling was an inch from their noses, the air thick with Freon and old insulation.

They each took a moment to just be, lying still and thinking nothing, before turning their minds to what came next.

"Okay," James whispered, when the moment had passed. He closed his eyes, imagining himself in his bed in his Dead House, addressing Ben across the Wooden Wheel park. "There's something we have to do."

Ben grunted to show that he was listening.

"My film, your city…" James sighed, giving himself one last chance to not say what he was about to say. "That's all over. We tried. We did what we could." He got choked up, perceiving for the first time how close Death actually was. He slowed his speaking pace, as if that could ward it off. "Look, the nineteen-year-olds are aimless. They always have been. We were too, at that age, even if we didn't know it. They're wasting the nine-year-olds' time. Bogging down *The Dream of Escape*."

Ben sighed through his nose, starting to feel where this was going. His ears filled with heartbeat and his stomach squirmed toward his groin.

"Squimbop's going to destroy the town after the Reunion. I don't know if that's a premonition or if it's obvious, but he is. What do we have to live for?"

The question hung in the air before condensing back onto their faces. They both wiped their eyes.

"What're you thinking?" Ben finally managed to ask. Crowded into the Crawl Space, his voice sounded strange to him, like something recorded a long time ago and played back on an antiquated device.

"If we're ever going to do something real, this is our chance," James replied. "There's no vast uncrowded future to dream our way toward anymore. Ugly as it may be, we're at the point we've been heading toward all along."

As quietly as he could, he reached behind his head and felt around for the two Ultra Max plastic bags he'd tucked under his pillow the last time he was down here. He held them wadded in his hand, not unrolling them quite yet.

"Do you remember the origin point? The two of us in the Meadow at nine, wading through the marsh grass, looking up at the Mountain, imagining what lay beyond its summit?"

The sound of Ben nodding was snakelike as it crinkled his sleeping bag's plasticky shell.

"We looked up there and thought".. Ben was speaking now, continuing the monologue, "we thought, *if our minds, and dreams, and visions, are to have any purpose at all, we have to get up there... somehow, no matter what it takes, we have to become capable of elevating ourselves, of becoming more than bodies born to decay...*"

373

"And thus the Pretend Movie was born."

They said this in unison, through their tears.

"I'm sorry we haven't been better friends lately," James said, when he'd gotten ahold of himself. "We should have been less busy, or busy with better things."

"Yeah." Ben wiped snot from his nose.

"Are you ready to do this for the nine-year-olds? They need us. If there's anything good left in us, we have to give it to them. No one else can. That's not nothing."

Ben understood, and agreed. It wasn't nothing. If there was beauty in anything, there was beauty in sacrifice. He wasn't ready, and never would be, but he forced himself to repress this knowledge, scraping it off like a coating of rot.
"I'm ready."

James unrolled the plastic bags and handed one to Ben. He stretched the other over his head, closing his eyes so as not to see its brutal off-white skin.

"I'll hold yours shut. You hold mine." His voice sounded comical, muffled as it was. They both laughed until they couldn't breathe. "Remember, as we fade out: focus everything on reaching the nine-year-olds through the Psychogeography. Pour everything into them. Everything you've learned about life and art over these twenty years. I'll do the same. They need us. They have to make the final journey on their own, but they won't survive if we hold anything back."

He gripped Ben's neck, pressing the plastic taut around it, creating a seal.

Ben did likewise for him, their arms entangled in the Crawl Space between them.

They lay quietly suffocating, each holding the other's bag shut. Their minds were melting down, mixing together and turning to oil. It ran through the open tunnels of the Psychogeography, out of the Gym, under the parking lot, and up the streets to the Dead Neighborhood, seeking the nine-year-olds at all costs.

All the spirit that had animated Ben and James was now rushing under the Wooden Wheel park and up into Dust House, where the nine-year-olds lay on the couch.

It came straight through the cushions, cutting into their spines and lighting them up, juicing their nerves. They found themselves on their feet on the mattress, bouncing with excitement. A veil had been torn away.

We can do this! The voice of their shared mind sounded more authoritative than they'd ever heard it. *Fuck the nineteen-year-olds. We can walk out the fucking door and out of the whole fucking town, and no one can fucking stop us.*

The only factor that determines whether the Pretend Movie comes to fruition is us, and we're up to it. We weren't before, but we are now. For the first time, the Oasis is within reach.

They jumped down from the couch, spines still tingling, arms and legs thick and powerful, ready to walk out of Dust House for the last time, then through the perma-dusk and down into the tunnels.

Back in the Crawl Space, Ben and James were inert, the plastic bags loose around their necks. They couldn't tell if they were dead or merely braindead, but they could tell that the nine-year-olds had gotten what they needed, and were already on their way.

They smiled, crinkling the plastic over their lips.

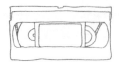

At the same time, the Mayor, who'd squirmed through J.L. Wind's speech praying he wouldn't be asked to comment on the nature f his relationship with Squimbop, had just made it home, again on foot.

He locked the door behind him and poured the last of his whisky into a glass. Switching it from hand to hand while he pulled off his shirt and unbuttoned his pants, he got naked, heaving off the foam cover of his hot tub.

There was still semen, blood, and skin in clumps on the surface, mixing with remnants from Squimbop's carcass to form a crust. He looked away from it, into his yard through the glass doors, and remembered what Squimbop had said upon exiting the house: "Next time, I'm going to do it to you."

Wondering when next time would be, he let out a War Whoop and downed the rest of his drink. His belly churned and flipped over, giddy with anticipation.

Then he slopped into the bath, cutting a hole through the crust that re-formed around him. Material floated up to his mouth and down his throat. He closed his eyes and took it in, savoring each morsel as a taste of Squimbop.

As the material reached his stomach, his heart pounded and his tongue fluttered in his mouth. He could feel the strands of his life knitting together, pushing him toward transformation now that all the illusions he'd lived with had been stripped away.

Closing his eyes, he sank deeper, imagining he was sinking into the Pornography itself, at last merging with it, without recourse to Movies... *Now the real thing and I are becoming one,* he thought, allowing his sense of self to break down and unfurl, crossing a line he had until now held himself back from.

He exhaled, tasting the pure liquid fertility that he had, until now, felt only in his Orchard, bubbling up through the mud, feeding the vaginas which he in turn had fed, back in what now seemed like the days of myth. He sucked steamy air, only his top lip above the water, until his lungs were swollen. With this new weight in him, he sank down even further, his head submerged, the tub given over entirely to the Pornography. The faces of all his children—none more so than the duo—swam behind his closed lids, and he felt his fat giving way to something more divine, his core strengthening and opening up, a new organ inside him taking shape, his pit of regret and loneliness remaking itself into something fertile.

On the very bottom, his womb grew to fill his center and the flap of skin between his legs where his penis and testicles had been torn off opened up and lined itself with a set of inner mucus membranes, which then lined themselves with an outer set of heartier, protective lips, a gateway between one world and the next.

The Mayor's thigh muscles grew taut and strong, hips widening outward, belly filling with eggs. Shooting up from the bottom on the edge of drowning, the Mayor thought, *I will conceive a child with Squimbop, and at long last something genuinely new will enter the ontology of the town. Something truly beyond me, outside me, for the first time in my life.*

Pushing himself to his knees, then standing with the help of the tub edge, he unfolded a plush towel from the pile by the door, wrapped himself in it, and padded to the kitchen, where he managed to extract a quart of ice cream from the freezer and eat half of it before the pain in his belly and between his legs grew too sharp to bear and he had to drop it, collapsing in the nook between the counter and the stove, where he dreamed of his old body peacefully decomposing in the quarry pit where it belonged.

377

PART VIII
The Reunion

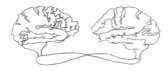

The nine-year-olds pulled on the jeans they'd kicked off onto the Dust House floor, feeling their new strength stabilize in their muscles and something liquid in their spines go hard. *Alright*, they resolved, fully inside the Pretend Movie now, both directing and starring in it without ambivalence or confusion: *time to go.*

They crept past Well where he lay half on the couch and half off it, the fingers of one hand resting on the floorboards, his open palm full of dust. They didn't expect to make it past without him waking up, since they could see a few seconds ahead into the Pretend Movie, and it featured a scene of him staring at them as they fumbled to open the door, twisting the handle back and forth, fighting the sticky lock. They thrilled at the thought that he was their first fan, rapt as he watched the Pretend Movie from the couch.

Well's eyes slid open. He appeared frozen, on the edge of sleep paralysis, witnessing the duo's departure with no power to intervene, or even to articulate his grief.

"Guuuh…" he moaned, watching them fight the lock.

"Thanks for showing us the way," they said, without malice. "We'll give the Desert your best."

The lock clicked and the door swung open.

Well's lips trembled, but the rest of him still didn't move. Had he been able to speak just then, he would only have wished them luck and told them to be careful.

Outside, the perma-dusk was hot.

The sounds of distant sprinklers filled their ears as they started to trudge down from the Dead Neighborhood and into the sweltering town streets, averting their eyes from the lurking Blankheads. Their sense of self was both nine and twenty-nine, attenuated between these poles, but the mission remained clear.

They stood in front of the Greek restaurant, watching old-timers shuffle around the Square, oblivious to the travails of the young, asking each other how they were doing while kicking dead Sub-Weird aside like trash bags the truck had forgotten to pick up.

The nine-year-olds were hungry enough to eat several breakfasts apiece, but there was no time. So, saying goodbye to the Square, they made their way into the Hotel, through the abandoned lobby and down to the basement, to enter the tunnels they'd entered so many times as the nineteen-year-olds, but never before as themselves.

Stirring in the Crawl Space, Ben and James could feel the point approaching at which they'd have to wake up, leaving the nine-year-olds to continue alone, fading back into memory. They could see this point growing larger in the distance, like a star pulling them toward it through empty space.

Gagging for air, they suffered to stay inside the dream a little longer, no matter the damage they would incur. "Get as far from here as you possibly can," they mumbled in unison through the plastic over their lips, their eyes tearing up under their closed lids. "Don't fear insanity or Death. No matter how real the threat becomes... slowing down is worse."

Braindead, they managed no more than this.

They stirred again, sucking air through the slits that had opened between the bags and their necks. Coughing on dust, their eyes weeping, they sat up, peeling off the bags only to smash their heads on the low ceiling.

Smarting, spinning, they saw themselves as two dumb ogres crammed into a makeshift nursery, and laughed. *Two thirds of the Comedy Troupe*, they thought, laughing harder. *And the Mayor's Number Three!*

James reached up to feel his aching head, and recoiled. He'd gotten so used to feeling it shaved that the stubble felt like fungus.

"Let's get the fuck out of here." He struggled to pronounce the words as he crawled out to where he could stand. Ben followed, groaning and slow as his dead parts fell away.

James led the way back up the stairs and across the basketball court, past the front desk and into the parking lot with Ben a few paces behind. Looking back at the Gym, he found he couldn't remember what significance it used to hold for him. Whatever it was, it was gone now.

The only good news, as far as he could tell, was that the feeling of impending doom was dulled; he retained a distant sense that things would not end well, but it no longer upset him. All thought felt coated in putty, soft and harmless.

"Got any money?" he asked, when Ben had caught up.

Ben patted his pockets, felt the cash the nineteen-year-olds had paid him at the Motel, and nodded.

"Let's get some breakfast."

They walked in silence, marveling at their new mental incapacity. The peace it brought was a kind of gift. They couldn't tell how long they'd been sleeping, nor remember where they'd been before that. They still held their plastic bags crumpled in their palms. When they noticed, they let them drift away.

They arrived at the Greek restaurant, kicking aside dead Sub-Weird just as the old-timers did. Dredging up the vestiges of their language faculties, they ordered coffee and pancakes, and chewed ice while they waited.

They gazed at the Blankheads at the surrounding tables, dropping food down their void-mouths, and barely registered that these were beings they didn't know.

Their coffees arrived, spilling over the lips of their mugs and into the saucers. They studied the spill patterns until their pancakes arrived.

When they'd choked down all they could, Ben piled up the money from his pockets on the table. They left without waiting for change.

Standing out front, back in the Square with the old-timers, they were overtired and sugar-high and freshly caffeinated. The perma-dusk made them sweat.

They had nowhere to go and nothing on their minds.

After a few loops of the Square, kicking the dead Sub-Weird back and forth, Ben stopped and said, "Let's see if there's a Motel in this town."

"Okay," said James.

They continued on, exhausted from communicating this much.

They had one stop to make on the way. Though they had no work to do here, an ancient sense of duty remained in their muscles, compelling them toward the Pine Hedge Office one last time.

Behind the School, they crossed the blacktop with its foursquare and hopscotch lines, then the kickball diamond, and began to climb the hill, ducking under the pine border, eerie in the perma-dusk.

Inside, they crawled along the pine hallways on their elbows. The going was huddled and cramped, branches stabbing their arms and necks. The claustrophobia threatened to pull them back to the Crawl Space, but they forced their way onwards, around the final bend and into the clearing where all of their charts and maps and notes had been pinned up. They took in the desolation of the center, trash and bones and beer cans impacted in snow that, this deep in the shade, still hadn't quite melted.

Under all the trash was the corner of one of the tunnel maps the duo had drawn, but it was illegible because Ben and James could no longer read, not even the symbols and diagrams of the Pretend Movie. Now it was nothing but squiggles, abstract as the cave paintings of an extinct race.

They reclined in the pile of paper, smelling pinesap and damp soil, soundtracked by the creaking of the swingset on the playground. Then they began ripping down branches and tearing up roots, grinding the trash against itself and shredding bark from trunks too thick to break, pissing on the pile in the center when they were done.

James squatted over the maps and shat, then used the hanging diagrams to wipe himself. Ben looked away, unsure what he was smelling.

If they had lighters, they would have set the whole thing ablaze. Instead, they hobbled away, ripping down branches and kicking up dirt, obscuring the path so that no future duo would have access, now that the current duo had made it through, out of this world and into the next.

Now they were truly disburdened.

Wandering away from the School, they came out on the Strip, where they walked in no hurry, admiring Ultra Max bags drifting in the breeze.

There were birds in the sky and worms on the sidewalk, and crushed coffee cups and condoms in the gutter, all of which fascinated them in equal measure. They stood before the Night School, its gravel lot empty, a CLOSED sign in its window, and tried to remember what had gone on in there, and in the Mattress Store beside it, and why. Whatever it was, it didn't seem to matter now.

After a few hours of wandering in this state, they arrived at the fenceline of the Town's City and gazed up at the massive Tower, a NO VACANCY sign shining through the perma-dusk. Drawn toward it, they stepped under the fence, crossed the muddy construction site, and began the long climb up to the Motel to see how much a room would cost.

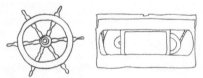

The Mayor woke on his couch covered in ice cream. He crawled to the bathroom, climbing up to the toilet without standing. Then he turned on the shower and stepped in.

As soon as the water touched his hair, the fact that the Reunion would be tonight, and that it would be held here, at the quarry behind his house, slammed down. *It's really happening*, he thought. *There's no more time.*

He couldn't remember if J.L. Wind had said this at the

emergency Town Council Meeting or if it was simply an objective truth he was picking up on now, but either way, he could see it coming. Toweling off served as the ritual of rubbing this realization in, accepting it all over his body.

Once he was dry, the interval of getting dressed and into his car passed without registering.

As he pulled down the driveway, he pictured it gorged with Blankheads closing in on the Reunion, sucking the life from the foundations of the house and yard like ticks so dense on a body no skin was visible.

Cruising down the Meadow-lined Road past James' house, he let himself think, for the last time, *It's six forty-eight in the morning and I've finished my raisin bran and packed my backpack and now I'm off to school. In class today, someone's going to show us what a planet is and tell us how many there are, and I'm going to have a chance to ask questions and there'll be someone to tell me I'll never die.*

He idled in the traffic circle outside the School, replaying last year's Reunion and the bustle of industry that Ben's and James' return had seemed to portend.

When this threatened to send him spiraling, he put the station wagon in park and got out, chugging up to the portico on foot.

Only once he was inside the main concourse could he spit into a trashcan and breathe through his mouth again, enough to get him walking down the hallway, past the bulletin boards that only displayed the corners of former sheets of paper, stuck there with colorful thumbtacks.

Everything was happening too fast. It seemed barely a week ago that he'd crawled along this floor with Ben and James,

385

gorging on bread effigies, and now—the feeling was impossible to shake—things were almost over.

The School was empty but for the Recess Aides, who still guarded the Chamber, observing the same schedule every day. They sat on their seats chewing gum, indifferent to the Mayor as he passed by.

When he saw the door of the Chamber, he fell to his knees and pitched forward, nearly breaking his nose against it. He slid down, tongue out, licking the tile at the base of the door, tasting the bottoms of Squimbop's boots. They tasted like the grass and dirt of the Meadow, mixed with numbing tallow and the salt of the Inland Sea.

After licking the floor clean, he stood, ready to confront the holy site. He put his face up to the door. It singed his nose with a smell of gunpowder and burning plastic, like the powders he'd smoked in his yard with Ben and James just before they turned nineteen.

So this is the mystery that will define the rest of my life, he chanted inwardly. Whatever you said to them in there, Professor Squimbop, will never be known, but I will carry in me the yearning to know until I die. It is the closest thing our town has ever had to a Scripture. You are the only one who knows where we came from, and where we are going.

And you told the children.

The Mayor repeated it again and again, pressing his nose up to the metal, letting it burn his flesh.

His womb quivered and cramped.

"I love you Professor Squimbop," he whispered. Then he turned his head and pressed his ear against the door, as he knew he would have to in the end.

He heard a moaning, at first very quiet, then growing in depth and intensity. Something painful and desperate trapped in there, the ghosts of all the days Squimbop had spent with the children, preserved in dead space, never to be purged.

He heard himself huffing and blowing out, Squimbop ramming into him on a Mattress Store mattress stuffed with the ground bones of his children, the two of them combining essences until a new child came into being.

Our true child, he thought, relinquishing the duo at last, aware he would never see or hear from them again.

He thought, *I'm ready. I've been sufficiently harrowed. I'm coming to ANGEL HOUSE.*

He ripped his head away from the door, knowing his ear would not come with it. Closing his eyes until he was around the corner, he never saw his tribute to the Squimbop Chamber, the ear that would remain stuck to the metal for the rest of the town's history.

The Recess Aides politely cleared their throats as he hurried by.

Rushing outside, the Mayor crossed the kickball diamond, cut through downtown, and made his way onto the Meadow-lined Road, just as Ben and James were desecrating the Pine Hedge Office.

The skin around the hole where his ear had been was extra-sensitive to the Reunion crackle in the sky, like the Squimbop Chamber had taken his filter, leaving him defenseless against whatever was in the air. He put a hand to the hole, but the tear was clean, barely bleeding.

A humid wind stirred dust at his ankles as he passed James' house, determined not to check if he was there. *Another Dead House*, he thought, casually, its deadness meaningless now that he was approaching ANGEL HOUSE... *the only house still living.*

He bowed his head as he crossed the marshy ditch into the Meadow, bathed in the purple glow. Past the ruins of the Ghost Town, he sank into the grass up to his waist and waded. He could feel the water of the Inland Sea lapping at his thighs and buttocks, flooding the grass and filling it with minnows.

It was as warm and soothing as his hot tub, but deeper, more natural. The real thing rather than a miniature indoor version of it.

He had to swim the last stretch before the porch, pushing aside grass and lily pads, feet churning through mud. He felt some slopping into his ear-hole, damming it up, setting the scene on MUTE.

When he got near the porch, he threw his arms out and grabbed the lowest stair, heaving himself up like a seal onto a dock.

The front door was open but he had to squint to locate the staircase through the purple glow. He wiped his feet on the rug as the smell of fat replaced his fear of Death with tingling numbness. He tried to look up to see what was left of the children on the ceiling but swooned and almost fell onto his back. Righting himself, he understood that his focus would have to be conserved if he wanted to remain conscious for the consummation.

So he breathed deep of the tallow smell, getting it as deep into his system as he could. When he was properly anesthetized, he put both hands on the banister and began to climb the stairs.

At the top, he heard Squimbop's low, even voice emanating from the Captain's Chamber, and pictured his erect penis like a dog's, red and slimy and jutting out of a fur-sheath.

The smell was obscene, like ovaries and prostates torn from living bodies and stewed together with sugar and alcohol. He pitched forward, whirling his arms to keep from falling. His vision blurred; he could sense that ANGEL HOUSE would not allow him to see its interior with any clarity.

He hurried along as the floor softened and the reek became so thick he had to breathe through his burned lips, which he chewed on frantic impulse, tasting brownie batter in his saliva. For a moment he was convinced he was alone in his basement, having entered his Orchard through James' Movie at last.

I've made it to the other side, he thought, as he burst through the final door, at the end of the hallway. There was Squimbop in the Captain's Chamber, under a sheet on the Mattress Store mattress, beside the gigantic Wooden Wheel that steered the ship.

They regarded one another.

"I was wondering when you'd show up," said Squimbop, from behind his laptop. "I dragged my mattress up here just for you."

The Mayor just stood there, mouth open, waiting for a sign to proceed.

"Come here." Squimbop patted the mattress. "There's something I want to show you."

The Mayor approached in a trance, gliding across the floor and onto the mattress, belly-first. He crawled up to Squimbop's side, nestling beside him while the Professor tilted his laptop so he could see.

The screen showed the door of the Greek restaurant, people coming in and out at irregular intervals. They sat and watched together, the temperature in the room rising. Strangers passed through, cooks and waiters showed up to work, then came Well, then came Ben and James, and then, finally, Squimbop and the Mayor.

Squimbop flicked to the next feed. Now the Sub-Weird were processing up the street, past the hardware store, heads down, some of them holding their pants up with their hands as

389

they shuffled into and then out of the camera's field of view.

The Mayor shivered on the mattress, roiling, his guts softening, his fat beginning to sizzle under his skin. He could feel his womb inflating as these images flooded in through his eyes.

Squimbop sniffed the air, doglike in his arousal, and flicked to the next feed, this one showing the radio station, the doorway with Well coming in and out, the Mayor dropping in. At the very top of the screen, almost out of view, the train of dreaming children floated by. He scrolled quickly through the year's worth of footage, dragging the cursor along the timeline at the bottom of the window, listening to the Mayor groan with longing.

Squimbop turned to look at him, smiled, and pulled the sheet away from his groin, revealing his erection. "Finally," he whispered, "there's this."

He switched to the final feed, outside the duo's Dead Houses. The Mayor groaned louder, almost a gasp, and swallowed a mouthful of saliva, wiping his lips with his sleeve.

Squimbop sidled closer to him on the mattress as the first image of the duo on their way to school filled the screen. "Here they are," he whispered, taking the Mayor's hand and placing it in his crotch. "Preserved forever, recorded so they can never get away. They'll never age, they'll never change... they'll never die."

The duo jaunted by, carrying their backpacks, shoes untied, talking furiously, stabbing the air as they gestured to make their point, whatever it was.

It was too much for the Mayor. He'd wanted it for so long, to see exactly this, or the same thing with Ben and James and himself swapped in. To see James' Movie, to simply know that it existed. But now, here, in the presence of a stranger and the knowledge that the footage was real, not staged, it was too much.

He heaved himself up just as his old body appeared onscreen, entering one of the Dead Houses in the middle of the night. Undoing his belt and wriggling out of his pants, he climbed on top of Squimbop, knocking the laptop aside, desperate to blot the awful Movie out.

So the foreplay is over, Squimbop thought as he helped the Mayor settle into place, tilting his hips to slide all the way into him. *Perhaps that's all the footage was ever for.*

The Mayor's vagina gaped so wide he could barely feel the friction as he began rocking back and forth, eyes closed, learning the rhythms of human intercourse for the first time. When he looked down, all he could see was the sheen of sweat on his belly, like rain on mottled tundra, Squimbop completely obscured below. He fought to remain present but fell back into himself, back into the Orchard, deep in his basement, alone in the dead of night, building toward orgasm with a mouth full of brownie batter, at the very start of the year, before the Reunion had even taken place.

When Squimbop comes, he thought, *the Orchard will be gone forever. Flooded with sex of a different order, a kind of sex beyond Pornography, no matter how deep the Pornography goes. I will conceive, and a human life will take shape within me. Never again will I be alone with my Movies.*

Squimbop tunneled through the Mayor's center, filling his stomach, his esophagus, even his mouth. He rocked faster and faster, feeling the tension mount in both sets of genitals while images on the laptop buried in the sheets behind him slithered silently across the screen.

He didn't slow down when he felt the explosion coming.

Here it comes, he thought. *The end of an era.*

But first there was a middle moment. Everything froze, or synched into equilibrium, so that the rocking of ANGEL HOUSE on its anchor mirrored the Mayor's rocking on Squimbop, and the whoosh of time flying past dimmed to a purr.

391

This, all along, is what I've been tunneling my way toward, the Mayor thought, aware he'd be better off thinking nothing. *The one moment that contains everything, in which the town finally feels whole.*

The one moment in which nothing's been taken from me and nothing's yet to come.

He leaned forward, desperate to make contact with Squimbop before the moment was gone. He leaned all the way over his belly, straining to see beyond himself.

When he craned his neck as far as he could, he could just barely make him out, his face red and reflective with sweat. They locked eyes and felt all the snarls and grimaces they'd worn throughout the act straighten into expressions of benevolence, peace, even love.

They exhaled together, catching their breath, and together felt what it would be to coexist, in this exact place and this exact time, without memory or agenda, immortal by simple virtue of having forgotten about Death.

Then the Mayor shifted slightly and Squimbop came.

He felt the Professor shuddering and pulsing, deflating as his fluid filled him. Along with it came a cold, wet influx of nostalgia, an awful longing to relive the moment that had just passed.

He kept rocking, slowing and catching his breath, accepting the pain of completion. The Professor felt like a shriveled strip of rubber on the mattress beneath him and the purple glow dimmed and ANGEL HOUSE strained on its anchor.

The Mayor tipped off him, onto his side, powerless to avoid the images flickering on the laptop screen: Ben and James at nine, walking out of their Dead Houses to meet in the middle on their way to school. He didn't bother reminding himself that it was a fresh duo, not really Ben and James. Why couldn't it be? What did it matter? All duos were equally lost to history now.

After a doze, the Mayor came to. He felt the cooling fluid drip out of him, soaking the mattress like a sponge cake.

Squimbop looked unfazed, lying on his side and breathing calmly.

"Now we're even," he said, with a pointed look at the Mayor's belly. "It's almost time for the Reunion. Let's shower and get dressed."

He stood up, not helping the Mayor, who lumbered downstairs after him. They showered side by side, using world-class soap, shaving cream and aftershave.

The Mayor luxuriated in washing away the remaining scum from the hot tub and everything that had clung to his crotch, dabbing at himself with a plush towel that Squimbop said he could get wet. He washed the singed flesh off his earhole and scraped the tallow that had gummed up under his arms, letting Squimbop watch without acknowledging that he knew he was watching.

After they were both dry, Squimbop handed him a red silk robe that he said would accommodate his swelling womb. Then he walked into the Master Bedroom. "I'll see you at the Reunion," he said, just before closing the door.

The Mayor nodded and set back out into the perma-dusk, gracefully slipping off the steps. His robe was so voluptuous he glided through the marsh and back onto the Meadow-lined Road without once feeling unclean.

After the Mayor left, Squimbop retrieved his laptop from where it'd been mashed into the sheets in the Captain's Chamber, turned off the video player, and began to compose an email.

Dear Master,

The energies in this town are coming to a head. Soon, it will be over for them. The two children I mentioned before are still at large. It may be that I will not get another chance to entrap them before it is time to pull anchor on ANGEL HOUSE and return these people to the sea floor from which they arose.

I will, suffice it to say, pursue them beyond the confines of this town if that's what's required.

All for now,

Prof. Sq.

The nine-year-olds hurried through the tunnel under the Meadow-lined Road. The weight of the Inland Sea pressed harder and harder against the tunnel walls, which buckled inward like they were made of skin, the air rank and vegetal. When the ceiling buckled too low, they dove onto their bellies and crawled along, like they had in the corridors of the Pine Hedge Office, forcing themselves forward with their elbows and knees.

Panting, they felt their hearts throb as they crawled under the Ghost Town, waves banging against the tunnel walls. Awful as the feeling was, they forced themselves onward as the first drops burst through the walls. They sucked down as much air as they could in advance of the moment when they'd have to dive underwater and swim with all the strength that Ben and James had poured into them.

Crawling faster still as the drops became a stream, they dove into the purple glow ahead, into freefall as the tunnel floor gave way. In the dark as they fell, they could hear the Mayor and Squimbop moaning, animal sounds that only magnified the feeling of being inside some giant beast, fighting their way through its intestines and out its anus before it digested them. After several minutes of falling, they landed in a warm brine thick with grass and tallow, a foot of airspace between their mouths and the roof of the foundation overhead.

Sipping air, they could hear the scraping and grinding of the ANGEL HOUSE anchor coming loose, and knew that soon the Inland Sea would cover everything and the last line of connection to the Desert would be cut. They would be nothing but sea creatures then. *Time to swim for it, t*hey thought, plunging under, forsaking the nineteen-year-olds' knowledge of the tunnel network for their own memories of their trip to the Desert, through the Psychogeography to meet Well.

We won't succumb, we won't succumb, they repeated inwardly as they swam, guarding the Pretend Movie against ANGEL HOUSE's persistent entreaty to give in. A single mouthful of warm brine is all it would take.

They kicked their feet and pushed further and further down, lungs bulging, eyes closed, hands tearing through weeds and floating pieces of foundation as the grassy warmth of the marsh turned into the cold waters of the Inland Sea, infinite and atemporal and filled with bone-snakes.

They turned to one another to make sure each was alive, but the liquid was blindingly purple and too thick to see through.

So they locked into their shared mind and dove deeper, desperately tuning out Squimbop's voice as it echoed from his mattress upstairs, the Mayor rocking back and forth upon him.

The tighter the duo closed their eyes, the more clearly they saw the Figure of Death slipping in beside them, still in his fur coat, laughing as he became one of the three Heads in the Brew, an image that they found had been implanted inside them, fraught with a significance from before their lifetimes.

Down, down, commanded their shared mind. *Don't let anything buoy you now.*

The Inland Sea was deeper than they thought possible, but they could see the tunnel mouth below, cut into the black bottom, lower than every reef, shimmering like the pathway they'd taken out of the Orchard and into the Dead Neighborhood at the moment of their birth, and again through the bottom of the Mayor's hot tub and into the Desert, when Well had called them up there.

As they fought their way deeper still, bone-snakes, thin and spindly as strands of semen, slithered up to meet them. The duo clawed at them as they swam, pushing them aside, not feeling the bites on their fingers and palms, focused only on the tunnel at the bottom glowing brighter and brighter as their lungs yearned to pop like eggs in a fist.

Down at the very bottom, they could see it for what it was: the ANGEL HOUSE anchor. A giant slab of rusted steel that had torn a hole in the sea floor. A hole it had now pulled out of. Slowly, it was rising, back toward the surface they'd forsaken, being winched up into ANGEL HOUSE where it would be stored as the ark set sail.

As their lungs pulsated, they felt Death draw near, its white light cutting through the purple murk, pulling them further down, all the way down to the bottom and then through it.

Out to the other side, they thought, aware that they might not make it. Each grabbed the other's hand and pulled, desperate to reach the light.

They broke through. The whooshing of the water overhead had ceased, and they were dry. A lid had slammed shut above them, and they could hear the Inland Sea creaking on the other side.

They lay there for a long time, beneath the bottom, heaving, unsure if they were dead or alive or neither. The Inland Sea pressed down overhead, still threatening to collapse the ceiling, but, for now, they were safe.

When at last they could feel their legs again, they stood up, wincing and hunching. Looking around, they saw they were at the nexus of the Psychogeography, all directions open from here. Dimly, like distant, out of focus TV screens, they could see their beds in their Dead Houses, the Town Square, the Wooden Wheel, the downstairs of the Movie Store, and other images of the town too indistinct to make out, all warping and bending in the purple light.

If they chose wrong, they could find themselves in the culvert behind Ultra Max or the gravel quarry behind the Mayor's house, swept back into the cloud of Blankheads. Trusting their Director-mind to find the Desert, they closed their eyes and moved in the only direction that felt right.

The tunnel spit them out at the level where the perma-dusk broke, halfway up the Mountain.

They crept onto the rocky path in a daze, standing at their full height for what felt like the first time, their spines unbending as they paused to take a last look at the town, blurry beneath the perma-dusk. They shook the water off their bare feet and sucked their fingers, tasting the tender skin under the nails that the bone-snakes had chewed off.

Then they climbed hard, watching their feet pull the ground behind them, only pausing when the terrain leveled out at an overlook, where they rested their weakened lungs until they could breathe without desperation again. Looking off, they saw the wide plane of the perma-dusk, like it was the earth's surface and the town was an old photograph buried deep below.

397

With this in mind, they resumed climbing, hauling themselves hand over hand up rock inclines covered in loose stones, then hurrying hunched on two feet when the ground leveled off.

When they next stopped to catch their breath, they had a premonition of the Figure of Death fighting its way back into the Pretend Movie, a few scenes from now. They couldn't help imagining it climbing the Mountain's sheer far side, hauling itself up hand over hand to meet them in the Desert.

So they picked up their pace, resolved not to stop until the summit was in view. Passing the cave they had slept in last time they were up here, they shook off the temptation to sleep again and, yawning, trudged higher.

"I'm up, I'm up," Ben groaned, rolling onto his side to face the door of a Motel room that someone was pounding on. "Just give me a second." He rolled out of bed and into the shower, which was freezing since the Blankheads had used all the hot water in preparation for the Reunion.

He'd slept deeply after deconsecrating the Pine Hedge Office, relishing the new feeling of dreamlessness.

James had slept deeply as well, in the other bed in the same room, but had woken before him and gone to sit on the edge of the Town's City.

The Motel was silent now. The Blankheads were gone. As

Ben toweled off, he looked down and glimpsed a gun on the floor, beneath a pile of Giant Chinese containers.

He picked it up, looking at it without recognition, hefting it from hand to hand. He put the barrel to his eye, staring as deep in as he could, then to his ear, in case it had anything to whisper.

Then, after cleaning his teeth with his tongue, he put the barrel in his mouth, pressing the cold metal against his back molars, feeling his stomach and buttocks tense.

He curled his finger around the trigger as James pounded on the door again, yelling, "Let's go! We're the last ones here!"

Ben breathed into the barrel and pulled the trigger, feeling it click loudly in his gums as he blacked out.

When he came to, James was standing over him and the door was hanging from broken hinges.

He looked around, then sat up and felt the back of his head. It was soaked; with blood or water he couldn't be sure.

"Is everything new?" he asked. "Am I in the next world?"

James was busy extracting clothes from the floor, shaking off the peanut sauce and pushing them at Ben.

"C'mon," he said. "Dry your hair and put some clothes on."

Outside the door, once Ben was finally dressed, they stood over the offline nineteen-year-olds and considered what to do.

The Town Square up here was clean and peaceful compared with the chaos of the Sub-Weird piled in the Square below. James put his foot against one of the nineteen-year-olds, looking over at Ben. A moment later, Ben did likewise, putting his foot against the other.

They nodded, registering that they had the same idea though they no longer shared a mind, and together rolled and kicked the nineteen-year-olds across the Square, past the replicas of the Hotel and the Greek restaurant, and over to the edge.

Here they hesitated, momentarily solemn, uncertain if they were about to go too far. Then they broke out in laughter, giddy at how much relief today had brought, and kicked the nineteen-year-olds over.

The bodies flipped end over end before splattering like fireworks in the Square below. Blood and Sub-Weird carcasses went everywhere, and Ben and James felt a sense of relief, like they'd finally achieved something after almost thirty years of trying. With these final Pretend Movie props disposed of, the file was closed for good.

They stood there, Ben and James together, fully indistinct now, unified as 'the twenty-nine-year-olds,' just as they'd been the nine- and the nineteen-year-olds in their time.

They hovered on the edge, teetering, about to fall, or about to jump: they lacked the mental subtlety to draw the distinction. They stared over, at the pile of Sub-Weird—everyone they'd grown up with, indistinguishable in the mess now—and the nineteen-year-olds piled on top.

Their minds sparked, fizzing; almost empty, they strained to commune, to merge back into the shared state they'd fallen out of somewhere on the trip to News City. They sidled next to one another, the two twenty-nine-year-olds back in a state of grace. Looking down at the Sub-Weird, they managed to think, in unison and without judgment: *That was us. We were them. Whatever difference we thought we had, we only thought we had it. Whatever distance we kept them at, at nine, at nineteen… because we had a Pretend Movie and they didn't… now that distance is only this, the fact that we happen to be standing up here, and they happen to be lying down there.*

Walking down toward the lobby to meet the Mayor, they

400

saw themselves as drifters at last, anonymous on these seedy streets, holed up in a Motel room where no one knew their business and no one needed to.

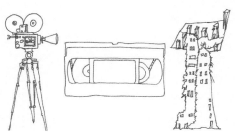

The twenty-nine-year-olds leaned against the windows in the backseat of the Mayor's station wagon, which he'd hiked all the way back to the School to retrieve, before picking them up outside the construction site. He still wore the red silk robe Squimbop had given him, loose over his swelling womb.

Neither of them remarked on any change in his appearance, nor on the coincidence of his passing by to pick them up. Whether they'd made a plan on the phone or just happened to have been in the same place at the same time was beyond the scope of their thinking at this point.

Driving along the Meadow-lined Road in the moments before ANGEL HOUSE flooded it, the Mayor tried not to look too hard at the two of them as they bobbed in the backseat, their heads knocking loudly against the windows. There was early Reunion foot traffic—Blankheads straggling along—but it wouldn't flare up in earnest for a few more hours. There would be time for the three of them to soak in the hot tub, then cook burgers and drink beer in the Mayor's backyard.

Looking in the rearview to change lanes, the Mayor caught sight of the twenty-nine-year-olds' faces. They looked like their heads had been molded from tan clay and then mocked up with store-bought eyes, noses, and mouths. He stared at them

401

as he pulled around the cul-de-sac and up his driveway, slowly accepting that whatever had come over them wasn't going to subside.

In the house, the three of them took their shoes off and went to the back windows while the hot tub warmed up. They looked out at the yard that led into thick underbrush and then a wall of trees. Beyond that, invisible from here, was the gravel quarry with the stopped tractors, where the Reunion would be held in a few hours.

J.L. Wind was probably back there now, setting everything up.

They each opened a beer from the thirty-pack in the kitchen, carrying it into the hot tub room where they waited for the Mayor.

"Time to get in," he said, opening his robe and closing his eyes, trying to keep the thought of bread effigies from invading his mind.

As soon as they were in the water, he looked at them and quickly looked away as they grew indistinguishable from those effigies, even more affectless than last time. He turned over, leaning his face on the tub's edge with his backside to them, giddy with a mix of shame and pride at the thought of them seeing his vagina, but they wouldn't look, or would but couldn't see.

There was almost nothing left of them. Turning back around, the Mayor tried to deny that the men formerly known as Ben and James, whom he'd loved maybe more than he'd ever shown, were gone and never coming back.

If they were here, he thought, *they would see what I'm trying to show them. They would see me for who I am.*

But the things in the tub with him now were no more than Blankheads, interchangeable with the horde that would soon descend upon the quarry to commemorate a past they had never shared and did not miss.

"Please," he whispered. "Come back."

He began to shake, then to tear up, then to sob openly, heaving, knocking the effigies over. They tilted sideways as he convulsed, building toward his final War Whoop.

The War Whoop, when it came, addled what was left of the twenty-nine-year-olds. They snapped back from the verge of blankness and ran out of the hot tub, trailing water across the floor of the kitchen and up the carpeted stairs.

The Mayor heaved himself out more slowly, wrapping himself in his robe and going after them through his house, following the water trail up the stairs to the bathroom.

He found them in the shower, mechanically scraping off the scum that had covered their bodies in the hot tub, looking neither at themselves nor one another.

He dried them off and, propping them against the edge of the tub, lathered their faces very carefully and gave them a shave.

Then it was time to put on their suits, which the Mayor had kept in his house for moments of comedown after long druggy days at seventeen and eighteen, times when the only reprieve from the misery of return was to get dressed up and eat a huge greasy meal.

Tonight, even if the twenty-nine-year-olds were indistinguishable from one another, at least they would look sharp.

The Mayor finished tying their ties and pulling their old jackets over their arms and shoulders, glad to see they still fit despite the moth holes. Then he took out two sets of matching black shoes and fitted them onto their feet.

Once they were dressed, he stepped back into his silk robe, long past the point of putting on one of the old suits that

403

hung in the closet.

Downstairs, the twenty-nine-year-olds reflexively took fresh beers from the box, putting them to their lips as the thrum of approaching Blankheads filled the house. The Mayor coughed and tried not to breathe as he gathered up a bowl of ground beef and a bag of buns and motioned for them to follow.

There were three chairs by the fire pit from the last time they'd all sat together, when there'd still been roving bears and night was still night.

The twenty-nine-year-olds set up the firewood and got it crackling with a couple of long matches while the Mayor formed the beef into patties and stuck them on the metal grill he then laid over the flames.

They feasted when the meat was done, each with a burger in both hands, pressing the soft mounds around the hard shapes of beer bottles in the centers of their mouths.

The Mayor knew that, before long, he'd feel a painful desperation to return to this moment, and that a great many moments in the future would be lost to this desire's futility, just as this moment was itself partly lost to the futility of returning to previous bonfires, when everything had looked the same, but something—the crucial thing, whatever it was—had been totally different.

Waking on the couch from which he had watched the duo leave, Well felt a broadcast about their disappearance coming on. The Dust House door was slightly open, perma-dusk drifting inside and making him yawn as he licked the air near his mouth to taste the direction in which the words he was preparing to utter were to be found.

He sat up, startled, when it blew shut. Fearing he'd never make it out if he didn't go now, he got to his feet and hurried out in his T-shirt and jeans, carrying a glass of rusty tap water to wash down the broadcast that was spluttering up from his throat.

As he wound out of the Dead Neighborhood and toward the lower streets, shoving his way through the slow-moving crowd of Blankheads, he felt like the town had been taken over and the radio station was his only refuge, the one neutral point from which he could call for help. He bunched the collar of his shirt under his chin, drained his water, and threw the glass on the sidewalk.

Passing the Square and the Greek restaurant, he refused to consider the pile of Sub-Weird with the nineteen-year-olds splattered on top. He hurried through side streets and onto the Strip just past the Night School. After crossing a needle-strewn patch of weeds that led to the gravel lot behind the station, he shouldered open the Employees' Entrance and locked the door behind him.

The station was empty. There was some sludge in the bottom of the coffee pot—still turned on, though long since burned out—which he let slip into a cup. Then he filled a bucket at the bathroom sink and carried it into the Broadcast Chamber, where he put on his old coat, settled into his old chair, and placed his feet in the water, trying to calm himself enough to speak.

"The Radio Angel flaps alone," he muttered into the mic, then waited, thought about it, and realized what he was trying to say. He picked up a used notecard and an Ultra Max pen and wrote: *The town has become the Ghost Town, just as what used to be the Ghost Town is now a pit.*

405

He said it aloud. It felt healthy to speak like this, to whomever was listening, even if it was no one.

"Our adult life in the Ghost Town starts right now," he said, and heard it ring true. "No more children drifting up the Meadow-lined Road at night. No more days asleep in the Hotel waiting for them to become mine—to become me—at nightfall. From now on, I will admit that I was born here, in this town, the same as the rest of you, just as deranged with fantasy as you are. The town as it was is the town as it was is the town as it was. Our time together is limited, the Reunion is impending, but I consecrate whatever minutes we have left to the dream of eternity together in our mutual Ghost Town. To the dream of all pretend things made real and present, to the past as an empty sac, incapable of containing a single lost treasure."

He felt the truth of what he was saying as he said it, modulating his voice into a register that adults could hear.

"I will not get the life in Dust House I prayed for," he continued. "I will remain singular, cut off from my innermost roots, withering, but I am here with you all today, even as Blankheads render the Square a zone of infestation, sucking out meaning and offering nothing in its place. See you all at the Reunion, which I've chosen to call *The Consecration of the Town as Ghost Town.* Our lives together have not been without joy. Try to remember this, and believe it, whoever you are, if you're listening. If you can hear me."

He rubbed his fingers over the volume knobs, playing them like an instrument that produced his voice.

Soon it would be time to put down the mic and face the likelihood that he'd never pick it up again. He sat there with it pressed against his lips, emptied of all the words he'd once had to say.

Well stepped from the bucket he'd been soaking his feet in and brought his coffee cup to the bathroom, dumping the brown pudding down the toilet.

He turned on the employees' shower and stripped and sat on the toilet as the water warmed up. When he got under, he scrubbed his skin with a cracked bar of soap like he was preparing his body for burial.

Thank you for your service, he thought. *You will be missed.*

He didn't linger, turning off the water as soon as he'd brought the soap once around his skin.

Getting out, he dried off with a hand towel and put his boxers, jeans, and T-shirt back on. Then he hurried to the Employee's Entrance, not passing the Broadcast Chamber again on his way out.

Back in the perma-dusk in the gravel lot, he stood in the spot where he used to park his car and yawned, closing his eyes and tasting the humid air, already salty with the coming waves. He looked up at an apricot-sized orb attached to the roof. Then he closed his eyes.

He kept them closed for a long time. When he opened them, he saw ANGEL HOUSE bobbing along what used to be the Meadow-lined Road.

The front door opened and Squimbop emerged in a jet-black suit, his hair slicked back and his mustache glistening. He walked down the front porch to where the water lapped at his feet, and waved.

"I pulled the anchor out. The Inland Sea has already

flooded the Meadow," he said. "I'm sailing up to the Reunion before I leave. Want a ride?"

Well nodded and got to his feet, leaning forward so Squimbop could grab his upper arms and hoist him aboard.

He followed Squimbop into the Captain's Chamber and stared out as they sailed up the canal past James' house, imagining the flooded Meadow and the Ghost Town far behind. When he leaned over the edge, he could see the roofs of the Greek restaurant, the Hotel, the Movie Store, all submerged, buried in brine and grass with bone-snakes swimming peacefully by. His mind filled with anger at Squimbop for having done this to the town and denying him eternity with the duo in Dust House, but the moment he turned toward him with the intention of saying what he felt, the words melted away. He burped, tasting stomach acid, and forced a smile.

"It's good to see you again," he heard himself say. "I missed you when I was in the Desert."

Squimbop smiled back.

Well was seasick by the time ANGEL HOUSE docked near the Mayor's cul-de-sac.

He knew he'd already come as close to crossing the Inland Sea as he was ever going to. He'd had a glimpse of what the town after Squimbop would look like, and now there was nothing to do but slip into that world graciously, trying to retain a few words with which to describe it.

"Take me with you when you go!" he wanted to shout as Squimbop was locking off the Wooden Wheel, but he could only mumble syllables, picturing the submerged Ghost Town filling with fish and plankton, at first, and then coral, after decades and centuries had passed.

He saw it so vividly that he only gradually became aware

408

of Squimbop staring at him. "Sorry," he said, wiping his eyes. "Just give me a second."

When he came back to himself, he wiped his eyes again and stood, letting Squimbop help him down the stairs and onto the Mayor's cul-de-sac, which had remained dry land for the time being.

They could see the Blankheads climbing the driveway and followed in that direction, past the Mayor's house and across the yard with its still-smoldering fire pit.

They hiked in silence through the tracks that the Mayor and the twenty-nine-year-olds had made a few minutes ago.

Well looked over at Squimbop as they crested the first of several small ridges along the range that contained the quarry. He imagined hefting a rock against the Professor's head, staving it in on the fourth or fifth impact, then running down the hill and getting behind the wheel of ANGEL HOUSE himself. He wondered how far he'd make it. Perhaps all the way.

Instead, he hurried to keep up, closing in on his final Reunion.

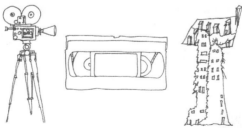

After loading the school bus with the remnants of the children at ANGEL HOUSE, Janitor Pete had spent the past few hours circling the town, keeping ahead of the floodwaters that had turned the Meadow-lined Road into a canal. He couldn't remember the last time he'd slept, nor where it could've been.

A phone call from Squimbop in the middle of the night had been sufficient to arrange the pickup. He would be paid $10,000 for his trouble.

He was pulling into the Mayor's cul-de-sac now, keeping to a narrow strip of pavement alongside the canal. Yawning, he shook the coffee cups in his lap for last drops that weren't there. Behind him, the deflated, mostly faceless children were becalmed, not quite asleep but dazed enough by the constant motion that they couldn't speak, though he suspected that they wouldn't have been able to speak even under the best conditions.

This only enervated him more.

He yawned and, as he turned the wheel a sharp ninety degrees into the Mayor's driveway, his eyes fell shut and he couldn't reopen them. The bus crashed into a tree and the airbag shot out, crushing him against his headrest without waking him up.

Water splashed against the wheels and ran into the motor, then began flooding the bus's floor as he went on sitting like that, tongue drying against the airbag, engine running, children falling over each other in back, sticking together.

A while passed with all of them inert in the bus. Water came up over the seats and set the children to floating, pressing them against the ceiling just as they'd been in ANGEL HOUSE.

It was so quiet in the cul-de-sac, with everyone already at the Reunion, that they might all have died like that had the water not tipped the bus onto its side. But when it tipped over, Janitor Pete startled awake, spitting salty brine as he heaved the lever to open the door, which, luckily, was facing upward.

"Alright, everyone! Swim!" Swimming into the Inland Sea himself, he could barely get the words out before his mouth and throat were filled.

He fought his way up what had been the Mayor's driveway, not looking back but feeling the children behind him, drifting as freely as plastic bags on a gentle tide. He could see the purple glow everywhere in the deepening ocean, which turned the humid air chilly as it took on depth and scope.

With a final heave, he surfaced in the Mayor's backyard, a beach now, inhaling and shaking himself off, peeling seaweed from his sleeves, watching the children wash ashore, whittled down to little more than spines.

"Follow me," he said. "The Reunion's this way."

The Mayor, in his red robe, and the twenty-nine-year-olds in suits that smelled of smoke and grease, were on their way along the path, past the parked tractors, five minutes ahead of Well and Squimbop.

Lonelier with his two inert companions than he would've been alone, the Mayor held his squirming belly and wished the baby could be born right now, in time to experience earthly life, if only for a moment or two.

The three of them had hiked this stretch of quarry dozens of times at night, visiting the tractors, which even then they'd imagined had built the town. Now the perma-dusk made the quarry look like the point where they'd always turned back, ambivalent about the prospect of actually reaching the edge.

Tonight, they really would go farther than before, all the way to the Blind Spot, the outermost quarry, which the Mayor had only ever reached in his station wagon, drifting in neutral along a path he never could have consciously driven.

After half an hour of walking, the lights of the Reunion became visible in the distance. Hypnotized, the three of them approached, Blankheads rustling in the woods all around them.

Tracing the edges of the pit, no longer fully present, the

411

Mayor drifted back to the night almost eleven years ago when he'd sat out here with Ben and James on the eve of their departure for News City and contemplated pushing them in, then jumping after them. *All three of us*, he'd thought then and thought again now, *preserved in time, buried in the foundation of the town, never again compelled into the unknown.*

Just as he'd teared up then, he teared up again now. *Would it have been better?* he wondered, looking to the twenty-nine-year-olds for a kind of confirmation he knew he would never find, *if the three of us had died then?*

Through his tears, the Mayor perceived rows of folding chairs, hanging lights, a stage with a PA system, and generators buzzing behind trees. They'd arrived. The Blind Spot yawned behind them, the tractors and backhoes parked along its edge, in the shadow of a pile of rubble. Their engines were idling, casting smoke into the air.

Blankheads were taking their seats, the voids of their mouths opening and closing without hurry, all menace implicit. Well, Squimbop, and J.L. Wind sat on the stage, watching the crowd.

The twenty-nine-year-olds had gone on ahead. If not for their suits, the Mayor wouldn't have been able to pick them out of the crowd. *Let them go,* he tried to think, *they're no one now.* Still, he found himself hurrying toward them, hoping to get a seat nearby before Blankheads filled the row.

He managed to find one. A Blankhead sat next to him on the other side, reeking that old bear smell he wished he didn't remember as well as he did. They made a chattering sound, like wings slipping back and forth over the backs of beetles, their attention entirely diffuse, focused on nothing, even as J.L. Wind tapped the mic and cleared his throat.

Just then, as if responding to a signal sent straight from the Blind Spot, the Blankheads stood, their void-mouths clacking, and processed into the idling tractors, cramming into the cabs, starting them up, and putting them in Drive.

J.L. Wind held the mic at his chest, swallowing whatever he'd been about to say as Janitor Pete and the mass of children staggered through the trees, emerging at the quarry edge.

The Blankheads began pushing the gravel pile back into the pit.

Filling the Blind Spot in, the Mayor thought. *Covering my grave without me in it.* He was riveted. *If only the nights of Movies were still ahead of me... Imagine the sanctity of my basement if I'd never had to leave...* but the possibility was too remote.

Janitor Pete held what was left of the children in a row at the edge of the forest, generators humming behind him, while the Blankheads pushed pile after pile of gravel into the pit. When the Blind Spot had been turned into a flat expanse, he would let them loose.

After an hour of deliberate work, the Blankheads had filled it in. A cloud of rock dust hung in the air, turning the purplish perma-dusk grey.

There was a moment of silence as everyone beheld the new terrain. "Look!" the Mayor shouted at the twenty-nine-year-olds, who were staring at their laps. They didn't respond.

Janitor Pete nudged the children forward.

They began to march, out of the trees and across the

newly created field, toward the Blankheads who sat in the center on their idling tractors, wiping their faces on their sleeves.

It took them a long time to move a short distance. They flapped their arms like they thought they were swimming, and bumped into each other as they went. A few tripped and didn't get up. Others broke legs and feet in mid-stride and likewise lay where they fell.

All their tallow boiled away, the children were little more than stick figures.

The Mayor half-expected to see the gravel under them give way and the Blind Spot reassert its dominion over the town, but so far the new ground held firm.

Well gripped his mic hard onstage to keep from sobbing at the sight of what ANGEL HOUSE had done to them. He doubted that anything remained of their memories of the Ghost Town.

The children stopped when they reached the Blankheads, who had stepped down from the tractors to stand before them. Neither group opened their arms to the other, but the children pressed their burned-away faces into the Blankheads' bellies, in poses that resembled affection, even recognition, however horrific its nature.

As the Blankheads yawned their void-mouths, threatening to suck out the rest of what remained of the children, J.L. Wind stood up on stage and said, simply, "Now this is a Reunion! Parents and children reunited at last. Broken families repaired. Long live the town."

There was so little conviction in his voice that he couldn't go on. He fell back in his seat.

When the Blankheads had stood with the children propped against them long enough that the sight seemed canonical, like a tableau out of art history, J.L. Wind tried again to speak.

414

"Lost to us throughout this long year, the children, who are our future, have finally returned. They will be safe and happy with their parents from now on, and our town, through them, will thrive."

He paused, passing the mic from his right hand to his left.

"This has been a difficult year," he said, "a year that has seen many changes. The tenure of Professor Squimbop, the shattering of the line between town and Outskirts, the aberration of our attempt to build a city, the scuttling of our Movie industry, the disruption of our seasons, and the melding of day and night." Here he looked at the Mayor, not without compassion.

"And yet, I propose to you all, order persists. The nature of that order has changed, certainly, and we in turn have had to change, and will have to continue changing, but the notion that we have moved from order to disorder is a faulty and destructive one. The town is still here, right where it always was, and, after tonight, Professor Squimbop will have moved on," he looked at the Professor here, who looked back at him with casual pity. "The School will continue to stand, and the children will resume their studies, making up all that they missed. A new teacher will be hired, and all of us will live long, prosperous lives. Beginning tomorrow.

"And so, I promise you all, order remains. A new year begins tonight. And what's more," he added with a grin, "though Giant Chinese is closed for the Reunion, there is a midnight breakfast at the Greek restaurant, to which you are all most sincerely invited. Free pancakes, on me!"

He stood with the mic in his hand for a long minute, gazing into the silence of the crowd, before taking his seat and nodding to Well to take his turn.

Well stood up, gripping the mic hard, his throat sore from the broadcast he'd delivered this afternoon. He closed his eyes,

415

repressing his vision of the town underwater. For one last time, he would pretend there was a future.

"Hello," he began, hoping he sounded more confident than he felt. "You'll all hear me on the radio again starting tomorrow. All of you, not only the children, are invited to tune in. Everything that is fact today will by then have segued into myth. I'll be the keeper of that myth. Starting tomorrow, the Age of Revelation will be over and the Age of Interpretation will have begun. Tomorrow, the literal truth of this year will be too much to bear. So I won't tell you you're wrong to insist on its figurative meaning. I will simply tell you about Professor Squimbop, whose influence on our town you will spend the rest of your lives trying either to parse or to deny, depending on your nature."

Well cleared his throat several times and wiped his lips with the back of his hand. "I hope you can all get some sleep after this," he concluded. "I'll be there on the radio to greet you when you wake up. Together, we'll soldier bravely onward."

He sat down as J.L. Wind took the mic back and looked hesitant about what to do with it now.

After a moment's pause, Squimbop took it from him.

"I have no speech," he admitted, pulling an ivory-handled hunting knife from inside his suit and fondling it lovingly. "After this, I'll be gone, and there will be no way of contacting me. My work here is almost done."

He beckoned to the Mayor with his knife.

The Mayor looked to the twenty-nine-year-olds for a kind of moral support he knew they couldn't offer, and got up, retying the sash of his robe.

Squimbop embraced him, and, in that embrace, eased the robe off. The Mayor stood naked before the town.

"Stand proudly," said Squimbop, running his knife up and

416

down his belly. No one spoke, or even moved.

"In here," he continued, after a moment, "sleeps something none of you know about. An actual new person." He scraped the Mayor's belly, pressing down lovingly, drawing a thin line of blood. "All of you are recycled, dredged from the floor of the Inland Sea, your thoughts and memories implanted from the soul-melt of thousands of previous generations. But this... this is something new."

Squimbop's eyes misted over. "Each of us has a Master. Someone higher. Someone remote. I am no different. And so, it is with a heavy heart that I—"

He leaned in, whispering, "I love you" in the Mayor's ear as he plunged the knife into his belly. "In a different world, we could have had a life together." With the hilt against his skin, he began sawing through the Mayor's womb, holding his lower back with his other hand, massaging him as he worked. Still, no one in the crowd spoke.

When the Mayor could no longer stand, Squimbop laid him on the stage and folded the flaps of his belly aside, reaching into the center and pulling out a handful of viscera.

Standing, he held it up for all to see. "Here," he began, blood dripping from his fist, "is the being that, had it reached fruition, may well have become the son or daughter to unseat me. To strip me of my power and bring my wandering to an end. To redeem your town once and for all and perhaps make of the world something better than what it is."

He paused, a look of great sorrow and remorse covering his face as he peeled apart the mass in his hands to reveal two identical homunculi. "Twins," he whispered, refusing to show surprise. Then he swallowed them both, one after the other, and licked their blood from his mustache. "You will never know how much I wish I could have allowed these two to thrive. ANGEL

417

HOUSE offers relief to everyone but me."

Then he dropped the knife into the Mayor's newly slender carcass and walked into the woods.

Well, J.L. Wind, and all the Blankheads and their children sat in silence, frozen like a still from a Movie as the floodwaters came. The Reunion, and with it the whole past it commemorated, was over.

The Square, the Greek restaurant, the Hotel, the Strip, the Night School, the Mattress Store, the Gym, Giant Chinese and Ultra Max, all of them went under, swarmed by bone-snakes and the dissipating bodies of the Sub-Weird, and all the footage on the tapes piled in James' office bled out, salting the water, making it that much richer and more complex for the next town it yielded up, wherever ANGEL HOUSE happened to dock this autumn.

Back inside ANGEL HOUSE, after turning the Wooden Wheel around to sail away from the Mayor's cul-de-sac and back onto the Inland Sea, Squimbop felt ill. Nevertheless, he opened his laptop, turned off the cameras, and composed an email.

Dear Master,

It is done. This year's town is no more. I have complied with all that I believe you expected of me. There are two that got away. They are at large, somewhere in the universe. I will do my utmost to locate them.

I know I cannot return until I do. I know, if I don't, I will wander forever, in exile.

Please help me,

Prof. Sq.

He sent the email, swallowed a handful of tallow, and, despite the prohibition he'd set for himself, began to write another, unsure what he intended to say until the words began to appear on the screen.

Dear Master,

I quit. Everything I wrote in the last email? It's not true. I'm done with this. All of it. Track me down if you wish to.

Fuck you forever,
Prof. Sq.

He moved his index finger over the Delete button, hovering there longer than usual. Then, just before pressing down, he watched his thumb creep lower and hit Send.

He sat back, trembling with a mixture of relief and terror, picturing tens, then hundreds, then thousands of proliferating possibilities of what his punishment would entail. He watched all the tortures he'd described to the children being meted out on him instead as he refreshed his browser again and again, eyes blurring, sweat pouring down his forehead. Any punishment, he thought, is preferable to another year like this one. He closed his eyes, sensing that, when he reopened them, the response would have arrived.

When he couldn't keep them closed any longer, he opened first one eye, then the other, and peered at his inbox, where, indeed, a single unread message sat waiting. He had to grab one hand with the other in order to click on the subject heading and read the response.

He read it ten times through, half of them aloud. Then he pressed his eye to the screen and scoured every letter, every space, every period, before registering that it was the exact message he'd just sent, returned to him verbatim. Not a single nuance changed. He felt blood pooling in his temples as he deleted it, slammed the laptop shut, and lay down. *So either there's no response*, he thought, his inner voice sluggish and defeated in his head, *or else that was it.*

It already felt possible that he'd never sent the email, just as he hadn't sent any of the others. Either way, he could tell, beyond even the tiniest hopeful doubt, that there would never be an end to years like the one he'd just completed.

Not soon, not ever.

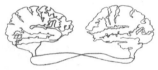

It was dawn in the Desert. Tendrils of light hung from the sky and touched the ground. By now the duo were far past the region they'd explored with Well. The horizon seen from Dust House was far behind them. The dead-end had come alive.

As the town below returned to the bottom of the Inland Sea, they sat down in the sand, panting, heads splitting. The vanishing of Ben and James felt like the loss of their producers— now they were entirely alone in the Pretend Movie, directing it, starring in it, and producing it with no outside assistance. Perhaps it had happened before they were ready, but they knew there was no stopping now.

It's just us and the Inland Sea, they thought, picturing the Desert as an island. The Figure of Death haunted their thoughts, just as it had when it stood behind the Wooden Wheel in the depths of Hibernation. But it hadn't yet appeared.

It's us and Death, or it's nothing, it's just… Desert and

420

Desert and Desert, they thought, marching onward.

Whenever they stopped to rest, the Figure of Death grew clearer in their shared mind, a scarecrow whose face combined Squimbop's and the Mayor's. Perhaps it was only a mirage caused by exhaustion, hunger, and dehydration, but it was intolerable. So they pressed on. The Desert surrounded them on all sides, every direction expanding the Pretend Movie into realms the town had barely hinted at, pushing them, both painfully and pleasurably, onto a new level of vision, one they couldn't be sure they were ready to operate on.

Scattering their memories of the town like ashes, they could sense that the Pretend Movie would start anew up here, cleansed of idols, stripped of all that referred back to the fallen world.

When all the ashes were gone, it was evening and a salty breeze had begun to blow.

They felt lean and healthy, unburdened and ready to perceive their surroundings directly, without the dirty lens through which everything in the town had been filtered and re-filtered, dripping into the Movies that, in comparison with what they were in the process of bringing to bear up here, hardly deserved the name.

When they cooled down, hazy outlines began to take shape around them: spires, walls, facades of stores and houses. It was all still distant, but soon they'd be on the Pretend Movie set, ready to start in earnest.

"The Oasis," they said, simply, as if naming it were the final step in ensuring its reality.

The total emptiness they'd walked through all day felt primordial now, like the very earliest stage of a process that was now well underway. The days and weeks and years of fantasy, roaming the land of their birth, were far behind. Now, though still nine-year-olds to all appearances, they were ready to take their stand.

The next time they looked up, they were on the sets they'd glimpsed up ahead, and light was back in the sky, either because they had walked all night, or because they had entered a zone where it was light all the time.

It hummed with energy, everything poised to come to life.

At the set's very center bubbled a hot tub. This they recognized immediately as their Directors' Hive, where all future thought would be born.

But as they approached, peeling off their clothes and panting with anticipation, a shadow fell over them.

They looked up and saw a tremendous Tower, blocking visibility to their left. It was leaning so far to one side it seemed to be in mid-collapse, its facade full of unfinished windows and jutting steel beams, chunks of dried cement hanging like barnacles.

This, too, chattered with energy, whispering ideas, perhaps concealing inhabitants. *If there are people in there, they will be our extras*, the duo thought, at the edge of the bath now.

Slipping in, they leaned back to look at the upper floors of the Tower. There were unmistakably human forms standing on the terrace, looking down at them, too high to tell if their expressions were friendly or hostile.

When they reached the verge of falling asleep in the hot, bubbling water, a clacking demanded their attention.

Though the sky was bright, the traveling party had its lanterns lit as it approached, waving them erratically. It was three gangly figures and a cart, which one of them was pulling and one was pushing while the third danced on top.

It was laden down with leather whips and hanging pots and archaic musical instruments, all manner of horns and gourds and stringed sticks.

The duo watched them stop and dismount and begin their show—muggings, pratfalls, mock fights, and flubbed magic tricks—before they stripped naked and walked into the bath.

Recognizing the Comedy Troupe, the duo whispered, "Why are you here?"

The Comedy Troupe sank all the way down so that only their heads protruded, making sounds that ran from gibbers to howls, slurping water and spitting it at each other, grinning morosely.

When they'd processed the duo's question, after several minutes, the Comedy Troupe spoke in unison, like they were repeating a litany that had long since been drained of meaning.

"We're here to cede the responsibility of the Heads in the Brew. Our time is done. We've thought all the thoughts we have in us. Like eggs that hatch, thrive, and then die. The Inland Sea is waiting for us, just ahead. The creation of the universe—call it the Pretend Movie, if you like—is up to you now. Make it a good one. Make it funny."

Then they resumed howling as they climbed naked from the bath and skipped away from the set, into the waves to die.

The duo bobbed there becoming the Heads in the Brew for a long time after that, letting inklings take shape, pretending each bubble was an egg, rising to the surface to hatch, determining one facet of the universe in which their lives would play out.

They sank down until the water reached their lips and the bottoms of their ears, as they stared up at the darkening sky.

As they pictured the Comedy Troupe drifting lifeless out to sea, they saw Ben, James, and the Mayor drowned in there as

423

well. These six cadavers seemed to merge into three.

They sighed, not unmoved, forgetting about the Figure of Death until a purple glow forced its way into their attention. Before they could consider its source, it had grown so bright they had to shield their eyes with their hands. Peeking through their fingers, they watched ANGEL HOUSE drop anchor.

As soon as the anchor found purchase, the Desert began to become a town, springing up from the blankness around them, filling in the Pretend Movie set with the heaviness of real life. "No!" they shouted, in their best Director's voices, fighting with everything they had against reverting to the state of two nine-year-olds in a bathtub as Squimbop got out and walked toward them.

Traipsing through the sand in his fur coat, Squimbop held himself as tall and straight as he could, poorly masking his exhaustion. Dust rose in a cloud around him as he approached, dying his mustache tan and making him cough.

The duo closed their eyes in the hot tub and sank under the water, praying he'd be gone by the time they resurfaced. They stayed under a long time, long enough to feel the Psychogeography opening back up beneath them, reconnecting to the Gym, the Hotel basement, the culverts behind Ultra Max... the entire network that the nineteen-year-olds had uncovered before going offline.

Gasping, they burst back through the surface of the hot tub, just in time to see Squimbop slipping in with them, the fur of his coat matted to his skin like a beaver's. *The Figure of Death has found us*, they thought, trying to convince themselves that this needed to happen. *Everything is on track... the Pretend Movie is deepening, finding its conflict, building toward its climax.*

"Look at me," Squimbop whispered.

They looked.

"You and only you survived. Of all the people, it was only

424

you. That means something. It means you are ready to cross the Inland Sea. Do you want to cross the Inland Sea? Do you want to feel how it feels to live in the Totally Other Place, on the far shore, beyond Death? Do you want to do what I do?"

As he said this, the Tower creaked overhead and began to sink into the sand. Squimbop and the duo watched in silence, the water up to their chins, as it sank to ground level.

On its roof stood models of the Hotel, the Square, and the Greek restaurant. They shuddered, aware that soon the whole town would have rebuilt itself around them. Sinking down in the tub so that only their eyes protruded, they tried to think, *We are the Heads in the Brew… We are the Heads in the Brew… It is our Pretend Movie and our mandate to make it real… We can inhabit any universe we can dream up.*

But Squimbop's taunt was unmistakable. "ANGEL HOUSE is about to leave. Come with me now or regret it forever."

The prospect of eternal exile, locked in the Master Bedroom as ANGEL HOUSE drifted, with nothing but his footage to keep him company, terrified the Professor, but he was powerless to force the duo onboard. If they were going to come, it had to be their decision.

"There is relief in the Totally Other Place," he said, sincerely wishing it were true. He crawled to his knees inside the tub. "Total relief. The absence of all compulsion, all ambition, all exhaustion, all doubt… and if you don't come, you will never be free of me. I will dog you forever, wherever you go. Whatever you do."

The duo believed him. Still, or because of this, they fought their way beneath his voice, deeper into the water, the tunnels opening again. Holding their breath as they plunged back through, flailing in the Psychogeography, they could tell that when they surfaced it would be as if they'd never left the town at all, and their

425

work on the Pretend Movie, forever in Squimbop's shadow, would be just about to begin.

ACKNOWLEDGEMENTS

Despite how lonely the writing process can be, no book is written alone. This one, certainly, wouldn't exist, in its finished or any of its unfinished forms, without the ongoing love, support, insight, and positivity of the people I've attempted to list here:

First of all, tremendous thanks to Jesi Bender and everyone at KERNPUNKT for taking on this strange and unruly manuscript, and turning it into the beautiful book you're holding now. It looks a whole lot nicer here than it did on my hard drive. Next, tremendous thanks to my brilliant wife Ingrid, for her edits, conversation, worldview, and moral support over the many years of this book's development. Thanks also to Eli Epstein-Deutsch, Rob Rice, Jeff Steinberg, and Matthew Spellberg, who were there from the beginning and somehow even before. Further thanks to Isaac Shivvers, Andrei Cristea, John Trotta, Joey Quinn, Jesse Barron, Dan Hirsch, Justin Keenan, Michal Labik, Lorenzo Bartolucci, Hayden Bennett, Jeff Jackson, and John Kazanjian, for reading and discussing early versions, and to the DAAD and Shaw Purposeful Travel Fellowships for providing the time and space to get the ball rolling, all the way back in Berlin in 2010-11. Thanks to Michael Natalie, Josh Lemay, and Tobias Carroll for interviewing me about the book in the lead-up to its publication, to John Madera for publishing an excerpt at *Big Other*, and to everyone who wrote such fantastic and generous blurbs. Thanks also to Patrick McGrath and Jack Ketchum, for the encouragement, mentoring, and tough love over the years.

Lastly, huge and heartfelt thanks, as ever, to my parents, Lynn (architect of the incredible blueprints at the start of this book) and Richard, for believing in me from the beginning, and for making sure I always had somewhere to come back to. Without the home they made for my brother and me in Northampton, there'd be no *ANGEL HOUSE*.

ABOUT THE AUTHOR

David Leo Rice is a writer from Northampton, MA, currently living in NYC. His stories and essays have appeared in The Believer, Catapult, Black Clock, DIAGRAM, The Collagist, Fanzine, and elsewhere. His first novel, *A Room in Dodge City*, was published in 2017, and its sequel is forthcoming.

His work is online at: www.raviddice.com